The House That Death Built

Mel Stone

The House That Death Built
Copyright © 2020 Mel Stone
All rights reserved.

ISBN: 9798664414684

All rights reserved, including the right to reproduce this book or any portion thereof in any form whatsoever, without prior written permission of the author, except in the case of brief quotations embodied in critical reviews and other noncommercial uses subject to copyright law.

All characters and events in this book are works of fiction.
Any similarity to any person, living or dead, is purely coincidental.

Cover and interior formatting by **MiblArt**.

To my Bubby.
I love you, baby girl.

Table of Content

Part 1 - The Cull ... 7
- Chapter 1 ... 9
- Chapter 2 ... 22
- Chapter 3 ... 30
- Chapter 4 ... 36
- Chapter 5 ... 43
- Chapter 6 ... 54
- Chapter 7 ... 63
- Chapter 8 ... 70
- Chapter 9 ... 78
- Chapter 10 ... 91
- Chapter 11 ... 99

Part 2 - The Farce ... 113
- Chapter 12 ... 115
- Chapter 13 ... 124
- Chapter 14 ... 131
- Chapter 15 ... 139
- Chapter 16 ... 149
- Chapter 17 ... 157
- Chapter 18 ... 162
- Chapter 19 ... 173

Chapter 20 179
Chapter 21 185

Part 3 - The Curse 191

Chapter 22 193
Chapter 23 198
Chapter 24 204
Chapter 25 213
Chapter 26 217
Chapter 27 223
Chapter 28 227
Chapter 29 231
Chapter 30 235
Chapter 31 238
Chapter 32 243
Chapter 33 249
Chapter 34 254
Chapter 35 269
Chapter 36 275
Chapter 37 288
Chapter 38 293
Chapter 39 300
Chapter 40 310
Chapter 41 314
Chapter 42 317
Epilogue 322

Acknowledgements 325

About the Author 326

PART 1
THE CULL

PART 1 - THE CULL

CHAPTER 1

The Journal of Arthur Graham Marco - vol 19, England 1818

I am off to visit the Hamptons. Sophie said they are still suffering from a lack of funds. It doesn't make sense. The estate and holdings should be producing well. I promised to look things over and present them with Diana's jewels if they wish to sell them. I do not expect a long visit.

He looked directly at me as I worked in the window of the tailor's shop. I lowered my face from his gaze and felt my cheeks burn from his impolite stare.

"You there! I need assistance." He pointed his walking stick at me.

A tittering came from the other women as I put my work down carefully and walked towards him. He tapped his walking stick impatiently and pushed his dark hair out of his eyes.

I took a deep breath and smoothed down my skirt. "How can I help you, sir?"

"I need a repair." He held out his long arm to show me where his shirt sleeve had ripped. The entire cuff was hung on by a few threads.

I examined where it had torn and looked up into his dark eyes. "I am sure you would rather have the tailor himself repair this. I'll find him and fetch you a robe…"

"There is no time," he cut me off, and to the horror of everyone in the shop, started removing his coat.

"Sir! What are you doing?" I asked as he tossed his coat on the counter and started undoing his waistcoat.

"You obviously can't repair it while I'm wearing it, so I'm taking it off."

"Oh sir, please..."

He tossed off his waistcoat and started on his buttons. His shirt came off. The other ladies gasped and cried out at the sight.

I froze when he threw the white silk at me. It bounced off my arms and hit the floor. I gawked at his chest. The chest of a hearty, healthy male.

Was this happening?

"Can you sew in a straight line!?" He pounded his walking stick on the floor with each word.

Shaken from my fit, I nodded. My ire was starting to rise and I found myself glaring at him in return. "Yes, I can."

"Then hurry, I am damnably late as it is."

I picked up the shirt and went back to my corner, finding thread to match the silk. The soft material was almost too much for my shaking hands, and I fumbled it a time or two. I could feel my cheeks stinging. He glared at me along with the other ladies. The longer I took, the longer a half-naked man stood in our little shop.

It was not my best work, but I did manage to repair the shirt without it looking like a complete idiot had done it. I hurried it back to him. He snatched it from my grasp and inspected it briefly before re-dressing. He slapped down some coins on the counter and stormed out.

"What a horrible and disgusting beast!" I declared as the door slammed shut. The other ladies rushed to agree with me. I pushed the incident away and returned to my stitches while the conversation returned to regular village gossip.

As the sun kissed the horizon outside, he re-entered our shop. His eyes were searching for someone. I ducked my head and focused on my skirt's pleats.

I heard his firm footsteps cross the hollow floor and stop at my side. The entire shop went quiet. I cringed and felt my cheeks begin to burn again at the reminder of his bare chest I'd seen this morning.

"Excuse me." His voice was still firm but less sharp than this morning. I glanced up at him.

"I behaved like a brute earlier today. I wish to apologize." He was still glaring.

I met his gaze. He certainly did not look sorry. I stiffened my spine.

"Do you really wish to apologize?" I gave him what I hoped was my best look of disdain.

PART 1 - THE CULL

"Yes, I do. I know when I am in the wrong. You did a fine job and saved me from embarrassment and a most unpleasant scene with my mother-in-law. I wish to thank you and make my appeal for forgiveness."

"You are welcome, and I accept your apology." I lowered my eyes and picked my needle back up.

I expected him to leave. He stood silently above me and I started to squirm.

"Is there anything else I can do for you?" I met his dark gaze with a glare of my own. His dark hair was too long to be in fashion, and he wore a beard. Rich gentlemen never wore a beard.

He quirked a brow at me, making me feel even more inferior.

"I need to get back to work."

I hoped he would leave. Forever. I focused on my needle and found the precise place to push it into the fabric.

He stayed at my side, staring down at me. I was starting to wonder if he was just a little bit mad. What possessed him to linger further?

"Can I help you, sir?" It was Mr. Cooper, our tailor and, hopefully, my savior. He smiled warmly at our visitor and approached us.

"Yes. This young lady did an exceptional job assisting me this morning, and I treated her like a complete brute. I came to make amends."

Mr. Cooper looked at me. "Miss Horton?"

I smiled up at Mr. Cooper. "I accepted his apologies, and appreciate his efforts to reconcile."

Mr. Cooper raised his brows and turned back to our visitor. "I see, Mr...eh?"

"Marco. Arthur Marco," he announced, offering his hand to Mr. Cooper.

"Mr. Marco." Mr. Cooper shook his hand shortly. "Is there anything else I can assist you with today?"

Mr. Marco looked back at me, his piercing eyes searching my face. I was sure he was counting every freckle on my nose and cheeks. "Possibly. Miss Horton announced to the world I was a 'horrible and disgusting beast.' I am trying to think of a way to convince her otherwise."

I flinched. "You heard me?"

"Yes, I heard you."

"Then it is my turn to apologize, Mr. Marco." I did my best to sound sincere.

"No, you were telling the truth, Miss Horton. I will agree I am a horrible man. Disgusting, however, is not something I have ever been called."

"You took off your shirt in full view of a shop full of women." I pointed out, meeting Mr. Marco's stare with a brave face.

Mr. Cooper's eyebrows rose up into his hairline. "He did what?"

At last Mr. Marco looked ashamed. "I did. In my haste and anger, I completely forgot where I was and my behavior was appalling." He looked at Mr. Cooper and bowed a little. "I shall promptly apologize to all your employees." He tucked his walking stick under his arm and immediately walked back to the group.

"I think he's mad," Mr. Cooper said. I was glad to have someone agree with my internal assessment.

"Shall I go fetch some help?" I asked.

"No, let us watch him. I may not be as young as I used to be, but I was quite the pugilist in my youth. I think I can manage to remove him if needed. At least I'll bloody his nose." His eyes remained focused on our visitor. I shrugged and returned to the pleats that demanded to be finished before the light dimmed.

I listened with one ear while Mr. Marco charmed each employee, young and old. They were suddenly amiable and chatty in his company. I wondered how he did it. I tried every day to have them accept me as an equal, even though my father was wealthy. They would politely remind me I was taking a job from someone else in the village who needed the funds and ignore me for the rest of the day.

He accomplished comradery in less than ten minutes, even after a scandalous introduction. I didn't know if I should be more disgusted with him or them.

He stopped at my chair. I looked up at him and gave him a glare before he could speak. "We've concluded our conversation already," I said, focusing on my work.

He tapped his walking stick lightly on the floor a few times and left my side. He gave one last word of remorse to Mr. Cooper and left.

I breathed a sigh of relief at his departure.

After I finished my pleats I was ready to go home. I set the skirt aside, tidied my work area, picked up my cloak and lunch packet, and said my goodbyes. The other ladies didn't lift their heads, but a few murmured farewells. It was progress.

PART 1 - THE CULL

The sun was setting and I had enough time to enjoy my walk home before dinner. It was a clear afternoon, smelling of growing crops, and sweet mowed hay, all the scents that went with a farming community. I stopped and closed my eyes, tipping my face to the sky to bask in the warmth of the sun.

"So, you are a sun worshiper? I wondered from all the freckles."

I opened my eyes and turned around at the voice.

Mr. Marco stood behind me, smiling and leaning on his walking stick.

"I enjoy the sun." I turned away. I began my steps towards home and found him keeping stride with me.

"You have no bonnet either?" He pointed to my bare head.

"They give me headaches. Not that it is any business of yours."

"No, no it is not." We walked in silence.

I finally broke the stillness. "Haven't you better things to attend to?" I stopped in the middle of the road and tried my best to match his earlier glower.

"Much better things, yes. But none are as interesting as you at the moment."

Politeness and all the manners my mother taught me about being a lady melted away in my brain. "I am sure I will prove to be more tiresome than anything else you've encountered."

"Possibly, but I would rather find out on my own."

I tossed up my arms, and set out at a faster pace. I heard him chuckle. He caught up with me and matched my pace.

"Do you take it upon yourself to torment women regularly?"

"I just started today. Tormenting you is now my new favorite occupation."

"I'm sure I could find someone else much more deserving than I of your attention."

"They would pale in comparison to your dagger-like tongue."

"You are mad," I pronounced.

"Probably. But if wanting to be in the presence of an attractive, interesting woman is madness, I'll suffer gladly."

Heat flooded my cheeks. I resolved then to ignore him.

He kept pace with me all the way back to my home, not speaking another word.

My spaniel, Pip, greeted me at the gate and I gave his head a pat and accepted a canine kiss. The traitorous dog then went to inspect my follower with tail wagging and bright, shining eyes in anticipation of a new friend. Mr. Marco greeted him and knelt to pet him.

I left them behind and made my way to the door. I turned in time to see him climb the steps. His eyes met mine and I smiled sweetly before I promptly shut the door in his face.

Smug and satisfied with my appalling behavior, I removed my cloak.

He rang the bell.

Our maid, Martha, came to answer it.

"Ignore it, Martha," I told her, taking off my dirty boots.

He rang again and Martha bit her lip. "Who is it?"

"An ill-tempered, rascal of a man trying to get my hackles up."

She looked uncertain. The bell rang again.

Mother appeared. "Is anyone going to answer the door?" She looked directly at Martha who pointed at me.

"It is nothing but an irritating pest, Mother. Ignore it and it will leave."

Another ring.

Mother herself reached for the door and I stomped to my room. I heard Mother welcome Mr. Marco inside before I shut my bedroom door.

I let my hair down and sighed with sweet relief when the few pins that held it out of my sight were taken away. I set to brushing my short wavy curls smooth.

The knock at my door didn't surprise me. The door opened and Martha's face appeared in my mirror.

"You have a visitor." Her eyes shone. "He's a handsome man."

"He is a wicked man who has been following me all evening, finding pleasure in teasing me."

Martha's face fell a little. "He said you were intimately involved."

"Intimate! I suppose so, if you call a brute of a man who disrobes himself in a shop full of women becoming 'intimately involved', then yes, I know him quite well."

Martha covered her gasp and she sat down on the bed, leaning forward to hear my tale. I spilled it all, adding a good dose of my own venom to it to sway Martha to my position.

"Maybe he is insane." She wrung her hands a little. "I should go find your father and brother."

PART 1 - THE CULL

The idea of my father throwing Mr. Marco out the door had great appeal.

She opened the door to leave and I heard my father's loud and rumbling laughter from downstairs.

It was too late. Mr. Marco was able to charm the other ladies at the shop, even after his abhorrent behavior. I feared my agreeable father had already succumbed to his charm as well. I heard men's voices conversing, rising in a crescendo, and then more laughter. This time with Mr. Marco and my brother Thomas joining in.

"Oh please, come down now with me. I can't say those things in front of your father with him in the room." Martha reached for my hand.

I took hers and patted it. "I shall go down and face the madman, Martha."

Pip ran up the stairs and circled around me. His tail wagged and pounded against my skirt. I could almost hear his simple thoughts, 'Oh mistress! Come see this wonderful new friend!' I smoothed a hand over his silky head and he calmed when we reached the bottom of the stairs.

"I don't suppose I could entreat you to bite him?" I asked.

Pip tilted his head, blinked, and then led me into the parlor.

Mr. Marco rose when I walked in, staring at me. He held a snifter of brandy and nodded at me.

"There she is! My dear, why didn't you tell us about your new friend?" Mother asked as I took a seat beside her.

"Because 'friend' is hardly the category I would place Mr. Marco in." I was happy to see my temper stayed firmly in my control. He sat down and took a sip of his drink.

Father raised his brows. "Really? Mr. Marco came here tonight to express his desire to court you."

All the blood drained from my face and my stomach grew warm. I looked at Mr. Marco. He hid a small, smug smile on his face behind the snifter. There was nothing more I wished at that moment but to reach out and slap it off him. Instead, I bit the inside of my cheek to keep my tongue civil.

"My dearest Father, I could think of nothing more disagreeable." I said between a clenched jaw.

Father laughed. "I told you she was a tough one."

Mr. Marco raised his glass for a sip and fixed me with a hard stare. "Which makes it all the more interesting."

I inhaled deeply to start a new tirade on what I thought of Mr. Marco.

Mother rose to her feet and stopped my words with a sharp look she'd perfected from raising five children. I knew I was in for more trouble when she smiled at Mr. Marco while taking my hand, gently. Once her fingers took mine, she clamped down hard and, oh so discreetly, dug her nails into my skin. I nearly yelped aloud.

"Would you excuse us please, Mr. Marco? I need my daughter's help with dinner. I'm so glad you'll be joining us."

I was whisked out of the room before I could utter a word of protest. Mother's grip had turned into a painful vice. She hauled me into the kitchen and plopped me into a chair like I was four years old.

"What is the meaning behind your behavior?" She hissed at me.

"My behavior! Maybe you should ask your newly beloved Mr. Marco about HIS behavior today!" I hissed back. I related my meeting with Mr. Marco and his bare chest to her. I finished my tale with, "I hardly think he is the kind of man you and Father wish me to be associated with." I felt a little vindicated at her wide eyes and blushing face.

She stood up and moved around the kitchen alongside our cook, Nell. They both had done the dinner preparation dance so many times they worked around each other flawlessly.

"So he is a rash man. That should hardly disqualify him as an acquaintance. I know for a fact you are prone to such acts as well." She sliced bread into even pieces.

"Mother! I have never disrobed myself..."

"I would hope and pray such a thought would never come into your head!" She shoved the bread towards me and took the saucepan from Nell to pour it into a more attractive dish.

"Then why when he does it you are not too harsh on him? His behavior was borderline criminal." I could see the workings in my mother's thoughts.

"You sincerely think he could be a good suitor!" I accused, rising to my feet.

Mother set the pan down with some force. "What I sincerely think is that a young lady with no prospects at the age of one and twenty should seriously entertain the thought of any man who wishes to be her suitor." Her eyes bore into my face, and I sat down slowly, dread filling me instead of anger.

PART 1 - THE CULL

"You wish to be rid of me," I said quietly.

"I said nothing of the sort, and it will do you good not to place words where they have not been spoken." She mixed the sauce vigorously. "Your first impression of Mr. Marco was not a good one, I agree. But as of this moment, he is a guest in my home and you will treat him as such."

"Now, go place this on the table and invite the gentlemen to join us for dinner." She nudged the bread closer to me.

Resolved to obey my mother, I took the plate of bread and walked it out to the table. I returned to the parlor where my father, brother and the horrible Mr. Marco sat conversing. They all stopped and looked at me when I entered.

"I have come to bid you all to join us for dinner," I announced sweetly, giving Mr. Marco my best toothy grin. I hoped it looked like I would bite.

He set down his drink and followed my father and brother towards the kitchen, stopping briefly before me. "I'm honored by your family's invitation, Miss Horton." He gave me a little bow.

"I'm sure your presence will provide us with delightful and fresh conversation," I lied, clenching my teeth.

"I'm sure yours will as well." He smiled at me. I glared back and his smile widened.

Mother waited for us at the table. "Ah, here we all are. You sit there, Thomas." She directed my brother. She took me by the elbow and steered me into a seat, right across the table from Mr. Marco.

I glanced across at Mr. Marco and found his smile was gone. He was scowling once again. Was it too much to ask to look at the man's countenance and expect a semi-pleasant glance?

"Mr. Marco, for some reason the sight of me vexes you. Every time I catch your eye you have a distinct look of displeasure aimed in my direction. Are you quite certain you wish to remain seated across from me?" I asked.

He cocked his head slightly. "Miss Horton, I can assure you there is nothing that would give me more pleasure than to sit across from you at dinner."

"Perhaps a blindfold then?" I shook out my napkin. "Then you could keep your seat and not see my face." I covered my lap with the napkin and smoothed it.

"But then I could not count each adorable freckle on your nose," he countered.

I felt the heat rise in me and glared down at my plate. Two could play at this game. "I don't mind your counting them, as long as you keep your shirt on while doing it."

My father laughed out loud while my mother hissed. "That's enough, Joy." Mother's pasted-on smile couldn't hide her horrified look.

"Joy? At last, I learn your name." Mr. Marco smiled at me.

"You followed her all the way here, said you were 'intimately involved' and you didn't know her name." Thomas chuckled. "You're a bit bacon-brained."

"Thomas!" My mother's voice was almost a shriek.

Father was kind enough to rescue her. "Joy is our fourth daughter. The others are Faith, Hope, and Charity. My wife's father was a passionate vicar. She wanted to name Joy 'Virtue', but I drew the line there."

My mother's face was beginning to turn a nice shade of purple. Good. She could share in some humiliation.

Mr. Marco's face showed nothing but pure amusement at my family's conversation.

Happily, Nell and Martha appeared with dinner and the conversation paused to fill plates and glasses. Mr. Marco appropriately gave my mother and Nell the right amount of praise which did wonders to calm my mother's apprehensions.

We ate a few bites before Mr. Marco dug another shot to my character. "Mr. Horton. With such a nice estate and comfortable living for your family, I find it odd I met your daughter working at the tailor's today."

Had he been closer, I would have kicked him under the table. Did he really have to pick at an open wound my family was already fond of scraping at?

"Ah, our Joy is rather an independent thing. Once she passed what she deemed, 'the age of marriageability' she took it upon herself to support herself." Father beamed at me. My father was always my champion. From the day Mr. Cooper had laid eyes on my first creation when I was twelve at my sister's wedding, he'd begged me to come to work for him. My father readily agreed to the apprenticeship.

Mother shook her head. "No such thing. Mr. Cooper had a large order for new livery at the Hamptons and Joy is just helping out." Mother took a drink of wine. A long one.

"If you want the truth, it's both." Thomas added his kindling to the fire. "Joy is fiercely independent, and she is also helping out. Father is extremely proud and Mother thinks she's a disgrace. She is a complicated thing, our Joy."

I was done with all of them. I scooted my seat back and stood, trying to keep my temper in check. "Please excuse me. I don't think I can take many more comments on my character without being ill."

Both Mother and Father called to me as I stormed away. I ignored them and was sure to slam the door hard.

The smell of warm hay and manure calmed me down when I entered the barn. I took a deep breath and slowed my steps. There was no reason to affect the animals with my current mood. I reached out and took a handful of grain from a bucket and walked to the stall of our old mare, Penny. She sniffed my hand and her lips accepted the treat. I scratched her head and rested my own against hers; inhaling her distinct scent soothed me. I had a wild thought of mounting her bareback and riding off into the wilds. Maybe I could find a troupe of wandering minstrels or gypsies who needed a good seamstress.

"Your family is wonderful." Mr. Marco's voice interrupted my thoughts. My heart hardened, gearing up for another verbal battle.

"I am glad someone thinks so."

"They were worried when you left. They are tender towards your feelings."

"I'm sure they are. So much so they sent a perfect stranger to soothe me."

"I volunteered to come." He stepped up beside me and reached out to pet the mare's nose. "Attractive thing, I'll bet she was a beauty in her prime."

"Yes. My father complains that she's a bit too independent."

"Your father must not be a good judge of horse-flesh." He dropped his hand.

"And you are?"

"I like to think so."

Enough banter. "Mr. Marco. I am not a horse."

He had the grace to look surprised. "I...never said you were?"

"You've been following me all day, judging me, sizing me up. I understand you wish to make amends, and I accept your apology and offer my own. But an offer of courtship seems a little much. Why won't you leave me alone?" I asked.

He was silent, digging holes in the soft dirt with his walking stick.

"My wife brought me here today," he started. "We had an arranged marriage. She had nothing but praises for me; like a dog I would cast off if she displeased me. I couldn't carry on a conversation with her without it making me weary. I felt nothing for her but duty to care for her and our families. I'm ashamed to say her death was more of a release to me than sorrow. Today I was to settle things with her family and resume my life as a bachelor. Then I tore my shirt getting out of my curricle. I found a tailor, and I found you. A woman who stood up to me and actually called me out on my rude behavior. It made me...feel...something."

"Feel what?" I couldn't imagine I had inspired many good feelings. I certainly hadn't had many from our first meeting.

"Shame." His harsh gaze met mine. "Self-revulsion is not something I have encountered much. I haven't felt the need to be in anyone's good graces for some time. But suddenly I wanted to challenge that I was a 'disgusting beast'."

"You made a pretty apology earlier. I accepted it. Now you may leave me to carry on with my life and you with yours."

He shrugged. "I tried, but you put a spell on me, you little witch."

"I did no such thing!" I countered.

"I left the tailor's shop ready to embark on the rest of my miserable life when you came out of the door with your bare head and freckles and stood in the sunlight; face up to welcome its rays. I was struck by how unconventional you were, and yet you radiate serenity. I think that's why I find I cannot leave so easily."

His words made my carefully-built shell crack a little.

"Mr. Marco. I'm flattered you find my faults charming. I am at peace with who I am." I had made peace a long time ago with my lot in life.

"I want peace." He stroked Penny's head softly.

I sighed. "It's not something I can give."

"Then I shall resume my study of you until I figure it out." He rubbed Penny's nose and took a step back from her. "Therefore, I must continue my courtship to remain in your company."

"I don't wish for you to court me."

"Oh come now, Miss Horton. I thought all young ladies dreamed of having a rich man come and sweep them off their feet."

"Only the daft ones who have feathers for brains," I mumbled.

"Such a hard-hearted little fairy! How did you become so?"

"I'm not hard-hearted, Mr. Marco. I just know you have a picture painted of me that is untrue. You know nothing about me but I'm willing to call a bully a bully; I sew for my independence, I like the sun, and I hate to wear bonnets." I gave him a small smile. "That alone should drive away any thoughts of courtship. You're obviously a wealthy gentleman with some rank." I motioned to his attire. "I'm a simple yeoman's daughter with no aspirations. Now please, leave me to my simple life."

He scowled at me raising his walking stick and smacked it hard against a bundle of hay on his way out of the stables. He stopped in the doorway, and turned back to me, pointing his walking stick at me. "I want a month."

"A month?" I asked, thoroughly confused.

"A month. A month to know you. To find out who Joy Horton really is."

"Oh please...don't...just go."

He stormed back towards me. He towered over me and glared. "A month to convince me you are not worthy of my attention. So far all you've done is frustrate and intrigue me. I don't think you know how attractive that makes you."

My heart jumped in my throat and threatened to choke me. "Mr. Marco..!"

He turned his back on me and strode away.

Chapter 2

The Hortons are delightful. Thomas Sr. is a wealthy yeoman who won't make the transition to a gentleman. He swore he'd go mad if he didn't have his hands in the dirt or sheep grease on his skin. Mrs. Horton is more genteel but has the same need to keep her hands involved in the household chores. Old habits die hard, I suppose.

Miss Horton is exceptionally delightful. I don't remember a day when I've had so much fun with a woman.

I was awakened early by my father's voice shouting through the house for everyone to help. It had rained all night and the sheep had managed to lay against the southern fence and push the posts over in the soft mud.

I dressed in a pair of my brother's old trousers and a faded woolen shirt of my father's and stumbled down the stairs.

Mother was handing Thomas his waterproof clothes. She scowled at my attire, but for once didn't try to dissuade me from helping. It meant the damage was substantial.

I pulled on my boots and found an old wool coat of Thomas's that would keep me well insulated. I had almost made it out of the house without a hat when Mother slapped a wide-brimmed leather one on my head. The look on her face stopped me from taking it off.

Thomas and I made our way to the fence. Father was there with our tenants. They were doing their best to hastily repair the fence while Brutus, our shaggy sheepdog, herded the sheep back from the opening they had made. Thomas handed me Penny's reins and jumped into the mud with Father.

PART 1 - THE CULL

Pip sat quietly at my side, having gotten in Brutus' way before. He wagged his tail a little and sighed. I stroked his ears and stood in the rain, waiting for instructions.

Father stepped away from the work and shook his head. "That'll have to do for now. We need to round up the rest of the flock." He took the reins from me and led the horse to Thomas. "Stay here, Joy. Make sure they don't knock it down again until we can come back with more supplies. Come on, Brutus."

Pip helped me keep an eye on the fence. His sharp barks kept any other wandering sheep from escaping. He shook in the rain and splattered me with more mud and water.

"Thank you, Pip," I sighed. I took off my hat, humming with relief when the weight left my head. Looking up at the sky I let the rain rinse my face. I wrung out my hair and went to put the hat back on.

I heard the bleat of a sheep and glanced around. They had started congregating when I had my back turned. Our big ram started leaning on the weak spot and stirring up the mud where father and Thomas had propped up the fence post.

"No, you don't. Pip! Get them away." I trudged through the mud. It stuck to my boots and slowed me down. Pip gleefully leaped towards them and barked, making them scatter.

I managed to go up the small incline, slipping once and getting mud on my hands and knees. I leaned hard against the fence to push the post upright. My feet sank deeper and deeper into the mud. Pip returned from his romp and sniffed around my feet before shaking off his mud and water all over me again.

I moved away from the post and watched it slip even farther down the embankment. Sighing, I moved back into position and leaned against it.

The sound of hooves clipped along the road. A lone rider appeared on the scene, bundled up in a blue woolen pea coat with shiny buttons and definite Royal Navy emblems. His face was hidden under the brim of his bicorne.

Pip held still and stared at him, then burst into happy barking and tail wagging. He raced off to meet the newcomer with wild abandonment.

"Hello there, Pip!" The rider slowed to allow Pip to come to the horse's heels. He dismounted and reached down to scratch Pip's ears. "What are you doing so far from home on such a nasty morning?"

It was John Turner, Thomas's best friend since childhood. I hadn't seen him in over three years. He had grown much since he'd left for the Navy, and his body had filled out into the size of a man instead of a gangly youth.

"He is not without a chaperone," I called out.

John raised his head, searching for my voice through the rain. He spotted me and his face grew into a smile. "Miss Joy Horton? Is that you?"

"Yes, Lieutenant John Turner. I would come and greet you properly, but I'm quite busy at the moment."

He led his horse towards me, shaking his head. "Found yourself in a scrape?" He sank a little in the wallow I'd made. "And digging yourself in deeper. Here, I think I can remember how to mend a fence. At least I can manage a temporary job until your father can do it properly."

"John, no! You'll get your uniform dirty," I protested.

He chuckled. "Trust me, it's seen worse than good English mud."

Without much effort, he righted the posts and managed to stretch the cables to keep them stable. It felt nice to relieve my back of the weight. I stretched my sore muscles while he finished the work, giving it a thorough shake to make sure it would hold. "There, that should do it. At least until they get back."

"Thank you for the rescue. Would you accept a dirty embrace of thanks and welcome?" I wiped my hand off on my breeches before reaching out for his hand. He pulled me in, squeezing me tightly. His embrace had become stronger after three years of work aboard a ship.

We released each other. "Thomas will be so happy to see you. I'm so glad you made it for Jane's wedding."

"She'll be so wrapped up with wedding plans she'll hardly notice I'm here." He smiled. "Where's Thomas?"

"He's off chasing sheep at the moment."

He tipped his hat and returned to his horse. "I'll call on your family later today."

"I'll be sure Nell makes your favorite pie and have it cooled before you come. I want to hear all the stories you have from around the world."

He grinned. "I look forward to it." He trotted away and left me with Pip and my vigil.

I was thoroughly chilled by the time Father and Thomas returned. My fingers and nose were red and numb and I could barely feel them. Father

PART 1 - THE CULL

briefly chaffed them, told me I had done well, and sent me home with a kiss on my forehead.

As I set my sights for home, the skies unleashed a waterfall. I kept my head down, letting the rain roll off the brim of my hat. The weight of it hurt my head, but the wrath of my mother kept me from taking it off.

Pip plodded along with his nose to the ground as the water saturated his fur. We were a soggy, sorry sight.

"Don't be so sad, Pip. I'll get you dried off and make you a nice bed in front of the fire." Lucky dog. He could spend the day on a warm hearth, while I had pleats and buttonholes waiting for me at Mr. Cooper's shop. My stiff fingers would take a while to be able to move fluidly with needle and thread. I pulled my sleeves over them to start the warming process.

I heard hoof beats on the road behind me. I glanced up and saw a curricle making its way briskly through the rain. Pip and I stood to the side to let it pass and then continued our journey.

The curricle slowed and stopped. The driver set the brake and climbed down from his seat. The brim of his hat tipped up and I saw his glare. For a man who claimed he was attracted to me, he had a strange way of showing it.

"What the devil are you doing out in such weather?" he demanded.

Mr. Marco marched towards me with a face as dark as a thundercloud. As if my morning couldn't get any worse.

"As you can plainly see, I'm walking home," I replied calmly.

"What possessed you to come out in this? Are you trying to catch your death?" He took my arm and started marching me towards the cab.

"The southern fence was damaged and the sheep escaped." I wrestled my arm away. "Some of us actually have to do some work to run an estate."

His face became darker if it were possible. He spoke quietly, with barely contained temper. "Get. In. The. Curricle."

My own temper shot out. "No."

Pip's head went back and forth between us while we shouted at one another.

"You stubborn little vixen," Mr. Marco growled.

"I don't want your help!"

"Are you daft? Why would you want to walk in the rain when I have a perfectly good curricle available?"

"Because you didn't ask me. You just grabbed my arm and started towing me where you wanted me to go. I'm not a child, and I don't belong to you!"

He stared at me and I glared right back. His fists clenched, and then loosened. "Miss Horton," he spoke softly, his eyes blazing. "It would be my utmost pleasure to give you a ride home. Will you please accept?"

I shivered. The rain was starting to seep down through my clothes and my fingers were almost impossible to move. I glanced down at Pip who looked as miserable as I did.

I looked back at him. "I accept your offer, Mr. Marco. Only if you will give Pip a ride as well."

He raised his brows at me and looked down at the soaked dog. Pip thumped his tail once and managed to look even more pitiful with sad brown eyes and drooping ears.

"What a sorry pair." Mr. Marco took my hand again, more gently. He placed it in the crook of his arm and guided me to his cab. He steadied me while I climbed in and then called for Pip, who bounded up into the curricle with zeal. The spaniel started to quiver, getting ready to shake. I wrapped my arms around him.

"No, Pip. Wait." The last thing I needed was Pip making a wet and muddy mess inside Mr. Marco's fine cab.

My canine companion looked at me as if I were asking the impossible and continued to shiver with anticipation of a good healthy shake.

Mr. Marco climbed up next to us and set us in motion. Once the rain was off my head I removed the hat. I sighed in relief when the weight left my neck.

"Bareheaded again. Why do you fight so much against propriety?" he asked.

"I am not fighting against it. I simply get headaches from propriety. It's a matter of comfort," I said.

Pip lurched again and I wrapped my arms around him once more. "Not in the cab, Pip."

"Let him go, my clothes will wash." Mr. Marco pulled my arm down from the wet dog.

Pip needed no further encouragement. He shook hard and splattered us both. I found a handkerchief in my coat pocket and wiped my face. Mr. Marco's face was also speckled with muddy dog water. I leaned over and wiped off his cheek. He jumped at my touch and then allowed me to continue.

"There." I tucked the muddy cloth in my coat.

"Thank you." He focused his gaze on the road.

We rode in silence and Pip panted between us.

"Do you often join your father and brother in the rain and mud?" he asked.

"Yes, as often as they'll let me."

He smirked. "Just to spite your mother?"

"No, that is just a bonus."

He gave me a stern look. "You shouldn't try to vex your mother. She is a good lady."

"Yes, she is. She and I just disagree on what is best for me." She wanted me married and raising a family. So did I, but one of us had to face the reality that it would never happen.

I brought my hands to my mouth and blew warm air onto them.

He glanced at my red fingers and scowled. "For heaven's sake, Miss Horton, a hat is one thing but no gloves?"

"I was in a hurry; Thomas would have left me and then I would have had to walk to the fence." I wiggled my fingers to regain some feeling in them.

He held the reins in one hand and tugged his glove off with his teeth. He reached over and took both my hands, tucking them in his long fingers. They started to sting against his warmth.

"You are like ice, Miss Horton, are you sure you don't need a keeper?" he asked.

"I'm quite sure. Except for my fingers and toes, the rest of me is perfectly warm. Some breakfast and a warm fire are all I need at the moment." I looked down while he rubbed my hands with his thumb. The initial stinging was going away, replaced slowly by warm friction. "Thank you."

"You are welcome. Anything to convince you that I am not the beast you think I am."

"Your first impression was not of a gentleman." I reminded him as he slowly rubbed my fingers with his in a comforting pattern.

"Something I am sure you will never forgive."

"I forgive you, Mr. Marco, but I will not forget, at least not in the immediate future."

"So, you are one to hold a grudge? A less attractive attribute for a young lady to have, but I can overlook it."

"I have warned you several times I am not wife material, but you are choosing not to listen."

"Who said I wanted a wife?"

The thought of the alternative brought a hard shot of anger to my belly. What kind of a woman did he think I was? I jerked my hands away and resisted the urge to slap him. "Stop this curricle right now," I hissed.

"Calm down, Miss Horton, my intentions are honorable towards you. I am more interested in your friendship at the moment. I have already been married once, and found the whole ordeal…stifling. You are a breath of fresh air."

I wiggled my fingers to try and find more warmth. "You are still a rash man. And I don't know if I wish to be your friend. I think you are too impetuous, which is why I was staring at your bare chest yesterday before you followed me home. You act before you think."

"Guilty as charged, Miss Horton. And far too old to change my ways."

I gave my best 'harrumph' and blew warm air again on my fingers. He couldn't be much older than thirty by my estimation.

"Don't be so stubborn, Miss Horton, give me your hands and let me warm them. I know you need to ply your trade today." He held out his hand towards me.

He was right. I reluctantly slid my fingers back into his palm. He squeezed them gently. Pip rested his wet head on Mr. Marco's knee.

"Why don't you have a driver or a carriage?"

He scowled and then shrugged. "Maybe I can't afford one."

I scoffed. "I've seen the fabric of your clothes, Mr. Marco. I suspect you can afford anything you wish."

"True." He gave me a little smirk. "Maybe you are not the only one who likes to buck tradition and propriety for independence, Miss Freckles."

I felt a smile tease on my lips.

"I find I have more freedom in driving my own transportation. And then I can take young ladies on thrilling rides through the countryside."

"Thrilling? At this sedate walk?"

"You wish to go faster?" He quirked a brow at me.

"You were going faster when you encountered Pip and me on the road." I pointed out.

He released my hand and took the reins. "As the lady wishes."

He gave the reins a crack and whistled sharply. The horses were more than happy to leap into action. Pip barked with excitement as we lurched forward.

I laughed and grabbed Mr. Marco's arm for balance. He took the corners sharp and we skidded in the mud. I gave an involuntary squeal when the rain pelted into my face. Pip barked louder when we sped through the puddles. It splattered up on our clothes and faces.

The freedom of the wind and rain in my face was exhilarating. That Mr. Marco was willing to indulge me was another definite crack in the armor I'd built against him. I released his arm as we slowed and came to a halt in front of my home.

"Would you like to come in for some breakfast? It's probably a simpler fare than you are used to, but it should be warm and filling." The invitation came out easily. Years of my mother's good manners were hard to withhold.

"I have already eaten, but I would be happy to accept a hot cup of tea or coffee." He climbed down from the curricle and reached up for me. I leaned into him and he lifted me easily by the waist and I slid to the ground.

It was an action I had performed hundreds of times, with several different men. This was the first time I blushed at the feel of a man's hands around me.

CHAPTER 3

I can't seem to stay away from Miss Horton. I should stop. I know better. I swore I would never look at a young lady ever again. But I'm laughing, I'm playing, I feel my cold heart thawing.

It seems I'm more selfish than I thought.

Martha met us at the entryway, her eyes widening at the sight of Mr. Marco and our mud-covered bodies.

"Oh goodness." She took my wet hat and started to peel off my coat. "Let me call for Mrs. Horton to help you, Mr. Marco." She took my coat and scurried away to the kitchen.

I reached over and took his hat, trying to brush off some of the mud. Mother appeared in the hallway. She took Mr. Marco's hat from my frigid fingers. "You two are a mess!"

"It is a definite mess out there," I agreed. Martha came back with two blankets, wrapping one around me. Mother peeled off his cape and coat then wrapped the other blanket around Mr. Marco before she led him to the fire in the parlor. Martha led me to my room.

"I was surprised to see Mr. Marco this morning out the window helping you out of his cab. I thought you disliked him?" She tugged my wet socks off my feet and placed them on a warm brick.

"I dislike being cold and wet more." My teeth chattered.

She looked at me with a big grin. "He is a handsome man. Don't you think?"

"I'm sure handsome men think enough of themselves and don't need my thoughts added." I pulled the blanket tighter. "Besides, he always has a perpetual scowl. Would it kill the man to smile once in a while?"

PART 1 - THE CULL

She shook her head and pulled clean clothes onto my body. "Honestly, sometimes I think you are doing all you can to drive off any man that looks your way."

"I did ask him to stay for breakfast," I said. I was enjoying the merry war we had going. It was energetic, and truth be told, fun.

She beamed. "You did? Oh, that will make Mrs. Horton so glad. She was sure you'd scared him away after last night."

"Not for lack of effort," I grumbled.

She started brushing my wet hair. "He's different from any other man around here. He might not care that you can't…" Her words trailed off before she could hurt my feelings. I closed my eyes and let her brushstrokes fill the silence.

"It's alright, Martha. I've made peace with it." I stood up and inspected myself in the mirror. The same face I'd seen all my life gazed back with big blue eyes and blonde hair that was currently smooth. Once it dried it would resume its unruly manners. Martha tried to come from behind with hairpins and pull it up. I shooed her away, ran my fingers through it, and headed down to the dining room.

I walked in and found Mother handing Mr. Marco a teacup. They both looked up at me, Mother with a smile, Mr. Marco with a scowl. He rose to his feet while I pulled my chair back.

I scowled back and slid into my seat. "What have I done to deserve such a look, Mr. Marco?" I placed my napkin on my lap.

"What look is that?" He sat down.

"Again, you look unhappy to see me," I answered.

"If you must know, I'm trying to hide my exuberance of seeing you once again behind a mask of indifference and disdain. All wealthy men perfect it at a young age. The more I glower the happier I am to see you."

His remark brought a smile to my lips. "I'm happy to know when I walk in the room it fills you with such delight that you must frown."

"You have no idea," he murmured.

"I was just about to ask Mr. Marco what brought him here this morning," Mother said, sliding into her own chair.

"I was on my way to offer Miss Horton a ride to the tailor's shop this morning to keep her head dry." He glanced at me. "Obviously, I was too late, but I was happy to give her and Pip a ride home."

"Pip?" Mother glanced over at the sleeping spaniel stretched across the hearth in an undignified pose, his belly facing the ceiling. "You gave Pip a ride in your cab?"

"Miss Horton insisted she couldn't leave her faithful companion." Mr. Marco gave me a wicked grin. I glared as my mother started a new tirade.

"Joy! How could you?"

Now he'd done it. "It was a simple battle of wills, Mother, I was trying to see how much Mr. Marco wanted my company. Apparently, I am more attractive than a dry, clean curricle that doesn't smell like a wet dog." I gave her my best penitent look. "I must say, it raises my esteem for Mr. Marco more than yesterday's first encounter with him."

"Touché." I heard him whisper.

Mother rolled her eyes. "The two of you are a pair. Now eat up, both of you are probably chilled."

She poured hot tea for the both of us. The warm cup felt comforting in my hands. I smiled and closed my eyes as sensation began to seep back into my fingers.

"The offer to warm your hands is still open, Miss Horton."

I finished a sip and set down my cup. "Has anyone told you that you are a flirt, Mr. Marco?"

"Yes, but you are the first woman I've ever flirted with who has cast aside my efforts. It makes me wonder if I'm doing it all wrong."

Unfortunately, he was doing it right. I did enjoy the warmth of his hands and fingers on mine, but I wasn't about to admit it.

"Your attention might be better spent on a young lady that will reciprocate," I said simply.

I heard my mother inhale. Mr. Marco cut her off before she could start. "The harder to get the better the reward, Miss Horton." He cocked an eyebrow at me.

Mother inhaled again, and I hoped her words would be directed at his inappropriate comment and not me. We were both saved by the sound of the doorbell.

"Oh, what now?" She rose to her feet and left us alone.

Mr. Marco chuckled. "I think her patience is wearing thin with our behavior."

I shrugged and picked up my cup again. "She'll forgive you before me. She's thrilled I didn't scare you away yesterday."

PART 1 - THE CULL

"You were trying too hard. Each cutting remark made me happier to be in your company."

"I see. So, if I become a simpering maiden begging for your attention, you'll go away?"

His eyes scanned over me, looking at my face and wet hair, then straight into my eyes, holding my gaze with his dark look. "If that's who you are, then yes, I'll leave. But Miss Joy Horton is not a simpering maiden, although I think it would be quite comical to see you try."

What did I have to lose but his company? I pursed my lips, then put on my sweetest smile. "Mr. Marco," I spoke in my best demure voice, adding a breathless tone I had heard my sisters speak in. "I cannot tell you how excited I was to see you this morning. Truly, you were my savior on the road. I don't know what I would have done if you hadn't come. You are my knight in shining armor. I don't think I can ever repay your kindness."

He sat back in his chair, threw back his head and let out a bellow of a laugh. His face softened and I saw old laugh lines appear. He was handsome without his scowl. "That was a powerful performance, but not convincing enough to make me want to run. I still find you intriguing."

"Oh, excuse me. I'm interrupting."

John's sister and bride to be, Jane Turner, entered the dining room. Her bright eyes looked back and forth from me to Mr. Marco.

We both stood. "Mr. Marco, please let me introduce Miss Jane Turner."

He smiled and bowed. "A pleasure."

"Mr. Marco, you must be new in our neighborhood?" Jane asked.

"Just visiting. I'm staying with the Hamptons."

"Ah, Lord and Lady Hampton are kind people. Relations of yours?"

"They are my late wife's parents," he answered.

"Oh, I am sorry," Jane said softly.

She'd only spoken three sentences with him and had already discovered more about him than I had. "I didn't know you were visiting the Hamptons. Lady Diana, was your wife?" I thought of the giggling dark-haired beauty that had been a fixture in our small village for so many years. She'd married her first season in London. News of her death had come almost a year ago.

He sobered and his face became dark again. "Yes, she was. It's what brought me to your shop yesterday. A torn cuff may not seem like much, but have a hair out of place and Lady Hampton will fuss over you like a mother hen. I don't like to be fussed over."

I searched his brooding face. Was Diana the reason for his sudden mood change?

The Hamptons were titled, but they were not wealthy. Father had bought a parcel of land to keep them from the poor house last year. How had Diana come to be attached to Mr. Marco?

"The shop is the reason I'm here," Jane spoke. "I've come for a fitting with Joy. I brought my dress with me. I can't wait to see what you'll do with it."

She turned to Mr. Marco. "She's an absolute miracle worker with the needle, Mr. Marco. She doesn't make clothes; she makes works of art."

Mr. Marco shook himself out of a daze. "A miracle worker, is she? I've seen the work of some of the finest dressmakers in London and Paris. I'm eager to see how Miss Horton matches up."

Jane waved off his remarks. "They are no match, I assure you. Will you be staying for the week, Mr. Marco? You could come to my wedding on Friday next and see for yourself."

It was a shameless play for her to get more attention. A wealthy son-in-law of the Hamptons would provide plenty of excitement to her wedding day.

Mr. Marco gave me a questioning look.

Don't do it. I willed the words at him with my eyes. If he didn't like simpering maidens, he was in for a deluge of them if he agreed to attend.

"I would be delighted to attend, Miss Turner." He bowed over her hand again. "Now, I must excuse myself. It sounds like Miss Horton has plenty of work to do, and she has told me plenty of times I am a nuisance." He shot me a wide grin.

"I'll walk you out," I said automatically. Once we were out of earshot I pulled on his sleeve.

"What were you thinking?" I asked in a loud whisper.

"Of attending a wedding. I enjoy them. Especially when they aren't my own."

I rolled my eyes. "Jane will have you meeting everyone in the neighborhood, all of them simpering maidens," I warned.

"I'll just have to let them know my heart is already taken by you." His wicked grin was back.

PART 1 - THE CULL

I resisted the urge to give him a push out the door. He accepted my help with his coat and tugged on his gloves before putting on his hat. "May I call on you again tomorrow, Miss Horton?"

"No, Mr. Marco, you may not." I tossed his cape at him.

He grinned and took my hand before I could escape. "Tomorrow, then." He gave it a squeeze and let himself out the door.

CHAPTER 4

I sent a letter to Sophie, telling her I was extending my stay with the Hamptons. I mentioned Miss Horton and her many charms. Now I'm waiting for her scathing response to bring me back to reality.

I expected Mr. Marco's face the next morning when I walked to the shop. I made my way through puddles with Pip by my side when a pair of dark boots stopped my progress. Instead of meeting the glare of Mr. Marco I looked up into the face of John Turner. His big grin brought one to my own face.

"John! Are you on your way to see Thomas?" I asked while Pip gave him a proper canine greeting.

"No, I was hoping to see you." He offered his arm the way Mr. Marco had yesterday.

It was like a foreign object, the arm of my brother's friend. He'd never extended it to me before. I felt a slow flush of warmth. I slowly took it. "You were?"

We continued walking. "I haven't seen you in three years. And when I did, you didn't look like the sister of my best mate anymore."

"Oh? Who did I look like? A drowned rat trying to keep a herd of sheep in line?"

He chuckled, then rested his hand upon mine. "A woman. One that I should have noticed before."

His touch was soft and my heart gave a little leap before I waved him off. "Oh, posh. You were barely a man when you left. You are hardly one now," I teased.

He grinned again. "We are the same age."

PART 1 - THE CULL

"Yes, you are coming in to being a man, and I'm nearing spinsterhood." I chuckled. "Such a double standard for the sexes."

"Extremely unfair," John agreed.

"And I'm sure there were much prettier women on your travels," I said.

"I will not comment on that. I can honestly say I find all women beautiful. The dark ones from the Mediterranean, the brown ones in the islands, and the pale ones found here at home. They are all different, and all beautiful in different ways."

"You made it all the way to the islands? What was it like there?" I was certain the black and white drawings in my father's atlas had not done them justice.

"Hot and humid," he instantly answered. "There were days when the entire crew was dressed down in their unmentionables and we were still drenched in sweat. I suppose if we had spent more time ashore than at sea it might have been more pleasant. The beaches were white and warm, even in the winter. And the fish were curious enough to investigate us. I wasn't sure if they had seen people before, the way they would approach us when we would swim."

"No man-eating fish?" I asked.

"No, thankfully, everything was smaller than us." He chuckled. "Leave it to you to ask about the frightening things. You always did enjoy a good scare." He nudged me playfully.

"I just find the world fascinating. I doubt I'll ever see the islands, colorful fish, or even man-eating fish, so I have to see things through your eyes."

"I am happy to oblige. Thinking of flora and fauna are much nicer things to remember than some of the other things." He became quiet, his eyes unfocused.

I gave his hand a squeeze. "You can speak of those things too if you wish. I won't mind. I'd be honored to listen. If that is what you need." I didn't know what else to say.

He stopped and studied my face.

"You are a dear friend."

"I hope so. I try to be. We all can use more dear friends." I pulled him back into motion. "We need to keep moving, I don't want to be late."

"Ah yes, the working Miss Joy Horton. Caught in the middle of her father's wealth and her own independence."

"It hasn't endeared me to the other ladies, so I don't want to give them a reason to complain."

He frowned. "They are unkind to you?"

I shook my head. "No, just not friendly. I cannot blame them really; I'm taking up a spot someone's sister or mother could hold and provide more income to their home. My father has tenants. They are tenants. I'm the odd one, not them."

"You are too forgiving. They should all be taking dressmaking lessons from you," he said, quickening our step.

"I am facing facts," I responded, finding I was tired of explaining my actions to everyone around me. "I wish others would as well."

"What truths am I ignoring?"

"The ladies at the shop have a legitimate reason to dislike me, but I cannot do much else with my life than what I know how." My words had become heated and my steps faster. John increased his long stride to keep up with me.

He grabbed my hand and stopped my tirade. Looking into my face, he said warmly, "I like you. I always have. Just the way you are."

I felt warm all over, a little thrill starting in my belly. He knew my faults, and the reason I wouldn't marry. Even though it didn't change anything, it was nice to be told I was liked. I turned my face away and re-tucked my arm into his elbow, calming down. "Thank you. It's nice to be with someone who doesn't expect much in return except for my company."

Something wet and cold nudged my hand. I looked down at Pip and stroked his head, calming down at his touch. My sweet little companion was so intuitive about my feelings.

"Thank you for the walk." I reached to open the door to the shop. The door opened and out barreled the Amazonian body of Lily Smith. She ran me off the stoop before she realized what she had done. John reached out and steadied us both.

Lily smoothly disentangled herself. "Oh Joy! I'm so sorry. Mr. Cooper wants me to go get more rags. I guess the rain seeped through the ... John Turner?"

John was awestruck. His eyes widened and his jaw slackened as he took in the sight of Lily Smith. I'd never seen a man so instantly smitten, not that I blamed him. Lily was an elegant creature. She wore her clean, threadbare clothes like royal robes. If her hair was out of place it looked like a romantic wisp done intentionally, and she glowed with kindness and strength.

The little thrill I'd felt by his attention was instantly snuffed out.

"I'm afraid…I am at a disadvantage," John stammered.

I laughed. "Surely you remember Lily Smith. She was perpetually at Thomas's heels when you were younger."

His smile widened. "Of course, little Lily Smith. I remember pulling your shoes out of the mud one rainy day."

She blushed prettily. "Yes, well, I finally grew into those large feet of mine."

"I apologize for not recognizing you, Miss Smith. So much has changed since I've been gone," he said sincerely.

"It's quite alright. But I must be going on my errand."

I felt quite invisible when John offered her his arm. "Allow me to accompany you, please."

She blushed again and glanced at me. I gave her a nod of approval. I had no claims on John Turner. Our walk had been pleasant, but the stirrings in my chest should and would be firmly tamped down.

"Thank you," Lily said. And they were off.

I made my way into the shop and put on my best smile for the ladies. Maybe today was the day I'd get some acceptance.

There was a little more warmth from them once they saw Jane's dress on the mannequin. I received many compliments, and the day passed pleasantly. I was even included in a few conversations.

My heart felt light when I gathered my bundles and headed home for the day.

"Joy, may I walk with you a bit?" Lily followed me closely on the way out.

"Of course." I managed to keep stride with her long steps.

"I had a pleasant walk with John Turner today," she said.

I grinned. "Lily Smith, you're blushing!"

"Yes, well, he was a complete gentleman. I just wondered if I had intruded."

I waved her off. "John Turner is an old family friend. Today was the first day he noticed I was a woman instead of a sister. Personally, I think he's been at sea a little too long and just needed some company of the female persuasion."

She blushed even deeper. "I hope his feelings can run a little deeper than just having something nice to look at. I have...admired him for so long."

I linked my arm through hers. "Do tell! I had no idea."

"It was the day he rescued me from the mud." She sighed. "I had just gotten new shoes, well, new to me. Old shoes that were still serviceable from our neighbors. They didn't have holes in them, and I could splash without getting my feet wet. I chose the wrong puddle and ended up to my knees. I don't know how long I stood there and cried before the young Mr. Turner rescued me."

"He's always had a good heart," I said.

"Are you talking about me, Miss Horton?" We looked up to see Mr. Marco approaching quickly. He smiled at me and then turned to Lily. Her tall stature met him almost eye to eye.

"Arthur Marco, at your service." He bowed. Lily grinned.

I rolled my eyes at him. "Mr. Marco, may I introduce Miss Lily Smith."

"A pleasure! Now I can walk two lovely young ladies home and be the envy of every man in the village." He tucked Lily's arm into his elbow and then took my hand in his. I'm sure I blushed, but I liked the way his hand felt in mine, how the warmth of his skin seeped through his gloves.

"And how are things at the Hamptons?" I tried to find neutral ground. Clearly I had never met anyone as persistent as Mr. Marco, and I couldn't bring myself to continue our merry war in front of Lily.

"Dull and cold. I spoke to Lord Hampton about it, and he admitted he had already spent his heating allotment for the year. I had a wagon of coal delivered this morning and it's almost to a decent heat before I left to walk you home."

"You would think with the amount of rent he demands he would have adequate heat," Lily said softly.

"You are his tenant?" Mr. Marco asked.

"My family is. The rent goes up every year and yet the roof never gets repaired. Sometimes I think he's trying to drive us all off the land. Or maybe he is gambling it away." She chewed on her lip in a charming way but stopped when she noticed she had Mr. Marco's attention. "I'm sorry, sir, I shouldn't speculate so."

"Nonsense! Say on, my dear," he encouraged.

She blushed at his words. I felt a tiny twinge of the green-eyed monster at his words of endearment but squashed them quickly. Lily was a beautiful creature with a kind heart. It was pointless to be jealous of her.

"We've been waiting for two years for him to fix the roof. Yesterday's downpour made for a damp night."

"I see. Have you appealed to Lord Hampton?" Mr. Marco asked.

Lily shook her head. "No. No one can get past the front door. His butler has us all neatly turned away and directed towards Mr. Lowell, his steward. All he does is make promises and tells us the rent has gone up before he demands payment."

"I see." Mr. Marco's bored scowl had darkened. I was beginning to tell the difference between his moods. When dealing with me there was a spark in his eyes as he was readying for the next verbal attack. This new issue had his eyes dull, pulled back into his brain looking for an answer.

"It's amazing. I can actually see the cogs and gears turning in your head," I teased him back into the present.

He squeezed my hand. "You should see what it does when I think about you, Miss Horton."

Lily laughed as I gave him a nudge. I admired the little laugh lines around his mouth and eyes, and I wondered if smiling had been more natural to him in his past.

The road was splitting ahead to our separate destinations. Lily dropped her arm and made a polite nod. "Thank you for the walk. It was a pleasure to meet you, Mr. Marco."

He made a slight bow. "The pleasure was mine." He watched her walk away, then placed my hand in the crook of his elbow, as was more proper, and pulled our bodies closer to one another, which wasn't. We walked in silence.

"Care to join me on one of my rash decisions, Miss Horton?" he asked at last.

"Does it involve removing one's clothing?" I replied in my sweetest voice.

"Imp! Will you never let me forget?"

"Not until they put my body in the cold ground. What would this rash decision entail, Mr. Marco?"

"Standing guard and acting as a distraction while I ransack Mr. Lowell's residence."

My mouth dropped open. He tugged on me and hurried our steps towards my home. "You suspect something?"

"I suspect a lot of things. The Hamptons are boring, not extravagant. Lady Hampton was complaining about the state of the crofters' roofs just the other day. She hates to see things out of order. Trust me, the woman is obsessed with having the world in order. Lord Hampton told her Mr. Lowell had used more of the rents to buy supplies to fix them, and thus why they were lacking in coal."

I tightened my grip around his arm to keep up. "Do you think Mr. Lowell…"

"And the butler, Dibble. I wouldn't put it past them to be in league together. He sends the tenants away from the Hamptons so Lowell can fleece them and pocket the money. Then they split it." Mr. Marco's steps had almost become a run when we rounded the corner to my home.

His curricle was parked nearby. He neatly lifted me off my feet and into the seat before leaping up beside me. He had just grabbed the reins when we heard a pitiful bay followed by loud barking. Pip came bounding out of the house followed by Martha.

"Come on, Pip, we'll need you too." Mr. Marco called. The spaniel jumped into the curricle and took his place on the floor between us.

"We'll be back for dinner!" I waved at Martha with a big smile before turning back to Mr. Marco with a more serious look, "If we're not in prison."

PART 1 - THE CULL

CHAPTER 5

I went over the books with Lord Hampton and found no discrepancies. I can not figure out why they are so far under the hatches. There is something rotten going on here. I mean to discover exactly what it is.

I held onto his arm as we took a corner fast and sharp. I was sure he was doing it just to make me grab him for balance.

"How do you suggest we infiltrate Mr. Lowell's residence?"

"*We* will not be doing that. I will be sneaking around while you keep his attention elsewhere." Mr. Marco snapped the reins again.

"Oh, I am? Do tell me how."

He slowed the curricle down and reached over to pick up one of my callused and dye-stained hands. He rubbed my fingers, paying attention to the callous on my index finger. My heart skipped a beat. "Simple, you need flowers for dying fabric. I'm sure there are some kind of blossoms on his property you would like to use."

I pulled my hand away from his. "Mr. Marco, must you always take my hand so much?"

"Yes. Yes, I must."

"You are improper." I folded my hands safely in my lap.

He was not a bit repentant. "Yes, I am."

He slowed down to a respectable speed as we approached Mr. Lowell's house. It was a tidy and well-kept cottage on the Hampton's estate. It was also surrounded by wild rose bushes which would make a lovely pink dye.

My heart started pounding in my chest as he pulled to a stop. "Mr. Marco, I suppose now is a good time to tell you I am a terrible liar."

He laughed. "I would expect nothing less from you, Miss Horton. Fortunately, I've had some experience in subterfuge. All you need to do is keep his attention." He leaned over and gave Pip's head a pat. "Pip will help. I'm sure he can be persuaded to dig around and make a nuisance."

Pip looked at me and panted with excitement. He leaped off the curricle as Mr. Marco stepped down. I went to place my hand in his and found his hands on my waist to lift me down. They lingered near my hips once my feet were on the ground.

"Mr. Marco!" I pushed away from him.

He gave me a soft smile. "I'm very improper."

"Extremely." I brushed down the wrinkles in my skirt while he called out to the house.

"Ho there, Lowell! Are you in?"

There was a moment of silence before the door opened and Mr. Lowell poked his head out. His large frame filled the doorway. He looked a little cross, but he softened at the sight of Mr. Marco.

"Yes? Can I help you?" He shut the door behind him.

"I hope so. I have a young lady on my arm who is pestering me for some of the flowers that surround your home." Mr. Marco pushed me forward. "Tell him, Miss Horton."

I said in a clear voice, "Your wild roses, Mr. Lowell, I could use them for my next project."

Mr. Lowell relaxed even more. "Of course, of course, help yourself." He waved towards the bushes. Pip trotted next to me while Mr. Lowell and Mr. Marco followed.

I leaned towards the flowers and inhaled their scent before brushing through them to find the most uniform in color. My mind raced with ideas of how to keep Mr. Lowell's attention. I plucked a few blossoms and turned to face the men. "I'm afraid I'm a little unprepared, I left my bag on the seat."

"I'll fetch it for you, be back in a moment." Mr. Marco offered and gave me a wicked smile before leaving. I took a deep breath and faced Mr. Lowell, wondering what to do next.

Pip began to growl. His sharp eyes stared at the rose bushes. With a short bark, he promptly chased a ginger-colored cat that darted out of the bushes.

"Peppermint!" Mr. Lowell shouted and chased after them both. I ran after them, shouting at Pip to stop.

Peppermint dashed through the grass and headed towards the nearest tree with Pip on his tail. He nimbly climbed it while Pip barked at the base of the trunk.

Mr. Lowell and I caught up to them. I grabbed Pip by his collar and pulled him back, scolding and apologizing. Pip strained against me, giving a few huffs at Peppermint who hissed from the tree.

"I'll take him back to the curricle. I am so sorry, Mr. Lowell." I pulled Pip away from the tree, giving him a sharp tug to bring his attention away from the cat.

Mr. Lowell paced beneath the tree and tried to coax Peppermint down. He raised his hands to his head and moaned loudly with despair. Mr. Lowell was not a small man. He was broad and sturdy. At that moment though, he looked small and helpless.

"Oh Miss Horton, please don't leave. We need to get Peppermint down," he pleaded.

"I'm sure he'll come down once Pip is gone," I assured him, tugging on Pip's collar.

"Are you sure? I can't have anything happen to him. He's too important." He tried to coax Peppermint down again.

"I'll help you get him down," I promised. "Let me tie up Pip." I turned around to head back to the curricle, hoping Mr. Marco was finding what he needed.

Pip reluctantly left Peppermint and followed me to the curricle.

Mr. Marco was standing at the head of his horses, and he was not alone. He carried in his arms something that looked like a cherub. Short, blonde curly hair adorned the head of the slight body he held. Big ice blue eyes with tears looked at me and at Pip. She wiped her nose with Mr. Marco's handkerchief and exclaimed with glee, "Oh! A dog! I love dogs so much!" Her tiny voice held nothing but joy and innocence.

Mr. Lowell's voice came from behind me. "Eva! What are you doing outside?" He rushed to Mr. Marco's side and plucked the small child from his arms.

"This sweet little voice was crying for her father when I was retrieving Miss Horton's bag. I intruded on your home to find the source," Mr. Marco said. He stood next to my side and murmured in my ear, "Things are not what I expected."

"Peppermint ran outside, Papa. I tried to follow him, but I got so tired." She coughed an unhealthy bark that came from deep in her lungs. Mr. Lowell pressed the handkerchief to her lips. It came away speckled with blood.

My face fell and Mr. Marco's scowl hardened. Consumption? I felt a prick of fear down my spine at the thought of the deadly disease. Mr. Marco took a step in front of me to shield me from the child.

Mr. Lowell scowled at us both. "It's not consumption. It's her lungs. She was born too early and her lungs are bad. She's not contagious. Sometimes she just coughs too hard."

Mr. Lowell's extreme concern about a cat stuck in a tree became clear. His face was kind and tender as he caressed his daughter's cheek. "Peppermint needed some exercise, sweetheart. I'm sure he'll be back soon."

Mr. Marco gave me a questioning look. "Pip was helping Peppermint exercise. Up a tree," I answered.

He closed his eyes and shook his head. "Your companion is most exuberant in all he does."

"*You* wanted to bring him along. *You* gave him strict orders to be a nuisance," I reminded him quietly. Mr. Marco scowled at us both. I smiled back broadly and Pip thumped his tail.

Eva's coughing subsided. More tears ran down her face from her exertion. She looked down at Pip and smiled with the sweetest and most honest expression I'd ever seen. "Can I pet your dog?"

I looked down at Pip who was panting and smiling with my hand on his collar. He yawned with a little yelp that made Eva giggle.

"Of course. Pip, sit," I commanded. He chose to be obedient for once. Mr. Lowell approached and Eva slipped from his arms. She reached out and took his silky ears into her small hands. She looked up at me with delight. "He's so soft." Pip leaned into her and rubbed his head against her small body, almost knocking her over. Eva giggled and threw her arms around his neck. He supported her small frame easily and managed to get a few wet licks on her face.

"Miss Horton, would you and Pip escort Eva inside? I have some things to discuss with her father," Mr. Marco asked.

Mr. Lowell gave Mr. Marco a confused look.

"It's about our mutual acquaintance, Dibble." Mr. Marco gave Mr. Lowell a meaningful look.

Mr. Lowell paled. He looked at me and Eva, and I thought he was going to gather up his child and run. He looked at Mr. Marco and clenched his fists. Was he about to start a fight? Then his shoulders sank in defeat. "Eva, stay with Miss Horton."

Eva and I walked back to the front of the house with Pip following.

"Can we sit outside on the porch and pet Pip?" Eva asked.

"As long as you feel well enough to," I answered.

She scowled. "I hate being sick."

"I do too," I agreed, sitting down on the porch and gathering my skirts around my legs. "There is nothing worse than being sick when there is so much more to do."

She nodded with too much wisdom from such a young child.

I opened my arms and pulled a willing Eva into my lap to keep her warm in the setting sun while Pip plopped down next to us. I wrapped my arms around her thin little body while she leaned over to stroke Pip. The feel of her small form in my arms soothed a familiar ache in my heart, the place reserved for the children I would never have.

"How old is he?" She rubbed Pip's belly when he rolled into a submissive pose.

I had to think. "Four. My father got him for me for my seventeenth birthday," I answered, smelling the scent of childhood on her hair. "How old are you, Eva?"

"Seven. I asked Papa for a dog, but he says Peppermint is a better pet. He catches mice, and dogs make Papa's eyes water." She scratched Pip under the chin.

I held her a little closer. Seven years old and so petite. I would have taken her age to be two or three years younger by her size. "Maybe Pip and I can visit you," I offered.

She turned her pretty blue eyes up at me and I was smitten. "Oh, would you? I would love to see him again. He's so pretty." She began to cough again. I held her while she shook, my heart breaking at the horrible noise that came from her chest.

She leaned back against me. "I hate being tired all the time. And I hate coughing. And I hate not having any friends because I'm sick." She sighed when I stroked her hair. "I shouldn't complain."

"You complain as much as you want. Pip and I are good at listening." I could tell she had so much to say. The way she had looked at her father with adoration told me she did her best to not worry him.

She rubbed Pip's ear between her fingers softly. "The doctor said I'm dying. Papa doesn't want to believe it."

"Neither do I." I rubbed her back.

"I wish…I wish he would just enjoy the time with me we have, instead of trying to make me better," she whispered.

I felt tears sting my eyes. I cradled her in my arms and scolded myself for worrying about my petty problems. "You have an awful lot of wisdom for one so young, Miss Eva." I kissed her head.

"And what do we have here? Miss Horton and Miss Lowell?" A friendly voice called from the road.

I looked up to see the tall form of John Turner standing at the gate. He waved to us and held up a basket. Pip gave a bark and leaped to his feet, leaving me and Eva behind.

John slipped through the gate, holding the basket out of Pip's reach when he leaped to inspect it.

"Off with you, mongrel! This isn't for you." He pushed Pip away.

He came to the porch and stood over us. "I wasn't aware you two were acquainted."

"Just recently. Eva and I were becoming fast friends before you interrupted." I smoothed her hair back.

"Miss Horton has a dog! He's so nice and soft, and funny!" Eva told him while Pip once again tried to stick his nose in the basket John was carrying.

"He's a pest." John pushed Pip back once more. He leaned over to the ground and picked up a stick.

Pip's form went absolutely rigid when he saw the stick. His tail wagged once, twice, then went still when John tossed the stick in his hand; his brown eyes followed every move John made.

"Off with you." John threw the stick hard and far.

Pip took off like a shot. Eva laughed as he bounded through the bushes after his quarry.

"I'll just take in the bread and jam my mother sent over. I think there is some stew as well." He reached down to touch Eva's curls. "You eat it all up, string bean." He went into the house then returned to the porch, sitting next to Eva and me.

"So, how do you know the Lowell's?" John stretched out his long legs.

"We only met this afternoon. I came to collect some blossoms for some dye. Unfortunately, Pip chased Peppermint up a tree. Miss Eva is kind enough to forgive him. Her father and Mr. Marco had business to discuss, so I am entertaining Miss Eva."

Pip came leaping back from his chase, dropping his stick at John's feet and sitting. He trembled, looking at the stick and then back at John. John picked up the stick and threw it. Pip flew into action once again.

"Can I try next time?" Eva pulled herself from my embrace and stood.

"Only if you promise to eat up all your dinner," John said. She nodded quickly.

"And how long have you known the charming Miss Eva?" I asked. Pip came crashing back, his ears were wet and a few burrs stuck in his fur. He dropped the slobbery stick at John's feet again. He handed it to Eva. She giggled and threw it. It only went a few feet, but Pip gladly leaped on it and brought it back.

"I was here when Eva was born. My mother was assisting and I was driving the horses. It was a mess, Joy. So much shouting, and crying, and blood. Before I knew what was going on I had this slimy wet thing in my arms they had proclaimed dead." He exhaled and called Eva over. "Let me show you a better way to throw." He taught her how to hold the stick by one end, and how to fling it. She tossed it hard and laughed when Pip tried to jump for it. It kept her conveniently out of hearing the rest of his tale.

He continued, "I just held it to me, staring at it. It was a tiny baby covered in heaven knows what. She was completely still and cold. Mother was yelling at me to find something to wrap it in while they worked on Mrs. Lowell."

His eyes looked off into memories. I felt his sorrow and leaned closer to him. I linked my arm through his and rested my head against his shoulder.

He smiled at me and squeezed my hand. "Steady on, as you can see my story had half a happy ending. Apparently, the jostling of a stupid fourteen-year-old boy trying to wrap a body was enough to rouse a baby from the grave. She started squealing. It sounded more like a cat than a baby. The doctor didn't think she would live out the week. She surprised us all."

Eva tired from her game with Pip. She brushed her golden locks out of her face and beamed at me.

The House That Death Built

"Miss Horton, John brought me a tin whistle yesterday. Can I get it, John? So you can play it for Miss Horton as you do on the ships?"

"That would be wonderful," I answered for him. She disappeared into the house. Pip plopped to the ground and gnawed on the abandoned stick.

"She's still too skinny. Mother said Mr. Lowell spends all his money on doctors. We've been supplementing as best we can."

"I'll start adding to the pot. All I have are nephews to spoil. It would be nice to have a girl to pamper." I was already thinking of dresses and shawls and bonnets and blankets I could make for Eva. I was sure my parents would add food and other supplies.

"What is Mr. Marco doing here?" John asked, nodding at the cab. His body tensed up when he spoke.

"I came with him. He is investigating something going on with the Hamptons."

John scowled. "Why are you with him?"

"Lily was telling us about their leaky roof on the way home today."

"Lily has a leaky roof?" John's frame straightened further.

"Really, John, it is going to be difficult to explain things if you keep interrupting."

He kept quiet while I told him of Lily's home and the lack of heat at the Hamptons. He shook his head. "I don't believe it, Joy. Hugh Lowell is a good man. He doesn't live like a king."

"He has a sick daughter. That would make the noblest of men resort to desperate measures."

"I still don't believe it. Besides…I know this is the country, Joy, but should you be alone with Mr. Marco?"

"It's no worse than being alone with you," I pointed out. He sighed, then perked up again when Eva appeared with a tin whistle.

"Play it, John!" she pleaded.

He smiled and took it from her hands. "As you wish. I learned this one from a Scotsman with only two fingers on his left hand, so it's verrra easy to remember," he said with a thick accent. Eva giggled when he started up a lively tune.

Eva tugged at my hands. "Dance with me!" she begged. I wanted to protest. She might not be well enough to dance, but I squashed the thought when I looked into her anxious face. She wanted to be treated like any other little girl, and I would do my best to give her that. We started a jig, pulling up our skirts ever so slightly to keep them out of the way. We giggled when we made mistakes and laughed when Pip started crashing into us to play along.

Eva started to cough when she bounced too much. She shook her head and scowled when John and I stopped to check on her. "Keep going," she said, holding Mr. Marco's handkerchief over her mouth.

"I think you've done enough dancing for today, little miss." I led her back to the porch and enfolded her once again in my arms to support her while her little body shook.

John's eyes met mine above her head. I saw the helpless look in his eyes that mirrored Mr. Lowell's. He wanted to do so much more than bring bread and jam and tin whistles. I stroked her hair and rocked her.

"I should go find your papa and take Miss Horton home," John said to Eva softly. "It's getting late." He strode away, his steps quick and frustrated.

"Will you come again, Miss Horton?" Eva rested her head against my bosom. I tucked her in tight against me, inhaling her sweet scent of sweat and mint. I couldn't recall a time where I felt less content than at that moment. My arms were still aching even though they were holding a child. It was as if my body knew this was only temporary and I'd be left wanting again.

"I'll come again," I promised.

"And bring Pip too?"

I kissed the top of her head. "Pip too."

"Eva, it's time for you to go in." I looked up at Mr. Lowell. He stood next to Mr. Marco at the bottom of the porch. His eyes were red and his face somber, but he managed a weak smile for his daughter who rose up and hugged him. She looked up at Mr. Marco and held out his wrinkled and stained silk handkerchief. Mr. Marco lowered himself to her height and tucked her fingers around it. "Please keep it, Miss Eva. I think you have a greater need for it than I do."

"Thank you." She disappeared into the house.

John came around the other side of the house "Ah, there you are Lowell. I brought you and Eva some supper." He ignored Mr. Marco and held his hand down to me. "May I take you home now, Joy?"

"Miss Horton came with me. I'll see her home." Mr. Marco's gaze fell on me. I knew he had a tale to tell about the Lowells and I was interested to hear it.

"I'm sure you've done enough for today, Mr. Marco," John interrupted, his eyes flashing, "I wouldn't want you to go to any more trouble."

"It's never any trouble when Miss Horton is involved." Mr. Marco's eyes narrowed. I might have seen his nostrils flare.

"As one of her family's oldest friends, I believe her father would prefer she didn't remain long in your company without a chaperone." John's eyes locked with Mr. Marco's.

"I'm fairly certain her mother would prefer she did," Mr. Marco said, his gaze not leaving John's face.

That was enough of that!

I stood up and brushed off my dress. "Pip!" My faithful companion raised his head.

"Pip, I discovered today that the males of my species are complete idiots, and would *prefer* your company above all others on my way home." I nodded to Mr. Lowell. "Good day. I shall be coming by to visit you and Eva again."

Mr. Lowell's face blossomed into a smile. "Good day, Miss Horton. We will look forward to it."

"Oh, come now Joy…" John started.

"Don't be a stubborn little imp…" Mr. Marco continued.

I glared at them both. I tromped by them with Pip at my side.

"Joy…be reasonable. It's almost dark." John fell in line next to me.

I watched Mr. Marco storm towards his curricle. I made my way onto the road.

It was worse there. John walked on one side of me, while Mr. Marco followed closely on the other side, leading his horses on foot.

Pip trotted next to me while I marched us down the road. I spent a few quiet, miserable minutes, gathering my anger and my thoughts before I stopped.

I pointed a finger at John. "You, John Turner, are not my parents, or my guardian or my chaperone. You have been gone from my life for three years, and you do not get to come back and assume you know what's best for me. I am of age and can go and do what I please with whomever I want. If you truly are one of my oldest friends, how could you doubt my judgment?"

"Joy, I just want you to be safe…"

I cut him off and pointed next to Mr. Marco. "And you, sir! How dare you insinuate my mother would consider entrapping you with me. And

PART 1 - THE CULL

how dare you think you have anything I want to…to…to stoop so low to such an entrapment! You have nothing I want. Nothing that would ever entice me to behave in such a way."

John's mouth gaped a bit. Mr. Marco blinked, then said softly, "I offer my deepest apologies, Miss Horton."

There was a low whistle and the familiar voice of my brother spoke from behind me. "You both worked her into a dither? At the same time?"

I turned around and saw him riding Penny, bareback. I was glad to see him and her.

"You're late for dinner, Joy. Father sent me out to find you." I took his forearm and swung up behind him in a move we had perfected since childhood.

"Don't you want to tell them goodnight?" his cheeky voice asked.

"Thomas, if you don't take me home this instant I will toss you off this horse and ride home by myself," I growled.

CHAPTER 6

I killed a man today. I'd kill him again if I could.

I didn't hear from John or Mr. Marco for two days. I had a bride to outfit and spent most of my time doing fittings for Jane. My curiosity about the Lowells and the butler Dibble had been placed firmly in the 'none of your business' corner of my mind. It stayed there with great difficulty until I couldn't repress it any longer. I decided to visit the Lowells and make sure all was well with little Eva.

I had stayed up late putting the finishing touches on Jane's gown and woke up near noon. I enjoyed a long stretch of my limbs before dressing and skipping down the stairs to forage for food.

There were two large floral arrangements on the dining room table when I arrived downstairs. Mother was there with Martha, cleaning up dishes. She positively glowed when I entered the room.

"You have flowers, dear. From two different suitors." She wiped her hands on her apron and pulled me to a seat. Martha poured me tea and milk while my mother picked up the cards.

I was confused. "I don't have any suitors."

"Of course you do, why else would they send you flowers?" Mother pushed forward the first arrangement for me to examine. It was a simple but elegant arrangement of violets and daisies. They looked like sunshine with splashes of color. I smiled and inhaled their scent.

"John Turner sent the violets and daisies. They smell so lovely!" She placed the card in my hand. "It says he's sorry. What on earth did he do?"

"Nothing to worry about." I sipped my tea. "He overstepped his bounds as my surrogate brother and I had to bring him back to reality."

PART 1 - THE CULL

Mother frowned. "He just wants to take care of you, Joy. He might even want to take care of you on a more permanent basis if you encourage it."

I groaned and pushed my teacup away, feeling my appetite leave with it. "Mother, please..."

"John Turner would make you an excellent husband. He is hard-working, kind, generous, and he cares about you. I fail to see how you could have any objections."

"He's fond of Lily Smith," I told her.

Mother grew silent and I almost felt smug at shutting her down. When it came to grace, beauty, brains, and kindness, Lily was miles ahead of me.

"He still sent you flowers, Joy." She pushed forward the other arrangement.

This one held strange flowers that would be grown in a hothouse. Exotic smells came from them. The colors were dark and bold, everything from a deep orange to a dark purple. Even the pink flowers were not feminine and light, but brash and loud.

"These must be from Mr. Marco."

Mother radiated excitement. "They are, all the way from a hothouse! I've never seen or smelled such flowers." She touched a dark blue petal.

"What does his card say?" I asked.

Mother's face softened a little. She handed it to me. "It says, 'I miss you'."

Those three little words brought me up short and caused a warm feeling to course through my skin and settle in my chest. "It says that?"

"Yes. And don't tell me you are not affected, Joy. I can see it on your face. You have feelings for him."

I pushed away the loud arrangement and reached for the bread and jam Martha had brought me. "I hardly know the man, Mother," I replied, trying to keep my voice light. I couldn't get her hopes up. I didn't want to get my hopes up either.

Instead, I told her about the Lowells and the charming Miss Eva. It had the effect I hoped it would. Mother busied herself finding old dresses and stockings that would fit. Jars of jellies and jams and other treats were added to a basket, as well as a haunch of lamb with a loaf of bread. Warm coats and mittens, scarves and blankets topped off the basket. Eva Lowell was about to be abundantly provided for.

I packed away Jane's dress and veil in paper and boxes while Mother found old children's books and dolls for Eva. Mother helped me pack a small cart. I loaded up the box with Jane's dress and she filled the rest with various things for the Lowells. I hitched Penny up to the cart and Mother brought me a bonnet. We had a silent battle of wills before I took it from her and slapped it on my head, leaving the ribbons loose.

"Come on, Pip," I called and he jumped onto the seat with me, circled a few times and sat down.

"Don't go too fast, or you'll break the jars," Mother warned.

As soon as I was out of sight, I tossed the bonnet into the cart and urged Penny to go faster. She picked up her steps and brought me quickly to the Turner household.

Jane insisted on trying her gown on one last time with me available for any changes. None were needed. Her mother and sisters showered me with praise until I had a swollen head. I definitely needed a trip to the Lowells to bring me some humility.

I pulled up to their house and grabbed a basket while Pip leaped from the cart.

"Hello, Mr. Lowell! Miss Eva! It's Joy Horton," I called out. The door was open an inch and I grabbed the handle and opened it wider.

"Is anyone home?" I peered into the room.

Mr. Lowell was face down on the floor. Blood pooled around his head.

I gasped and dropped my basket. The jelly jars smashed when they hit the ground and Pip yelped as I ran to Mr. Lowell. I knelt next to him, shouting his name and rolling him over. He groaned, and I sobbed with relief. He was alive. Lightly, I slapped his cheeks and tried to rouse him.

"Mr. Lowell, wake up! What happened?"

Where was Eva?

"Where's your daughter?" I demanded, shaking him harder. His eyes rolled open but remained unfocused when he tried to move.

"Eva..." he whimpered. "Don't...don't let him find her." He lapsed again into unconsciousness.

I was on my feet, shouting for her. My heart pounded faster. Racing through the little house, I searched frantically in every wardrobe and under every bed, table, and chair. Pip sniffed everywhere, retracing my steps and looking at me with confusion.

"Oh Pip, we have to find her," I sobbed. I ran to the back door and threw it open wide.

"Eva!" I called, waited for a response and then started to make my way towards the wild roses and the woods beyond. Every few steps I cried out her name and listened intently. I walked farther into the trees and my searching was rewarded with the sound of a child's coughing.

"I'm coming, Eva!" I pulled up my skirts and rushed towards the sound.

As I drew closer, the sound of coughing mixed with crying. Pip dove ahead of me and into a thicket of grass and shrubs.

"Pip!" a tiny voice cried out. I knelt and made my way through the branches and leaves that poked and scratched at me. Under the thicket a tear-stained Eva hugged Pip tightly. He held still and rested his head against hers, before breaking the embrace and lapping at her tears.

"Eva, what's wrong? What happened?" I reached out for her hands and I gently tugged her out of the branches.

"A bad man came and fought with Papa. He had a pistol." She sobbed and wheezed. I enfolded her into my arms and we both trembled.

"He said he was going to kill me and make Papa watch. They fought and I ran. I ran as fast as I could and then I hid. He's trying to find me. I heard him yelling at me and saying such terrible things. I needed to cough so bad but I couldn't let him find me." The words she spoke chilled my blood.

"Who was this man?" I rose to my feet.

"I don't know." She took my hand. I looked around for any signs of danger.

"Come along, we'll go straight to Squire Patterson's house," I said. The local magistrate was the safest place for her to be. Once she was secure, I'd send someone back for her father.

She took a few steps before her coughing started again, horrible and hard until she was choking and gagging. I waited until it passed and lifted her into my arms to carry her. She sighed and wrapped her arms around my neck. "I'm sorry I'm so weak, Miss Horton," she whispered softly in my ear.

"You were a strong, brave, and smart girl. Don't ever think of yourself as weak. Look what you did today," I encouraged her while I made careful steps out of the woods. We had just reached the rose hedge when a figure stepped out from behind it.

It was a pale, white-haired man dressed in Hampton's new livery. His fine clothes were dirty, stained and torn. He looked haggard and tired until he saw us. At the sight of Eva, his eyes lit up with a fury. He drew a pistol and pointed it at me. "Put the child down."

She whimpered and buried her head in my neck. Her limbs tightened their hold around me.

"She's done nothing," I whispered.

"He's got to suffer. She's got to die, so he can suffer." His eyes were wild, staring through me. The barrel of the pistol shook.

"Please, Mr. Dibble." I assumed this was the butler. "She's just a baby. She has nothing to do with whatever you and her father have done."

"It was the perfect plan!" he shouted, spittle flying from his lips. I heard Pip growl low at my knees, but Dibble carried on. "It was all about her as far as he was concerned. Why else do you think he did it?"

Eva began to cry. Her hot tears ran down my neck.

"He did it because he loves her," I said more for her ears than his. She cried harder.

Dibble's eyes hardened, "I'm not going to Newgate. I would rather go to the noose. And if I'm going to the noose I'm going to go there with a smile on my face knowing that the bastard is suffering more than I am. She's his world, and I'm taking it with me."

He took a step towards us, aiming his weapon. I cried out when a furry brown and white body flashed into action.

Dibble screamed as Pip's jaws locked around his wrist. I'd never heard such ferocious noises from my lazy, loveable companion. His snarls and growls were terrifying! He latched onto Dibble and shook his head so quickly the pistol dropped.

I turned and fled. Holding tight to Eva, I crashed through the woods. I could still hear Pip's growls and snarls. I could hear Dibble's screams and shouts while I tried to find my bearings.

I plunged ahead when I heard the sharp report of a pistol and the cries of a dog in pain.

"Pip!" I called out, feeling my heart being torn from my chest. Eva's cries grew louder and tears blinded me. I had to keep going, I had to keep her safe.

Her weight was starting to slow me down and I gasped for air. We crashed our way through the woods. The branches tripped me and tugged at my skirts.

PART 1 - THE CULL

"I can hear you!" Dibble called out from behind us in a high pitched voice. He was getting closer to us.

I looked around for a hiding place. I would move much faster without Eva, and I could draw him away from her. A large dead tree surrounded by a thorny holly bush was my best idea.

I set Eva down carefully and wiped her tears as she wiped mine. "Eva, dearest, I need you to hide again and be so quiet," I whispered. I handed her my handkerchief. "Cough in this if you must, but hide your face well. I'm going to lead him away and find help."

Her face was filled with terror. "Oh Miss Horton!" she sobbed.

I caressed her cheek. "You are so brave and clever. You can do it." I pointed to the log and the holly bush. "He won't think you went in there. He'll think you didn't want to get poked. I need you to crawl in there and hide." I could hear the crashing of Dibble's movements getting louder.

I pulled the holly bush aside, flinching at the thorns as she crawled in. I whispered to her, "I'll be back soon. Stay here, and be silent."

I drew in a deep breath and ran away from her, breaking branches and making as much noise as I possibly could. I heard Dibble curse behind me and I ran faster. The territory became more familiar and I realized I had turned around in a circle back towards the rose hedge. The pink flowers were a welcome sight. Penny and the cart were close and unless he had reloaded his pistol I was about to outrun my pursuer.

I put on a burst of speed and broke through the rose hedge, into the arms of Dibble.

"Got you!" he shouted in triumph. I screamed and squirmed as he held me tight. His thin size hid a tremendous amount of strength.

"Where is she?" he demanded, shaking me so hard my teeth rattled.

"Leave her alone!" I shouted back, pounding against his chest.

He threw me to the ground. Air left my lungs. I inhaled long and hard before my breath came back. I tried to find my feet when the side of my head burst into pain. I cried out and rolled away from the agony, catching a glimpse of Dibble's booted foot coming at me.

It hit my ribs this time, and I screamed and gagged when the air left my lungs once more. He kicked again and again. I gasped when Dibble crouched down next to me, grabbing me by the shoulders and shaking me once more.

"Where is she?"

For an instant, I saw the pure madness that radiated from him. Determination hardened his face. He slapped me. His eyes were wild when he shook me again. I knew he wouldn't let me live, even if I told him.

"I'll never tell you," I hissed. His hands wrapped around my throat and squeezed. I struggled in his grasp, digging my nails into his wrists while my battered body fought for life. Darkness seeped around the edge of my vision. I heard my heart pounding in my ears. I looked at Dibble's face, thinking irrationally how disappointing my last view of life would be his matted hair, scratched pale skin, and hard eyes bent on killing me. My hands released their hold on him and darkness crept in.

I was just about to give in to the void when my ears rang with the sound of gunfire. Dibble's eyes widened and his hands released my throat. His body toppled on mine.

I couldn't see, I couldn't move; but I could still hear, I could still feel.

"Joy!" a voice shouted. The heavy weight of Dibble moved off me and I could breathe again. I gasped for the sweet, fresh air and tried to move, my body still not responding. Arms lifted me and embraced me carefully.

"What has he done to you?" The voice whispered softly, with a great amount of anger infused in it. Hands touched my face carefully, brushing my hair back. When they reached the place that had exploded with pain earlier it brought a new wave of torment and I heard myself moan.

"Oh, my Joy." I was brought closer to a thick chest, my head resting in an embrace and I inhaled the scent of Mr. Marco's cologne. Peace and safety enveloped me, and I felt myself relax even as my body protested being touched.

I willed my eyes open and looked up into the face of my rescuer. His face was blurry with the darkness slowly moving away from the edges of my vision. I saw his neat beard, his black hair, and his dark eyes formed into the scowl I was familiar with. It made me want to smile but my body still couldn't respond to my requests. I had the absurd idea to thank him for the flowers. Truly, my brains had been scrambled.

I opened my mouth to speak and thankfully a rational thought croaked out. "Eva?"

Mr. Marco's scowl deepened. "Where is Eva?" he asked. My vision was improving and I saw there were more faces peering down into mine. Lord Hampton stood at his shoulder, his face a mask of anger. Squire Patterson came at me from above, his face upside down and full of concern.

PART 1 - THE CULL

"Holly bush…" my voice sounded like it was being dragged along sandpaper. "Log…" The pain throbbing from my head became worse and I moaned again. I closed my eyes and buried my face in Mr. Marco's chest. I couldn't breathe enough air to satisfy my body's need for it. The darkness played around the edges of my sight. I gave up and closed my eyes.

"I have her, go find Eva." Mr. Marco commanded. He lifted me without much effort and carried me as carefully as he could. I still whimpered whenever I was jarred too much.

"My curricle is too tall, I'm going to put you in the cart," he told me, gently setting my body down. I hissed when my ribs touched the hard surface and then sighed when he tucked his coat around me to cushion the ride.

It was painfully long. I knew Mr. Marco was torn between speed and my comfort. He chose the latter. He called out to me a time or two to make sure I was still conscious. How could I not be, when every movement brought more agony?

We finally arrived at my home. His arms wrapped around me carefully and lifted my broken body from the cart. I managed to open my eyes and the sight of my doorstep mingled with his scent helped me relax. He carried me up the steps, shouting and ringing the bell.

There was a flurry of activity when Martha opened the door. She was not one to remain calm in a crisis. She screamed and wailed at the sight of my battered form. Mr. Marco strode through the door and shouted at her to shut up and show him where my room was.

Mother appeared on the scene and took control. The sound of her voice made me moan with relief. She directed Mr. Marco to my room and he placed me on my bed while explaining what had happened with Dibble.

"I'm taking Penny for the doctor," he spoke sharply once he'd been relieved of his burden. I opened my eyes when I felt someone touching my face softly, lightly caressing it. His warm fingers left my skin and I watched him turn around to exit.

I needed to say something, to thank him somehow. I opened my mouth.

"I missed you too," I managed to croak out softly.

They were not the words I intended to say. My brain was still rattled.

The words stilled him. He stopped in the doorway and stood, not turning around to face me. He then punched the door frame, making Martha give out a yelp, and stormed off.

My heart fell into my stomach and a traitorous tear trickled down my cheek.

"Come, Martha, let's get her in her nightgown." Mother directed. I whimpered when they maneuvered me out of my dress. They tucked me in bed, Mother sat next to me and washed my face with a cold cloth. It felt heavenly on my face, and I sighed when Martha brought me a cold cup of water to drink. I lay back on my pillow. The darkness and pain swarmed in again and I let it overtake me this time.

I hissed when the doctor prodded my face. I flinched when he cleaned out the wound and let out a long wail when he touched my ribs. He then listened to my chest and prescribed rest and laudanum for the pain.

I shook my head when the doctor brought the cup to my lips. "I don't want laudanum."

"Joy, please..." Mother started.

"You will be a good patient and do what the doctor says." Mr. Marco commanded me sharply. What was he doing in my room?

"What are you doing in my room?" I demanded, trying to sit up. I grimaced while I moved back into a sitting position. My muscles failed and I fell back onto my pillow with a sob.

"I knew you were going to try and bully the doctor. I'm here to make sure you behave." He took the cup from the doctor and pressed it to my mouth. "Now drink up."

"It makes me ill." I turned away.

"You're already ill. You need to rest." His arm came behind me and lifted me carefully. I hated that he did it so easily. "Now, we can sit here and fight, or you can drink your medicine and start to heal so we can fight properly later."

I glared at him but sipped down the laudanum. He made sure I drank it all before he gently laid me back and disappeared from my view. Mother tucked the blankets around me and stroked my hand. I could hear the doctor and Mr. Marco talking in the background, Martha bustling around stoking my fire, and Mother humming softly while she rubbed my palm. The drug took effect quickly and everything faded into silence and sleep.

PART 1 - THE CULL

CHAPTER 7

She's feeling better today. I've never been so relieved to be on the receiving end of a stinging tongue. Miss Joy Horton is a magnificent creature.

I really did hate laudanum. It made me nauseous and dried out my mouth. The lines between reality and dreams were also blurred.

I heard my father softly telling me I was his darling little girl, but his face was Mr. Marco's and he was pushing more laudanum down my throat. I heard Thomas cursing from John Turner's lips and swearing vengeance and then John saying the man was already dead. He looked odd having a conversation with himself. I saw Martha barking like Pip and it made me weep bitterly until Mother made her leave the room. Time wavered. Waking up felt as if only a few moments had passed but I was sure it was more. Disoriented and cross, I woke up feeling sore, thirsty, and annoyed.

Sunlight lit my room through the sheer curtains. I tried to move and found my body was responding once more but protested every movement.

I reached out slowly for the glass of water that sat on the table next to my bed. Large warm hands enfolded mine and brought them up to soft lips for a kiss. I focused my blurry vision on my father's face. He smiled at me and released my hand.

"Let me help you, Joy." He brought the glass to my lips and helped me drink it down. I didn't taste the bitterness of laudanum so I eagerly drank, feeling it wash away all the sticky grime that had built up in my throat. Swallowing hurt, and I was sure my neck was a bruised mess. I laid back down and thanked him.

"What time is it?" I blinked away more sand from my eyes.

"Early afternoon. Your mother was here but I convinced her she needed some rest. She didn't move from your side all night." He softly kneaded my hand in his.

"Eva?" I asked anxiously.

Father smiled. "She's fine. They found her. She's a bit scratched up from the holly bush, but she's wearing her battle scars proudly. She told us what you did."

I squeezed his hand quickly and looked into his face. "And Pip?" My voice broke. My poor little champion.

Father's smile widened. "He hasn't left your side either."

I saw a pink nose rise above the bed and heard loud snuffing. Tears flowed freely as my dear companion whined to see me.

"Since your mother isn't here to stop me, we'll indulge in some naughty behavior." Father bent down and lifted Pip up to the bed. "He's a little battered, but should recover."

He limped to my side. I ran my hands along his silky coat that had recently been bathed and brushed. There were no bandages on him. He licked my tears and plopped his body down on mine. I gasped in pain but when Father went to move him I held on tightly to Pip's furry body.

"Oh, my sweet boy. You are such a good boy." I crooned and kissed his nose. He licked me with exuberance.

"That's enough, don't injure your mistress again." Father pushed him away from my face. Pip circled around his tail once and laid down next to me, worming his head so it rested under my hand. I stroked his ears softly and closed my eyes. He huffed out a soft snort of contentment.

"Are you in much pain?" Father asked.

I shook my head. "Only when I move. It's nothing like the agony I was in yesterday."

"Two days, my dear. You've been in bed for two days."

That despicable laudanum. "Two days!" My mouth dried up the more I spoke. "Is there any more water?"

Father poured me a glass, "Mr. Marco slept in a chair outside your door. Every time you refused to drink he fought you to take more laudanum until you finally rested on your own."

"That bully!" I spouted and took the glass from him. "He had no right. I don't know where he gets the idea he's suddenly in charge of my welfare."

Father laughed at my temper and leaned over me, pressing a kiss to my forehead. "You are going to be just fine, Joy."

"I see her tongue was not injured," Mr. Marco said from the door.

I scowled back at him. "You should not be anywhere *near* my bedroom, Mr. Marco."

Pip caught my irritation and stood up to bark at him. He managed to sink a paw right onto my injured ribs and I cried out, arching my back against the pain.

"Pip, get down." Mother entered the room. The look on her face silenced everyone. Pip jumped down with a guilty look and limped out of the room with his head down low and his tail between his legs.

"My daughter has been severely injured and needs her rest. It would be best for her if both of you take an example from Pip and leave." She pointed at the door and glared at both men. They sheepishly left the room.

Mother muttered something unladylike under her breath that made me smile. She pulled a chair up next to me and stroked my face. "You brave, foolish girl. How did you get caught up in this?"

I sighed. "Mr. Lowell was unconscious when I found him, and Eva was nowhere to be found. I couldn't let anything hurt her."

Mother gave me a stern look. "You should have run for help."

"I would not leave a child alone with a madman, Mother, and I would do it again if I had to." I leaned into Mother's palm when she rested it on my cheek.

Martha entered the room carrying a tray with tea and a bowl of something that smelled delicious. My stomach sprang to life. She beamed down at me. "Mr. Horton said you were awake. He said to bring you some tea and some broth and bread."

Mother and Martha propped me up to eat. I managed the spoon for myself while they filled a tub of hot water. They placed me in it when my meal was finished which felt heavenly on my aching body.

I flinched at the sight of my bruises that ran up my ribs. On my arms were distinct purple handprints where Dibble had held me and shook me. I didn't even want to look at my neck and face to see what kind of mess was there.

Mother helped wash me and spent time scrubbing my scalp carefully enough to make me sigh. If I were Pip I probably would have my leg quaking with happiness.

"Jane postponed her wedding." Mother told me. "Said there was too much fuss going on to have a wedding. Squire Patterson has been investigating the whole affair and reported his findings to us. Dibble had been stealing from Lord Hampton and blackmailing Mr. Lowell to do it. He was bound for Newgate when he escaped, injuring one of his guards. The guards made it to Lord Hampton's where he and Mr. Marco rounded up the Squire and headed straight to Lowell's. They saw him attacking you..."

Stray droplets dripped into my bathtub and rippled on the surface.

I looked up and saw Mother's tears falling into the tub.

"Oh, Mama." My childhood name for her rolled off my lips. "I'm safe now, please don't cry."

She nodded and wiped her eyes with her wet hands and laughed at herself for doing so.

I contemplated the fear I felt when I couldn't find Eva, and how I'd risked my life for a child. I understood a little why Mother chided me for not finding help instead of running to the rescue.

"I'm sorry I scared you, Mama."

She wrapped me in a blanket and hugged me gently. "You don't have to be so…" She stopped and sighed. "It's what makes you my daughter." I hugged her back as tightly as my sore muscles would allow and let her help me back into a clean nightgown and clean sheets that Martha had placed on my bed.

The exertion of eating and getting clean had taken all my energy. Laying back on the bed, I found a comfortable position, and went back to a restful sleep.

***

I awoke early the next day and managed to get myself dressed without too much flinching. My limbs were feeling looser and the pain was slowly subsiding.

After breakfast, I made my way to the parlor and sank to the floor. I joined Pip at the fireplace, enjoying the warmth and petting his soft fur while he let out little dog sighs of bliss. He let out a tiny yelp when my hands touched his back hip.

"Poor little man." I rubbed his head and ears until he relaxed again. I wish I knew what Dibble had done to him, but he acted normal and was

PART 1 - THE CULL

eating and drinking according to Thomas and Father. I trusted their judgment and promised to sneak him more treats while he was recovering.

"We've had quite an adventure for two avowed homebodies, haven't we?"

He thumped his tail once.

"I'm having a great deal of confusion too, Pip. I've never had so much male attention, except you. At least with you, I know what's expected." He gave me another thump and slowly rolled over for a belly rub.

I obliged him, "What about you? Do you ever wish for romance or are you settled in your bachelorhood like I am in my spinsterhood? Do you wish for a four-legged lass with a wet nose and beautiful brown spots? Or maybe you like black spots better? And long curly fur?" I grinned. His tail thumped quicker and harder and I rubbed faster.

I slowed down and found myself resting my hands on his head, thinking of Mr. Marco. "Black or brown?" Once in a while, I indulged in thinking I had a different future ahead of me instead of the one I'd carved out. One with a dark-haired gentleman who declared himself a 'horrible' person, but cradled a sick little Eva to him carefully.

I knew a future with Mr. Marco was impossible. He must have a title he had not disclosed to me or any of our neighbors. Lady Hampton would not have married Diana to anything less than an earl or a baron and I could not remember the details of her wedding since it had taken place in London.

My father made the money of a gentleman, but he'd never stop working. I was certain he'd go mad if he tried. My world and Mr. Marco's were separate places, and I snuffed out my fantasy.

Mother came in and let out a great sigh of exasperation to find me on the floor with Pip. "Can you get up? You have visitors."

"Who is it? I cannot bear a visit from Mr. Marco right now."

Mother gave me a worried frown. "Would you have me turn him away?"

I nodded, relieved that she would protect me for a bit. "Yes, please. He can be...exhausting."

Mother smiled. "Most men are, dear. But your visitors are the Lowells."

Martha led in Mr. Lowell and Eva who ran to me and threw her arms around me.

"Hello, little darling." I hugged her tighter and ignored the pain.

Her big blue eyes rested on me. "Are you hurt?" she asked seriously. "Pip was hurt bad. He found me in the holly bush, and he was walking on three legs."

"We're both doing much better, see? He's using all his legs now." I pointed to Pip who was limping quickly to Eva. "I think he missed you."

Eva knelt down and hugged Pip, petting him softly. "I'm going to miss him so much! We're moving away."

I glanced at Mr. Lowell. "Lord Hampton has turned me out without references. Hi...er, Mr. Marco agreed to take me and Eva on one of his other estates. He needs a gamekeeper there. He promised to pay me enough to keep Eva healthy and safe."

"That's wonderful. A gamekeeper? Poor Peppermint. He is going to be surrounded by dogs!" I grinned at Eva. She beamed back and ran Pip's ears through her fingers.

"But no dog is as good as Pip," she said solemnly.

"No dog is as good as Pip," I agreed. Something else was niggling at me. "You said something." I pointed at Mr. Lowell. "Just now. You were going to call Mr. Marco by another name."

His ears turned red. "His title, but he gave me strict orders not to disclose it. Especially to you."

"I'm sure he did." I laid back into an unladylike slouch. Mother didn't correct me and we chatted with the little family until Mr. Lowell declared it was time to leave. I hugged Eva again, wished briefly she was mine and released her.

Mother saw them to the door. She came back into the room and wrapped my shawl around my shoulders again. "You could probably use another nap."

"He is hiding his title from me," I groused.

"Of course he is. You would only use it against him." She smoothed my blanket across my lap.

"Do you know what it is?"

She pressed a kiss against my cheek. "Get some sleep. John Turner is coming by to check on you later, and you don't want to be drooping while he's here."

"Mother!"

She gave me a look that brokered no argument. "Sleep." She left the room.

"The entire world is conspiring against me," I told Pip while he turned a circle and laid at my feet. He let out a long sigh that I echoed.

CHAPTER 8

Mrs. Horton is a veritable dragon! I've tried for a week to see Miss Horton and she has turned me away soundly at every attempt. Luckily, I've found a sympathetic ear in Mr. Horton.

Sunshine made it too perfect to stay inside and rest for an avowed sun worshiper. Nell pressed me into service instead.

"Go catch us dinner." She placed a fishing pole and a basket into my hands. "Your father has been hinting about trout for dinner for a month now and I haven't had a chance to catch any."

I took the basket and pole and left the house before Mother could insist on a bonnet or hat. Pip trod alongside me, his limp nearly gone. We made our way down to the small river that provided our community with life.

Pip explored near my shady spot near the riverbank, keeping me in sight while he snuffed through the bushes and trees. I cast my line and flinched when my ribs protested the movement. But my cast was good and I felt happy with the progress of my healing body.

The air was blissfully quiet and fragrant with the smells of spring in the country. The sun was warm, the sky was blue, the air smelled of flowers and animals and moss. I inhaled deeply, laid back in the grass and closed my eyes, letting the sun warm me.

"I've never seen that technique before." My eyes flew open to see the smiling face of Mr. Marco. "Does it work well?"

"You would be the one to cut up my peace." I strained and shifted back into a sitting position.

"Pax, Miss Horton!" He held out his hands, which were full of more fishing implements. He was dressed more casually as well in just shirtsleeves, a tweed waistcoat, and a neckerchief. "I honestly didn't know you were here. Your father showed me his favorite fishing hole yesterday and invited me to use it today."

"Oh did he?" I gave him a skeptical look.

"Yes. I think it was to make up for his daughter being most disagreeable and refusing to see me." He sank down next to me and unloaded his equipment to the ground.

"I'm trying to heal, Mr. Marco. I couldn't continue our merry war when I was injured."

His dark eyes washed over me and warmed me more than the sun. "I only wish I could kill the bastard twice."

"Your language leaves much to be desired." I reeled in my hook and released myself from his gaze.

"Yes, Miss Horton, I am well aware I have been found wanting in your eyes." He prepared his own pole for use. "I've been called the finest catch in London…in England! But I can't get a little country girl to look at me with sincerity."

I recast and inhaled. "You have a title."

He glared at his pole, his bait, the water, even at Pip when he plopped down beside us with a canine huff. He was still glaring when he cast his line a little too hard and it landed on the bank across the river. He muttered under his breath while he reeled it back in.

"Will you tell me what it is?" I wanted to hear it from his own lips, to know exactly how out of place I was in his company.

He cast his line out again and grunted when it landed properly in the river. "Yes, Miss Horton, I will tell you what it is. But only if you promise we will never speak of it again, and you never call me by it."

"Ever?" I asked.

"Ever." His lips were tight and his eyes firmly on mine. This was serious business for both of us.

"I promise," I vowed softly.

He looked away from me, back to his line in the water, and told me his title. His long, dignified, ancient title.

I gaped like the fish we were trying to catch. "You're a *Duke?*"

"Stop," he warned. "You promised."

I clapped my mouth shut and stared at the water where my pole was dancing a merry jig as my mind raced.

"I think you have a fish." He pointed out.

I reeled in too quickly and my catch escaped.

We sat in uncomfortable silence as I recast.

"I'm still the same person, Joy," he said quietly.

"I haven't given you leave to use my name."

He chuckled and reeled in a fish. He placed it in my basket and cast out again. "May I call you Joy?"

"Considering who you are, do I even have a choice?" I growled the words before I could stop them from escaping. He looked hurt and I hung my head. The man had saved my life. Frankly, he could call me whatever he wished. "That was rude of me and I apologize. Yes, you may call me Joy."

He smiled now. "Will you call me Arthur?"

"No, Mr. Marco, I will not."

"Why not?"

"Because of the thing we are not to speak of. It's not proper to be on anything less than formal terms with you."

He pursed his lips, "Very well, but if you get the rash idea to call me by my name someday, I would welcome it."

"Duly noted." I recast.

The silence between us was comfortable again while Pip snored next to me.

"Are you feeling better?" he asked after a few minutes had passed.

"I am, thank you. And thank you for your timely arrival at the Lowell's and your excellent marksmanship."

He cursed again, "I put you in that situation. You wouldn't have been there if I hadn't dragged you into the whole affair."

I snorted. "Don't be ridiculous. I was there of my own accord to visit Eva. Just because you introduced us doesn't make you responsible for anyone else's actions."

"I should have seen him safely in Newgate myself. I should have pushed to see you instead of taking your brother's advice to let you calm down after I insulted you."

"You speak as if the whole world revolves around your actions. Is that what one thinks when they have a title like yours?"

His eyes lit up with fire when he saw my grin. "Imp! I should never have told you."

"Probably not, but I did make a promise and I will keep it."

PART 1 - THE CULL

"Unless you use it to pester me. This is the first time I've ever had a woman use my title against me."

"I'll keep using it against you if you choose to keep this disagreeable mood." I felt a jerk on my line and reeled it in.

He exhaled loudly. "It seems all I do is apologize to you."

"Is that what you are doing now?" The fish was strong, pulling hard against me. I tugged and reeled. My aching muscles started to complain.

"I'm trying to. Although it is a bit difficult when you are reeling in your catch. Do you need help?" he asked when I flinched.

"No, I've got…" I hissed loudly. My pole jerked hard and I almost lost my grip.

Mr. Marco took over. His look of surprise at the strength of my catch made me feel better about my weakened muscles.

"Whatever have you caught? A sea serpent?" He dipped and tugged the pole.

"I don't think they swim this far upstream," I replied, rubbing my arms with relief.

I watched him brace himself and slide a little in the wet grass when the fish jerked hard on the line. Pip leaped to his feet and watched with a wagging tail. I slowly stood up and scowled at the angle of the pole.

"It's going to break!" I exclaimed.

"It might." Mr. Marco grunted, trying to straighten the pole. "Or the line might snap. I hope your father invests in good equipment."

"He does, but it's meant for trout, not sea monsters." I was at his back, my pain forgotten. His footing slipped again and he inched closer to the water.

"Careful. It's slippery the closer you get to the bank." I reached out and touched his elbow to rebalance him.

"Back away! I don't want you getting hurt again," he snapped, sending me a warning look. He stumbled forward, his boots splashing into the shallow water before he righted himself again and stepped back onto dry ground.

"Maybe I should just cut the line." I flinched when the pole bent into itself.

"And let this devil escape? No, he's going to have to earn it." He reeled on the squealing pole.

"You say that until you are impaled in the eye by a splinted pole," I grumbled, digging for the knife kept within the basket.

I stood up to face Mr. Marco once more when the line snapped. The pole jerked back and hit him directly in the face. He let out a yelp as he fell backward onto the ground with a loud thump.

Pip reached him first, sniffing and licking him. I heard him curse. "I'm alright, Pip. I wish your mistress would show me half as much concern." He glanced up at me, standing over him with a knife in my hand. A large welt was forming on his forehead and nose. I bit back a grin.

He nodded at the knife. "Come to make an end of me, have you?"

I laughed. "No. I was going to cut the line. Are you hurt?"

"Just my dignity, but then again you knew I had none on the day we met." He grinned at me and I gave him a snort in response.

I picked up the pole and examined the frayed line. "I don't think it was a trout. Have you another hook?" I cut the end of the line evenly.

"Just use my pole. After that battle, I think I'm done for the day." He collapsed onto the ground again, rolling onto his side and watching me bait the hook. Pip flopped down next to him and sighed with bliss when Mr. Marco rubbed his ears. I cast my line and sat down next to them.

We were quiet. I watched the water, aware of Mr. Marco's eyes on me.

"Why do you think it is that we have such spirited discussions?" he asked.

I grinned. "Is that what you call them? I like Shakespeare's term 'merry war' better."

"Ah, so I am Benedick to your Beatrice, am I?"

"I suppose we are when I think about it." I reeled in my line a little.

"Good. There's hope for you to fall madly in love with me yet."

I shook my head. "I doubt that, Mr. Marco. Besides, a 'fish and bird may fall in love but where would they live'?"

He was quiet.

I reeled in my hook and recast. "Really, I don't know anything about you. I know you are rich, you're spontaneous, and you have a large attachment to your name we can't speak about."

"My dear Joy, you know more about me than that. Don't you?" His eyes searched mine, a little fear creeping in around the edges of his gaze.

I nodded slowly. "I know you are humble enough to apologize when you are wrong. That you have a soft spot for those in need, quick to fight for justice." I glanced down at his fingers making small circles on my knee. "And you can't keep your hands to yourself."

"A fine young lady once said I was 'inappropriate'." He released my knee and lay back in the grass, resting his head on his arms. "But my other fine attributes should be enough for any young lady to decide I have an excellent character and give me her heart."

I let out a cry of disgust and was about to begin a tirade on what he could do with his heart when my line jumped. He sat up quickly, hovering to help me. It was an easy catch to land, and he dispatched the fish and put it in my basket for me.

"What else do you want to know about me?" He wiped his dirty hands on his breeches.

I shrugged. "I know nothing about your family, or where you grew up. I know nothing at all about your past. While my family is more than happy to supply you with every sordid detail of mine."

I saw him cringe a little. "Does one's past matter so much?"

"If one is a criminal, one's past matters."

"Then you have nothing to worry about. I am not a criminal."

"So you say, and yet you keep a beard like a pirate." I pointed out.

He ran his hand along his jaw. "I have scars from the war. I try to keep them hidden; they are frightening to some."

Now we were getting somewhere. "What did you do?"

"The unglamorous, nasty, and mostly boring job of financing the whole sordid affair." He huffed. "I'm unpopular with the *ton*. I have the stink of trade about me because I wanted to keep our men fed and supplied. Everyone wanted to beat Boney but no one wanted to do the real dirty work to get the job done. Those of us who did are shunned worse than…" he trailed off.

"A yeoman's daughter who plays in the mud with the sheep?" I plugged in.

"I think they'd embrace you more than a nobleman turned tradesman." He scoffed. "Anyway, Boney's spies found out who was keeping the coffers going and decided to take me out. I was set upon when I left my house one day. I was glad I only got a few scars." He rubbed his hand along his whiskers.

"I'm grateful for the work you did," I told him. "Did your family approve of your work? Or did they abandon you as well? I've heard familial ties in the *ton* can be…strained."

He laughed aloud. "Strained, yes that's one way of putting it. No, my family consists of me and my mother. She approved of what I was doing.

She's known as an 'eccentric' and gets away with anything she does. If someone questions or disparages me, she's on them like a tenacious bulldog with a prize and won't relent until they've publicly sung my praises."

"Your relationship with her isn't difficult?" I ventured.

"No, not at all, we are quite fond of each other," he said with a wistful smile.

A fish decided to jump on my line. It jerked hard and he took the pole from me without a word. I thanked him and rubbed my sore muscles while he reeled in my catch and took care of it for me.

"How many more do we need?" He baited the hook.

"Nell would appreciate one more." I leaned back into the grass while he cast the line back into the water. He didn't return the pole to me.

"You are kind to employ Mr. Lowell after all of this terrible business." I stretched out my legs. Pip came next to me and rubbed his head against my side until I pet him.

Mr. Marco scowled. "Lord Hampton turned him out without even listening to his tale. Dibble had loaned Lowell money for the doctor, and then he employed the doctor's help in squeezing Lowell. The doctor gave the poor man false information on his daughter's health and no hope for her future except in radical and expensive treatments only he could provide. Meanwhile, the doctor gave Dibble back half the money Lowell was paying him. When Lowell couldn't pay back his loan, Dibble threatened him with prison unless he started stealing from the tenants. Can you imagine that sweet child in debtors prison with her father?"

"Eva is not as ill as we thought?"

"I'm sending out my personal physician to check her over once they get settled and then we'll know more. I still haven't dealt with the other devil who calls himself a physician."

"Dr. Morris?" I thought of the kindly old country doctor who prescribed treats and rest for sore throats and believed that bleeding was a macabre and deadly practice. I couldn't imagine him doing such a thing.

"No, a Dr. Findlay. Lowell refuses to see Dr. Morris after the death of his wife."

"I see." I gazed out at the river, listening to its soothing sounds while it rushed over the rocks and reeds around us. He reeled in the final fish and placed it in the basket. He secured the poles, shouldered the basket and reached a hand down to me. "Come along, Joy. You've been yawning for the past five minutes. Let me walk you home so you can nap."

"I have not." I tried to subdue a yawn sneaking up on me. I failed and he gave me a knowing look. "Oh, hush. It's only because you suggested it." I took his hand.

His grasp was warmer than I remembered it. We were skin to skin, without gloves impeding anything. His grip was firm but gentle when he pulled me to my feet. He didn't release my hand as we walked back towards my house with Pip.

CHAPTER 9

Miss Horton seems immune to my charms. My wealth has no appeal to her. She despises my title. Every day I try to find some little crack in her armor but when I try to find what's under it she thwarts me with that tongue. Maybe it's for the best. Sophie's letter warned me away, and I know she's right. I know I cannot take Joy Horton as my wife.

As true as that statement is, I cannot bear to leave her side either.

Jane was radiant in her gown, covered in glass beads that sparkled in the sunlight. Her face beamed with happiness when they came out of the church. Everyone in our community cheered and the celebration began.

John Turner was especially handsome looking in his dress uniform and hat; his buttons shining brightly as well as his boots. He grinned at everyone as he followed his family out of the church. Children ran up to him and begged to touch his coat. He bent down and let them smudge the buttons with little fingerprints. He placed his hat on those that asked and laughed when they raced around the churchyard as tiny naval officers.

I watched him from the sidelines. My nephew held onto my hand and swung it hard. I refrained him from getting dirty. My sister, Hope, adored weddings and had come for a visit. She mingled with her husband, Lawrence, among the crowd while four-year-old David and I tried to find things to keep his attention. I would have let him play with the other children, but knew his mother would scold him if he got his fine clothes dirty.

"I like his sword." David's eyes were locked on the shiny weapon on John's hip. "I wish I had one like that. I only have a wooden one."

PART 1 - THE CULL

"A wooden sword is a fine weapon for you to practice with," I told him. "You are so fierce I would be afraid to see you with anything else."

He gave me a ferocious smile, full of teeth. "I want to be a pirate. They don't have to worry about their clothes." He looked at his mother with a scowl.

"A pirate, eh?" John Turner had approached us and overheard David's declaration. "I chase pirates." He growled and picked up David who started to scream with delight.

"And then we make them walk the plank!" he said to the writhing child before tossing him high in the air.

I laughed with them. He swung David by his legs, "Or we hang them by their ankles, and tickle them!" He held out the squirming child for me to attack.

I enjoyed his squeals and John tipped the breathless boy back upright in his arms. He plopped his large hat on David's head and the boy beamed in his arms.

"Now, I know you are a fearsome pirate, but your dear Aunt Joy is still recovering from being…sick." He gave me a knowing look. "And you need to take good care of her. You are so strong, you might accidentally hurt her."

David gave me a worried look. "Did I hurt you, Aunt Joy?"

"No, dear heart, but I am a little tired from trying to keep up with you."

"Let's go find your Uncle Thomas. I think he wanted to be a pirate once too." John gave me a look that warmed my cheeks. "Your lovely aunt needs to rest so I can dance with her later."

"Thank you, John."

He leaned down towards me and directed David. "Give your aunt a kiss."

I received a wet little boy kiss on one cheek and a dry warm masculine kiss on the other. John's actions surprised me and I drew away quickly.

"Save me a dance, Joy," he commanded and walked away with David.

I watched them leave, touching the spot on my cheek where John's lips had rested so briefly. What had gotten into him? He had shown a *tendre* towards Lily all week long. What was he doing?

I felt a presence at my side when my hand was tucked into a warm arm.

"Mr. Marco." I looked at the fine glove that covered my hand. It was white, silk, expensive, along with the rest of his attire.

"My dear Joy. You look stunning." He lifted my hand and ghosted a kiss across my knuckles.

I looked down at my own gown, a simpler creation of dark plum and silver stitching with a high neck and long sleeves to hide my sickly yellow bruises. Hope had powdered my face to cover the others. I thought I looked a bit dowdy but would take the compliment. He led me towards the tables and found me a seat, taking the one next to me.

"This is unlike any wedding breakfast I have ever been to," Mr. Marco admitted, looking at the hodgepodge feast provided mostly by everyone in the village. I knew the celebrations would go on long after the bride and groom had left.

"Have you ever attended a wedding outside of London?" I asked.

"Not for a long time. Everyone here is much more friendly," he clarified, looking at the bride and groom who greeted well-wishers and held each other's hands. "There is a great deal of affection between them."

I watched Jane and Bruce. They looked at one another like they were the only ones present. He kept his hand on the small of her back, his presence steady and sure but not demanding while she laughed and gave his arm or hand a caress every chance she got.

"I hope so. They will have to put up with each other's company for a long time."

"I wish them every happiness." His eyes clouded and his jaw relaxed. I watched him, wondering where his mind had wandered. Was he thinking of a dark-haired beauty who loved to laugh?

"Are you thinking of Diana?" I asked quietly.

He shook himself free of his musing. "What? No. Not Diana. You'll think I'm a cad, but I hardly think of her at all."

"You are, indeed, a cad," I declared and rolled my eyes. "What were you thinking of?"

He grinned. "I was thinking of the new Mrs. Lassiter's spectacular gown. She was right. Your work would surpass anything found in London. It would be more fitting to find it in an art museum than being worn on a beautiful country maiden."

"You flatter me." I admired my work as well. "I think on anyone else it would be just another gown. That is Jane's gown. Made for her and only her. I put a lot of time and energy and…" I stopped before I could spill any more of my usually guarded thoughts and gave a small chuckle. "Forgive me. I'm carrying on." No one really understood my work. I'd tried to explain it so many times to my family what compelled me to work so hard on my projects, what drove me to have dye-stained hands and calloused fingers when I should be focusing on needlepoint more suitable for a young lady.

"No, please tell me. I want to know." He turned towards me. "I'm still trying to figure out the mysterious Miss Horton, and suddenly she is opening up to me. What else did you put into that gown?"

"You'll think me simple." I tried to wave him off.

He tipped my chin up, his eyes full of sincerity. "Never."

I took a deep breath and jumped in. "Love. It's a labor of love. I love Jane, for all her loud laughter and flighty thoughts. Even if she is a 'simpering maiden', I still love her."

His smile was warm as I continued. "Because I love her, I wanted her to look like royalty on her wedding day. We fought, you know, over her dress. She wanted one thing and I saw another. I wouldn't say she was wrong; she just wasn't seeing what she really could become. She finally trusted me and I am happy to say I didn't let her down."

"You have a gift. Should you go to London your work would be clamored for."

"I don't think I could do it. Making things for strangers, or making copies of the same dress. Jane's dress would look wrong on anyone else but Jane."

"Ah. Spoken like a true artist."

I rolled my eyes. "If you say so."

A tap on my arm drew my attention to John Turner. He smiled at me and bowed. "Forgive the interruption, Your Grace, Miss Horton, but I have come to claim my dance. I assume you still know how to dance a reel?" He held out his hand to me.

I slid my hand into his. "But do you remember how to dance?"

"We'll find out together." He looked over my head at Mr. Marco, his eyes shining like he'd won a prize. I glanced back at Mr. Marco who had affixed a darker glare on his face. Before I could reason with them both, John had tugged me away from his presence and into the dance.

I let the moment overtake me and my body moved freely for the first time since the incident. My aching muscles twinged ever so slightly, but they stretched nicely and warmed quickly to the exercise. I was glad to be whole once more.

John Turner hadn't lost a step since he'd left us. He made an attractive partner, looking splendid in his uniform on the dance floor.

"You still dance like a native country gent." I took his hand for a turn.

"Yes, well, the Navy didn't beat all of my learned habits out of me. Just the less desirable ones."

"Such as?" I asked.

"Sleeping regularly, eating good food, drinking clean water…" He grinned at me.

We made another turn and I saw out of the corner of my eyes Lily's lone figure. She watched John's every move while we made our way through the group, her hands wrung tightly on a handkerchief.

I could see her heart breaking.

I stumbled and John reached out to correct me. I looked up into his concerned face as he took my elbow and pulled me from the set.

"I'm fine, John," I promised. He led me from the dance.

"Are you still hurting?" He placed a hand around my shoulders carefully and steadied me against him.

"Not as much as Lily is."

"Lily?" His puzzled face immediately scanned the crowd. His eyes found her and his face fell. "Lily," he whispered.

"I thought you two had a *tendre*, but perhaps I was wrong. If not, you should be dancing with her, not me." I pushed him away.

His lips pursed and he scowled, never taking his eyes off her. "I need to set some things straight, Joy. I'll be back." He gave my arm a light squeeze.

"Take your time." I watched him stride through the crowd to her side.

I made my way back towards the tables. Mr. Marco was not in sight, but my father was, along with David. They both were stuffing themselves with small cakes and other sweets that were smudged and smeared across David's clothes. Quite a few crumbs littered my father's cravat.

"I assume his mother has not seen him yet." I sat next to my father. He leaned over and kissed my cheek.

"Nor your mother. We escaped the two harpies and made a successful pillage of the desserts." My father proudly patted his belly. David grinned at me, his lips stained with dark berry filling.

"I'm sure Mother and Hope would love to know you are referring to them as harpies." I removed one of my gloves to wipe at David's cheek.

"The loveliest harpies I know." Father reached for his beer and took a long drink.

"I saw you dancing with John Turner. Are we going to have another Turner wedding soon, only I'll be paying for the food and beer?" There was a hint of concern on his face.

"Possibly. I'm sure Lily Smith and her family would appreciate it if you picked up the bill," I teased.

"Ah! Lily Smith, is it? Fine girl. He would do well to marry her." His face relaxed.

"Better than me?" I asked.

"Of course, better than you. You'd make a terrible wife for a Naval man."

"Oh? Why is that?"

"All that moving around and worrying. Not to mention he wouldn't be able to support your silk and thread habit. I want better for you." He sipped his beer.

"I'm afraid you will be the one supporting my silk and thread habit for a long time." I leaned over and rested my head on his shoulder. He felt warm and safe against my cheek and smelled like home. I closed my eyes and enjoyed his presence.

"Papa…Aunt Joy…" David's little voice drew our attention. The little man was shaking and his face had turned distinctly green. "My belly…" his eyes grew wide.

My father leaped up and grabbed the child, carrying him quickly from the tables. I went on a quick search for some water. The best I could do was a glass of lemonade.

I found the pair next to some bushes. David was no longer green but pale and exhausted. He rested in my father's arms.

"Here, little pirate. Have a drink." I helped him sip some of the liquid. He swallowed and sighed, resting his head on my father's shoulder. My father gently rubbed his back.

"Too much celebrating for this powder monkey. I should take him home before the harpies find us."

"I'll let them know." I kissed David's sweaty brow. "See you at home."

I returned to the tables to tidy up the mess they had made when a strong hand covered mine. I looked up into John's scowling face. "I apologize, Joy, but I must speak with you."

"Of course. How's Lily?" I asked.

His scowl deepened. "She's fine. I…" He shook his head. "I need to speak with you now."

"Very well." I gave him a nod. He led me from the party into a more secluded corner.

As the sun began to set, the world was turning a lovely golden color. He didn't speak a word as we drew farther from the crowd toward a copse of trees. His brow was furrowed and he practically marched me out of sight.

He released my arm. I watched him pace back and forth, making my heart beat faster. Was it bad news? Or good news? What would he say? Where was Lily? A battalion of butterflies marched in my belly. John was rarely this serious. Was he going to…? Oh dear.

He finally took a deep breath. "I'm afraid I have ill-used you."

I was instantly confused. "Have you?" I couldn't think how. Did he want me more than Lily? Had I read the signs between them wrong?

He took another deep breath and gathered my hands in his. My heart leaped into my throat. This could be a disaster.

"My dear Joy, I have, as of late, been spending a great deal of attention and time with you." His speech was more formal than anything he'd been using in the past two weeks.

"Yes, much to my brother's dismay. He is quite jealous," I said. "And I have enjoyed our time together, and your tales from the Navy while I recovered."

"I have as well. And I care for you deeply, Joy. But I'm afraid my actions have not been entirely honorable."

"How so?" I felt a twinge of discomfort in my gut. I pulled my hands from his grasp and crossed my arms across my chest, feeling suddenly defensive.

"I have been competing for your affections, but not for the right reasons. I have no intentions towards you of love or marriage." He spoke in a rush.

It was a relief to hear but I was still confused. "You were competing for my affections?"

"Yes, I was."

"And now you don't want them?" I had to clarify. I'd been oblivious the entire time!

"Yes, that's what I'm saying."

"I see." I swallowed. "Mr. Turner, I assume you have a good reason for trying to play with my affections?" My voice came out clear and cold. What had he been thinking! While I was glad his intentions were not towards me, why would he try to string me along? What had I done to deserve such treatment? What had Lily done?

He sighed. "A selfish one. The duke is the reason behind my actions."

"Mr. Marco?" I was even more confused. "What does he have to do with anything?" I sounded a little more shrill than I wanted to.

He scowled. "I've met many men like him. He's arrogant and selfish, tossing around his wealth and turning the heads of any woman he wants. When I saw him vying for you, it made me angry. I could not let him break your heart."

"So you thought it would be better if you would break it instead? Your attention towards me was nothing but a…a…contest? Between you and Mr. Marco?" My face flushed with embarrassment and anger.

"It was a one-sided contest. He had no part in my plans," John confessed. "I wanted to prove I was a better man than a rich and titled one. You are a dear friend, and I wanted to keep you from harm. But today I realized I'm the worst kind of man. I'm dancing and flirting with you, while I want to be with another, just to make you lose your interest in him."

My mouth went dry. Anger and humiliation swept over me from the tips of my toes to the roots of my hair. I wished the ground would open and swallow me whole.

John wasn't much help.

"Joy. I care…" He reached out a hand towards me.

"Don't try to soothe me, John! I am angry with you!" I felt the traitorous tears stinging my eyes and forced them back before he could see. Everyone had seen him dancing with me, had known he'd visited my house daily. That kiss on my cheek. And I had gone off alone with him! Oh, I could hear the gossip starting even now. Going to the tailor's shop was going to be absolute torture!

He had the grace to look ashamed. "I let it go too far, Joy. I've hurt you and I've hurt Lily, and I ask for your forgiveness."

"And someday you might get it. But not tonight." I pointed back towards the party. "Leave me."

"I should escort you back to the party." He offered his arm.

Was he insane? That was the last place I wanted to be!

"I do not wish to be seen with you. Nor do I wish to be in your company another moment!" I hissed.

He hesitated, then gave me a short bow and walked away.

Wiping away the stray tears of humiliation that had bullied their way through, I focused on putting myself back together. I grabbed a nearby tree and used it for balance while I gathered my emotions. Laughter and voices drifted from the party I had no desire to return to. An escape plan was in order. I gulped down a breath before it could become a sob.

"What a horrible, rotten waste of flesh. I should beat him soundly!" A voice growled from behind me.

I was startled when Mr. Marco appeared from the shadows. He took my elbow to support me as I stepped away from the tree. His scowl was not focused on me, but on the retreating back of John Turner.

"Mr. Marco." I hurriedly wiped my eyes again. Thankfully, no sobs escaped but I felt tired. I wasn't up for another battle with Mr. Marco right then.

"Just give the word, Joy. It would give me great pleasure to call out that villain for your honor. I would do so now, but I won't leave you in your distress." His eyes were bright and furious as he watched John Turner disappear into the crowd.

"You were spying?"

"I saw him lead you away and feared he had less than honorable intentions. I was ready to intervene if necessary. Every ounce of restraint I had was required not to." He took both my hands in his and squeezed them tight. He looked intently into my face. "My sweet Joy, please. Let me strike him, just once. I want to break his perfect nose."

I bubbled up a small chortle at his enthusiasm. "No, no thank you. I'm not sure I could take a confrontation between you two right now. I might wish him harm."

"That's my girl." He squeezed my hands once more before he handed me a handkerchief.

"Don't encourage me, Mr. Marco. I'm feeling very weak-willed at the moment." I took it from him and wiped my eyes and blew my nose.

"I have some experience with tearful ladies. Rest assured I have the best remedy you can find at my fingertips." He brushed his lips against my fingers.

PART 1 - THE CULL

"What is that?" I took a deep breath and blinked rapidly to clear my eyes. I was enjoying the feel of his hands in mine entirely too much. "Knowing you, I'm afraid it involves something rash? Or perhaps plying me with drink?"

"Joy!" he said with mock horror. "I can't believe you would think drinking is the first thing I would recommend for a young lady with sorrow to take up."

"Indeed, Mr. Marco. Apparently I am not myself tonight. What wholesome activity would you have a young lady take up when she is unhappy?" I tucked his handkerchief into my glove.

"Dancing, of course! One simply cannot dwell on unhappiness while dancing. And while I don't know all the steps of your country reels and jigs, they are currently playing a waltz, and I excel at waltzing."

"You are modest, sir." I felt a smile creeping up on me.

"Aren't I though? It's quite maddening that you don't have a better opinion of me. At last, you can finally recognize one of my many virtues." He dramatically puffed his chest out and gave me a condescending look that brought out a giggle from me.

"Stop your teasing." I chuckled again. "I'm quite sure your ego is already well-fed by many a simpering maiden, and you broke their hearts while yours remained intact."

"You are so harsh with me. And I dare you to find one lady who can call herself ill-used of me. Come, we must finish your treatment." He placed my hand upon his arm and directed my steps back towards the mass of people.

"I'm afraid the party holds no interest for me at the moment. I'm thinking of how to slink away like a coward." My eyes were gritty and my chest felt heavy.

"Nonsense! The Joy Horton I know stands up to bullies. We'll give him an eyeful and plenty for your neighbors to talk about. It's just the thing you need. Trust me."

His words were spoken with the playful tone we'd taken with one another, but his eyes were more serious. They pleaded with me to accept him. To trust him.

I felt warm inside that this man was wholly focused on my well-being. No one had ever done so before. It was heady and addictive. I quickly squashed it down and reminded myself that it wasn't for me.

I managed a friendly volley and forced out a smile. "Only because you are an expert on the subject."

He looked pleased. His hand wrapped around my waist and swept me into the dance. I found Mr. Marco, indeed, was a good dancer. My feet barely touched the ground as we moved and swirled to the music. I found his arms strong and firm while he guided me around. Heat radiated from him in the cooling night air. I found it hard to keep an appropriate distance from it. It promised warmth and comfort if I would just come closer.

His face peered down into mine and said softly, "They are all staring at you."

I glanced around. "They are staring at you, Mr. Marco. I thought that was your goal."

"To make all the other men here jealous, yes. It is too easily done with you in my arms."

"Your flattery will get you nowhere. Especially when I know the truth. They are all speaking about how daft you are for setting your gaze upon me."

He glared at me. "It isn't flattery. I think you have gone a great deal of your life without compliments, and I'm doing my best to make up for it. You are a beautiful woman, and they can't ignore that." He adjusted his grip and pulled my body closer to his, so his lips were at my ear instead of being face to face.

"Let's give them more to talk about." His voice whispered roughly in my ear.

I laughed a little as he swept me away into his heat again. He took the lead and I followed instead of stumbling or forcing my way through things. I had to admit he was right to face the issue instead of slinking away.

I saw John standing with Lily on the side of the dance floor. Her arm was linked in his, her face soft and happy while she watched us dance. John's was a mask of fury.

Mr. Marco spun me away from the couple; his voice warm and soft in my ears. "See, he's already regretting it."

He was suddenly ripped from my arms. I cried out and stumbled backward in time to see John with a firm grip on Mr. Marco's arm.

I let out a little cry of alarm. "John!"

They exchanged fierce looks.

"Stop!" I commanded. John couldn't hit a duke. The repercussions would be…

Mr. Marco growled and planted his fist in John's face. I gasped loudly.

John barely flinched and hit him back. Could you hit a duke if he hit you first?

Mr. Marco staggered a little, holding his jaw before looking up at John. He wiped his lip to look for blood. He had a mad grin on his face and fire in his eyes.

John and Mr. Marco then simultaneously descended into a mess of flying fists. In another moment they were on the ground wrestling. The music stopped while groups of men and women surrounded the two brawlers, screaming and cheering.

"Stop! Stop!" I shouted, trying to shove my way back through the turmoil. I had to break them up, to pull them apart. What madness had overtaken them? Was Jane still here? I desperately hoped she had left before her wedding had turned into such a scandal.

A pair of soft but strong arms held me back.

"Let them go," Lily said to me, putting an arm around my waist and holding me back. "It's been brewing all week. Let them have at it."

"They are acting like animals! We need to stop it!" I protested. I saw my brother working his way through the crowd. Hopefully, he would be the voice of reason. I latched onto him. "Thomas! You need to stop them! John and Mr. Marco are fighting!"

Thomas's grin was wider than Mr. Marco's. "Finally! It's about time." He peeled off his coat and tossed it my way before jumping into the fray.

I didn't think I could close my mouth if I tried. Lily shook her head and tugged me away. "They've got some steam to work off. Just let them go. Thomas will make sure no one gets really hurt."

"I don't understand them. They are all idiots!" I cried. I pressed Thomas's coat to my chest while Lily steered me from the spectacle.

"You're right. They are," she soothed. "John told me everything he did tonight. He's been an absolute villain. I hope Mr. Marco gets a few good hits in to knock some sense back into him."

"I don't know what he was thinking to try and string both of us along! He's horrible!"

"He thought he was rescuing his dear friend from the grasp of the wicked Mr. Marco."

"I didn't ask him to! I'm perfectly capable of handling Mr. Marco on my own."

"I know that. Everyone knows it but John." We flinched when we heard a solid punch hit behind us. The crowd cheered. "John does care for you, Joy."

"I know." I sighed, linking arms with her and walking away from the fight. "But I'm still angry with him. Come along, Lily. I think we both need some sherry."

"That sounds delightful." She rested her head on mine as we walked home.

PART 1 - THE CULL

CHAPTER 10

I can't remember a day when I've had so much fun. I danced with Joy. I got into a fantastic fight with a man who didn't pull his punches because I was a duke. I drank something I am wholly sure is unfit for human consumption and got into an inebriated brawl with Joy's brother. We cursed, we sang, we pounded out our frustrations. It was a glorious time.

And I held Joy in my arms.

I tucked Lily into one of our spare beds, insisting she spend the night. She was much more drunk than I.

We'd spent a pleasant evening with a bottle of sherry, some of Nell's fairy cakes, and a lot of talk about idiot members of the opposite sex. It felt good to laugh and cry with Lily. Going to bed knowing I had a true friend in her felt even better.

With my head slightly but not unpleasantly dizzy, I dressed in my nightgown and sat on the end of my bed looking out the window at the moonlight. I curled my arms around my knees and rested my head on them.

I didn't want to face the next day. John's good intentions towards me would be seen the wrong way, especially if he continued to court Lily. I would be the cast-off woman, not the dear friend he was protecting. On top of that, Mr. Marco started a fight at Jane's wedding…correction; the Duke of Ironwood brawled at a country wedding over a nobody yeoman's daughter with a Naval Lieutenant. That was sure to be a horrible scandal.

I groaned and crawled into bed, hoping I had imbibed enough sherry to tamp down my worries. I closed my eyes and took a deep breath to welcome a dreamless sleep.

Loud, drunken singing interrupted my peaceful slumber.

I grabbed my shawl, wrapped it around my shoulders and left my bedroom.

Thomas and John were entering the house with Mr. Marco being carried between them. All three of them were drunk and singing loudly with random bursts of laughter. Mr. Marco sported a cut above his eyebrow and a split lip. John had a black eye and bruises along his jaw. Even Thomas had a bit of a swollen nose.

I gaped at them all, especially at John and Mr. Marco laughing together like old chums as they staggered into the parlor. Thomas and John managed to get him to the couch, dropping him without much care how he landed.

"Ow! Are you chaps trying to start up another skirmish?" he bellowed, rubbing his head.

"Just trying to make sure both your eyes match," John responded. His face sobered a little when I entered the room. "Uh oh."

I shook my head, trying to quell my anger and disgust. Fighting, and now this! "You're loud enough to wake the dead! I'm amazed Mother hasn't appeared yet." I hissed.

"Mother's here now." I heard her voice behind me and turned to see her glaring at all three of them. She looked rather formidable in her wrapper and nightcap. I was glad to not be in their shoes.

"You two." She pointed at Thomas and John, "In the kitchen, now." She looked at the inebriated Mr. Marco who was making a pathetic attempt at trying to stand to attention. "Stay where you are, Mr. Marco. I can smell what these two have plied you with, and you won't be standing until morning." She placed a hand on my shoulder. "I'll get him some water and a blanket; you make him a bed there on the couch."

John and Thomas quickly ducked from the room before she could grab them by the ears. I approached Mr. Marco.

"I'm afraid I am not at my best right now," he admitted, staring at his boots. He looked rather pitiful with mussed hair, along with cuts and bruises on his face to match his torn, disheveled clothes.

"I can see that." I knelt before him to pull off his boots.

"Your mother is not impressed with my behavior. I can tell," he slurred.

"You are perceptive," I agreed, pulling the other boot off.

"And we didn't finish our dance." He glowered. I pulled on the sleeve of his jacket.

"I'm sure we'll get another chance," I soothed, pulling the other sleeve off. I turned to lay the coat on a chair when a pair of strong arms wrapped around my waist. He promptly pulled me into his lap and against his chest.

"Mr. Marco!" I protested. His arms held me tightly to him.

"I don't get drunk, I want you to know that. I haven't been this drunk in…years…" His lips were pressed into my neck when he spoke. His beard tickled my skin as he nuzzled me.

I held still, trying not to let his actions affect me. Strange sensations took over my body, making me shiver. I managed to swallow and exhale. Keeping calm would work better than screaming my head off. "I think you should let me go now."

"When's the last time anyone held you, my Joy?" He tightened his grip around me. His warm breath rested on my cheek. I didn't answer him. The only man who had ever held me tightly was my father when I was young, and his embrace felt entirely different than the one Mr. Marco held me in now.

"Mr. Marco, your behavior is appalling." I ignored his question. My head warred with my heart. His arms felt good around me, even better than when we were dancing.

He ignored me. "You're not held enough, I imagine." His nose trailed along my skin. "You smell so good." He pulled me tighter to his warm body.

"I'm sure in the morning you'll be horrified at your actions," I spoke sternly. My heart pounded and I tried again to gently squirm out of his arms.

His bearded cheek rubbed against my skin. "I doubt it."

I tried to convince myself I didn't enjoy the sensation. "Mr. Marco, my mother is going to return at any moment. I'm sure she will find your actions inappropriate and call in John and Thomas to remove your drunken carcass into the drive." I managed to hiss when his lips brushed against my hair. He stilled, his breath on my cheek was warm but my words stopped his actions.

"Damn. Both those fellows know how to throw a punch." He slowly released me, his hands sliding reluctantly from the embrace. I stood up and swung his legs up onto the couch, pushing him back into the cushions.

Mother entered with a glass of water, a blanket, and a bottle of witch hazel with a rag.

"Clean him up. I'm getting Thomas and John settled. Idiots." She shoved the items into my hands before I could beg for a release of duty.

With a sigh, I turned back to Mr. Marco and found him snoring on the couch, blissfully unaware of the inappropriate attention he'd just displayed. Irritated, and now in control of the situation, I doused the rag with witch hazel and applied it to the open wound at his eyebrow.

"Aaargh!" His eyes flew open and I smiled wickedly at him.

"Drink this." I handed the water to him and continued tending to the rest of his wounds.

"Fiend! Do you have to smile so much? One would think you are enjoying my pain." He gulped down the water.

"One would be right." I dabbed at his lip.

We sat in silence while I worked. He flinched as I wiped the blood away and closed his eyes when I finished. I stepped back and tossed the blanket over him.

"Thank you, Joy." His words slurred.

"Go to sleep, Mr. Marco."

He was gone before I came down the stairs the next morning. I found my father at the breakfast table with Thomas and John who were both looking green. I found great enjoyment in clattering my dishes and speaking loudly to them. "Mr. Marco didn't stay to enjoy breakfast?"

"He snuck out before any of us woke up," Father said. "I don't know how he managed, seeing how out of sorts these two are." He dropped his spoon onto his saucer and grinned. John and Thomas groaned loudly.

"Grandpa!" An exuberant David raced into the room. Thomas made an agonized sound and John buried his head in his arms. David came to stop and looked back and forth from the suffering men to his grandfather. "What's wrong with Uncle Thomas?"

"He had too many sweets," I said.

"Oh." David acknowledged solemnly, putting a hand over his stomach. "Just throw it all up, Uncle Thomas, you'll feel much better." He spoke with all the wisdom of a four-year-old. I let out a laugh while Thomas groaned and covered his head.

"Now, what's got you so excited this morning?" Father asked David, pulling him into his lap.

"There is a fairy princess upstairs! A real one, not pretend!"

My father's brows raised and he glanced at me. "Is there now?"

"Yes, I went into the wrong room this morning looking for my mama, and she was there, asleep. She is extra pretty, so I kissed her like Sleeping Beauty. She woke up, and then she talked with me, and we cuddled in her bed while she read me books until Mama woke up to dress me."

"That would be Lily." I rose to my feet. "I should go invite her down for breakfast."

John's head flew up. "Lily's here?" His black eye was more pronounced this morning, along with the yellow bruises along his jaw and the dark circles under his eyes. His naval jacket was covered with dirt and the buttons had lost their luster. His cravat was untied and stained and his top button hung by a thread. He ran his hands through his messy hair. "I'm a complete wreck."

"Good, you can propose to her and get this mess sorted out," Thomas mumbled.

John was on his feet. "You don't propose to a girl right after a night of drunken brawling! I still need to speak with her father!" He stormed out of the room towards the front door.

David watched him leave, looking up to my father for answers. "What's wrong with Lieutenant John?"

Father laughed. "He wants to marry your fairy princess, David."

David's face screwed up with anger. "He can't! I saw her first! I kissed her and woke her up, not him!"

Thomas started to laugh. "You got to kiss her before he did? Well done, little pirate."

Lily entered the room, looking as radiant and ethereal as David had described her. "Good morning."

"Lily! Come sit by me!" David demanded. Father sat him in a chair and prepared him some toast.

"Thank you." Lily accepted the heaping plate Martha placed in front of her. I smiled at our intuitive maid and was about to take a bite out of my own toast when the bell rang.

"I've got it, Martha." Father left the table. My mouth was full of eggs and ham when he returned with Mr. Marco at his side.

He'd apparently had a bath and a change of clothes. He was wearing bold colors and a layered traveling cape that made him look larger. The cut above his eye was a little pink and the wound on his lip had disappeared. He looked hale and hearty for one who had been so drunk the night before.

"Good morning Horton clan, Miss Smith!" He made a bow. Pip rose from his spot under the table and nudged his nose against Mr. Marco's leg until he was scratched behind the ears. "Good morning to you too, Pip."

David's eyes were agog when he took in Mr. Marco's long hair, dark beard, and black eyes. "Aunt Joy…is he… a real pirate?" he whispered.

I laughed as Mr. Marco bowed to the child. "This is Mr. Marco, David. And I'm pretty sure he is a pirate."

"I am not a gentleman," Mr. Marco pronounced. "Not after the spectacle I made of myself last night. I have come to offer my deepest apologies and sincere thanks for your hospitality."

"You are forgiven." Mother came to her feet. "Will you join us for breakfast?"

"No, thank you, I need to be going. Might I have a private word with Miss Horton before I leave?" he asked.

My entire family's eyes rested on me. I felt my cheeks redden. I nodded and followed him out of the room with Pip at our heels.

We stood on the front porch and faced one another in the morning sunlight.

"I suppose you think I owe you an apology for my behavior last night." He tapped his walking stick lightly on the step. There was a twinkle in his eyes and I saw the prelude to a merry battle.

"A gentleman would apologize. But you, sir, are a pirate, and I will not hold my breath waiting for an apology from a scoundrel."

"Good! Because I'm not sorry at all, and it would be wasted breath for me as well."

"I should be angry at your behavior, Mr. Marco. It is a wonder I am not telling my father to shoot you on sight."

He leaned towards me and tugged on an errant curl that had fallen across my eyes. "That's because you like being in my arms as much as I like having you there." He spoke for my ears only.

I didn't know whether to melt or be outraged, so I chose the safer route. "Pip! Bite him! Hard, on the leg. I would like a pound of flesh," I commanded the cheerful dog who wagged his tail back at me.

"Luckily, Pip is firmly in my camp." Mr. Marco rubbed the spaniel's ears. "You'll have to find another champion since John Turner should be asking the fair Lily for her hand today."

"Yes, I noticed you two are suddenly fast friends after pounding each other's faces all night."

He shrugged. "It's the fastest way for males to work out our disagreements. Mostly I just wanted to give him a good thrashing for making you cry." I felt my insides warm at his words.

"He and I have reached an accord. He gets the fair Lily, and I get to court you without his interference."

I let out a laugh. "I really am going to teach Pip to bite you. And John."

"I received Thomas's blessing as well as your father's. You, my dear *Joy*, are officially being courted." His emphasis on using my name was grating.

I was getting annoyed now. "We agreed to be friends, *Mr. Marco*. That's all we can ever be."

"I am changing the agreement."

"You can't change the agreement unless I agree to change the agreement as well." I protested.

"I changed it without you."

"Then change it back!" I demanded.

He laughed now, throwing his head back and letting his shoulders shake. "I am going to miss you, my dear Joy."

My temper faded away. "You are leaving?"

"I find I need to return to Town. I face a summons from my mother and an important vote in Parliament." He reached out for my rogue piece of hair that had again fallen across my face. His fingers lingered when he tucked it behind my ear.

I felt equal parts relief and disappointment at his departure. "I think I will miss you too, Mr. Marco."

"You *think* you will?" He smiled at me.

"I think so."

"Will you think about our courting while I am gone?"

I shook my head. "There is nothing there to think about."

He scowled now, his hands clenching the top of his walking stick. "I can tell from the stubborn little look on your face it will take something rash and inappropriate to change your mind. Perhaps I should kiss you soundly while your entire family watches." His eyes darted to a place behind my shoulder.

"They are not…" I turned around to see the window curtains quickly close on Hope, Mother, Martha, Lily, and even little David's face. "Oh for goodness sake!" I turned back to Mr. Marco, recognizing the dangerous look in his eyes. I placed the porch pillar between his body and mine. "Stop right there. You keep your lips far away from mine!"

He took my hand, chuckling as his warmth invaded my skin and he brought my fingers to his lips. "We'll discuss our agreement at another time," he said before kissing each finger softly, making my knees knock and my brain melted.

Bending down and he gave Pip one last scratch before placing his hat on his head. "I'll be back in a month's time. I'll miss you." He turned and skipped down the steps.

Tell him! The little voice in my head screamed at me. *Tell him now!* I held on tightly to the pillar for support before, "You should consider not coming back. I…I cannot be who you want me to be!"

"You already are everything I want you to be!" He climbed into his curricle and took up the reins and whip. "I'll write to you, every chance I get."

My stomach dropped like a cold stone. "I won't respond!" I shouted back.

He shook his head and flicked the reins. "I cannot believe you would be so unkind as that," he shouted and the horse broke into a quick clip.

"But I cannot write…" I whispered like a coward while I watched him disappear.

PART 1 - THE CULL

CHAPTER 11

Sophie saw it right away. She railed at me for an hour. She's right. I cannot have Joy Horton as a wife, but I need her in my life like I need air to breathe. A mistress then? Is Arthur Graham Marco, Duke of Ironwood, going to break his lifelong rule and take a mistress? Would she even accept?

Mr. Cooper released me from the shop. My recovery had taken too long and my place had been filled by another. I felt a moment of dejection but knew it was for the best. He promised to call on me if he was behind and needed an extra hand. He encouraged me to continue to design and create. "You're too good for my shop, Joy Horton. You need to go and make your mark elsewhere."

I spent the next couple days with my sketchbook, thinking up designs for Lily's wedding gown when Mother entered the sitting room. She was flushed with delight and tossed her bonnet onto the couch next to me. She held out the mail.

"You have a letter, Joy! From Mr. Marco."

I stared at it before taking it from her, not believing it was real.

My first letter. Ever. Even my sisters had never written to me when they moved, not that they had reason to. Mother kept me apprised of their lives with her own letters.

I looked at the thick handwriting and the red wax seal with the elaborate monogram letter above it. If I concentrated, I could make out my first name, and that was about the extent of my understanding.

Mother beamed. "Do you want me to read it to you?"

A feeling of horror washed over me. "Mother, the last thing a young lady wants is for her letters from a man courting her to be read aloud by her mother."

Mother's face fell. "I was just trying to help."

And now I had hurt her feelings. "Thank you. I told him I would not write to him, and he brushed it off as nonsense. He'll find out I was in earnest." I set the letter on the table next to me and picked up my sketching once more.

"Did you tell him why you would not be responding?"

"No. I did not feel it was any of his business." I felt old wounds being picked open.

"He's openly courting you, Joy. How could you keep it from him?"

I looked up into Mother's face. "Mother, please. I've told him repeatedly I would not make a good wife and his attention would be better spent elsewhere."

"Why do you say such things? You would make an excellent wife for anyone. You have wonderful skills, talents, and you are pretty, quick-witted, and bright. I won't hear any more of such talk."

I gave her a small smile. "You only say that because you are my mother."

She took my face in her hands, angling my chin. "I say such things because they are the truth, Joy. Please stop being so hard on yourself. Open up to other possibilities." She leaned down and kissed my forehead.

Once she was gone, I picked up the letter from Mr. Marco and examined it.

My first letter.

I cracked the seal and examined the contents, an entire page in length. His script was bold and the lines on his letters were thick. The signature at the bottom was messy but elegant, with the letters running into each other in round tall form.

Which Mr. Marco had written? The fun and witty one? The bully demanding a response? Perhaps I held a private love letter that would make me blush?

There would not be a merry battle if he returned. My silence would send a volley to start a full-blown war. If he did come back I knew he would not back down from it.

The next day I convinced Mr. Cooper to release Lily early, promising to make up her wages with whatever task he would assign me. I took her home and tried gown after gown on her. I looked at the different colors against her skin, the different lines of the dresses and how they hung on her along with what fabrics would suit her best. Ideas and designs flowed in my head and onto my sketchbook until Thomas interrupted us.

"Oy!" he called from downstairs. "Come here and help me clear out this mess!"

We gathered ourselves downstairs and found Thomas grinning in the doorway.

"Gift arrived for you, Joy." He opened the door.

On the porch sat crate upon crate of bolts of fabric. Wool and silk and lace and everything in between were displayed in a multitude of colors. Another crate was full of threads of varying thickness and pigments. A large box of bottles filled with dyes from all over the world sat next to it all.

Mother put her hand over her chest. "Oh, Joy...that man definitely knows the way to your heart."

"This is a small fortune," Lily gasped.

I was stunned into silence. I knelt down and gently touched the first of many fine fabrics. "This is too much." I groaned, thinking of how much he was going to hate me by the end of the month.

"He knew you would like it better than flowers or anything else." Mother lifted another bolt of fabric into her arms and carried it inside.

She was right. He'd just pounded a hole straight through the wall around my heart. He'd not only listened to my ramblings about fabric and thread and Jane Turner's gown, but he'd actually heard me. He knew what my passion was and now he was courting me with a grand gesture of support.

"Lily, you are going to shine brighter than the sun on your wedding day," I vowed.

"You can't use this on me!" she protested.

"There is enough here for me to make a new gown for everyone in the village. Of course I'll use it on you, and one for Mother, and one for Martha, and even one for Nell if I can get her to accept one. I'm sure my sisters will faint dead away at the sight of it all and demand something new."

"I'm sure he'll expect one on you, Joy," Mother chided.

"When I get to it," I promised her vaguely.

"Here." Thomas handed me another letter. "This came with it."

Mother lifted her brows at me as I accepted it. "Do you want me to read it, dear?"

I tucked it into my pocket and shook my head. "No, no thank you." I gestured at the mound of fabric. "Clearly, I received the message he wanted to send."

Father beamed at the mess. "Now there's a fool in love if I ever saw one." He gave me a squeeze. "One who can take proper care of my baby girl."

"Father..." He slipped out of the room before I could protest further.

I threw myself into making Lily's gown, stitching and dying and cutting and layering. I received a new letter every couple of days, each one getting shorter and shorter. The last one was only one line long, in thick letters, as if the pen had scraped across them over and over. There was even a hole where the pen had punched through the paper.

Now he's getting angry. I smoothed it down and touched the letters, tracing them carefully with my fingers. I wished they would hold still, instead of squirming and running into one another while my vision blurred and my head ached.

Two weeks after his departure he gave up writing to me and wrote to my father instead.

I was elbow deep in smelly, purple dye when Father confronted me.

"Joy, I have a letter here from Mr. Marco." He held it up for me to see. I recognized the red seal and expensive paper, along with the thick handwriting.

"How is he?" I carefully wiped my hands on my multicolored apron.

"Very concerned. It appears you haven't answered any of his letters and he is inquiring about your health. He's under the impression you are at death's door."

I groaned. "I informed him I would not respond to his letters."

My father's frown matched the one Mother had given me when I had received my first letter.

"Did you tell him why?" he asked.

I shook my head. "No...it's...none of his business."

He shook the letter at me. "The man thinks you are dying, Joy! I never thought you would treat someone so horribly."

I cringed at his words. Was I being harsh and petty? I dredged up all the reasons why I was doing this and it strengthened my resolve. "I was hoping he'd get to London and forget all about me."

Father snorted his disbelief. "I have an entire bedroom filled to the brim with the biggest courting gift I've ever seen, and you hoped he would forget you?"

I nodded, "He's...we're...not a good match." I wanted to rub my eyes but the thought of streaking my face with purple stopped me. "Now that he is gone, I am hoping to keep him away."

"Yes, well, as your father that's my job, not yours. And he would make an excellent husband for you. I'll write to him at once and end this nonsense."

"Oh, Father! Please, please don't!" I cried out, throwing away caution and placing a large purple handprint on my father's sleeve.

"Joy! The man thinks you are dying" he shouted, waving the letter in my face.

"It's not my fault he's too stupid to believe me when I said I wouldn't write back!" I shouted back.

Father and I glared at each other. My heart pounded and my face flushed. I tried to get my voice back under control. "Please, Father, please respect my privacy. Kindly inform Mr. Marco I am in exceedingly good health and I appreciate his concern. Express my thanks for his gift and that I am putting it to good use. Remind him I told him I would be...unable to write him back. Use those exact words. Nothing more."

He sighed. "Foolish child." He leaned in and gave me a kiss on my forehead. "I will do as you ask."

My next letter from Mr. Marco was two pages long. I could almost see the anger radiating from the pages. The words were tall and sharp, slanted to the right and peppered with ink spots and smeared letters.

"I wonder if you found any new creative names to call me besides Fairy, or Imp. Most likely you've gone with something worse," I whispered, smoothing out the pages and setting them with my other letters, certain it would be my last one.

I was wrong.

Another letter arrived the next day. Short and just a few sentences, but the words were loopy once more and even. Neat and clean like his first letter.

I received one every day. Each one a page long and full of graceful loops and his strong thick lines. He wasn't giving up, and that made my heart beat faster and my spirits dampen. I looked forward to seeing him again and fretted and worried at the same time.

The month came to an end, and the letters stopped coming. I felt a sense of relief until I heard Pip's joyful barks while I sat in Mother's flower garden working on the embroidery for Lily's veil.

"Hello, Pip!" Mr. Marco's voice filled the air. I could hear Pip's tail rapidly smack against his legs. Concentrating on my work I prayed silently I would survive this confrontation.

Mr. Marco stood over me while I plied my needle. His shadow blocked out all the sun and I could feel his glower and displeasure radiating. I gathered my nerves and looked up. This would probably be our final verbal battle.

His glare was harsh enough to burn a hole through my conscience. A true glare on his face, instead of his resting bored scowl. I swallowed and met it with a steady gaze of my own.

"Mr. Marco," I greeted, giving him my full attention. "I did not expect you to return to our little neighborhood."

"Was that your plan to keep me away? Absolute silence? I wrote to you," he snapped.

"Yes, you did."

"You did not write back."

"No, I did not."

His chest puffed up with anger. "Did you even read them?"

"No."

He walked a few steps away from me, muttering. He took an angry passing swipe at a lavender bush with his walking stick before he stormed back. "And why not?"

"Because I cannot read," I answered simply and held his gaze. His features softened a little into skepticism.

"I find it hard to believe your most excellent father did not educate you."

"He did. Or he tried," I admitted.

He waved his walking stick at me. "Move over, I wish to sit by you."

"I did not invite you to do so," I pointed out, but moved my project out of the way to make room.

"I don't care," he growled and pushed himself onto the bench next to me. I found his presence comforting, especially since I was about to pour out my greatest fault to him. He came back to me. He deserved to know.

"Now, I would like you to explain this amazing lack of ability from someone so articulate, sharp-witted, and bright."

PART 1 - THE CULL

I smiled and tried to renew our playful war. "You think I am sharp-witted and bright? Why Mr. Marco, you have never paid me such a compliment before. One would think you missed me."

He glared at me. "I did, dammit. Explain now, Joy."

I drew in a deep breath and picked up the veil. It was easier to talk while not looking at his piercing gaze.

"In all fairness, my first governess did try her best. She had successfully taught my older sisters and was certain I would be another smart Horton daughter. I could recognize pictures, I could sing, I could add and subtract and even recite. Everything was going well until we brought out the paper and pen to write. Things went swiftly downhill.

"The alphabet became my nemesis. I knew all the letters, backward and forwards, even from the middle and the sounds they made. All until it came to putting them down on paper. My governess would write on the paper, and tell me, "That's an 'A'. Now you write one."

"I would reproduce it the best I could. My letter never looked the same as my teacher's. It was upside down or slanted wrong. Sometimes the lines would touch, and sometimes they would not. When I looked at it, it would move and change, wiggle and squirm into something else. I would race and scribble as fast as I could to capture it before it moved around the page.

"She tried begging, pleading, praising, rewarding, punishing, and sometimes she fell into a heap on the rug sobbing trying to get me to read. I did all she asked. I wanted to please her, so very much; I wasn't doing it to vex her. I just couldn't communicate what I was seeing.

"My governess gave up, and they hired another. One who favored placing a stinging rap on my knuckles with a switch for every wrong line I drew. On our second day of lessons, after being struck five times repeatedly for writing the letter B wrong, I flew into a passion. She ended up with tiny teeth marks on her nose, and I was put into my room for the rest of the day. It was the shortest employment she'd ever had.

"My third teacher took a different approach. After working with me for a day she told my parents I would never amount to much and they shouldn't waste their time and money trying to teach me. She said an asylum would be better for me than a home. For a five-year-old because she couldn't read! My mother cried and my father paced around the room, stealing glances at me that wavered between frustration and failure. He dismissed the governess and took me into his arms, telling me I was pretty and smart and his precious girl. He assured me, and my mother, that not being able to read was nothing to be concerned about and plenty of people lived in this country and made their way through life without the written word. I would just have to work harder at other things.

"Mother wasn't satisfied and took me to doctors to confirm my governesses' observations that my brain did not work the way it should. They informed her that my condition was sometimes passed from parent to child."

I scrutinized my tiny daisy that had taken shape during my narrative, brushing a few loose threads aside. I looked at Mr. Marco, trying to interpret his scowl. "That is why I did not read your letters and respond. Now you know."

I felt free. My disability was finally out, spoken aloud to Mr. Marco the reason I could not be with any man, or have any children. "Now you know why I would make an unsuitable wife. Especially for a peer. I cannot answer mail, I cannot organize meals, keep a budget, or keep up with current events unless I am read to. And I cannot promise my children will not be born with the same problem. I cannot provide an heir. I am not wife material."

I expected and was almost certain Mr. Marco would leave, and I could finally get back to my comfortable little life. Mr. Marco sat in silence next to me. I would not look at him, would not meet his gaze.

Gently, he reached out and took the veil out of my grasp, setting it down carefully next to him. He took both my hands and looked into my face. His fingers were bare as he rubbed them softly over the back of my hands. His eyes gazed into mine with intensity. "You are an amazing woman, Miss Joy Horton. And I am glad to know you." He brought both of my callused and colored hands to his lips and kissed both of them.

"Mr. Marco…" Warmth rose up my neck and cheeks.

"Arthur."

I shook my head with a chuckle, "I cannot call you Arthur."

"Friends do. And you are my friend. You don't trust a story like that to just anyone. Arthur. Try it."

"Arthur…you are still a pest." I tried to lighten the mood.

He grinned. "It's because you bring out the best in me."

"You shouldn't be my friend, Arthur. It's not proper."

"I don't give a damn about propriety, Joy. I care about you."

PART 1 - THE CULL

"Why?" I really wanted to know. What made a rich and powerful man care about me?

"Because I'm happy when I'm with you," he said simply, and kissed my hands again, his warm breath lingered against my skin.

"I've been perfectly awful to you," I pointed out.

"It's been a challenge, I'll admit. But that's what makes it so enjoyable. If you were dull and drab and without so much personality and wit, I'm sure we wouldn't be friends. I adore verbally sparring with you. You and I are well suited, Joy."

I gave him a skeptical look. "I doubt you are going to renounce your title and sell all you have to become a farmer."

He laughed. "No. No, I'm afraid I have too many dependent on me to sell it all off and leave them at the mercy of a new master at the moment." He looked at me carefully. "But I'll bet you could help them become independent, couldn't you?"

"I'm not a miracle worker, Mr. M…Arthur."

His eyes lit up. "Yes, you are, Joy. You just don't know it." He was quiet, looking intently at my face. He then released my hand and stood up abruptly. "I must take my leave. I'm about to kiss you if I don't."

I gasped and watched him turn away, my heart pounding in my chest at his declaration.

He tapped his walking stick on the ground a few times, turned around and marched back towards me. "But then again, you already know about my lack of self-control."

He pulled me on my feet with a quick jerk that caught me off balance. I stumbled closer to him, and found myself caught in a full embrace while his walking stick clattered to the ground. His grasp did not hurt, but was firm and gave no illusion of who was in control of the moment.

"Arthur…!" then his lips were on mine. His lips were moving on mine. And mine were moving back! My hands were no longer trying to push him away but hold him close, gripping his waistcoat to keep him near. My body betrayed me while my mind wrapped around the feel and smell and delight of kissing Arthur Marco.

He finished his gentle kiss and pulled my face back into his gaze. I was speechless as we gazed at one another. His thumb reached up and brushed along my cheekbone. I turned my face away and my cheeks flamed.

"All those freckles…" he admired.

"Arthur..." I tried to interject. My head was spinning from his kiss, and I couldn't make a complete sentence.

"Another kiss? Is that what you want?" he asked. His lips came crashing down this time, abandoning his previous gentleness. One hand held me close by the waist and tight to his body, and the other dug deep into my hair and held my face to his.

This kiss started a fire, one I quickly abandoned myself to, wrapping my arms around him as tightly as he had me. I kissed him back with all the frustration and desire I'd felt since he'd come into my life. Letting go of the all pent up energy, I gave it to the one it belonged to.

He released my lips and held me to his chest, his breath coming faster, his fingers plundering through my curls. "My Joy, I must have you." His lips pressed against my hair, murmuring his words with hot breath against my skin.

"No," I moaned, trying to regain my sense of balance. Things were spiraling quickly out of control, even though I was as inflamed as he was. I really needed to get my fingers out of his waistcoat.

"Don't fight me anymore. Our courtship is over. I will have you." He kissed my forehead.

"I can't." I tried to call up all my old arguments.

"Why?" His lips covered my cheeks and took my lips again briefly, tenderly. Each kiss weakened my resolve. "My sweet Joy. Why can I not have you?"

My eyes were closed, my head reeling from his attention. "Because I cannot be a wife for you." One of us had to remain sane.

He stiffened then, pushing me back. "Wife." He stared at me long and hard. I could once again see his mind working, the cogs and wheels churned to settle on what he would do. "Yes, you could have nothing less than that." He murmured. He straightened and took me by the shoulders, staring down at me with intensity. His gaze seemed to last an eternity while he waged a silent battle with himself. His grip tightened and then he released me.

He adjusted his cravat straight and took up his walking stick. "I shall meet with your father. Now."

"Wait, what?"

"For your hand."

The bottom fell out of my stomach and hit the ground. "You can't..."

PART 1 - THE CULL

His smile was almost cruel. "You can't kiss me like that, dear Joy, and not make me think you don't want me too."

I couldn't deny it, but a kiss was one thing... "I can't marry you."

He turned around and marched towards my house. "It's too late, Joy. I will have you."

My knees turned to jelly. I sat down hard on the ground and watched him disappear from the garden. Marriage? Talking to my father? Did the man not understand the meaning of the word 'no'? I groaned, and buried my face in my hands. I wanted things I'd never wanted before. But one of us had to be rational.

Mother was waiting for me when I walked inside. Her eyes were bright and her face flushed with pleasure. "Mr. Marco is here, speaking with your father. I think he wishes to propose!"

"That is his exact intention, Mother. But I do not intend to accept."

Her countenance fell. "Joy. You can't be serious. When a smart, handsome, wealthy man asks for your hand, you accept."

"I cannot." His kisses had not weakened my resolve to do the right thing. "I do not expect you to understand. I know you see it as a good match. But I would not make a good match for any man. I accept this and I wish you would too."

"You have spent a great deal of time convincing yourself of that, haven't you?" Mother's voice was filled with quiet fury. "You think you don't deserve happiness because of your handicap, or you have to prove something because of it."

"Mother..."

"I have three married daughters and delightful sons-in-law. I have never seen any of those fine young men look at your sisters the way Mr. Marco looks at you. That man is *in love*. For all your faults he looks upon you as if you hold the moon." She pointed her finger at me. "You may have convinced yourself that you don't deserve what you really want, but will you deny the opportunity to him? Would you deny yourself the chance of happiness with him? Or will you refuse because it doesn't fit in your carefully crafted world?"

I gulped. "His happiness shouldn't depend on me, Mother."

"He is a rich and powerful man. He could buy up the entire country if he wanted. And all he wants is you, Joy! I dare say the only person in the world who can really hurt such a man is you. I've always thought you were the brightest of my children, but all I see right now is a fool."

My mother's words were harsher than a slap. I said nothing as she left me, gasping to keep my emotions in check. I forced myself to retreat back behind my mental walls of wisdom. I turned towards my father's study and stood outside the door, touching it lightly.

I could hear my father and Arthur talking softly inside. I slumped to the floor, resting my head on my knees to contemplate my upturned life. How could I ever make things go back to the way they were?

Did I really want them to?

The study door opened. I made a small cry as I fell backward onto the floor into the doorway. I looked up into the faces of my father and Arthur. Both had similar expressions of bemusement.

I remained on the floor, looking up at them. "I assume you had business to discuss concerning me."

"Your name has come up in conversation," Father agreed.

"And what has been decided?" I asked.

"Mr. Marco is to be your husband, if you accept," Father said.

"I see."

"Joy, for heaven's sake, stand up!" Father demanded, reaching down and pulling me to my feet.

I stood and smoothed my gown. "Mr. Marco, I am afraid I cannot accept your proposal." Both of them glared at me. "I was going to tell you earlier, but you stormed away so quickly."

Arthur took my arm. "Excuse us, Mr. Horton." His voice brokered no disagreement and his face had gone from his usual scowl to one of sheer anger.

He pulled me out of the room and I didn't fight him. We marched down the hallway and into the parlor. Once we were alone he took me by the arms, forcing me to look him in the eyes. "Why, Joy? Why must you fight me so much on this?" he demanded.

I tried to wrestle away from him. "Arthur, I have nothing but kind and fond feelings for you..." I started.

"Kind and fond," he hissed, releasing me. He paced then pointed at me. "I have more than 'kind and fond' feelings for you, Joy. Do you need another demonstration of my passion for you?" His eyes raked over me and I shuddered. I wasn't sure I could resist another encounter.

"No, but I need you to see reason."

"Reason? I'm quite sure you are the irrational one. I have good health, land, and money! I even have a title! What more could a woman want?"

"That is precisely why I cannot marry you! Titled men with money and land do not marry illiterate farmer's daughters who should not have children!" I shouted back.

We glared at one another, both of us seething

He took a deep breath and ran his hands through his hair, let out a furious cry and paced away from me. I wrung my hands.

His voice shook, "As you may have noticed, my dear Joy, I am not like most men. I don't give a damn about my money, or land, or even the title. The only thing I want is you. I love you, Joy."

My heart jumped into my throat and my hands fell at my side. I couldn't speak. All I could do was stand there and watch this man tear down the wall around my heart brick by brick. Mother was right? He loved me? Truly?

He reached for me slowly and took my hands carefully. I felt powerless at his touch and glanced down at our hands.

He continued, "I love you, you hard-hearted little fairy. I love your freckles. I love your quick mind and wit. I love your unruly hair. I love your loyalty to your friends and family. I love your compassion for others. I love how talented you are with your needle and your eye for making works of art. I love how independent you are." He pulled me closer as the rest of the wall came crumbling down with his embrace. "I love you, Joy Horton. And I want to be the husband of such a wonderful woman." He leaned down and kissed me.

It was impossible to resist.

So I didn't.

I gave up entirely and kissed him back, feeling my knees buckle and sway as he supported my weight. He felt right. All of it felt right.

He ended the kiss and rested his forehead on mine. "And now Joy, what do you want? Forget everything else, me, your family, and your… affliction. What do you want?" He ran his hands gently up and down my spine. I trembled and the dam broke.

I felt a little sob rise in me. "I can't…" I'd never said them out loud. Ever. "Yes, you can." He kissed both my cheeks softly and pulled me further into his arms, holding me against his chest and stroking my hair. "What do you want?"

The answers came spilling forth before I could stop them, bursting free after spending so much time hidden. "I want a house… a comfortable house… with sheep on the lawn and spaniels tripping everyone when they come to visit." I started to sob.

I felt the rumble pass from his chest and into mine. "I can give you that. What else do you want?"

"I want a husband who thinks I'm brilliant, even though I'm illiterate." Tears ran down my face and stained his waistcoat.

"My Joy." He kissed my hair. "I can give you that."

"And…" I sobbed harder while the desire I had chained up so deep came bursting out, refusing to be silenced ever again.

"Yes?"

"I want children! I want babies and children and grandchildren and everything in between." I cried, gripping his coat as my tears watered his cravat.

He tipped my face up, wiped a thumb across my cheek to remove a tear and lowered his face to mine. "I will give you that," he promised.

PART 2
THE FARCE

PART 2 - THE FARCE

CHAPTER 12

I'm a damned soul. I'm a greedy bastard.
But I could not give Joy anything less than what she deserves.
I'll take my happiness. I'll fight for this one, fight a losing battle just like my father and his father before.
I'm absolutely terrified.

Arthur beamed at me when my father and I entered the chapel. He was in full regalia befitting his title. I thought he looked like a peacock. I hardly looked at my father until he placed my hand into Arthur's and placed a kiss on my cheek.

We turned and faced the vicar. He addressed the congregation, and almost immediately his voice droned into the background. I glanced at my husband to be.

"I like your hair," Arthur whispered and I couldn't hold back a smile. I fingered my newly cut locks. My mother and sisters had all cried when I appeared with my short hair. I knew Arthur would find it amusing. I was right.

He took my hand and slipped a ring onto my finger when he spoke his vows. A pink, teardrop shaped diamond solitaire sparkled back at me when I looked at it.

"Something simple." He whispered. I rolled my eyes and gave him a subtle shake of my head when the vicar demanded our attention again.

"I love you, Joy Horton Marco," he said before we kissed as man and wife.

And we were married.

Well-wishers crowded us when we exited the church, surrounding us with shouts of happiness and laughter. We were hugged and kissed and jostled by family and friends. Arthur helped me up into the open carriage then laughed when Pip jumped up behind me and sat on the seat cushions looking as if he owned the vehicle.

The crowd laughed. My mother shouted. "Pip, you scoundrel! Who brought him along?"

My brother grinned slyly at me and blew me a kiss. Arthur climbed in next to me, wrapping an arm around my shoulders.

"Don't fret, Mother Horton. I knew he was part of her baggage," he called out to her. Pip leaped from cushion to cushion, sniffing every new scent. He stumbled a bit when the carriage started to roll but eventually found a spot where he could stand with his face in the wind.

I rested my head on Arthur's shoulder while the carriage driver made our way towards the party. He tugged off his gloves and sighed happily as he ran his bare fingers through my shortened hair. "I really do like it." He twisted the curls around his fingers.

"You're going to ruin the hard work Faith did to make me presentable," I scolded but didn't move to stop him. His fingers felt good on my scalp.

"One of my favorite things about you is that you keep your hair loose and let me touch it freely without being swatted at." He entwined my bare fingers with his, pressing our joined hands to his lips.

The carriage passed village center, and kept moving.

"We didn't stop." I sat up.

Arthur tugged me back into his arms. "No, we didn't. We are headed on to the inn."

"Does my mother know this?" I imagined the look on her face when we didn't show up to our own party.

"No, but your father does. Thomas brought Pip here so we can leave the inn early in the morning. I supplied the entire village with enough food and drink to make them completely forget we aren't there. I even paid the musicians an obscene amount of money for their services," he assured me.

"We're going to the inn." I echoed, trying to reorganize my thoughts. "Why the sudden change in plans?"

He gave me a wicked grin. "I promised my new bride a few things. A house with sheep, spaniels, and a great many babies. I couldn't wait to get started."

I rolled my eyes. "I see. How many were you planning on?"

PART 2 - THE FARCE

"Spaniels or babies?"

I elbowed him softly. "Babies, you scoundrel."

He shrugged. "As many as she wants. Ten or twelve, I think."

"Ten or twelve! Is that all?"

"To start with, more if she wants them."

"Let's start with one and move on from there." I rested my head on his shoulder again when the inn came into view. My stomach gave a leap when the carriage rolled to a stop and Arthur climbed out with Pip.

He held out his hand and I took it, feeling my heart beat faster.

"Nervous, Mrs. Marco?" he asked as I stepped down. His gaze met mine, quirking a brow.

"No. Excited." I tucked my arm in his.

Both his brows raised. "Excited," he repeated slowly.

"Yes." I grinned at him. "I've spent a good many years repressing every…procreative… feeling I've ever had." I reached up and ran my fingers through his beard, and trailed them down his neck to his chest. "And now, I don't have to. I have a great many…feelings…to explore. I hope you're up to the task."

He squared his shoulders as we entered the inn. "Damnation…now I'm nervous."

***

I looked out the window while we traveled towards London. I quietly watched the farms become smaller and smaller and the houses closer together.

"Now are you nervous?" he asked.

"Yes," I replied. "I haven't met your mother yet, I have a load of new responsibilities, and I still can't read."

He waved off my concerns. "You're a brilliant woman who adapts to everything around you. You'll be magnificent."

"I might embarrass you."

"I'm a peer who is neck-deep in trade. I'm already wildly unpopular." He tucked me closer to him. "We'll be extremely happy being social outcasts together. Hopefully, people will just leave us alone. I didn't realize what a wonderful side effect of trade was until I was involved in getting funds for the war. Almost immediately I was uninvited to parties and mothers stopped throwing daughters at me."

"I imagine it made your job at Parliament more difficult?" I asked.

"At first. But you need to realize one thing before we arrive in London. The *ton* is filled with debt."

I furrowed my brows. "How did that help?"

"I am saturated with money. It's a simple thing to buy up someone's debts. They are remarkably willing to do anything to remain in their comfortable houses with servants and food and trinkets, especially when faced with debtor's prison. Dinner invites and ballroom appearances magically appear in one's hand when you own their life."

I shook my head. "You really are a pirate."

"I think you once called me a scoundrel as well. And a disgusting beast."

"You are not a disgusting beast, but you are still a scoundrel." I rested my head in the perfect niche between his arm and chest.

I hadn't realized I'd fallen asleep until the carriage came to a sudden halt. I sat up and found my nose instantly assaulted. The air smelled of unwashed bodies and sewage, rotten food and smoke.

"Oh!" I covered my face. "What is that horrible stench?"

Arthur snorted. "That is London." He shook out his deadened arm I had been sleeping on. I dug out a handkerchief to cover my nose.

"It's awful!" I peered out the window.

The view wasn't much better. The air was thick with soot and fog. Carriages shuffled and struggled against carts and people. There was no color anywhere except on a few storefronts. Even the people were dressed in some shade of grey and black or brown. Eyes filled with despair looked up at me, with dark shadows and sallow faces. No one smiled. The air was full of horses screaming, people shouting, crying.

I turned to look at Arthur, unable to express the shock and sadness welling inside of me. I'd never seen anything like it. The sights, the sounds, and the smells. My heart fell into my stomach.

He gave me a puzzled look. "Joy?"

I looked out the window again, feeling their eyes upon me. Children with no hope. Women sold themselves and looked at me with disdain. Men fought for every scrap they could find, and looked at me with hatred.

"Have you brought me to Hell itself?" I asked quietly.

"Come away from the window." He tugged at me. "We don't live here; we just have to travel through here to get home."

PART 2 - THE FARCE

This would never be home. This chaotic mess of smells and sounds and colorless people would never be comfortable to make a home. Even if I lived in the palace, this place would never be home.

"Just because you can't see them doesn't mean it doesn't exist." I cried out. "We have to do something."

"I know. Joy, stop struggling. I see them." He ran his hands up and down my arms to soothe me. "It's overwhelming. I've forgotten how overwhelming it can be."

"What can we do?" It was so much…too much to be done.

"It's why I'm here for Parliament, I do the best I can for them. I try to save as many as I can, but I can't save them all. You can't either."

"It's too horrible." I tried to look out the window again.

"Look at me. Joy, look at me." He gave me a little shake until I looked into his dark eyes. I saw sorrow reflected there and I knew he understood.

"You can't save them all. Do you understand? You can't save them all. You'll put yourself into an early grave if you try."

I nodded and took a deep breath. "I understand." He wrapped his arms around me while our carriage inched forward until the road opened. I either became used to the smell or it lessened while we moved through the city. The noises changed too, from shouts and screams to the simple sounds of hooves against the stones and people calling out greetings or news. I saw more color in the window. Trees and flowers dotted the landscape. The houses became bigger and the road became smoother.

We stopped and my heart leapt in my throat. Arthur straightened up and put on his hat. I straightened my clothes and clenched my hands. He gave me a glance. "Ready?"

I nodded and he opened the door of the carriage.

He stepped out first and Pip leaped out after him.

He helped me step down and pressed a hand to the small of my back to steady me as I took in the scene.

The house was huge.

Enormous.

Gigantic.

It was an awe-striking, jaw-dropping, gargantuan monstrosity. I immediately felt my stomach drop into my toes. The staff was waiting outside, lined up in their livery and uniforms, looking polished and professional.

"Joy, this is Byron, my right-hand man." He gestured to the first man who gave me a bow. He wasn't much older than Arthur, with long curly brown hair tied back in a queue. His face was scarred and pocked but his eyes were bright.

"And Mrs. Poulson." He nodded at the housekeeper with the belt of keys around her waist. She gave me a curtsey and lowered her eyes. Beautiful silver hair was tied up under her cap and laugh lines raced around her face.

"Your mother is in the salon," she said to Arthur.

If my stomach could drop any lower it would have.

Arthur's face brightened, and he tucked my arm into his elbow. "Excellent! We'll go straight in, bring us some tea? Once she leaves, we'll greet the staff."

"Very good," Byron said with another nod. Arthur led me through the line of servants. I smiled at them as we walked past, keeping my head up and meeting their gazes. I tried to look confident and friendly as we entered the gaping maw of the house.

Where I immediately drowned in pink.

The rugs, carpets, paint, wallpaper, flowers, the furnishings. All pink.

And it was hideous.

"Oh my..." I gasped, gaping at the majestic marble bust at the base of the staircase resting on a light and airy mesh of pink tulle.

"Revolting, isn't it?" Arthur handed his walking stick and hat to Byron. "I let Diana do whatever she wished with the house as long as she left my bedroom, my study, and the servants' dwellings alone. It kept her happy and busy."

I walked over to the bust and lifted a corner of the base to pull out the frothy fabric. I could swear the stern face set in stone sighed with relief when I removed the offending piece from its presence.

"Come along, you'll have time to strip the house of unnecessary frills later," Arthur assured me.

I followed him into the salon, taking in the tall ceilings and doors and the many shades of pink scattered about the room.

The only thing in the entire room not doused in pink was a grand lady sitting on the pink striped couch. She rose to her feet and I took in the size of her. She was as tall as Arthur and broad with no womanly curves to speak of. Her face split into a grin when she saw Arthur and she opened her arms wide.

PART 2 - THE FARCE

"Hello, my darling girl," he greeted, embracing her tightly. She squeezed him back tighter, before releasing him and peering into his face.

"You're a brute!" she declared, in a perfect feminine voice that contrasted with her masculine body. "Running off after a bride I've not met, and keeping me waiting almost a week. You know I can't leave once the Season starts." She swatted him.

"Calm down, my love," he soothed, putting an arm around her. "I want you to meet my Joy. And I expect you to shower her with as much affection as you do me. Joy! Sophronia Marco, my mother."

Bright brown eyes looked me over with a thin smile. I gave a deep curtsey, feeling it was the best greeting I could give.

"Oh Arthur, she's delightful! Look at all those adorable freckles! You weren't lying about them!" His mother left his side and came to mine. "Welcome to the family." She squeezed the breath out of me.

"And don't you dare call me anything but Sophie. Arthur only introduces me by my full name to vex me." She gave him a glare.

"I can imagine." I glanced at my husband. He gave us both a look of pure innocence.

She settled into the couch when Pip appeared and rested his head on her knee.

"Who is this little charmer?" she exclaimed.

"That is my wife's dowry," Arthur said.

"Dowry! Your manners are deplorable. I'm amazed she agreed to marry you." Sophie ran Pip's silky ears through her fingers.

"It took a great amount of persuasion," Arthur admitted.

I ignored Arthur. "This is Pip."

"Aren't you a handsome fellow?" she said to him, bending down and resting her nose on his. "I'm so glad you are a dog person, Joy. I never trust people who don't like dogs. This bodes well for our relationship. That and you have Arthur smiling again, I thought he never would after Diana died." She gave her son a fond. "He shut himself up in this house and only appeared when summoned. He was a drab at parties and members of Parliament wanted to remove him just because of his sour face."

I looked over at Arthur who was starting to squirm. "Enough of that, old girl. A new bride doesn't need to be given other people's old memories."

"Then why did you let her memory live so long in this house?" Sophie demanded, gesturing at the pink décor.

"Because I'm a terrible decorator," Arthur snapped back.

She gave him another look I recognized from my own mother's facial repertoire. "Stuff and nonsense! I would have gladly helped. Or at least hire someone."

Arthur let out a long breath. "Soph…you are the most trying creature…"

Sophie's eyes glittered as the tea was brought in. I rose to my feet and took the tray.

"Well, I'm famished," I said to break the silence. I poured the tea and passed a cup to each of them while they glared at one another. They were definitely related.

"I'll be redecorating the house. Starting tomorrow." I tried to soothe the situation. "I would love some advice or thoughts about where to start."

Sophie took a sip from her cup and smiled at me. "That would be delightful. I tried to get Diana to take some advice but she was so adamant to do it all on her own."

"She was finally free from her mother to express herself," Arthur grumbled.

"Are you speaking ill of my friend, Lady Hampton?" Sophie asked.

Arthur closed his eyes. "I wouldn't dare."

She huffed and set her cup down. I started in on a finger sandwich, giving a sliver to Pip.

He gobbled it up and sat down, his big eyes begging for more. I snuck him another piece.

"What do you think of London? Arthur said it is your first time here," Sophie asked me.

Loud, dark, smelly, disgusting, sad… "It's different from what I thought. I feel completely like a fish out of water."

"I'll take you driving to help get you oriented while Arthur is out fighting for the rights of the people. I'm sure my friends will be delighted to meet you."

"No, not your friends." Arthur glowered at her.

Sophie glared back. "They are perfectly respectable people who will be enchanted with her."

"That's what I'm afraid of. No introductions without me."

Sophie huffed and set down her teacup. "I shouldn't impose any longer, after all you are newlyweds, and I'm sure you want to get settled." She rose to her feet. I stood as well.

Part 2 - The Farce

"I'll call on you tomorrow," she promised me with a light kiss on my cheek. "I am happy to see him smile again."

"Come and give me a kiss," she demanded of Arthur, who obliged and saw her to the door.

He came back into the salon and plopped onto the couch next to me. I took a little fairy cake. "And now you've met my mother." He sighed.

"She…"

"Is a tyrant? Overbearing? Exhausting?" he supplied.

I pinched his lips shut. "I haven't formed much of an opinion of anything except she loves you."

He scowled. "And I love her too, even if she gets me all worked up over nothing."

I pressed the fairy cake to his lips. He took a bite and groaned. "I've forgotten what a marvelous chef I have."

"We still need to greet the servants." I brushed crumbs off my lap into a handkerchief.

"A moment first, Madame Wife." He leaned in and gave me a kiss. "I want to compare your lips to this cake. I can't decide which one I like to taste more."

CHAPTER 13

She's trying to bankrupt me.
I now own a soldier's hospital and two orphanages.
The house is being gutted and an army of craftsmen is taking more of my blunt.
Go ahead and try, my darling. We'll never run out of money. I'm glad you are putting it to good use.

I tossed open the double doors to the library with a flourish and set my hands on my hips, overwhelmed at what needed to be done.

"Oh, sweet Diana." I started picking up the feminine doilies littered about the room. I thought of Lady Hampton's tight control and smiled a little. "I'll bet you were thrilled to get to do things your way."

I made my way to the curtains and cringed at the pink stripes hanging from ceiling to floor. I grabbed one from each side of the window and threw them open.

The maid sitting in the window seat screamed simultaneously along with me. We both grabbed at our chests to keep our hearts from bursting forth.

"I'm sorry! I didn't know anyone else was here."

"No, Your Grace, I need to apologize." She climbed out of the window seat. "I should have been cleaning, dusting the shelves, but I saw this book..." She held it out for my examination.

"What book is it?" I didn't even glance at it.

"*Gulliver's Travels.* I find they always bring a smile to my lips." She looked down at the cover and then back at me.

Part 2 - The Farce

Her speech was impeccable. I took in her face and curly auburn hair poking out from under her cap. She couldn't have been any older than I was, possibly younger. Her speech and posture spoke of breeding.

"Do you have a copy?"

"I used to." She placed the book back on the shelf.

"I have a feeling you used to spend time reading in libraries, rather than cleaning them," I said.

She sighed. "Please excuse me. I shouldn't be taking up your time." She offered a quick bob and turned to leave.

"Don't go."

She stopped turning back to me. "Yes?"

I motioned to a chair. "Please, sit."

She came back cautiously and sat on the edge of the seat, her back straight and her hands clasped in her lap. I sat across from her, taking in the sight of her. Her posture and poise were perfect, her eyes didn't waver from mine. This wasn't a maid. This was a Lady.

"What is your name?" I asked.

"Alice. Alice Graves," she answered in her perfect voice.

"Alice. Were you educated by a governess?"

Her face fell a little. "Yes."

"And times have become difficult for the Graves family." There was no other answer to why a well-bred lady was dressed as a maid.

Although her posture remained straight and her face impassable, I saw a tear in her eye. "They have as of late become a little difficult."

I sat closer to her and covered her hand. "I won't pry anymore, Miss Graves." I rose to my feet. "Please follow me." I directed her and led her out of the library to the salon. I walked to the large pile of correspondence I had sitting on the small desk and motioned for her to take a seat.

"I have a feeling you would be better suited to be mistress of this house than I am," I told her.

"Oh, Your Grace! I would never assume...!" Alice protested.

"Hush now. It's no secret." I picked up the stack of letters. "Servants know everything. I informed Mrs. Poulson yesterday about my shortcomings and I'm sure everyone knows by now."

She lowered her gaze. "No one has said anything but kind things about you."

I let out a sigh of relief. "That is good to know, I was sure they were going to say I was an idiot."

I dumped the pile of letters in her lap. "I cannot read, Alice Graves. And I think your talents as a maid are lacking, especially since *Gulliver's Travels* has more appeal to you than cleaning the windows."

"I'm not very good at windows," she admitted, gathering the letters into a neat pile.

"But you excel at reading?" I handed her the letter opener.

"Yes, I do."

"Excellent. Now, while I go through this room and gather up every pink frippery dear Diana has left us, you will read every letter addressed to me."

She agreed, opened the letters, and read in a soothing alto voice. I could not believe how many invitations I had, or cards from people calling when I said I was not home. I hadn't been here for more than two days.

"I'm sure they all just want to come and get a look at the country girl who married…" I stopped before I spoke of the title.

Alice shrugged. "That's mostly the way of it. They are going to come and look at your flaws, or what they consider flaws, and use them to build themselves up because of how horribly they treat each other."

I made a face. "Like animals eating their own."

"That's exactly what it is." Alice grinned.

"Then I'll need someone to guide me." I made a new pile of pink ornaments. "I'd like to offer you a better position. I need someone to handle my correspondence, to help me navigate these shark-infested waters, and to occasionally read a novel to me."

"You need a companion," Alice said.

I nodded. "Yes, I need a companion. Desperately."

She smiled as a million cares were taken off her shoulders. "I am a horrible maid. I think Mrs. Poulson would be much happier if I didn't try to clean a single thing in this house again."

I chuckled. "That bad?"

"I streaked the windows and broke the china. I can't get spots off silver, and somehow, I managed to make a stain on the carpet grow larger instead of disappear. I can't even start a fire or carry water without spilling it." she lamented.

"How did you come to be in our employ?" I asked.

PART 2 - THE FARCE

"My father is Lord Edgington. He's an infamous gambler." She twisted her apron in her fingers.

"And now an invalid as well." The voice of my husband filled the air.

We both rose when he entered the room. I received a kiss on the cheek. He sat down on the couch next to me and motioned for Alice to sit again.

"Invalid?" I prompted her to continue. Arthur wrapped an arm around my waist and pulled me into him.

"He had a stroke. He was able to do well enough at the tables and races to keep the debts away and for us to live comfortably until then. When he had the stroke his creditors came calling."

"I sold everything I could to. There was enough to keep my brother Charles at Eton for the rest of the year, find a room for Father and my younger sister. But there was no way around the fact that I needed to work."

"Why a maid?" Arthur leaned forward. "Why not a governess or companion."

"Father is…still ill. Abigail stays with him all day to take care of him, but she's so young. His temper has become volatile. I needed to stay close, to go home every night and take care of them." She bit her lip.

Arthur leaned back against the cushion. "Sounds like Lord Edgington needs to be sent off to rusticate. How old is your sister?" he asked kindly.

"Abigail is eleven."

"And Charles?"

"Fifteen."

"Well then. I'm sure your new position as my wife's companion will cover the cost of your brother's tuition, send your father and a nurse off to Bath to recover, and find your sister a boarding school." He rose to his feet. "I'll just be off to make the arrangements."

"That's too much," she protested.

I rose and took her hand. "Let him go, Alice. It's best not to let him get idle, it gets him into trouble."

"I heard that, Madame Wife! And don't think you'll go unpunished for your impudence," he called from the hallway as his footsteps trailed away.

Alice gave me a wide-eyed look. I shook my head and laughed. "Go get your sister and your father, let them spend the night here and explain everything. I'll have Mrs. Poulson prepare rooms for you." I said, leading her out of the library.

I watched her disappear and made my way to Arthur's study. He was already at work writing letters and dispatching them to a small regiment of footmen waiting for their orders.

He looked up at me and smiled. "We can't save them all."

"But we save who we can," I said, understanding him better now.

***

Alice jumped into the renovations with me. We tackled the library with enthusiasm. The door was removed and ordered to be painted a shade of cream. I happily climbed a ladder to remove the floral pink curtains.

"We can paper over the walls." Alice stood beneath me, ready to catch the falling fabric.

"Something light and plain. I want everyone to be comfortable when they come in." I worked on a ring that just wouldn't release.

"A light blue or green," Alice offered.

"Or a mixture of both. Maybe in a striped pattern." The ring let go and the curtains fell with a heavy whoosh.

I heard a loud giggle coming from the doorway and smiled when Abigail Graves appeared with Pip at her side. Her term didn't start for a few more weeks, so Arthur had given her the keys to the attic and encouraged her to explore.

"Look how cute he is!" she gushed. Pip sat next to her, a paragon of patience wearing an old baby bonnet and gown. His tail wagged quickly out from under the hem of his new apparel.

"Oh, poor Pip! Really, Abby!" Alice scolded, which just brought more giggles from her younger sister.

"Very cute. Perhaps you can find something a little more dashing for our handsome boy," I suggested.

"Of course! Come on Pip!" she said and the pair took off again for the attic. I enjoyed hearing the stomps and rattles of her excitement tearing through the enormous house. It definitely needed children.

"Thank you for your indulgence." Alice folded up the curtains. "She hasn't been this happy in months."

"Mail's here," Byron announced and brought it in on a silver salver. I was amused at such service and the white gloves he always wore. Mail at home was usually somewhat damp and spotted with rain. Here things were pristine, crisp, and clean.

"Thank you." Alice took it from him and sorted it while I made my way down the ladder.

"And the paper catalog you asked for." Byron produced a book full of wallpaper samples.

"Excellent!" I took a chair next to Alice at the desk and flipped it open.

"Several invitations to a rout, a ball, and a dinner party," Alice reported. "I'll bring them to the attention of His Grace to see if he needs to attend for any political reasons. And a letter from your mother."

Alice's voice was smooth and clear. Everyone was doing well. Thomas missed having Pip and was looking at finding another dog to get under everyone's feet. Father missed his baby girl, and Mother hoped everything was getting settled well and said to expect a visit from Hope.

I dictated a letter back to her, watching Alice form the letters perfectly before they swam away into a murky mess.

"Can you sign it?" Alice held out the pen.

"I can make an 'x' as well as anyone can." I took it from her.

"What about a J? I've seen your sketches, and there's no reason you shouldn't be able to draw your name. Just think of them as pictures instead of letters." She brought forth a clean sheet of paper. "Luckily your name is short. Think of a J as a fish hook. An O is just a circle. And a Y could be…" She drew a large Y on the paper. As the only thing in my vision it was easy to make out.

"It looks like a slouching scarecrow without a head," I declared.

Alice laughed and handed me the pen. "Wonderful! Think of it as exactly that. Draw a fish hook." I obeyed.

"Good, now a circle. Oh, your circles are perfect. Now, a slouching scarecrow without a head." I obliged. She beamed at me. "There! You did it! That's your name." She underlined my work.

Put together again they started to muddle. I concentrated on one character at a time and could see it. Fish hook, circle, slouching scarecrow without a head. Joy. I had written my name!

"It really looks nice too," Alice said. I repeated the actions on the letter to my mother, my hand shaking a little with excitement. "Your letters are neat and the same size."

I looked down at my name once more while Alice dusted the ink. Something warm and wet started running down my cheek.

"Are you alright?" she asked. Another tear joined the first.

"I'm wonderful." I threw my arms around her, not caring in the least about propriety or personal boundaries. The happiness in my heart couldn't be contained. "You are a miracle worker! No one has ever explained it to me simply so I could follow. I can write my name! I've never done it before."

Her soft arms enfolded me. "Oh, now you're going to make me cry too."

Abigail came bounding into the room, with Pip at her heels wearing a new costume. They both came up short at the sight of us weeping and smiling.

"Are you both ill?" she asked.

"No," I wiped my face, "Just happy. Your sister is an amazing woman."

Abigail snorted. "Everyone knows that!"

PART 2 - THE FARCE

CHAPTER 14

She does charity work, she's remodeling the house, and still finds time to fit everyone into new clothes. She greets me with a smile and a kiss when I return from Parliament. We laugh and argue over the news. We read novels and make love. My wife is remarkable.

Does a condemned soul deserve so much?

In the mornings, the park was quiet with few visitors. At Arthur's insistence, both the driver and my bodyguard, Neville, took us in the open carriage and kept a distant watch over us. The weather was cooler in the morning and I could smell fresh growing things over the usual stench of London.

Pip brought me a stick, placed it at my feet, and pounded his tail against the ground. I picked it up, gave it a hard throw, and watched him race after it.

"He's so fun! I wish I'd had a dog growing up. Father despised animals." Alice was sitting pretty and proper on a bench, wearing a spencer and bonnet with a book on her lap.

Pip returned and spat out the stick when I reached for it. We both felt the freedom of being outside and doing familiar things again.

Female voices coming from the path broke me from my thoughts. I took the stick from Pip and told him to sit when they came into view. I was certain they did not want to get trampled by an exuberant spaniel who was quickly becoming covered in his own drool.

They were well dressed, wearing bonnets with elaborate embellishments. One was older than the other, but they were similar in size and appearance. They walked leisurely, speaking to one another in pleasant tones. A maid and a footman followed at a proper distance.

"Oh dear." Alice whispered and came to her feet as they approached. They stopped next to the bench when Alice greeted them. "Your Grace, Lady Arnette," she said demurely, bobbing at each lady.

"Lady Alice Graves! I didn't think to see you here. I had heard your life had become quite the predicament. Someone told me you were looking for work." The older lady spoke, eyeing Alice up and down.

"Thankfully, I was able to set our lives back in order." Alice smiled at me. "May I introduce the Duchess of Ironwood."

Both ladies turned and looked at me, as well as the maid and footman who had caught up to their mistresses. I nodded at them, repeating what Alice had done. "Your Grace, Lady Arnette."

Her Grace eyed me up and down. Her eyes searched out my every flaw, every freckle, every hair on my uncovered head, down to the slobbery stick I held in my hand. Lady Arnette's face was pinched, her eyes stayed on mine.

Her Grace suddenly turned up her nose, twisted her head and marched off without a word.

Alice gasped loudly.

Lady Arnette blinked rapidly at her mother and then addressed me. "Good day, Your Grace," she mumbled and hurried off. Their wide-eyed servants followed silently behind them.

I gave a short, bewildered laugh. "What just happened?" Pip knocked his head against my hand and I threw his stick for him.

Alice plopped down on the bench, her eyes wide. "She gave you the cut direct."

Now my eyes widened. That's what that was? The cut direct? Not a snub, or even a public shaming, but the worst social attack one could receive.

"Oh," I replied. The ramifications of what had just happened swept over me.

I didn't exist to Her Grace. I didn't belong in her social circle, her city, her town, her country, her world. I didn't belong with Arthur. It was beneath her to even address me as a human being. It stung but wasn't unexpected. "That was the Duchess of…?"

"Leighton," Alice responded quietly. Her face had become as bewildered as Lady Arnette's. Was she going into shock? I sat next to her and picked up her hands, chafing them a bit.

"Alice, relax. You would think I've just been shot or stabbed."

"No. This is worse, much worse." Alice buried her face in her hands.

Pip brought back his stick and dropped it at my feet. I picked it up and tossed it again, but he remained. He butted his head against Alice's knee and let out a soft whine.

"There, you see. Now you've upset Pip!"

"I can't…I can't fix this. I'm supposed to help you and bring you into London society. His Grace asked me to take care of you and now…" She moaned again, tears spilling from her eyes.

"If my husband could not foresee this kind of thing happening when he married an illiterate yeoman's daughter then he's the delusional one, not you." I pointed out.

Alice gasped. "You shouldn't say such things about your husband."

I waved it off. "If he's happy, and I'm happy, what does it matter if some woman I've never met doesn't want anything to do with me. I don't care."

I only made her cry harder.

"Alice, please stop. I'm not upset. I'm certain Mr. Marco will be more upset at the Duchess than at you."

"You say you don't care, but when everyone finds out what she did, no one will accept you!" Alice wailed.

"You mean I'll stop being inundated with visitors and cards from people I don't know? This is sounding better and better." I handed her a handkerchief.

"Oh Mrs. Marco, you don't understand. This is an act of war against you. I know Her Grace. If she has her way, you'll be snubbed everywhere you go by everyone you meet. Even shopkeepers and tradesmen won't dare to do business with you for fear of her wrath."

Now that did make me angry. Taking action against me was one thing, to take it out on other people and their livelihoods was something else entirely. "Well, if this is an act of war, we need to go home and come up with a strategy."

I took Alice back to the house and dictated a quick note to Arthur, asking him to come home as quickly as he could and sent it off to Parliament. If I was going to battle I needed someone who knew the rules of engagement.

I calmed Alice down with a glass of sherry and paced around the no longer pink salon. I'd gone with a sea green color on the walls and light blue furnishings. The dining room was next on my sights, beginning with stripping any paint on the walls and finding the wood beneath. What did it say about me I was more concerned about cornices and carpets than the goodwill of a Duchess?

"Joy!" My musings were interrupted by my husband bursting into the room. I was swept up in his arms before I could even greet him.

"Are you sick? Are you hurt?" he demanded, his hands running over my arms and face.

"What? No." I pushed his hands down.

He took a step back. "There's nothing wrong with you?"

"Not physically, no," I assured him.

He let out a long breath and started pulling off his gloves. "I nearly broke my neck getting here thinking you were at death's door!"

"I asked you to come as quickly as you could, not that I was dying."

"My dear Joy, that's what 'come as quickly as you can' means to most people." He threw off his cape and enfolded me in his arms. "Even though I'm overjoyed to escape the monotone of Lord Perkins' voice for the rest of the day, I would love to know what emergency has brought me home." He kissed me, then made his way to the sidebar and poured himself a brandy.

"Alice and I met the Duchess of Leighton today." I took a seat next to Alice, patting her hand calmly.

Arthur wrinkled his nose. "Harpy. I hope you had a somewhat civil conversation with her."

"She gave me the cut direct," I informed him.

Arthur's eyes blazed. He stood in silence, his face becoming a mask of anger as he grasped for words. The snifter of brandy met an untimely end shattering between his fingers.

"Arthur, stop. You'll cut yourself!" I rose to my feet and carefully took the shards from his hands with my handkerchief.

"She did what?" he demanded while I wiped the blood and brandy away.

"She gave her the cut direct," Alice said miserably. "I was there to witness it, along with Lady Arnette and two of their servants. I failed you, Your Grace."

"The devil you did," Arthur growled and stormed away from me.

I followed him to the doorway. He opened the door and bellowed for Byron.

Part 2 - The Farce

"You still have glass in your hand." I forced him to hold still while I picked out tiny shards.

"Leave off, Joy! I'm fine." He tugged his hand away from me. I grabbed it once more and wrapped it with a clean handkerchief.

Byron appeared.

"Fetch my dueling pistols and inform Lockton I need a second right now," he snarled.

I choked on my next breath of air as Byron dashed out. "Dueling pistols? What on earth are you planning?"

"I'm going to call Leighton out at once. A cut towards you is a cut towards me."

Alice let out a wail.

"Arthur, are you mad?" I gave his shoulder a shove, hoping to snap him out of his delusion. "She cut me! You and Leighton have nothing to do with it. I called you home to ask you how to proceed."

"These are the rules of engagement, Madame Wife. Husband and wife are one flesh, what one does reflects on the other. This is inexcusable behavior. Leighton has let his wife run roughshod over people for too long, and now he will answer for it."

"If anyone should challenge anyone it should be me and the Duchess." I pointed out.

He gave me an incredulous look. "A petticoat duel?" He sized me up and down. "You really don't care what they think, do you?"

"And neither do you, which is why this whole argument is ridiculous. I shouldn't have even called you home."

Byron entered the room with a dark wooden case. Both Arthur and I leaped for it at the same time. Byron wisely retreated. We tugged on it back and forth.

"Then why did you call me home if you don't want me to fix it?" he shouted, yanking the box towards him. I didn't release my hold and jerked it back harder.

"Because Alice was upset and I wanted your immediate counsel on how to proceed. Not for you to start challenging peers to a duel," I shouted back.

"Dueling is the correct counsel on how to proceed!"

"Then I'll challenge her, not you!"

"We're going in circles, Joy!"

"Then let go and listen to reason." I pulled and twisted my body so hard the case of pistols came away from his grasp and I stumbled with it.

He glared at me, I glared at him. Alice hiccupped loudly. We both turned to face her.

"I've never seen a married couple act like this," she whispered in awe as the tears dried on her cheeks.

I glanced at Arthur who gave me a sheepish look, and I returned it.

"I'm very passionate about my wife," Arthur said to her, his eyes on me. His face started to relax and warmth returned to his eyes. "So much so I lose my head when someone disparages her."

"My husband is my greatest champion. Even when I don't need one," I returned, giving him a small smile. I hugged the pistol case to my chest.

Byron interrupted by clearing his throat loudly. I hadn't noticed him returning.

"The Duke of Leighton is here, and seeks an audience with you and Her Grace," Byron spoke calmly.

Arthur's face went dark and he glanced over at me. I clutched the pistol case tighter to my chest and twisted it out of his view. "Arthur, don't you even think about it."

"Only because you just replaced the carpet. Show him in, Byron."

Alice excused herself and slipped from the room. I placed the case on the couch, thought better of it, slipped it underneath the cushions, and sat down on it for good measure. I went to rise again when Byron led Leighton in.

"Don't stand, Joy, not for him," Arthur growled.

The Duke's step faltered. He was a fit man, as tall as Arthur with beautiful white hair and laugh lines around his face. He bowed to Arthur and then faced me and gave a deep bow.

"Ironwood, please introduce me to your wife so I can make a proper apology to her." He did not take his eyes off me.

Of course, Arthur wouldn't let it be easy.

"I shouldn't even let her be in the same room as you! You are not worth the air it would take to speak the words to introduce you."

"Arthur, please." I calmly stood. "Let him speak."

Arthur exhaled and came to my side. "Leighton, this is my beautiful, charming, and stubborn wife, Joy Horton Marco, Duchess of Ironwood." Arthur took my hand.

PART 2 - THE FARCE

"And calm," Leighton said. "I always thought you needed a calming influence, Ironwood."

"I wouldn't say I am always calm, Your Grace. We were just having a bit of a row before you arrived." I offered my hand and he made a proper bow over it.

"I fear it had to do with me and my family." Leighton released my hand.

"Your name was mentioned," I said. "Along with pistols and seconds."

"That serious already?" Leighton sighed.

"She was convincing me she should call out your wife instead of me calling you out," Arthur reported.

Leighton's eyebrows raised, and he gave me another appraising look. "As much as I would like to see that, Her Grace is currently unavailable. She's on her way to Scotland." He looked at Arthur now. "And she is not to return to London if you and your wife are in town. Ever."

"You've exiled her?" I asked.

"She's taking a well-deserved rest away from the pressures of the *ton*," Leighton corrected me.

"I see." I looked up into Arthur's face. His face was still a mask of anger. Was it enough?

"Your Grace, I offer my honest and sincere apologies on behalf of my family about the way you were treated today." Leighton's apology was sincere.

I forgave him at once. It wasn't his fault; he had no more control over his wife than Arthur did over me.

Arthur glared down at Leighton. "You shouldn't have let it get this far. She's been terrorizing people for years."

"You're right." Leighton met his gaze. "And it stops now."

Arthur's face softened a little. "I'm finding my thirst for blood waning."

Leighton offered a smile. "I would be most pleased if you would both attend a ball tonight at my home. My daughter, Lady Arnette, is hosting for me. She was quite distressed over the actions of her mother this morning and thinks we should present a united front for our neighbors and friends."

I wanted to refuse. So far, I'd managed to politely decline every invitation we'd received.

"We'll be there." Arthur patted my hand.

Leighton turned to address me. "Excellent. I would be honored if you would lead the dancing with me, Your Grace."

My heart plummeted into my shoes. "It's not necessary, Your Grace."

"I'm afraid it is." Arthur nodded at Leighton. "She'll be honored to join you."

"I shall see you both tonight."

He left the room in Byron's care. The door had barely closed before I was panicking.

"Arthur! How could you?"

"You asked me how to proceed, this is how you do it! Battles in London are fought in ballrooms."

"Arthur. I can't dance," I hissed.

"Nonsense. I've danced with you. I'm quite excited to finally finish the waltz with you."

"Country reels and jigs! My sisters taught me the cotillion and quadrille when they came home from school, along with the waltz, but I've never danced them outside of my mother's parlor."

"You'll be happy to know the ballrooms of London have stolen heavily from their country cousins." He led me to the door and called out for Alice. She appeared from out of the library while we made our way down the hallway.

"To the piano, my dears! I hope you are somewhat accomplished, Alice. My wife is about to get years of dancing lessons crammed into one afternoon."

PART 2 - THE FARCE

CHAPTER 15

She went into the fray like Boudica of old.
If only she knew they were not worthy to be in her presence.

A hush fell over the crowd when our names were announced. I could feel everyone's eyes shift and stare at us as we stood before Leighton and Lady Arnette.

"Put on your battle face," Arthur said under his breath and I forced a smile. He pushed me forward with his hand on the small of my back.

"Your Grace, I'm delighted to see you again. Welcome." Leighton spoke loudly for those eavesdropping and kissed my hand. "I'm looking forward to our dance."

"You might rethink that once I step on your toes." He laughed and released me. I slid over to receive two air kisses from Lady Arnette while Leighton and Arthur shook hands. The crowd released a huge sigh and everyone started speaking again.

Lady Arnette took both my hands. Her voice was soft and warm. "I am glad you are here, and I am sorry."

"I know," I cut her off. "Let's never speak of it again." I gave her my warmest smile. She looked relieved and gave me a nod before turning to her next guest as Arthur's hand returned to the small of my back and started driving me through the crowd of unfamiliar faces and gaudy clothing.

"I'm a fish out of water," I whispered.

"You are the loveliest fish here," he assured and lifted my gloved hand to his lips for a quick kiss. Ladies whispered behind their fans at his behavior.

"We need to get this over with. Hopefully, this will be the only engagement we will have to attend this season and everyone will return to gossiping about who wore what to where." He took my arm and led me through the room.

"Ironwood!" A voice carried across the ballroom. We both turned to see two men approaching.

"My cronies. I apologize in advance."

"You didn't tell me you had friends in Town. They haven't come to the house."

"I warned them not to. I wrote each of them and told them I was entrapped in the arms of ecstasy and if they interrupted us, I would run them through," he whispered in my ear.

I blushed. "Mr. Marco, you are a scoundrel."

He laughed aloud. "I've managed to get you to call me Mr. Marco and a scoundrel in a single sentence. It must be a new record."

"I have plenty of other names to call you, but we are in polite company," I replied, giving his arm a proper swat with my fan as his friends assembled.

"You've brought out the little wife! Finally, the mysterious lady is revealed." A short, stocky middle-aged man with a kind face reached for my offered hand and bowed over it. "Sir Reginald Lockton, your servant, madam."

"Reggie, this is my wife, Joy Horton Marco, Duchess of Ironwood." Arthur introduced.

"Joy! How wonderful. This grumpy old man needs some joy in his life." He gave my hand a squeeze. "Let me introduce the rest of our motley crew."

I was warmly welcomed by a young Mr. Carter. "Enchanted," he said over my hand.

Reggie kept a tight hold of me. "Now then Arthur, tell us all about the woman who has you leg shackled again. I thought you'd sworn off the fairer sex."

Arthur's eyes lit up. "She's nothing like the fairer sex you know, Reggie, and I'll thank you to release her before I plant you a facer."

Reggie's eyes lit up as well. "Oh ho! That's the way of it, is it? I can see there are many mysteries about the new Duchess I must uncover. My dear, please promise me a waltz so I can find out your secrets and seduce you. I do enjoy the jealous look in Arthur's eyes."

Part 2 - The Farce

"No one waltzes with my wife but me." Arthur gave Reggie a dark look.

"It's worse than I thought, Carter." Reggie shook his head. "He's gone topsy turvy for a woman."

"Head over heels," Arthur agreed. "Completely in her pocket."

"Madness, Ironwood. You've been taken over by sheer madness." Reggie gave me another appraising look. "But she's quite lovely to look at, not as pretty as Diana, but lovely nonetheless."

"No one was as pretty as Diana." I heard Mr. Carter speak under his breath.

I'd had enough. "Yes, well, *she* is tired of being talked about when she is standing right in front of you. *She* has also promised to open the dancing with the Duke of Leighton and will excuse herself now and hope when *she* returns, she'll find you all have better manners." I released Reggie's arm before turning my back on them all. I glanced back and saw Arthur grin at me with approval before I left to find Leighton.

He'd just finished welcoming guests when I arrived and took my arm at once.

"Ready, my dear?" I warmed at the endearment. He really did want all to be well between our families. I gave him a nod and let him lead me to the musicians.

"What shall we start with?"

"A quadrille?" I'd managed to get the steps and turns correct after a day of drilling. I was grateful Leighton allowed me the choice and wondered if it was his idea or if my dear husband had put a word in for me.

"A quadrille," he directed the musicians and then took his place on the floor with me.

There was a great silence, as if everyone was holding their breath. Then the music started and I took Leighton's hands. There was a collective release of air and everyone started talking again. We led the set and talked briefly when we met. I managed to keep my eyes up and my face relaxed. I felt hundreds of eyes watching me for any flaws. Voices murmured through the room, low and unfriendly.

"I don't belong here, do I," I said to Leighton when we next met in the turn. He pursed his lips as we touched hands.

"No, my dear, I'm afraid you do not."

I looked over at Arthur who was watching with his cronies. His eyes radiated fondness and pride.

"Do I belong with him?" I asked quietly.

Leighton laughed. "Definitely. I haven't seen Ironwood laugh or smile about anything…well, ever. I have never seen him work up such a passion as I did today. You most certainly belong with him. You'll never be accepted, but I do think you'll be tolerated. For the sake of every husband or father who wants to keep from being shot, the women will keep peace."

It was the most I could ask for. I pasted on a smile and renewed my steps to match those of Leighton's. I didn't miss one step or turn.

Afterward, there was a lot of bowing and mingling, instead of the applause and laughter I was used to in the country. I took Leighton's arm and he escorted me back to Arthur's side.

Arthur tucked me close and kissed my cheek. "Well done," he murmured.

I leaned up to him and whispered, "Can we leave now?"

He laughed aloud and shook his head. "Not yet, my love, I still need my waltz. And we still need to be seen."

"Yes, and on that happy note, is there any chance I can steal your husband away for a game of whist? Another partner would be most helpful, and I'm pretty sure his sharp eyes would prove Sir Henry Danvers is a dirty rotten cheat." Reggie's voice lowered to a conspirator whisper.

I released Arthur's arm. "Of course, gentlemen, I'm sure I'll find something else to occupy my time."

Arthur was less sure. "I'm not so sure I'm ready to leave you to the wolves yet. Your dance was flawless, but no one is looking at you kindly."

"I'm tolerated, and that's enough. I'll expect to see you for every waltz, and I will update you on my every movement, or lack thereof. You've got to let me out on my own."

He frowned at me, digesting my words while his friend gazed on with a hopeful, boyish grin. "You're sure?"

I nodded. "Go. You don't want the *ton* to think you're too leg shackled to be without me."

He kissed my hand and walked away with his friend.

I found myself wandering the room, taking note of the latest fashions and making silent notes in my head of how and what I would do differently. There was an awful lot of décolletage. I glanced down at my own gown and was glad of the coverage I'd given myself. Mine was different from every gown here, and I had been getting looks from others. Of envy or repugnance, I wasn't sure.

"Joy!"

I jumped at the sound of my name and turned to see Sophie frantically waving at me through the crowd. I felt sudden relief at seeing her friendly face and made my way through the crush to her side.

She grabbed my hands and kissed both cheeks. "It is so good to see you here! Finally getting Arthur out of the house. It must be some kind of miracle."

"It has more to do with politics than miracles," I said.

"And your gown! Breathtaking. I've already had two women demanding to know your *modiste*. Naturally, I tell them it's a big secret you will not divulge, even to me. Imagine their faces when I come out wearing the new gown you are making me! Green, they will be absolutely green!"

"You're giving me a big ego, one I can't keep up with," I protested.

"Oh, posh. Where's Arthur? Left you alone to face the gauntlet?" She looked over my shoulder for his face.

"Whist," I answered.

She scowled. "Reggie got to him already. He thinks Arthur is his good luck charm, but it's his vanity. He refuses to wear his spectacles at the tables and that is why he loses. Now, come meet my friends!" she demanded, taking my hand and marching me to her corner of the room.

All of her friends were male. And young. Barely out of school, young healthy men clustered and crowded around her. She was old enough to be their grandmother!

"Hush!" She commanded and they all stopped their carousing. "This is my daughter-in-law, Joy, the new Duchess of Ironwood. She is straight from the country and doesn't know our modern dance steps well. Now, I expect every one of you to help her look magnificent on the dance floor."

Oh dear.

Like a pack of exuberant puppies, they crawled and pushed each other aside to get to me.

"Ten pounds I can teach her the minuet in one dance," one announced.

"Ten says I can do it in one set!" another boasted.

"Oh my," I gasped as more bets were thrown about.

Sophie's eyes glittered with amusement and she spoke in a quiet voice to me, "I know, aren't they horrible? I adore them so much. They have no clue about anything. They are just a mass of energy. I've found it's best to direct them in different ways. They are so amusing."

Hands grabbed mine and I was taken to the side by a boy barely old enough to shave. He started giving me firm instructions as to what I should do. "Please, Your Grace, I hate losing to Prescott. He gloats so." He went over the steps with me a few times until he was certain I would succeed before ushering me back onto the floor under the close scrutiny of his peers.

I did my best to fulfil every request from all of Sophie's boys, but I was having a difficult time remembering their names along with all the steps and turns. It all became a muddle. Soon I was laughing along with Sophie while the young men fought over how much I would learn in so little space and time. The betting became more heated and I was certain several fortunes had switched hands. Eventually, I begged off their attention and found a seat next to Sophie as she started directing them to the wallflowers for their next round of attention.

The room was getting warmer. I wasn't sure how people continued to dance in the heat and the crowd of bodies. My fan was little help on keeping my face cool and my wrist was getting tired.

A little breeze caught my attention and I turned towards it. Large French doors were flung open to a balcony and the cool air of the night flooded the room. Everyone let out a collective sigh of relief and couples left arm in arm for the gardens. I rose from my seat and followed the mob. "If you see Arthur, I'm stepping out for some air," I told Sophie while her pack started in on another round of dares and bets with one another.

The cool breeze was refreshing. I inhaled deeply when I left the room, but I made the mistake of stopping too quickly outside the doors and found myself pushed along with the crush. I fought my way through them and into a corner of the terrace. Leaning on the railing, I inhaled the scent of the gardens below, relaxing as the cool air and fresh fragrances worked their magic on my heated skin.

Suddenly, strong arms wrapped around me from behind and pulled me close to a warm broad chest. I gasped and froze.

"There you are, Suzanna. I knew you would come." Warm breath tickled my ear.

I instantly started to squirm in the unfamiliar grasp, fear crawling up my spine. His arms tightened around me. "Stop! Please! I'm not Suzanna!" I protested.

PART 2 - THE FARCE

Instead of letting me go, he held me tighter and whispered, "Ah...so that's the game tonight." His tongue flicked out and licked my earlobe.

I let out a yelp and smashed the heel of my boot on his foot. He swore.

"I am not Suzanna!" I elbowed him in the belly and when he doubled over, I turned and smashed the heel of my hand into his nose. It exploded with blood and he crumpled to the ground like a puppet.

My assailant moaned and twitched while I gaped at what I had done. The training Thomas and John Turner had given me had actually worked, a little too well. I gathered up my skirts and hurried back into the hot ballroom.

I pushed my way through the horde and found a seat next to the wall away from people. I opened my fan, furiously waving it in front of my face. It felt hotter now than before I'd left the room.

What had I just done? Would the constabulary come? An inquiry? At least there would be a huge scandal. All my hard work on the quadrille had just come undone. What about Arthur's reputation? Had I just ruined it further? Would I even be tolerated anymore?

I thought about going to search for Arthur, but I didn't want to seem I was incapable of taking care of myself or show weakness to his cronies. Weak? I had just attacked a gentleman!

All too soon a loud scream came from outside. I cringed and waved my fan faster as faces turned towards the uproar and the music came to an abrupt stop.

I watched the man I had assaulted being carried into the room between two others, covered in blood and moaning. Cries and shouts of alarm filled the air. Men hurried outside to find the culprit. I closed my eyes and wished I was anywhere but in a ballroom full of peers while the crowd grew louder.

"What in blazes is going on?" My eyes flew open. Arthur stood over me and his friends were gathered around. They all were peering over the crowd, trying to get a look at what was taking place.

"I'll go find out," Mr. Carter mumbled and pushed his way through the crush of bodies.

Arthur rested a hand on my shoulder. "Have you any idea what the fuss is about?"

I felt my face flush and shook my head. "I'm not sure." My voice sounded high and abnormal. I couldn't meet his eyes with my own and my skin flushed from my cheeks to my ears and down my neck.

His eyes narrowed. "Joy?" He strung my name out like a warning.

I shrugged and waved my fan faster, gathering my courage. "I'm really not sure, Arthur." My voice was at its normal tone and I met his eyes with as bold a look I could muster.

He gave me a glare. The voices around us twittered with excitement. He leaned down to me and whispered, "Why is there blood on your gloves, Joy?"

My fan froze in place. Slowly, I glanced down at my hand resting in my lap. Big, red drops of blood splattered up my white gloves. My hand shook and I dropped my fan. Arthur bent down, picked it up, and laid it over the glaring evidence of my attack, placing the strap around my wrist.

He finished standing and placed his hand between my shoulders. "I think all the excitement is making my wife tired. Please excuse us," he announced and pushed me out of my chair. "Good night Reggie."

His hand was again in the small of my back, steering me through the crowd to retrieve my wrap and his hat and walking stick.

Mr. Carter joined us at the coatroom. "It's the youngest son of Lord Fredericks. Martin Fredericks. Someone has beaten him soundly. It looks like they broke his nose; there's blood everywhere. Ladies are fainting and someone is calling for the constable." I flinched.

"That sounds quite serious. Please keep us apprised of his condition." Arthur placed a firm hand around my glove to hide the blood.

Mr. Carter snorted. "I'm sure it's not serious. Everyone knows he's always got a lady on the side. Perhaps this one had a husband instead of being a rich widow."

Arthur draped my wrap around my shoulders. "I'll expect a full report tomorrow."

Mr. Carter nodded. "I look forward to it. Good night Ironwood. Your Grace, it was a pleasure to meet you." He gave me a small bow.

Arthur's arm effectively guided me out the door and into the carriage. He sat across from me with a scowl, knocked on the roof and the carriage started off.

He started taking off his gloves slowly. "Well, Joy. I'm waiting."

"Waiting for what?" I asked innocently.

"To hear the reason why there is blood on your gloves." He slapped his own gloves on his thigh.

"I had a small accident in the ladies room involving a hairpin," I lied, avoiding his gaze.

Part 2 - The Farce

He shook his head. "That's too much blood for a pinprick, dearest. There's also the small fact you don't use them. I know what a terrible liar you are, remember?"

I sighed, knowing he would not relent. My cheeks burned. "There were so many people… and it was hot. I went outside the doors to the terrace to get some air. I was just barely out the door, Arthur, I promise you. I did not stray into the gardens. The crowd pushed me aside into the shadows behind the door. He was waiting for someone there."

"Young Martin Fredericks?" Arthur guessed.

I nodded. "He wrapped his arms around me and started calling me Suzanna."

Arthur's scowl grew; I reached out and placed a hand on his leg. "I struggled and told him I wasn't Suzanna, and he should release me. He thought it was a game, and… licked my ear." I shuddered.

Arthur's hands grabbed mine. "He did what?"

"It was then that I struck him. Thomas and John Turner taught me to defend myself after the encounter with Dibble. I stomped on his foot, elbowed his guts and planted my fist up his nose."

Arthur grew still, his eyes widened.

"I didn't know there would be so much blood. He hit the ground hard. I rushed back inside and found my seat before anyone saw. I think you were the only one who noticed the blood on my glove. I don't want to embarrass you…or cause a scandal. I'm worried about undoing everything we've tried to do tonight and…Arthur? Are you laughing?" I demanded, jerking my hands away from him and his shaking body.

He laughed louder, tossing his head back with mirth.

"It is not funny!" I exclaimed.

"It *is* funny, Joy! I don't know if I should call out Young Fredericks or go apologize to him for the assault by my wife!" He laughed even harder.

Folding my arms across my chest, I turned away from him as he continued to laugh. He wiped tears from his eyes before he moved to my side of the carriage. He pulled me unwillingly into his arms, still chuckling, and pressed a warm tender kiss to my cheek. "You are magnificent, Joy."

I softened a little and snuggled into his embrace, relaxing and resting my head against his chest. "I find more and more that your opinion is the only one that matters." I told him.

"Good. Now please, the next time someone cuts you or tries to take liberties with you, let me know so I can outright shoot them. You're starting to make me feel like an emasculated husband. I'm still not sure I don't deserve to plant Young Fredericks a proper facer."

"At least wait until his nose heals," I suggested and he burst into laughter again.

PART 2 - THE FARCE

CHAPTER 16

I introduced her to Reggie and Carter. They've started hanging about the house again. Both of them are enchanted with her. I am a green-eyed monster every time Reggie flirts with her.

I hope this wasn't a mistake.

I was the last to breakfast the next morning. Alice was there, reading the paper and my correspondence. There was no sign of Arthur. He hadn't been in bed when I had awoken either.

"Have you seen Mr. Marco?" I filled my plate.

"Yes, he and Mr. Carter said they had some errands to run and would return to finish breakfast with you."

She started presenting my correspondence. "A thank you from the Leighton's. A letter from your sister Hope, and several notes from all the flowers you've received." She passed over a stack of cards.

I wrinkled my brow. "Flowers?"

Alice's eyes sparkled with mischief. "Yes, from all your dance partners."

"From all my…oh no." I rose to my feet. "Where are they?"

Alice's grin widened. "I had them all put in the parlor."

I groaned and hurried to the parlor. The room was stuffed full of vases and bouquets. Every color imaginable burst forth from them. It smelled like springtime had deposited itself into the room.

"Arthur is going to hate this." I started to laugh.

"I would say you were somewhat of a success," Alice smirked.

"No, it's not like that at all. These are all from Sophie's boys. They were all betting they could teach me the minuet in less than ten minutes. Did you know she surrounds herself with young men fresh from school. She said, 'Who better to show them how to deal in London than a kindly old grandmother.' Ha! She had them all dancing to her tune and she makes them think it was all their idea."

Alice laughed. "I will definitely accompany you to the next ball."

"Oh Alice, there probably won't be a next ball. Leighton was gentlemanly and kind, but he made it clear to me I would only be tolerated in the *ton*, never accepted." I wasn't truly sorry for it, but I had hoped I could help her meet someone who could help better her circumstances.

Alice shook her head. "The *ton* turns on a whim, and you are its latest oddity. I've got another stack of invitations received this morning. There are still more people who want to gawk at you and snub you."

She said it with such flattery I laughed.

"Such joy in the morning, after such a turbulent night!" Arthur appeared with Mr. Carter at his heels. "I trust you rested well…good gracious! Did a hot house vomit in my parlor?"

"Arthur!" I scolded.

He glared back at me. "What's all this then?"

"Flowers from my dance partners. Since you never danced with me, I'll assume you did not get me any flowers." I teased.

"Dance partners? Wha…we weren't there long enough for you to dance with so many people!" He gestured at all the vases.

"I met your mother's friends."

He groaned and Mr. Carter laughed. "All those young bucks were dancing with your wife while you played whist."

"Yes, thank you, Carter," Arthur snarled and roughly handed me a parcel. "Here."

I opened it quickly. "New gloves?"

Arthur nodded. "From Fredericks. I bought him a new cravat, and he bought you a new pair of gloves. We strongly suggested he verify his lovers before he grabs them."

I heard Alice gasp, and I had to ask. "Did you hit him?"

"No, he was going to." Mr. Carter grinned. "Until we saw Fredericks with his two black eyes and a broken nose. Well done, Your Grace."

I flinched at the description of his injuries. "Has he seen a physician?"

"Joy, stop thinking about that jackanape and tell me what you are going to do about all these flowers," Arthur demanded.

Part 2 - The Farce

"Enjoy them? They are lovely and it was kind of them to remember me, even if they were more worried about winning a bet instead of me trotting on their toes," I teased.

"They were using you for their idiotic bets. I'm going to have harsh words with Sophie."

"If you insist." I was not worried in the least; Sophie could handle him. "Breakfast is getting cold." I turned him back towards the dining room. "Mr. Carter, will you be joining us?"

He nodded and offered Alice his arm. She smiled and blushed before taking it.

We had just finished eating when Byron announced the arrival of my sister Hope and her family.

Arthur's eyes were as wide as mine with surprise when they entered.

David was never one for ceremony and rushed forward with an exuberant, "Aunt Joy!" His small arms wrapped around my knees and he almost knocked me over.

"Oof! You're getting much too strong." I bent down to embrace him. I let Arthur make the introductions. I took off David's hat and gave him a kiss.

"I didn't know you would be here today." I leaned in to give Hope a kiss on her cheek.

"I wrote to you," she defended. "I wasn't sure if you would respond, so…" She looked down at the table where her letter was sitting. "You just got it today? Oh, this is embarrassing."

I rubbed her arms. "It's wonderful!" I was glad to see her face and David's as he dove under the table to find Pip while her husband, Lawrence, shook hands with Mr. Carter and nodded to Alice.

"Lawrence had business in town this week, and I thought we could come to visit you instead of staying home alone waiting for him."

"Of course. I'll be glad for your company. We'll see whatever sights you want and then I'll put you to work." I gestured at the pink décor.

She looked up at the fresco on the ceiling, "Are the cherubs wearing pink underthings?!"

I giggled as Arthur's voice broke through the conversations. "Come with me, gentlemen! My wife has just received an entire hot house of flowers from a dozen different young bucks, and I must perform better. You too, David, I'll need your advice. No, Pip, you stay with the ladies."

I watched them leave and got Hope settled into a bedroom with one adjoining for David. She joined me for a walk with Pip, admiring the park and the people in it, along with the horses and vehicles. Neville followed at a discreet distance.

"It's so busy!" she exclaimed while we walked along the banks of the river. Pip scouted ahead of us and returned regularly to check on our progress. "So many sounds and smells. Oh, I almost turned around at the gates with the smell. I'd like to blame it on the fact that I am expecting again."

"Hope, that's wonderful!"

She beamed. "Yes, I'm excited and nervous all over again. Hopefully, this one will be easier than David. I didn't mean to show up on your doorstep unannounced. I just wanted to visit you before I was too fat to roll out of a carriage."

I giggled. "You never got fat, even with Lawrence bringing you all the sweets you demanded."

"I'm sure you'll be following shortly right behind me with a little heir to the kingdom." She gave me a squeeze.

"I hope so." It was too early to guess if I was carrying a child. All I wanted to think about was a new niece or nephew to spoil. "A girl this time, Hope, we need a girl."

"MAMA! AUNT JOY!" a loud voice called from across the park.

Hope sighed. "A little girl might be quieter…"

Pip gave a joyful bark at the sound of my nephew's voice and ran back towards us with his tongue lolling out. A smart-looking phaeton was heading our way with Arthur driving. David was standing and waving at us while Lawrence kept a steady hand on him. Mr. Carter lounged in the rear.

They came to a halt and David leaped from the carriage. "Aunt Joy! We got you the best present!" He grabbed my hand and pulled on it as the other men climbed to the ground. His hand was sticky and his face was a mess of sweets that hadn't made it to his mouth. I grinned at Hope and followed him.

"Come on! Look! Look!" He dragged me to the back of the phaeton where a horse was tied to the bumper. "We got you a horse!"

I looked up at the old stallion who blinked and looked down at me. He was a fine-looking boy, with beautiful lines and a dappled grey color. He leaned forward and began to nuzzle my arm and search my pockets for

Part 2 - The Farce

treats. I ran a hand along his neck. He was warm and soft and smelled like home.

"His name is Toady!" David exclaimed.

I laughed. "Toady? What an odd name for such a handsome old man."

"His name," Arthur corrected as he put an arm around my waist, "is Alistair DeFrogney, but your nephew found out all the stable hands had rebranded him as Toady, and that's what he answers to. He's an old racing horse who was about to be sent to the glue shop. I think he's got a few more good years in him to prance you around."

I adored him immediately. "You are going to become a fat, spoiled, old man," I whispered to him.

"Better than flowers?" Arthur asked.

"Much better than flowers." I placed a kiss on his cheek. I reached out and untied Toady from the curricle. "I want to walk him home. Will you join me?"

He scowled a bit. "Nothing would give me greater pleasure, Madame Wife, though I fear to let any of these other males take a hand at the phaeton. Carter smashed the last one I let him drive."

"It was raining and slippery. I was in a hurry to get out of the weather," Mr. Carter protested.

"David would like to try his hand, but these two are a little more spirited than I could trust him with." I rolled my eyes. "Lawrence would be a better choice and I did already offer to let him take a turn…"

"I would feel nothing but guilt if I gave it so much as a scratch." Lawrence finished, placing an arm around Hope. "Although I would like my delicate wife to ride back with us. You've already taken too much of a walk, my dear." He looked at her pointedly.

Arthur raised his brows. "I see. Then it is up to me to return us all safely. We'll have to crowd together…Neville can hang off the back…"

"I'll walk back with Her Grace." Mr. Carter climbed out of the vehicle.

Arthur's eyes narrowed. Mr. Carter stared back, his face serene and calm. The silent conversation between them became more heated. "That's quite alright, Carter."

"Oh, leave off, Ironwood! Neville is a perfect chaperone. She'll be holding onto a lead rope, not my arm. Stop being mule-headed and take the others home," Carter said.

I nodded in agreement. "I'll be perfectly fine with Mr. Carter. Take my sister home and come back to meet us halfway."

Arthur scowled down at me. "Very well."

Lawrence lifted Hope into the vehicle and Arthur climbed up behind Pip who cleaned the sweets from David's face while the boy giggled. He gave Mr. Carter another meaningful glare and slapped the reins. I watched them disappear around the corner before I gave Mr. Carter a small smile. "Shall we?"

He gestured with his hand. "After you."

I tugged a little on Toady's rope and he obediently followed, glancing and nipping at patches of long grass as we walked back towards the monstrosity where I lived. Mr. Carter walked next to me, his hands clasped behind his back. Neville kept a proper distance behind us.

"I must confess I am a little disappointed in you." Mr. Carter broke the silence.

I furrowed my brow. "Oh, how so?"

"I bet your husband a box of sweets for David you'd scold him for purchasing an old horse."

I smiled. "David will be delighted and I'll be able to remind Arthur about his own betting habits when he goes to chastise his mother and her friends. Let me guess," I scratched Toady's neck, "you didn't see any worth in my old friend here."

"Not much more than paste," he admitted.

I shook my head. "That doesn't surprise me. We are surrounded by excess here, no one takes the time to see anything of worth anymore."

"I'm more surprised you didn't demand he return it and come back with something flashier and expensive. I'm sure you know he certainly could afford it!"

I turned my face away from him. "I see." And I did see. In the politest terms possible he'd placed me in the position of being nothing much more than a fortune seeker, that I'd somehow captured Arthur in order to spend his money.

I shouldn't have been surprised. I knew it was bound to happen when I knit my soul with his. But knowing didn't stop the outrage. Anger filled me and I quickened my steps. Toady bobbed along to match my pace.

"Your G-!" Carter started.

PART 2 - THE FARCE

I stopped so quickly, Toady tossed his head back and almost stepped on Mr. Carter. "Don't call me that! I am Mrs. Joy Horton Marco. That is my name to you now. I didn't want anything more than that."

"I apologize…"

"Don't do that either!" I was shouting now, and Toady let out a whinny of displeasure so loud people turned to see what the commotion was. "Don't apologize. Not when you don't mean it! I refused his proposal for this very reason. I'm sure it's too impossible for you to think a man and a woman simply wanted to find happiness with each other. Rank and title and birth don't matter but love and respect do."

So much for not gathering attention. I could feel the redness in my face as I glared at Mr. Carter, daring him to make another comment. I felt other eyes on me as well, and heard a few gasps and murmurs.

"Alright there, Your Grace?" Neville called out as he approached. He looked ready to plant his fist on Mr. Carter's chin if I asked him.

"Everything's fine, thank you, Neville." I turned from Mr. Carter, took a deep breath and began my walk anew.

He was silent but kept pace with me. I kept my eyes on my destination.

"Did you really refuse his proposal?"

I nodded.

"How did he take it?"

"Not well, if you know Arthur at all."

Mr. Carter chuckled. "I can imagine. How did he change your mind?"

I sighed. "He asked me what I wanted. I told him, and he said he would help me get that."

"What do you want?"

"That is none of your concern." My glare silenced him.

We continued out of the park in silence. The sound of Toady's hooves against the stones was all I heard while we both gathered our thoughts. He broke the silence first.

"I do owe you an apology, Your G- Mrs. Marco. Arthur told me this morning you were the most genuine person he'd ever met. I didn't believe him. I didn't believe there was such a person in existence. But anyone who instantly falls in love with an old stallion and denounces her own newly elevated status can only either be genuine, or mad."

I managed a smile. "I wonder if it might be the latter."

"But you are wrong if you think I don't want a man and woman to simply find happiness with each other, no matter who they are." He gazed into the distance, a wave of sadness washing over his face. He was filled with longing, with regret and words unspoken.

"You lost someone."

He blinked back into reality. "Yes. Someone I shouldn't have been with. Someone whose rank and title kept us apart."

I chewed on my lip. "Is there any hope for you to be with her?"

He shook his head. "No. No, she's passed on now."

I placed my hand on his arm, slowing our pace until we stopped. "I am sorry, Mr. Carter. I cannot imagine your heartache. I wish I had more than words to console you with. But I am truly sorry I misjudged you," I said earnestly.

"Thank you, Mrs. Marco. We were both in the wrong," he admitted. "But I see your husband coming down the street. If you don't take your hand off my arm, he'll run me through and eat my heart here in public as a warning. And please don't let him know I upset you, I have never dueled and his marksmanship is exceptionally fine." The light was back in Mr. Carter's eyes.

I removed my hand and looked up the street to see Arthur marching towards us with a glower. Pip was at his side with his tongue lolling about.

"At least Pip is happy to see me," I said when they reached us, rubbing his head.

"What are you talking about? I'm thrilled to see you." Arthur glared at Mr. Carter.

"If you were any more excited I would send the women and children running for cover." I placed a kiss on his cheek and felt him relax immediately. "I watched over Toady, Mr. Carter kept watch over me, and Neville kept watch over him. We're all carefully watched over," I assured him. He tucked my arm into his elbow.

"I prefer my own eyes on you." He took Toady's rope from me to lead our small entourage home. "As well as other things," he spoke for my ears only.

PART 2 - THE FARCE

CHAPTER 17

I've never had a business investment fail. Ever.
I was giddy about losing the money but managed to keep a straight face in front of Carter.

A month later Carter burst into breakfast with a sheaf of papers in his hand.
"Ironwood! We have a problem! The *Newhaven* has sunk, and everything is lost!"

Arthur was speechless for a moment. "And the crew?"

"Most survived. Captain Moss went down with it like a good captain should. His first mate made it to Plymouth with the survivors. I just got his missive." He handed the papers to Arthur who scanned the contents.

"Arthur?" I reached out to touch his sleeve.

"A lot of fortunes have just been lost, Joy." He sighed and rubbed his forehead. I could see his brain trying to salvage the situation.

"We can sell this monstrosity, move to the country, and live off my sewing." I offered hopefully, trying to bring some levity to the room.

His smile didn't quite reach his eyes. "This is a drop in the pond for us, but not for others." He looked up at Mr. Carter. "I assume you're packed and ready to go?"

Mr. Carter's mouth was a grim line. "I know your horses are faster."

Arthur nodded and stood.

I stood with him. "You're leaving?" I had the distinct feeling I was not invited on this journey.

"It's a big mess with investors at each other's throats. If I don't get there and throw some coins around, there will be bloodshed."

"I'll help you pack," I offered.

"No time. I'll leave now with Carter. Send Byron with my things later." He pulled me close. He kissed me firmly on the mouth before releasing me. "It's no place for you, Madame Wife. Stay here and behave yourself."

He kissed me again, while Mr. Carter and Alice both tried their best to look away.

"Alice?" Arthur gave her a meaningful look.

"I'll keep her occupied," she promised, linking her arm through mine.

I squeezed it in a show of female solidarity and gave him a smile. "We'll be fine."

And they were gone.

The house felt empty without him. The servants were kind and helpful with everything that needed to be done to move his things to a new location. Mrs. Poulson and Alice ran the rest of the house like clockwork with little input from me. The remodels were underway and didn't need my constant supervision. The craftsmen converged on the rooms to replace and repair with order and precision. I'd finished Sophie's gown, two more for Alice and one I'd started on for Hope before she left.

After two days without my husband, I was well and truly bored. I missed my morning races with him and Toady, and my afternoon entertainment of what went on daily in Parliament. Arthur's reading of the newspaper at breakfast now fell to Alice. While she was a great companion, she lacked Arthur's wit and humor about the news we debated over. The novel we were reading together lay on the table next to our bed. It felt like cheating to continue it without him.

"When did a man make such a difference in my life that I should miss him so much when he's gone?" I asked Pip aloud while we played fetch. I threw a ball for him and watched him race off. Alice sat on a nearby bench with Neville hovering nearby.

Pip retrieved his toy and returned it promptly, sitting and staring at the ball.

"I was perfectly happy and occupied before I knew him. I should be able to be so without him." I threw the ball again and he took off after it.

He brought me back the slobbery toy and dropped it at my feet.

"Obviously, I was not meant to be a lady of leisure. I'm sure I could find more charity work to do, but Arthur warned me to stay out of trouble. He'll be upset if I start a new project without him investigating first." I threw the ball a little harder and farther and watched him race after it.

I rotated my shoulder. It was getting sore from throwing. Pip came and sat down, dropped his ball, and laid on top of it, signifying he was done chasing.

"I think…I think he's quickly becoming my favorite person, Pip. Even more than you," I confessed, kneeling down and stroking his silky fur. It wasn't something that had taken over me suddenly or an overwhelming feeling that had struck me, but something sweet and steady that was growing more and more each day.

I smiled down at Pip and scratched his ear. "I suppose if one is to have a favorite person, it's best to be one's husband. Arthur complained I had too much power over him. I see now what he meant. He's only been gone two days and I'm suddenly at a loss without his presence." Pip licked my hand quickly in response, gave a deep doggy sigh, and laid his head down on my knee.

"Now then, how should we occupy ourselves?" I stroked his ears. He responded with a snore.

"Joy! I need your help at once!" I turned and saw Sophie in a curricle with a crying young woman.

"What's wrong?" I asked, hurrying to her side.

"What's wrong? Just look at her!" She gestured wildly at the woman in her curricle. "Her grandmother is sponsoring her coming out and she's dressed like I did three decades ago. It looks completely wrong on poor Amelia here. Wrong, wrong, wrong!" Sophie's voice boomed across the park.

I looked over at the young woman whose hair was definitely out of fashion in a high towering updo and wore far too much face powder. Her face and body had pleasant curves but had been enrobed in so many flounces and frills she looked like an overdone cake rather than a fetching young woman.

"Oh. Oh, I see."

"I was visiting her grandmother this morning and when she introduced me, I was horrified. I gave her a good scolding and stole Amelia away immediately. Hurry up now, there's no time to waste! There's a ball tonight and she's going to be the talk of it. I wagered twenty pounds on it with my bucks. They don't think I can do it."

"Oh heavens, Sophie!" I said as 'poor Amelia' burst into another round of tears.

"Hush now, once Joy is finished with you, they won't even recognize you. We'll have the pleasure of watching their faces when I reveal who you are. I love making their jaws hit the ground. It will be so delightful to watch them act like idiots and fawn over you."

"I'm not sure you are making her feel much better." I knew then exactly where Arthur's rash behavior came from. Sophie had practically kidnapped the poor thing. "Go back to my house and have Mrs. Poulson show you to my room. Alice and I will be there shortly and we'll get started."

***

Amelia stood in front of the mirror, her eyes wide. It had taken all day, many cups of tea and sandwiches, a haircut, and a small army of maids, but she looked stunning.

"She looks like she's wearing starlight…how did you do that?" Sophie asked.

I looked down at my callused fingers. They were a little battered and blistered after the race I'd put them through. The old-fashioned gown was discarded in a corner. A new white silk dress in a modern style sat upon her form. I wished she could wear something other than white, but Sophie had insisted she was too young to wear anything else.

I'd worked with Alice and my other maids frantically to sew on tiny jeweled beads onto a dark tulle overdress to look like the night sky. I'd marked each place carefully, placed it on the mannequin, and got to work. Sophie had cleaned Amelia's face and found a smooth complexion underneath with little need for cosmetics. She'd then summoned her hairdresser. With her hair trimmed and smoothed into something simpler and more elegant, she looked like a different young woman than the one I'd met this morning. Once she'd gotten dressed, I placed her in front of the mirror. She hadn't moved in over a minute.

"Thank you for bringing her today," I told Sophie softly. "I needed some kind of a challenge to get me out of the doldrums."

Sophie smiled at me. "Missing our boy?"

I nodded. It wasn't hard to admit now. I did miss him, but I found the new Joy Horton Marco could still find pleasure in the simple things without him.

Part 2 - The Farce

Sophie pressed a dry, warm kiss on my cheek. "I do like you, Joy, so very much. I'm glad he found you. You are so much kinder and more fun than the others."

Others? What others? Was she talking about Diana? I opened my mouth to ask for clarification but Sophie was already ushering Amelia out the door before my tired brain could catch up. Without her energy, Alice and I and four other maids collapsed into a tired heap. I laughed at us all wearing similar expressions. We were dazed, but beaming at a job well done.

"I'll have Mrs. Poulson give you all the rest of the night off. I'm sure your fingers are as sore as mine." I rubbed my callused digits together. "You all did wonderfully." Their cheeks flushed and they each gave me a smile.

Mrs. Poulson walked into the room with a letter. "This just arrived, from His Grace." I took it eagerly from her and told her my instructions for the weary maids. They left together except for Alice, who took the letter once I opened it and scanned his handwriting. Tall and loopy, not too dark. He was in a good mood when he wrote.

"Dear Joy ... and Alice," she giggled. She took a deep breath and continued reading. I didn't listen much after I heard the first sentence. *"I'll be home in two days."* I relaxed, imagining how to welcome home my favorite person.

CHAPTER 18

I've been tricked, and there is no sign of Carter.
I'm not sure what's happening but my gut is roiling with fear.
I can't get back to Joy fast enough.

"Please, Alice, you are being ridiculous," I told her for the fifth time. "There is no reason for you to keep me company all night long waiting for Arthur."

A week had passed and the entire household awaited the return of its Master. I'd tried not to stare at the front door like a mooncalf, but it had become harder and harder as the day progressed with no sign of him. I'd taken to the library with Alice, working on a new waistcoat for Arthur while she read to me.

There had been a flurry of excitement when Byron had returned with the carriage. I'd watched out the window with a huge grin on my face when it pulled up. When the servant had been the only occupant exiting the vehicle, I left the window to meet him in the hall. Apparently, I didn't look welcoming.

Byron hung his head. "Please don't look at me like that, Your Grace. I'd have dragged him back if I could. He was delayed by an urgent problem that suddenly came up. He sent me ahead with the carriage and told me that he'd be 'riding with the hounds of hell at his heels' to get back tonight." The tips of Byron's ears turned red at this confession.

"I'm sure he will be," I assured him as the footmen unloaded the carriage and I sent Byron off to rest for the evening.

Alice had continued to read to me after dinner until the light dimmed and her voice became soft and scratchy. I insisted she go to bed and I would continue my vigil alone.

Part 2 - The Farce

"I can stay up with you and keep you company," she offered again.

I gave her a pointed look. "I honestly don't want you to observe our greeting. I'm planning on giving him an exuberant homecoming."

She giggled and yawned. "I'll leave you to it then." I finished dressing in my nightgown and robe. I put on my slippers and made my way down to the library.

I had a nice fire going and plenty of light to work on my latest project. When the clock chimed midnight I found my eyes drooping. I set my project aside and lay back against the couch cushions, closing my eyes to rest and promising just a quick nap before Arthur came home. It couldn't be long now.

I woke up when I heard the library door quietly open and close. I kept my eyes closed but started to stretch. "Welcome home, Mr. Marco."

A hand came around my throat and another clamped down on my mouth. My eyes opened wide and I looked up into the face of Mr. Carter.

His breath was hot and heavy with the stink of liquor. I started to squirm, trying to tear his grip from me. His hand tightened around my throat. I gagged and struggled as horrible memories surfaced. I remembered being kicked, my ribs aching, my lungs screaming for air. I saw a flash of Dibble's face before it melded back into Mr. Carter's.

He shook me hard until I stilled. "None of your tricks, Mrs. Marco. I'm well aware you know how to defend yourself. And if you scream again…" His hand left my mouth and pulled a pistol from his pocket, pointing it at my forehead. "I'll shoot you and everyone else who comes to your rescue. Am I clear?"

Fear struck me and I froze. I managed a nod and he removed his hand from my throat. He backed away so I could sit up. I felt my limbs tremble as he kept the gun held on me.

"Why are you doing this?" I tried to keep my voice steady.

"Because that bastard husband of yours has made my life miserable."

He sat down next to me on the couch, the gun still pointing at my chest. His eyes were red and he hadn't shaved or bathed in a few days.

"What has happened to you? Are you in need of money? I'm sure Arthur would help you; he counts you as one of his dearest friends." My voice wavered.

He snorted. "I wish it were that simple. I've got gobs of money. I can buy whatever I wish except what I truly want. What I need."

I clutched the fabric of my robe. "What do you need?"

He looked at me and smiled weakly. "Love, Mrs. Marco. Isn't that what we all really want?"

He suddenly rushed towards me. I raised my arms to ward off his attack, then gave a yelp as he grabbed me and pulled me onto his lap. I struggled and thrashed while he held me to him. Then he lifted the pistol and pressed it against my skin. "Shhh. We don't want anyone else to come into the room and get hurt, now do we?" He shoved the barrel into my ribs.

"No." I trembled. His arms closed around me and pressed me closer to his chest, the gun now pointed at my neck.

"You're so soft." He inhaled my hair and sighed, "And you smell so good. How do you women do it? You are flesh and blood like any male and yet you make us long to touch your skin."

I didn't respond. He took my curls in his hand and started to run them through his fingers, mimicking the action Arthur had done a hundred times. "I can see why he is infatuated with you, why he spends so much time at home now instead of his usual haunts. I would keep you close too until I grew tired of you. It's been months since your wedding. Why hasn't he tired of you yet?"

I remained silent and refrained from jerking away while he played with my hair. My heart was pounding so hard I could see it moving beneath my robe.

"That's another feature you have I find so attractive. You never speak unless it is necessary. No useless prattle or begging from you, just this quiet, solid strength. Yes, I can see why he fell so hard for you." He brushed a finger along my cheek. "I'm truly sorry. I honestly believe your husband loves you. If I wasn't so positive I would have left you alone."

I found my voice. "Why does that give you distress?"

"Because I like you. I admire you and have found our time together to be most enjoyable." He rested his cheek against my hair softly. "But now I have to kill you."

My heart fell into my belly like a stone.

"Please." I begged, "I don't understand."

He rested his head against my shoulder as if he were tired. "I suppose you do deserve an explanation. It's something to pass the time until your husband arrives. We wouldn't want him to miss it."

Part 2 - The Farce

I felt a bit of rage and shrugged his head off me. "Are you going to kill him too?" I demanded. The will to fight rose up within me and I started to squirm. There had to be a way to escape.

His arms tightened around me. "Calm down. I've never struck a woman before. I don't want to start now."

I scoffed at his misguided chivalry. "You won't strike a woman, yet you're going to kill me?"

"It's not personal, it's revenge. For Diana."

I was even more confused. "What does Diana have to do with this?"

"I loved her. Sweet Diana… I adored her. And your husband killed her."

The fight seeped out of my bones. "That's not possible. Arthur would never…"

"Save your breath. He's a murderer. A clever one, but still a killer."

"He didn't kill Diana. She died of pneumonia." I repeated what I had been told.

"That's what he told everyone. Paid the doctor a large sum to say that too. I've just come from Ironwood. The servants were tight-lipped about the whole thing. I questioned the doctor over and over. His story never stayed the same about what happened. His guilt finally wore him down and he told me the truth. Diana never had pneumonia. She was hale and hearty until the day she died."

"Then what was it?" My mind was racing with a million thoughts in a million directions. Murder? Revenge? How did I get caught up in all of this? I was a simple country girl.

"Poison," he whispered into my ear, his hot breath making me shudder. "She was at Ironwood all alone, vibrant and beautiful until he joined her there. Within a day she was dead."

"Why would Arthur kill her?" It came out as a sob.

"Because I loved her." He nuzzled my cheek with his nose. I flinched and turned my head away.

"Stop it," I hissed.

"You don't believe me? There was no love between them."

"I know that. He married her to help her family. Their mothers made the match."

"He never touched her. Ever. He never gave her more than a kiss on their wedding day. He brought her here to London and promptly ignored her. She was so lonely. I danced with her one night; Ironwood never would dance with her. She lit up when I took her in my arms. She was charming and witty, bright and fun. All she needed was some attention and she blossomed. I took her on drives and to parties. People fell in love with her. Ironwood never batted an eye that I was wooing his wife. She told me of their farce of a marriage, of how lonely she was. I was the first man to ever touch her."

I shuddered again when he pulled me tighter against him. "She was exquisite. So much passion just waiting to be released. I fell madly in love with her. We confronted him together, telling him we wanted to be together." He paused.

"Was he angry?" I whispered. I could imagine him being so. I'd seen his passion during the fiasco with the Leightons.

He inhaled and shook his head. "No. The bastard calmly gave us his blessing. Said he would work it out so we could be together. He told Diana to leave London until he got things sorted so she would be safe from scandal. I was going to follow her once I got my part of things situated. I never saw her alive again."

"That doesn't mean he killed her."

"Who else would? Who else didn't want a scandal of being cuckolded by his wife and friend? He was finally gaining respect in Parliament after being attacked for his part in the war. A divorce would be a huge blow to his status. He had every reason to kill her. He took her away from me." He pressed a warm kiss against my cheek and caressed my face. "Which is why I'm going to take you away from him."

I caught another whiff of liquor on his breath. "Mr. Carter, I don't think you're thinking clearly."

He snorted. "How else would I work up the courage to come and kill another man's wife while he watched? I've had hours in a carriage by myself with a few bottles to contemplate what I'm about to do. I just wish there was another way." His voice trembled.

"You don't have to do this." I tentatively touched his arm. "Please. It's not what Diana would want."

"Diana isn't here!" he bellowed. "And all you've tried to do since you got here was eliminate her memory. You've gutted this house and all she did here!" He tipped the gun up into my chin.

I met his eyes, and I saw the madness. I saw his agony and frustration, loneliness, and anger. I saw a man grieving for the woman he loved and

PART 2 - THE FARCE

could never have. I saw the anguish of how he had almost had happiness only to have it wrenched from him. I pitied him as much as I feared him. "I don't believe you really want to do this. But if you do, you'll have my forgiveness."

"Shut up!" he hissed and shook me once before he collapsed and cried into my hair. I held still while he sobbed, the pistol once again aimed at my ribs. He wept, crushing me to him tightly, murmuring Diana's name over and over. All I could do was pray.

He became still. I could feel his composure returning. He wiped his face with his free hand and let out a deep breath. "I'm sorry, Mrs. Marco. I have to even the score. You have to die." He brushed my cheek softly with his and rested his forehead there.

I couldn't reason with him, couldn't change his mind. This was sheer insanity fueled by liquor. I was ready to struggle and scream now, his threats be damned. If I was going to die, it was not going to be in front of my husband. I'd take a piece of Mr. Carter's flesh with me. I would not let him have his perfectly planned execution. Joy Horton Marco would go down fighting!

I was planning my attack when the library door opened and Arthur entered. My heart gave a giant leap. He took in the sight of me sitting on Mr. Carter's lap, locked in an embrace, and his face filled instantly with rage.

"What the devil goes on here!"

"Don't be too hard on her, Ironwood, she's under duress." Mr. Carter held the gun up and pointed it underneath my chin. I bit my lip to keep from crying out, my eyes locked onto Arthur's.

All color drained from his face. He stared at us and then gave a slight nod. "I see. And why have you chosen to take such liberties with my wife?" He walked calmly over to the side table and poured a drink.

"'Eye for an eye'. Isn't that what the Bible says?" Mr. Carter said. "You took what was mine, I'm here to repay you."

Arthur swirled his brandy. "Ah. This is about Diana."

"You killed her," Mr. Carter spat.

"I most certainly did not!" Arthur snapped.

"Don't lie! I've got the truth now. Dr. Bartlett finally gave in to his conscience. Diana didn't die of pneumonia. You paid him a lot of money to say so."

"Dr. Bartlett is a spineless weasel who shouldn't be practicing medicine. How much did you pay him to get him to say what you wanted to hear?" Arthur shot back.

"He's not the only one! She was seen in the village, at the shops, laughing and visiting tenants on the day she died. She was healthy and whole. She was fine until you got there." The gun had begun to slip from its position under my chin. It wavered and began to tip towards Arthur.

"I never even saw her when I got there. She'd been making visits, came home, sent me a message with the footman that she was tired, and went straight to her room. I never laid eyes on her."

"You had her poisoned. None of your servants will breathe a word about that night, a word about you or her. One of them helped you do it."

"You are grasping at straws, man. Diana fell ill and died. Dr. Bartlett is a quack doctor and probably misdiagnosed the cause of death. I didn't kill her."

"No one goes from being vibrant and healthy to dead overnight!" Mr. Carter shook, the gun was pointing at Arthur now.

Arthur tossed his drink at us. It splashed into our faces and stung. I cried out, and so did Mr. Carter.

I felt hands shoving me aside. I fell onto the floor, blinded by the liquor. I could hear Arthur and Mr. Carter struggle on the couch while I tried to crawl away.

"Help! Please help! Mrs. Poulson! Byron! Alice!" I cried out. The tears in my eyes washed away the stinging liquid.

Doors slammed and voices shouted while the fight continued. They grunted and swore and scuffled for control of the pistol. I backed away and ran to grab the fireplace poker.

I heard a solid punch and turned to face them with my weapon. Mr. Carter had gained the upper hand. Arthur had taken a hit and staggered. Mr. Carter wiped his eyes and found where I was standing.

He raised the gun and pointed it at me.

As he raised his pistol, I heard Arthur roar. His body plowed into me from the side. I fell hard with his form covering mine, hitting my head on the floor. My ears were ringing from the gunshot. Stars filled my vision. Arthur's weight pinned me down. I felt something hot and wet seep through my clothes.

Arthur lifted himself off of me and looked down. Blood covered us both, staining his white shirt and spreading across his chest. It covered my robe and I glanced down to see the hook of the fire poker embedded in my chest.

Arthur's eyes widened. "Joy?"

I gasped with surprise, staring at my injury. I reached up to touch it, to make sure it had really happened. It didn't seem real. My hand wrapped around the handle of the poker and the pain radiated sharply from my chest. I moaned.

"You bastard!" he roared. I watched him fly across the room and attack Mr. Carter, who was standing motionless with his smoking pistol. He stared at me with wide eyes.

Arthur showed Mr. Carter no mercy. The ferocity of his assault shocked me. He knocked the pistol from Mr. Carter's hand and then landed a fist in his face, followed by another and then another. Mr. Carter stumbled back, bloodied and bruised, but he didn't put up a fight.

The room filled with people and noise. Byron ran to Arthur. Footmen tried to pull Arthur away, shouting and struggling to stop him from pounding Mr. Carter to death.

Mrs. Poulson stood above me. "Oh, Your Grace," she moaned, the blood draining from her face when she took in my injury.

"Please, Mrs. Poulson." I reached for her hand. My hand shook as she took it in both of hers. Her grasp was warm and soothing. My own fingers were icicles.

"Please, send for the surgeon." I was amazed I could speak so clearly when my body began to shudder. I should be crying or screaming. Instead, I felt strangely detached from it all.

She gave my hand a squeeze and disappeared from my vision.

"Mrs. Marco!" Alice collapsed next to me, her face pale. "Don't move. Stay still," she commanded, pulling her robe off and wrapping it around the hook to stabilize it. She stroked my hair calmly and held my hand. "What happened?"

"Where's Arthur? Mr. Carter?" My voice trembled and my body shuddered harder.

"He's safe. Byron has him, and Mr. Carter is being taken out. Someone has gone for the authorities." She caressed my face. "Just lie still."

"I think...I think Arthur has been shot. He was trying to stop Mr. Carter from killing me." My arms and legs were jumping by themselves. I tried to get them to behave to no avail.

"Joy!" Arthur's voice preceded his face. He knelt next to me and took my hand from Alice. He was covered in blood and the stain on his shirt continued to spread.

"You're hurt." My teeth started to chatter.

"Get some blankets," he ordered Alice and kissed my fingers. "The surgeon is coming. Just stay quiet."

"But you're hurt!" I raised my voice. "He shot you." I felt a tear prick my eye.

"Just a scratch," he assured me. "I'll have Byron clean it up and bandage it after you are cared for." He kissed my fingers again, holding them against his lips. "You need to lay still."

Alice returned with blankets, and she and Arthur covered me with them. My eyes stared at his shirt, watching the stain bloom. It was worse than what he was telling me. There was too much blood to be a simple scratch.

"Look at my face, Joy," he ordered. He tipped my chin up to force me to look into his eyes. I met his gaze.

"That's more than a scratch." I tried again weakly.

"You need to relax. I'm fine. Just be still." He stroked my cheek as the pain started to radiate from my wound to the rest of my body.

I reached up and held his hand, keeping my face focused on his. "I missed you."

"I missed you too. I should have been home earlier. I should have... dammit. I was delayed. I'm certain Carter had something to do with it."

"He said he loved Diana..." I suddenly found it hard to focus on his face. His features were becoming foggy.

"He did, and she loved him. It was a giant mess. Stay with me, Joy." He tapped my cheek lightly. "Keep talking."

"He hates you. He's sure you killed her." My limbs had stopped leaping about and my eyes were having a hard time staying open. I was suddenly weary, the pain in my chest becoming dull instead of sharp.

"I didn't kill her. I was seeking an annulment so they could be together. It was sure to be a phenomenal scandal, but I didn't care. I tried to help them. Eyes open, Joy!" He spoke sharply.

PART 2 - THE FARCE

I opened my eyes wider, taking in his concerned look. I focused on his shirt. The blood was soaking through his waistcoat now. I glanced over at Alice who was at my other side, stroking my shoulder and arm. "Alice, Mr. Marco is hurt."

"Joy, you are like a terrier with a dead rat!" he snapped.

"Please, dear Joy, just stay still." Alice's voice shook. She looked up at Arthur. "I promise I'll look after His Grace after the surgeon arrives to care for you."

"There, you see! You've got another nagging female attached to my simple scratch. Will you stop worrying now?"

"Yes," I moaned.

"Dr. Porter is here," Byron announced, in the most informal voice I'd ever heard him speak.

Another face swam into view. A bald man with lines and wrinkles all over his face knelt beside me. His eyes were kind and clear as he pushed Arthur out of the way.

"Let's see what we have here." He pulled away the blankets and Alice's blood-soaked robe.

"Nasty piece of business." He grimaced. "Let's move this into the dining room. Get all the light you can there, with blankets and rags. Boiling water and I'm sure you have an excellent selection of brandy to supply as well. Grab her legs, let's keep her as straight as possible." Strong arms lifted me and I whimpered. My grip was still fastened hard around the poker.

I moaned when they set me down. Arthur was directing servants with the doctor's orders while Mrs. Poulson cleared things from the table and chairs.

"Your Grace, you are going to have to release the poker for me to take it out." Dr. Porter calmly reached for my hands. He peeled my fingers away and had Alice take one hand. The other he tucked into his own, taking my pulse.

I trembled and shook. "I'm...so...cold..." I managed, my teeth chattering.

"I think we had better get you more relaxed. Just let me get my bag and we'll get you more comfortable. Ironwood!" he called out softly and transferred my grip into Arthur's. "I'm going to put her to sleep as much as I can." He left my field of vision.

Arthur leaned over me and kissed my forehead. "Just relax, Joy. Everything will be fine. You'll patch right up, I'm sure of it." He stroked my face gently, then froze, looking at the blood on his fingers.

"Your blood or mine?" I tried again. He glared at me.

Dr. Porter's voice interrupted. "Drink this." He tipped a bitter liquid into my mouth. I coughed and sputtered and he poured more between my lips until I had swallowed a sufficient amount.

I shivered and clung to Arthur's hand. I watched Alice waver. "She should leave." I released her from my grasp. "Alice, go."

Alice's eyes narrowed. "I'll stay." She firmly took my hand again. "I'll just keep my eyes on your face," she promised.

The room spun and I wavered between pain-filled consciousness and a drug-induced dizziness. Blurry forms moved around me as things clattered and moved into different positions. I heard Dr. Porter giving directions, his words melting into a buzzing murmur. I felt pressure on my limbs, hands holding me down. Faces peered down at me, with wide eyes and scowls, muttering things I couldn't understand. There was a searing fire in my chest when the doctor pulled out the poker. It caught on my ribcage, ripping and tearing. I screamed and felt strong arms struggling to pin me down while I thrashed to get away. I heard Alice sobbing and Arthur cursing. I felt Arthur's forehead press against mine and inhaled his scent, his familiar cologne mingled with sweat and horse.

"Please, Joy, just hold still," he begged, his own voice wavering. The shapes around me became darker and darker, voices grew quieter and quieter. And then there was blissfully nothing.

PART 2 - THE FARCE

CHAPTER 19

It's a coincidence. It has to be.
London is safe. It couldn't attack her here.
Could it?

When the world began to take shape once more, I felt the pain return, but it was dull and not unbearable. Faces were still shrouded in darkness and voices muttered strange things around me. The little amount of light in the room wouldn't hold still. It raced around trying to banish the shadows with no luck. A face neared mine… it was Dibble! I whimpered and tried to squirm away. He came closer and morphed into Mr. Carter. I screamed and tried to run, feeling my limbs being restrained. I heard voices cry out, shouting and cursing along with… growling? I heard Arthur sharply order silence. I was weeping when I felt his arm across my neck, cradling my head in his embrace. I begged him to save me. He pressed his lips to my temple and whispered in my ear. "It's the fever, Joy. Please relax and let the doctor examine you. I'm right here. No one will hurt you," he promised, running his fingers through my curls.

I inhaled his scent again, clean now, his favorite cologne mixed with the flavor that was completely him. I relaxed and took deep breaths of him while he murmured words to me that still didn't make much sense, but his voice was deep and warm and his hand stroked my cheek. I was safe.

With a shudder, I let the shadows move around me without trying to follow them. It was easier to close my eyes and let them do what they wanted. Dibble wasn't coming to choke the life out of me. Mr. Carter wasn't seeking his revenge in my death. Arthur had me.

"You need to drink this, my Joy." He lifted me carefully up a few inches. I tasted the bitterness of laudanum and other medical remedies on my tongue. My throat was parched and I was happy to swallow them down. Things were a muddle but one thing was still clear in my mind. Arthur had also been wounded. I stiffened and tried to look at him, my sight was blurry as I tried to open my eyes wide enough to see.

"Your chest…" I mumbled.

"Damnation, Joy! You have a bigger hole in your chest than I do."

I heard Alice's voice at my side, soft and insistent, her light hand rested on my arm. "He's fine, Mrs. Marco. He's fine. I saw him get patched up. It was just a scratch," she promised me.

I nodded, finding it made the world spin even more.

"Back to sleep, harridan." Arthur's lips rested against my ear again. "It's the best thing for you."

I didn't have the strength to argue.

The next time I was coherent it was daylight. The drapes muted the light, but it was still warm and soft. I wanted to feel the heat of it on my face. I managed to move a little and heard a soft rustle at the foot of my bed. I tried to sit up, but the pain stopped me short.

I gave a little grunt and I tried to push myself up to see the damage. My vision was then filled with a furry spaniel who insisted on exuberantly licking my face. I managed a smile for my favorite canine. "Hello, Pip." I lifted a weak hand and placed it on his head. He ceased bathing my face and plopped down beside me, ramming his head and body under my arm before settling there with a content sigh.

I managed to stroke his ears between my fingers. "What's happened?" My mind was still foggy with laudanum. I was thirsty and a bit hungry. He rubbed his head against my fingers and lay still again.

"Have they all abandoned me?" I asked. "Given me up for dead?"

"Don't be ridiculous." Arthur's voice came from the doorway. "I leave for one moment and that's when you decide to wake up." He made his way across the room in quick long strides and sat next to me, taking my fingers off Pip and into his own warm grasp. "Are you in pain?"

"Only when I move. I'm thirsty and hungry," I said with a scratchy voice.

He brought more pillows and propped me up carefully, then helped me sip some cool water. I managed to look down my nightgown and see the lump of bandages piled between my breasts.

PART 2 - THE FARCE

"How bad was it?" I asked. He rang, for a servant then returned to my side.

"The wound was deep, into the bone. But it kept the important bits inside from getting hurt. The infection afterward was the worst." There were dark circles under his eyes. His cheeks were pale and his face scruffy.

I ran my fingers lightly over the long whiskers that covered his neck. "You haven't shaved."

"I haven't had a proper scrape since I've been home. There were other pressing things to attend to." He captured my fingers and kissed them.

Mrs. Poulson appeared and he asked for tea and broth. She disappeared and Arthur focused on me again.

"Carter?" I asked.

"Hanged. He pled guilty and walked to the gallows like he was some kind of martyr."

I flinched and felt tears come to my eyes. Even after the whole ordeal, I felt pity for him. "Arthur..."

"Don't cry over him, Joy. He's not worth it."

"He loved Diana."

"He tried to kill you. I let him into our home and he was a serpent waiting to strike. He gets no pity." Arthur's hand cupped my face softly and wiped the tears away. "No tears for him. I just want to know what he did to you. He wouldn't confess to anything."

The anxious look in his eyes softened when I shook my head. "Nothing. He didn't hurt me. It was so odd. He showered me with physical affection while he calmly told me he was going to kill me." I shivered a little at the memory.

Arthur stroked my cheek. "What other venom did the serpent say?" he pressed softly.

"That you killed Diana, poisoned her to avoid a scandal because you were a cuckold."

He shook his head. "I was seeking an annulment, nothing more or less. I sent her away to avoid the scandal while I worked things out so they could be together." He then gave a short snort. "If you need proof, I'll have my solicitor tell you how he pleaded with me not to seek an annulment on the grounds I was impotent."

"Impotent!" I tried not to laugh, it hurt too much.

"Well, yes, we both know that's not true, now don't we." He grinned at me and I gave a short laugh that stopped when my chest protested the motion and turned into a groan instead.

"You need to rest and get better."

"What does that entail?" I grimaced when I shifted my weight to a more comfortable position. "No more laudanum," I added when he saw me wince.

He smiled. "There's my girl. You eat and drink and I'll send for the doctor. Now that the fever's gone I can hire a nurse instead of taking on the job myself. You threw quite a fit if anyone else touched you. Pip even bit Dr. Porter once when he was cleaning your wound and you started to cry. Now we have to lock him in the kitchen when the good doctor walks in the door." He gave the spaniel a glare. Pip stared back without remorse.

"My little champion," I praised and stroked his head. He settled in closer to me.

"Little monster," Arthur retorted. The food and drink arrived and Arthur settled in to help me manage it. I insisted on lifting the cup myself. He looked like he wanted to protest, but allowed it.

"You should hear the rumors flying now, Madame Wife." He mentioned as I sipped the warm broth.

"I shudder to think of them." I reclined back on the bed. The simple task of drinking was exhausting. "What new scandal have they come up with now?"

He tenderly brushed my hair away from my mouth and lifted the cup again to my lips. "The most newsworthy has been that after a week of never leaving her bedside and acting as her personal nursemaid, Arthur Marco must truly love his wife."

"Idiots. I could have told them that." I scoffed before I took another drink.

***

Shortly thereafter my mother descended on the house like a tyrant.

She hadn't even removed her bonnet before she was in my room. A simple look from her had Pip hanging his head and he slunk off to hide under the bed.

"Byron, is it?" she asked in clipped tones. She removed her gloves and bonnet and handed them to him.

"Yes, ma'am." Our broad-shouldered and scarred servant shrank in her presence like a small boy.

"I want the door knocker removed at once, and the bells silenced in the entire house as well. I need to see the housekeeper here now."

Byron was more than happy to disappear.

Mother sat next to me, brushing a hand on my forehead. I inhaled her clean scent and sighed. I felt a thousand times better already.

"My dear girl. I had to come. Arthur may be a wonderful husband, but he's still a thoughtless male."

I laughed and flinched.

"Still hurts? Let me guess, you refuse anything for the pain."

I nodded.

"Always a stubborn little lamb. Lay back and relax. I'll take care of things." she promised, laying a kiss on my head.

"Mother Horton! This is a surprise." Arthur entered the room cheerfully with Mrs. Poulson.

A look from her immediately silenced him. "I am not happy with what I have found. Bells going off so she can't rest. You haven't even darkened the windows to muffle the sounds outside. And when is the last time she had a bath?"

Arthur blinked. The silence in the room was thick.

"I think I'll go hide with Pip under the bed." He turned to leave.

"You aren't going anywhere," Mother said sharply and he stopped midstride. She pulled a list from her reticule and handed it to Mrs. Poulson. "Please have the kitchen prepare these for me. Then find me some thick fabric to cover the windows," she commanded. Mrs. Poulson took the list and slipped out.

The nurse had been sitting quietly in the corner this whole time. She cleared her throat with hesitation and asked quietly, "Am I being dismissed?"

Mother gave her a predatory smile. "Oh no, I have quite a few things for you to do. Your presence will definitely be needed." The little nurse looked slightly relieved at keeping her employment.

"And as for you, my son." She took a deep breath and walked to Arthur. She embraced him calmly. "Now that you have borne the brunt of the frustrations that I've carried through the countryside, I'll thank you for being patient with me. I get quite passionate about my children."

"Now I know where *she* gets it from…" Arthur nodded towards me, then returned her embrace. "If you can get my Joy back to her passionate state as well, I'll be glad you intervened."

Mother proceeded with her plan for my recovery. She and the nurse bathed me, careful of my stitches. Having clean skin and hair made me feel like I was finally, truly, on the mend. I was tucked back into clean sheets and presented with a meal of beef and potatoes and cream which my stomach was happy to consume with no ill effects.

Mother was on hand when Dr. Porter arrived. Pip growled from under the bed and was silenced when Mother snapped her fingers at him. He didn't come out from his hiding place but gave an indignant doggy huff.

"Dr. Porter. I have been anxious to meet you," Mother said with a smile. She took his measure like a cat about to devour its prey.

"Mrs. Horton," Dr. Porter greeted. "The pleasure is all mine."

"Oh, I doubt it will be for long. Because I promise you now, Dr. Porter, if my daughter so much as flinches during your examination I will flay you alive."

The doctor gaped. He started to stutter a response when she cut him off.

"I have no doubt you are a brilliant surgeon, and you saved my daughter's life," Mother continued. "And I will be eternally grateful to you. I also have no doubt you are used to treating soldiers and rough men, and Joy told me your bedside manner reflects it. So, gently, if you please." She motioned to me.

His touch was much more tender than it had been. "All looks well. I'll be back in a couple of days to take out the stitches." He closed my gown and gave me a gentle pat on the head. "I'll go inform your husband."

Mother watched him leave and smiled down at me. "Get some sleep," she commanded softly.

I lay back and felt the weariness overtake me. My eyes shut and I heard her dowse all lights and exit the room with the nurse.

Sometimes one just needs their mother.

PART 2 - THE FARCE

CHAPTER 20

She is recovering slowly. Too slowly. I want to crush her to me, to whisk her away somewhere safe.

I want to smother her with kisses and assure myself she is real.

I want too much.

It was a dream. I *knew* it was a dream. But it didn't stop the fear overtaking me, it didn't stop a cold sweat covering my entire body as I ran for my life.

I was in my nightgown, barefoot, and running in the dark. Sticks and thorns pierced my feet. I stumbled and raced for safety. I kept running into the rose hedge outside Lowell's house. No matter where I turned, or how fast I ran from it, it always appeared ahead of me. I heard Dibble's voice in the dark, taunting me while he crashed through the woods. He promised me death and pain.

I ran away from the rose hedge and into the strong arms of another man. For a brief moment, I thought it was Arthur's embrace and relaxed until I looked up into the face of Carter. He smiled at me and held me close like I was a lover, even while I railed against him to escape. No matter how hard I hit, no matter where I hit, he never let go.

"I've got her!" he announced loudly, caressing my face with the barrel of a pistol.

Dibble's hands wrapped around my throat, squeezing hard. Carter brought the pistol up to my forehead.

"Shall we see who wins? I'll give you to the count of ten, Dibble, then I take my turn."

I gagged and struggled between them.

"One..."

The hands tightened. My eyes bulged with the pressure.

"Two..."

I started to cry. I couldn't fight them both.

"Three..."

I heard whining and then barking, right next to my ear.

"Pip?"

My eyes opened and Pip was next to me, barking, whining, licking. My heart was still pounding as he burrowed into my side.

"I'm awake, boy. I'm awake," I reassured him, bringing my hands to my throat and taking a deep breath.

Unsatisfied, he plopped down on my sore chest and huffed in my face. I reached up and pet him. His weight calmed me, the feel of his fur a comfort. I forced myself to breathe slowly. He muttered something in his doggy language and rested his head down on me.

I heard the door open and Alice softly called, "Pip! Don't wake her!"

I rested my hand on his head. "I'm awake, Alice. I was having a nightmare and he woke me from it."

Alice entered the room and opened the darkened curtain to let a little more light in. She took one look at me and frowned. "You're covered in sweat."

"It was not a pleasant dream." I tried to put the images from my mind.

"Get off her, Pip." Alice pushed him off my chest. He grumbled, turned in a circle, and then took his place at my side.

"Let me get you some water." She helped me sit up a bit. I let her help, feeling more exhausted now than when I had first fallen asleep.

I wiped the tears and dog licks from my face as she brought me a cup. I trembled while I drank.

"Thank you, Alice. Where's Mother?"

"Sleeping, although it took a great deal of persuasion to get her there. Mr. Marco threatened to lock her in her room if she didn't rest."

I managed a small smile. "I'm sorry I missed that discussion." My hands still shook. I rested them on Pip and absorbed his warmth. "Will you stay, please. And read to me? I don't want to be alone," I admitted.

Alice took my cup and nodded. "I'll need a little more light, though." She stood up and opened another curtain. "What do you want me to read?"

"Anything." My voice was weary. "I just want to hear your voice while I sleep."

"I have a horrid gothic novel I've been reading before bed," she admitted with a grin of mischief.

I loved her ridiculous taste in books. "Perfect."

Alice's reading while I slept became somewhat of a routine over the next week. My stitches were removed, the nurse dismissed, and the doctor stopped visiting after reminding me I needed to rest and eat. I was agreeable to the terms; I just couldn't complete them.

Whenever sleep found me, Carter and Dibble were there waiting.

I could rest with Alice's voice in the background. She took turns with Mother, reading or chatting while working on various projects. If I could hear them, I could sleep somewhat shallowly on the edge of consciousness.

But even they had to rest.

And the nights were long when I was alone.

I tried to keep Pip with me, which brought a scowl and a finger snap from Mother.

"He barks every time you stir, Joy. He's not helping you rest." She wasn't entirely wrong. He was so loud when chasing my nightmares, getting back to sleep was impossible.

Ever since Mother had arrived Arthur's visits had become twice a day. He'd kiss my forehead good morning and bring me tea, then disappear. He'd appear in the evening and ask about my well-being, kiss my cheek chastely, and disappear again as quickly as he could.

I was going to put a stop to it.

I entered his study quietly. The house was quiet, all the servants in bed. But I was done with bed. I'd recovered as much as I could and it wasn't enough. My face was still pale. Sleep was elusive, full of nightmares and fear that left me even more exhausted than being awake.

Arthur was sitting at his desk, poring over some work. He was in shirtsleeves with his waistcoat unbuttoned, his idea of working comfortably. I watched him, his gaze going back and forth from ledgers to letters. He looked like my Arthur, the rash and clever man I had married, but he didn't act like him. He was becoming withdrawn from me. Ever since my attack and illness, he'd stopped sharing the same room with me. I understood at first, he wanted me to rest, but now his absence was the reason I couldn't sleep. The one person who made me feel the safest was keeping his distance so I could heal. What a pair of idiots we were!

"Arthur."

"Joy! What are you doing up?" He rose to his feet and strode towards me, taking my hands in his. "You should be in bed."

"So should you," I said, nodding at the clock.

"I'm just finishing up a few things and then I was going to retire." He leaned forward and gave me another chaste kiss on my forehead. "Back to bed with you."

I held onto his hands. "Come to bed with me."

He was silent, then reached up one hand to cup my cheek. "I don't know if that's a good idea."

"I want you." I leaned into his hand and closed my eyes at his touch. Safe.

He ran his thumb along my lips slowly. "I want you too. Please get to bed and get better."

I shook my head. "I can't sleep. I try but...I have nightmares."

"My dear girl." He gathered me close, rubbing my back. "Carter?"

"And Dibble," I added.

I rested my head against his chest and inhaled his scent, feeling myself relax when I wrapped my arms around him. "Please, let me sleep with you tonight."

"I won't let you rest. I want you so badly it's unhealthy."

"Is that why you've been avoiding me?" I rubbed my face against his shirt.

"You've noticed. I'm certain I'll make things worse if I take you to bed." He sighed, embracing me tighter and then releasing me abruptly, dropping his arms like I was aflame. "I will hold you firmly to me when you are healed," he promised. "Go back to bed."

I didn't let go, resting my head on his chest and shoulder. "I won't break."

"You might. I've seen you damaged twice now, and it's a sight I never want to see again." He tried to pull my arms off him. I held firm, even as my strength waned and he peeled me away from him.

He held my wrists in his hands, gently pushing me away. Enough! I'd had enough of what everyone else thought was good for me. I knew what I needed, and only he could provide it. "Arthur. I want you to take me to bed and love me," I commanded him.

Part 2 - The Farce

I felt him stiffen. I could almost hear the argument he had with himself in his head. I knew the second he lost. His arms surrounded me and his lips possessed mine, holding me and supporting my weight. He kissed me breathless, with all the feelings he was holding back for my sake. I think he meant to scare me with his ardor. I kissed him back, meeting his every move with one of my own, feeling his grasp becoming tighter as I showed him physically I was up to whatever he wanted. He cried out and pulled back, looking down into my face with a scowl. "Go to bed now!"

"I will as soon as you take me there," I responded in the same tone.

He snapped.

I was in his arms, being carried into our room, and he locked the door behind us.

He loved me over and over, sometimes holding me so tightly I could feel my bones creak. I enjoyed every moment of it, digging my fingers into his skin to match his fervor. I heard him whisper things to the air, promises that made no sense as he clasped me to him and we worked ourselves into one.

"Not this one..."

"I need her so much..."

"I'll give up everything..."

Every time I tried to question him, he'd stop me with kisses until I begged for more.

I collapsed on his chest, finding my familiar niche there between his shoulder and ribs where my head fit perfectly. I stroked his skin softly, feeling whole once more. His arms came naturally around me, his lips against my head.

"I think I can sleep now." I yawned, nestling down into his embrace and closing my eyes.

"I did my best to make you weary."

I relaxed, feeling the nightmares running from our presence. I was drowsy and could barely hold onto consciousness while he stroked my skin.

"Go to sleep, we'll discuss your sleep therapy in the morning." I gladly obliged, closing my eyes and surrendering to the rest I needed.

I'd like to say it was a peaceful night of blissful sleep, and for the most part, it was. Whenever Dibble appeared, I'd try to run from him, and hear Arthur's voice speaking calmly to me, "It's not real, Joy. You're safe in bed with me." The villain would disappear and I'd fall deeper into sleep.

Carter appeared only once, holding me to him in a deathly embrace until I felt Arthur's beard rub against my skin. I sighed and relaxed in the arms of my husband as he kissed my face. "Go back to sleep, Joy. I've got you."

So I did, back to oblivion where I could finally rest my body and mind.

I awoke feeling stronger, wrapped up against Arthur's chest. He snored in my ear and I smiled at the familiar feeling and sounds of waking next to my husband. This was what I needed most of all.

I turned in his embrace and he rolled onto his back so I could rest on his chest. I ran my hands along his skin lightly until they ran across a new scar. The one Carter had given him.

I sat up immediately and examined him in the morning light. He cracked one eye open to see what I was doing and sighed loudly. "Honestly, woman. You are becoming tiresome."

"Hush." I pinched his lips shut. I looked at the pink flesh. It was a round scar, the size of my thumbnail.

"You were shot." I didn't give him a chance to deny it.

"Yes, I was shot. It was slowed through my clothes and embedded itself right there in my skin…what are you doing now?"

I rolled him over to look at his back, to see if there was an exit wound. It was smooth and clear.

I pushed him back down onto the bed and peered into his face. "That doesn't make sense," I remembered the blood seeping through his clothes. There had been too much of it to be such a simple wound. "You were bleeding badly."

He shrugged. "What can I say? It's a miracle." He pulled me back down onto him, his arms holding me tightly as he kissed me. He rolled me onto my back and lightly touched the pink scar on my chest. "Now, permit me to examine you as well."

It was only fair.

PART 2 - THE FARCE

CHAPTER 21

Ironwood has been robbed! IT'S MISSING!
I have to find it! What new plan of death is it trying now?

Arthur's warm hand was in the small of my back as he ushered me back into the house after our morning curricle ride. He still wouldn't let me ride Toady, and our morning drives were more sedate than usual, but I enjoyed the sunshine and air. After three weeks of reclaiming my place at Arthur's side, I was almost completely recovered. My cheeks were nicely filled out and the shadows were gone from my eyes. I tired easily, but was finding more energy day by day.

"Your mother is still planning on leaving today?" he asked. Byron and Mrs. Poulson appeared to take our gloves and Arthur's hat and walking stick.

I nodded. "I told her she could take a carriage, but she still refuses. She doesn't want to be a burden."

He rolled his eyes so much like Mother I gave him a playful shove while we walked to breakfast. Alice and Mother were both at the table eating while Pip was under the table looking for crumbs.

"Ready to leave off with the London heat, Mother Horton?" Arthur sat down.

"Yes, I don't know how you can abide it," she said, fan in hand. "I might come back for a visit in the spring when you return for the Season. Where are you going after Parliament lets out in two weeks?" I was also happy to see our stay in London coming to an end. It had been a time I wouldn't soon forget.

Arthur shrugged. "My wife hasn't told me yet."

"Your wife hasn't been given any options yet," I objected.

"That's easy. Simply pull out a map, tell me where you want to go and we'll go there."

"What if you don't have a house there?" I asked.

"I'll buy one."

I shook my head. "Don't be ridiculous. I would rather you buy another orphanage or soldier's hospital. Just tell me where your holdings are and we'll pick one."

"I'll have Mrs. Poulson bring you a list later."

The list Mrs. Poulson presented me with was lengthy.

Alice perused it with Mother, both of their eyes wide.

"I don't think he would need to buy a new house. He appears to have a residence in almost every county. Even Scotland and Wales." Mother shook her head. "Your husband truly has the Midas touch. Your father told me he's never lost an investment and his holdings do well. He simply can't fail."

Good. There was another workhouse I knew of that needed updating and uplifting.

"Yes, but one seems to be missing." Alice's eyes flitted along the list. "He is the Duke of Ironwood, but I don't see it here."

"Ironwood? Where's that at?"

"Norfolk, on the coast." She lowered the list. "I wonder why it's missing. I've heard it's beautiful there. My grandmother used to tell me stories of the parties that went on when Sophie was mistress."

"Maybe he just assumed I already knew about it." I shrugged. I laid a hand on my stomach as it began to churn. Breakfast was not settling well with me.

"That's probably why. Do you want me to read the whole list to you?" Alice asked.

"Not without a map." I sank back into my seat and took a few deep breaths. Nausea started to take hold of me. "Which is closest to you and Father?" I asked Mother.

"Ironwood isn't too far. It's right on the coast. I know you love the water, Joy. It would be just the thing to help you regain your strength." She gave me a concerned look. "Are you feeling ill?"

I waved her off and took a deep, calming breath. "Too many scones at breakfast."

PART 2 - THE FARCE

Byron then appeared in the doorway and made his way to us. "Apologies, Madame. This just came from Parliament." He handed a note to Alice with a bow.

"Thank you." I took another deep breath to ward off increasing nausea.

Alice opened it and read immediately. I always appreciated that about her, she never scanned a letter before reading it to me, she just jumped in so we would each receive the news at the same time.

"Dearest Joy, I've been called away to take care of an urgent matter. I'm not certain of how long it will take me, perhaps weeks, but I will return as soon as possible. Yours, Arthur."

I sat in stunned silence. "That's it?" Alice nodded, flipping the paper over to double-check if there was something additional written.

"What does he mean by that? Is someone dead or dying? Where is he going?" I demanded of her, sitting up straight. My head protested the quick motion with another bout of nausea.

She shrugged and handed me the note, not that it would do any good. Even I could see it was a single line of correspondence followed by his familiar signature.

"And I'm supposed to wait behind like a good little wife and not worry?" I plotted a slow and intricate torture for him. What would make him act like this?

"Calm down, dear heart." Mother tried to soothe me, taking the note and squeezing my hand. "You're looking a little green."

It was just like Arthur to take off on a rash expedition without a thought about the consequences. "If he thinks I'm just going to sit here and do nothing, he had better think again." My belly was rolling now, I took a deep breath to keep the scones in place.

"Joy, dear. He probably thinks he's helping you by not upsetting you with details." Mother said.

"If Father had taken off for parts unknown and left you with a vague note you would be furious," I pointed out, taking the note and shaking it at her. "And it obviously didn't work, because I *am* upset!"

I stood up to call for the carriage. Sickness rushed upon me before I could speak a word and the extra scones came back to haunt me and the new carpet.

Mother pushed me back onto the couch and rubbed my back as I moaned. She pulled my hair back from my face. Alice raced to help, throwing an empty vase in my lap to empty the rest of my stomach. Mother pushed my now sweaty hair back from my face. "So much for going home today. I think you need me a bit longer."

All I could do was groan. I had been doing so well!

Dr. Porter was called for and I was bundled back into the bedroom. Mother conferred with him before his examination, and he confirmed her suspicions.

"You are increasing," he informed me, giving me a gentle pat on the shoulder before he left. "Tea and toast before any activity and you should be fine. Your mother will be a better source of information than I."

I sat in silence, trying to gather my thoughts. I was going to have a baby. Arthur and I were going to have a baby! And he wasn't here to celebrate with me, to share this moment with me. I was an equal mix of ecstatic and furious.

"I am so angry with him," I shouted once Dr. Porter shut the door. I threw off my blankets to re-dress. I was going to hunt him down.

"Call for Byron. I'm sure he knows something." I growled as I became entangled in my dress. Mother straightened it out and pushed me into a chair.

"Tea and toast first," she insisted. "You'll need strength for your battle."

I grumbled but agreed. Byron appeared shortly with the tea and toast. He swore to me by all his scars he didn't know where my husband was. He'd received no instructions to forward any clothing or supplies to my errant husband's unknown location.

"Sophie's next." I grabbed my gloves and called for the carriage.

Sophie rose when we came into her sitting room, looking tall and regal and calm, as usual. She took my hands and kissed my cheeks. "Dear Joy! You are positively flushed. Sit down and I'll call for refreshment." She placed me on a couch and motioned for Mother and Alice to sit.

"Where is your son?" I demanded.

"My son?" She looked confused before her eyes cleared. "Arthur? He's not at Parliament?"

I handed her his note and she read it quickly. "Oh dear," she sighed.

"What is it?" I demanded. "Do you know where he is?" My stomach dropped as I finally gave voice to a fear I had thought so ridiculous at first I refused to entertain the notion. "Is there another woman?"

PART 2 - THE FARCE

"Another...no. No, no of course not!" Sophie took my hands in hers. "Arthur loves you more than anything in this world. If he's run off it's for your benefit, I'm sure." She squeezed my fingers tightly.

"Then where would he go and not tell me?" I slumped into the couch. "And why?"

"I'll bet he's gone to Ironwood," she said instantly. "That's the only place that would take him from you like this without an explanation. Rest assured; he'll be back before you know it."

"What's at Ironwood that would take him off in such a hurry?"

Sophie hesitated. Her brain worked in the same way Arthur's did, forming and plotting before she spoke.

"I'm sure it's probably something to do with Diana and all this unpleasantness with Mr. Carter," she said at last. "He wouldn't want to upset you further."

"Well, he's failed on that account." I smirked as an idea came to me, he wasn't the only one who could make rash decisions. "We'll pack up the house and join him there."

Sophie's face drained of all color. She was a large and vibrant woman, bigger than life at times. To see her shrink in fear made my heart skip a beat. Her hands gripped me tightly, almost to the point of pain. "No! No, you cannot go to Ironwood." The desperation in her voice caught me off guard.

"Sophie? What's wrong?" I asked as Mother and Alice came to provide support.

"You cannot go there," Sophie whispered. "Please Joy, promise me."

"You're scaring me, whatever is wrong with Ironwood?" I asked. Mother fanned her and Alice poured her a cup of tea.

Sophie's mouth gaped as she sought the words. "It's haunted."

Alice gasped, Mother stopped fanning, and I drew back with disbelief. "Surely you aren't serious."

Sophie nodded. "Please, dear Joy, he can't lose you too."

Her words mirrored those Arthur had spoken to me in his passion. What was going on? Was Ironwood really dangerous? "Lose me? Sophie what...is Arthur in trouble?" I demanded.

She shook her head, trying to smile, to calm me down. "No Arthur will be fine. The spirits are only hostile to Marco brides."

"But you threw such big parties there!" Alice protested. "My grandmother would tell tales of your Twelfth Night festivities for days. She never mentioned a word about ghosts."

Sophie glanced at her. "I wasn't a Marco bride. I was an heiress, a full-blooded Marco. My husband took my name..." her words trailed off and so did her gaze. I was starting to wonder if this wasn't a fantastical tale. Sophie wasn't young by any means. Was her mind slipping?

I slumped back and released her. "This is an incredible story, Sophie. I cannot believe it." I didn't believe it. A haunted house whose specters only attacked women married to a Marco?

Sophie shook her head to refocus. "We don't speak of it. Had Arthur and I known Diana was going there instead of to her parents..." She bit her lip and took her tea from Alice. Uncomfortable silence settled over us.

"Are you saying the ghosts at Ironwood…killed Diana?" This really was getting farfetched. Mother wore the same bewildered face I did. Alice gazed on in amazement.

Sophie sipped her tea and shook her head. "Ghosts killed Diana? What nonsense." She set her tea down. "She was sick. That's all there is to it." She wrung her hands in her lap. "It's that nasty Carter who kept digging and digging into things, stirring things up that should be left to rest."

She was making even less sense than before. My head hurt with all the thoughts bombarding me and my stomach churned again. I needed a nap and a conversation with my favorite spaniel to make sense of everything.

"Thank you for supplying me with a guess on Arthur's whereabouts, dearest. We'll leave you now." I leaned forward to press a kiss to her soft wrinkled cheek.

She kissed me back. "Don't worry. Arthur can take care of himself. You just stay safely here in London and everything will be fine. You'll see."

Mother took my arm as we waited for Neville to assist us into the carriage and muttered. "That was the strangest conversation I've ever been a part of."

"Do you think Arthur…?" I trailed off. There were so many endings to that sentence, each one I didn't want to voice. I rested my head on Mother's shoulder as we made our way back to the house. So many questions rammed together in my brain that didn't make sense. Diana and Carter at Ironwood? Ghosts?

The only thing I could grasp onto was the answers would be at Ironwood. And I would go there to find them.

PART 3
THE CURSE

PART 3 - THE CURSE

CHAPTER 22

I hate this place. I hate it down to the marrow in my bones.
I need to find it. I need to get back to Joy.

Pip and I had our heads out the carriage window when we came onto the Ironwood estate. After three days of travel, he wanted a good run and I wanted to stop moving so my stomach would hopefully settle.

"It's so beautiful," Alice sighed as we rolled through the gates.

It truly was. The land was green and smelled of sheep and mowed hay, and it smelled like home.

The houses were in good repair and the road was smooth and level. The landscape erupted in trees and flowers and color. I inhaled the familiar scents deeply when Ironwood came into view.

Ironwood was a mismatched house of history. I could see where one ancient ancestor had built a home, and then the next generation had added, then the next, and the next. The smashing contrast of different architecture from different eras became a beautiful hodgepodge of history and stories to be discovered.

I loved it immediately.

Arthur stood at the door with an army of servants. I'd sent Byron ahead that morning to let him know I was coming. I was certain if I'd given him any more warning he would find a way to send me home.

He was at the carriage door when it came to a stop. He opened the door and reached for my hand. I accepted his help and reached out for the door handle to steady me.

"I missed you," he growled in my ear.

"I missed you," I said back softly, finding I truly meant it. My fears and suspicions melted in his presence, even if I was still put out with him.

One of us had to bend a little, so I smiled up at him and saw his eyes soften when my feet touched the ground. At least, they appeared to touch the ground. I did not feel it. All I felt were sharp little pins that pierced my feet and legs when they straightened from their long trip. I saw his look of alarm when my legs crumpled.

"Oh dear." I had a brief moment of confusion, my vision narrowing to only the buttons of his waistcoat. I heard the chattering and bustle of the servants while Arthur shouted. I was pressed firmly into his chest and his arms tightened around me. Then I was swept up into his embrace and being rushed towards the door.

"Out of the way!" he bellowed and carried me into the house and sat down with me in the parlor.

Hands loosened my cape and clothes and I tried to push them away. "Please, I am fine."

"Fetch me some brandy!" Arthur barked.

"No, no brandy," I protested and tried to sit up.

His arms held me fast to him. "Sip some brandy. It'll help rouse your blood after such a long trip."

"No, I cannot." I pushed the snifter away. My boots were being pulled off and Alice rubbed my feet.

"My Joy, please," he entreated, taking the glass and pressing it against my lips.

I turned my face away. "I cannot! Mother said drinking spirits was not good for the baby."

The room instantly went silent. All the servants stopped moving and I was fairly certain I felt Arthur's heart skip a beat where my cheek rested against him.

I felt my cheeks blaze and clenched my eyes shut. "I did *not* mean to announce it in such a way." I opened one eye at a time to judge his reaction.

Arthur's eyes were wide with surprise before he began to laugh. He gave out a great and wonderful noise of happiness. It brought me delight.

"No brandy for Her Grace." He passed off the glass to someone and stood with me in his arms.

"Please, I can walk," I protested.

PART 3 - THE CURSE

"That has yet to be seen. I have never seen my fiery wife wilt like a debutante before," Arthur pointed out. "Byron, please be good enough to send for Dr. Grant."

"I sat too long without taking a stretch. Mother warned me my body would do strange things." I wrapped my arms around his neck and happily rested my head against his. Safe.

"Yes, well, your mother is not here. And your husband will take no chances with his precious wife and child." He carried me up the stairs and tucked me carefully into bed to wait for the doctor.

Dr. Grant was a kindly old grandfather who calmed Arthur down by assuring him I was well. He told me to rest in bed for the remainder of the day and he'd be on hand if I had any other needs. He left the room and I was finally left alone with Arthur. Now I wanted answers.

"Now tell me exactly what are you doing here?" I demanded.

"What am I doing here? What are you doing here? This is the last place I wanted you to be."

"What? Why? What are you hiding?" There had to be something, some explanation for the abrupt way he left, some reason I had spent the last few days in a swinging carriage with my head out the window being sick to come to his side.

"Hiding? I'm hiding nothing. It's old and drafty and not the place for you, especially now." He gave a pointed look at my still flat belly.

"It doesn't matter where we are. What matters is you ran away from me without any explanation." I crossed my arms over my chest.

"There wasn't time." He paced and ran his fingers through his long dark hair. "I had to leave at once."

"Yes, I know. I had Byron pack for you. You didn't even take a proper coat or boots." He was working up to something, but I didn't know what. His face was agitated. My heart sank into my stomach.

"Arthur." He stopped and looked at me.

"Is there someone else?" I asked softly, finally getting out the question that had been lurking in the back of my mind.

"What? Is that what...how could you..." He came and knelt next to me, taking my face in his hands. "Is that why you are here, to come and tear me apart over an imaginary woman?"

"No." I suddenly felt warm tears sting my eyes. Where were these emotions coming from? I blamed the baby entirely. "You ran off so quickly.

No one knew where or why. You've never done anything like this before." I wiped my eyes. "What was I supposed to think?"

"You're supposed to trust me." He pulled out a handkerchief.

I took it and wiped my eyes again. "Yes, well, you are supposed to trust me too."

He glared. I glared back. He sighed, caressing my face before he stood up. "Ironwood was robbed."

I slowly nodded. "I see." Not really. What was stolen that was so important he had run off with just the clothes on his back?

"My study was broken into, my safe was torn out of the wall and carried off. A few of the staff were injured. Ironwood is the family seat, it is where I keep all my deeds, titles, and contracts. Paperwork was strewn all over the countryside. It's all a mess now. I had to get here and start cleaning up."

Now it made more sense. "Who was hurt?" I demanded, trying to rise from the bed.

He pushed me back down. "Relax, my little Valkyrie. Dr. Grant has already taken care of things. Everything is back in order and the solicitor is coming from London with copies of my files so I can restore things."

"Was there money in your safe? Jewels?"

He shrugged. "A hundred pounds, some old coins and jewelry pieces that were more for history and sentimental value than monetary worth. If they are smart, they'll sell everything, keep the money, and burn all my papers." He slid next to me in the bed and tucked me up under his arm. "I'm sorry if I worried you."

"You should be," I groused, snuggling closer to him. "I was more upset about being in the dark than anything else."

He stroked my hair. "Do you need to know everything? Am I allowed any secrets?"

"No, you're not."

He chuckled. "Well then. My first confession is we can't stay at Ironwood."

I snorted. I already loved the place. "Yes, we can."

"It's not safe here. It's just been robbed."

"They won't come back, and you can use your vast wealth to hire more security. I'm sure someone needs a job." I brushed it aside.

"It's old and drafty, not a place to have a baby."

"It's vastly better than that monstrosity in London. I'm sure there's a small army of craftsmen I could hire to set all things right."

"Joy. It's not safe here. We need to leave as soon as you are rested."

"Is this about the ghosts?" I looked up at him for a reaction. I wanted to see him laugh it off, to be able to laugh it off together.

It didn't happen. Instead, his eyes widened. "Who told you about ghosts?"

"Sophie. She discouraged me from coming here, saying something about Marco brides being under attack at Ironwood by specters." I watched his face grow solemn. A little sliver of fear crept up my spine.

"I see." He tucked me closer to him. "And if it were true?"

I closed my eyes and rested against him, thinking of the noise and crowds of London, and the peace I already felt at Ironwood. "I've already been attacked twice by the living. I'll take my chances with the dead."

CHAPTER 23

She's here. I don't know how, but she's here. My heart drilled into my stomach when I saw her exit the carriage. I was the one to almost faint until she wilted. My dearest Joy is carrying a child. I've never been so thrilled and so terrified at once.

So completely terrified.

The next morning Ironwood's butler opened the door to the breakfast room and announced in his most regal voice, "You have a visitor, Your Grace. Miss Eva Lowell." His eyes sparkled with mirth and he gave an overdone bow. A child giggled and burst into the room.

"Eva?" I stared as a little blonde hurricane ran to me.

"Ooof!" I gasped when strong little arms embraced me. I hugged her tightly and then pulled her back. It was Eva, but it wasn't. This child had bright eyes and fat pink cheeks, not pale and thin like the Eva Lowell I had known.

I smoothed her hair back from her face, beaming at her. "Look at you. You look wonderful." I gave her another hug.

"I feel well! Dr. Grant said I just needed sea air and lots of food." She did a spin and Alice watched with amusement. "I got the dress you made me! I wore it today."

I laughed and examined the tight seams and shortened sleeves from her growth. "It's a little too small now. I'll have to make you another one. Alice, this is my dear friend Eva Lowell. Eva, this is Lady Alice Graves."

Eva made a proper bow to Alice. She then took a seat next to me and helped herself to a plate as if she had done it a thousand times before.

PART 3 - THE CURSE

I immediately suspected the staff had a great deal to do with her rapid growth.

"I'm so glad you are here." Her mouth was full of toast. "I can't wait to show you everything at Ironwood! Is Pip here?"

At the sound of his name, the lazy spaniel appeared from underneath the table, stretched, and yawned loudly. He took the gleeful greetings from Eva with a great amount of patience and licked the jam from her face.

"He and I had a long trip. And I think he stayed out too late exploring." He huffed and laid at my feet.

"Do you think he'll still want to play with a stick still?"

At the word 'stick', Pip's head rose from the floor and his tail started pounding rapidly.

"I don't think he will ever be able to resist chasing a stick," I said solemnly.

Pip happily chased a stick and a ball for Eva after breakfast. I watched them play while I soaked up some sunshine and inhaled the clean sea air. So much better than London.

I was pleased Eva's cheeks were flushed pink and she was breathing hard but clear. No cough rattled her lungs.

"Do you want to see the hedge maze?" she asked.

"We have a hedge maze?" I answered, rising to my feet. I wanted to see everything Ironwood had to offer. I held out my hand to her.

"It's not really a maze, not anymore," Eva informed me as we entered between two giant hedges. "Just a winding path now. Peter, he's the head gardener, said he was tired of chasing after people who got lost in it. So he left the true path and ripped out all the false trails then 'dared Himself to give me the sack'." She finished in a deep voice.

I laughed and she pulled me along through the winding path. Pip kept pace with us, taking a few moments to sniff out new scents and discoveries.

I inhaled the scents of country air. Sweet hay and grass, the hint of animals, a wisp of summer flowers in the air. It smelled like home. It felt like home. "I never want to leave Ironwood," I announced.

"I don't want you to leave either." I felt Eva's head rest against my arm. "Why would you?"

I snorted. "Apparently, it's haunted."

Eva gasped, her face brimming with excitement. "Really? Haunted?"

"I take it you aren't afraid of ghosts."

She shook her head. "My mother is dead, so she might be a ghost. And I'm not afraid of her."

I smiled at her simple logic. "I'll bet your mother is an angel instead of a ghost."

She frowned. "What's the difference?"

She had a good point. "I guess one just sounds nicer."

"So nice ghosts are angels and mean ones are 'ghost' ghosts?"

I laughed. "That's as good an explanation as any."

"If there are ghosts or angels, they'll be at the end of the maze. That's where the crypt is."

"There's a crypt too?" Pip followed us through the rest of the winding path.

"Yes, that's where Mr. Marco's family is. The dead ones, anyway," she informed me. I chuckled at her forthright statement.

The path ended into a wide, bright clearing where the crypt stood. There was no door on it, just a large archway for an entrance. Inside was tall and open, with glass tiles on the ceiling to let in light. Roses and other flowers surrounded it, giving off a sweet fragrance.

"This is the friendliest crypt I've ever seen." I walked up to the archway and peered in. Shadows played about while my eyes tried to adjust to the change.

"Mr. Marco said he doesn't care if I come and visit his relatives. It's a nice quiet place to come and think," Eva said.

Pip suddenly stilled outside the entrance.

"What is it Pip?" Eva and I watched his ears twitch and his nose sniff rapidly. We stood still and listened, wide-eyed, for any noises.

Pip's lip curled into a snarl, but he made no sound.

"Do you hear something?" I asked my furry companion again. I reached over and took Eva's hand. She squeezed mine back and we held our breath. Silence.

"Does he hear a ghost?" she whispered.

"I don't know," I whispered back, watching him carefully.

His ears flattened, he let out a growl, and dove into the crypt. We heard him sliding around inside and barking madly. Eva and I took a few cautious steps back when something burst forth out of the entrance.

We both screamed when a rabbit sped out, running right between me and Eva, followed by Pip who almost knocked us over.

PART 3 - THE CURSE

We started laughing while Pip took off after his quarry.

"Unless ghosts have giant ears and furry tails, I think it's safe to go in."

We entered the Marco family crypt together. Everything was neat and tidy with tombs stacked on all sides of the walls. Two large ones sat in the middle with statues of the dead resting atop it. One was a man holding a sword. He was dressed in clothing from the crusades. Next to him was a woman, dressed from the same period. Her hands were clasped around what appeared to be a Bible, holding it to her chest.

I walked over to them, running my hand on the stone as Eva climbed on top of it. She laid down next to the statue of the man.

"Look! His sword is longer than I am. Do you think he was really this big?" She stretched her toes to make herself longer.

"It's possible."

"I use it as my measuring stick. I used to be this long." She pointed at a rune in the sword. "But now I come up to here." She patted the base of the hilt.

"Using a dead man's tomb to chart your growth. You are truly fearless." A voice came from the archway.

I looked up to see my husband's frame filling the entrance.

"I heard screams." He scowled at me.

I smiled. "Pip flushed out a rabbit that almost climbed up our skirts," I explained, crossing over to his side to receive a one-armed embrace.

"We're here to find the ghosts or the angels." Eva slid off her perch.

"You'll definitely find ghosts and no angels. I'm sure he will find offence at the blasphemous use of his sword and come back to smite you with it." Arthur said in a wicked voice, chasing after Eva who screamed with delight and ran to the other side of the tomb. I watched them duck and circle around the statues before she made a mad dash towards me.

"Mrs. Marco! Help!" She hid behind my skirts, giggling as he made his way back to us.

Arthur raced to us both and with a loud growl, scooped us both up into his arms and spun us in a circle. Eva squealed. Pip returned to bark at us until Arthur set us down.

"Would you like to introduce us to your family?" I asked once everyone had calmed down.

Arthur heaved a great sigh. "Why would you want to know about a bunch of dead people?"

"Because if I meet a ghost, I want to be polite and address them by name," I answered.

"Imp." He took my hand and led me further into the crypt with Eva and Pip.

"Who is this distinguished couple?" I gestured at the large tombs in the center.

"James and Marguerite de Marco. He came back from the Crusades and was rewarded with this property and title. They built the first home here, which has been torn down and rebuilt several times."

"So they started Ironwood." I slid my arm into his elbow.

"They started it, yes." He glared at the statue of James de Marco with a hint of malice.

"You are not fond of him."

"He was a greedy bastard who didn't deserve the life he got," Arthur spoke low so Eva couldn't hear.

I had no response to his vehemence so I pulled him away. "Where is your father resting?" I redirected.

He led me to a nameplate, reached up and then backed away. "No sorry, he's over here." He led me to another place. "There we are, Nathaniel Jacob Woods. Sophie's true love." He ran his hand over the name. "He let Sophie keep her last name so I could carry on the Marco line."

I could make out the large letter 'N' but that was all.

"And Diana?"

He gave me a somber look and led me to the newest nameplate that was still shiny and the letters sharp. "Diana Hampton Marco." He rested his hand there softly.

I touched it, giving a thought to the vibrant beauty who loved pink. "Eva, I think you should bring her some pink flowers when you come for a visit."

Eva looked at it carefully. "Any pink flowers?"

"Any pink flowers will do," I assured her.

"And bring some for my grandmother as well." Arthur walked to another tomb. He rested his hand there reverently. I could make out the first letter and decided to try reading it if it would hold still long enough for me to finish.

"O...ol" I started to pronounce before I hesitated. The other letters started scrambling together to frustrate me.

"Olivia." He finished for me.

"You knew her well?"

He nodded. "Yes. She was a remarkable lady. I loved her very much."

"I'll bring her lots of flowers," Eva promised solemnly.

He smiled at the child. "Thank you, my dear. It will do my heart good to know someone is looking after her. Now, since I'm sure the two of you have scared off any ghosts who might have been lurking about, I'm going to take you both back to the house so they can resume their normal haunting." He pushed me out of the crypt. "I'm sure you both could use a nap about now."

"I hate that you are right." I stifled a yawn as Eva hid hers behind her hand.

CHAPTER 24

She loves it here. Of course, she loves it. It's green and quiet and beautiful to the naked eye. She doesn't see the corruption. She doesn't hear it whisper to her. London was safer for her. Even with its thievery, mobbing, and murders, London was better than here.

I met Alice on the stairs after my nap. "Sophie's here. I'm going to prepare a room for her."

I gave her hand a quick squeeze of gratitude. "Thank you, where is she now?"

"In the parlor with His Grace," she said.

I hurried down the steps and made my way through the hallway, grinning to myself. Haunted, indeed. I wanted her to point out where the ghosts were residing in this lovely old home. I certainly couldn't find any.

I could hear their voices through the slightly open door when I approached.

"I came as soon as I found she'd left. Is she sick or … has she gone mad? I warned her to stay away." Sophie's worried voice floated from the parlor.

Mad? Why on earth would *I* be suddenly insane? I thought she had a better opinion of me! And while my mother had taught me all about the deviltry of eavesdropping, I promptly pushed aside her teachings.

"No, she's…she's quite well. I don't understand it," Arthur responded.

"She's well? Truly?" I heard the rustle of Sophie's clothes as she moved about the room. "How…? It doesn't matter. We need to take her away from here at once," Sophie commanded.

"Don't you think I've tried? In one day, she's already in love with this cursed pile of rocks! I have half a mind to burn it down."

PART 3 - THE CURSE

I crept closer, biting my lip. Why did he hate it here so much?

"...you have no idea where it will take up residence if you do." I'd missed the first part of what Sophie said and listened closer. Residence? Were they talking about the ghosts?

"That's not the worst of it. Joy is...*enceinte*," Arthur said softly.

I heard Sophie gasp and the furniture creak. I can only guess she'd sat down at the news.

"Oh, Arthur. It's so...horribly wonderful." Her voice quivered with emotion.

Horribly wonderful?

"I was going to kidnap her, drag her from here kicking and screaming if I had to, but her condition..." He trailed off and gave a growl of frustration. "She was in declining health when she arrived. Alice said the trip here was hard on her. I spoke to the doctor. He doesn't want her to travel any time soon."

I wasn't leaving Ironwood. I would confront this mystery.

"I don't know why you both are so determined to make me leave." I threw the doors open wide and banged them loud when I stormed in. "I love it here. It's perfect."

They both gaped at me a moment. Sophie recovered first.

She stood from the sofa and approached me with an embrace. "Joy! Arthur has just told me the happy news. I'm ecstatic!" She gave me a tight hug. Her eyes were full of affection and tears as she gazed down at me. "I never thought I would live to see the day our family would expand."

"Thank you, Sophie." I embraced her back. "But you are changing the subject. I haven't seen a single ghost since I've been here."

"Yes, she and Miss Eva were in the crypt looking for them this morning," Arthur said with a scowl.

Sophie's face became aghast. She was the most accomplished person I'd ever seen at changing her emotions in a heartbeat.

"The crypt! Why would you want to go to that dirty old mausoleum? Really, Joy. It's hardly the place for you or little Eva to play."

"We were looking for the ghosts you warned me about. I wanted to confront them," I told her. Sophie ushered me to the sofa and sat me down.

"Of course you would," Arthur muttered.

I shot him a look. "As you can see, I've not been assaulted by any ghosts." I glanced between her and Arthur. "Will one of you please finally explain to me what's going on? What's wrong with Ironwood? And don't tell me it's haunted." I warned Sophie.

Her face softened. "Of course, it's haunted. All old houses like this are haunted. I'm just happy the spirits have taken a liking to you." She squeezed my hands affectionately. "But it is old and hasn't been updated in years."

"I haven't seen anything that a fresh coat of paint and some new carpet won't take care of," I countered before the argument that it was a creaky old house waiting to fall down came into play. The house was well taken care of from what I could see, it just needed some updating.

"I haven't let you into the dangerous parts where it is drafty and moldy and probably infested with rodents and disease," Arthur said.

"Your servants are too well trained and you are too efficient to let that happen," I retorted.

"I doubt the walls are going to fall down around our ears, but Arthur is right. Some sections of the house might be… dangerous." She cast him a worried glance. He glared back at her.

"But there is no question of moving you anywhere until the doctor says you are fit for travel," she said, bestowing a smile on me. "We want to keep that wee one safe and secure and keep you healthy and happy. In the meantime," she cut me off before I could protest the need to travel anywhere, "Arthur can open up the house and make sure *everything* is safe and secure before you send in your army of craftsmen to make it habitable."

She sent him a hard look that dared him to argue with her. He met her gaze, his face putting up a silent argument. An uncomfortable and silent battle of wills followed.

Sophie never faltered until finally his face fell and he sighed. "I can't fight you both…That's acceptable."

Sophie squeezed my hands and stood up. "There, now. Everything will be fine. I'm going to take a bit of a rest and then we'll tackle your needs for a nursery." Her cheeks flushed. "I'm so excited!" She swept out of the room.

I watched her go and then turned to my husband. He'd walked across the room and was staring out the window, his hands clasped behind his back.

I crossed to his side. I didn't touch him but I could feel the warmth coming from his body. I took in his frustrated countenance and followed his gaze out the window.

PART 3 - THE CURSE

All I could see was the beautiful landscaping and a tidy drive. The flowers were blooming but fading as the season was coming to an end. The leaves were changing slightly in the trees, reds and browns mixed in with the green. I saw Eva running with Pip, laughing when he tried to leap and grab the stick she was holding. I could see the army of servants going about their work in an efficient manner, content and healthy. I saw the horses and fat sheep grazing on green grass, crops growing in the distance, the water reflecting from the far-off river. I saw a veritable paradise.

"Why do you hate it here?" I asked softly.

He stiffened, then reached over and took my hand, entwining our fingers together. "It's difficult to be here." His thumb traced a pattern on the back of my fingers as he gazed back out the window.

I didn't want to hear any more about ghosts, something about all this had to be grounded in reality. "Did something happen here? Something to you?"

He exhaled sharply. "Yes."

"Will you tell me?"

"Never."

***

The next day Arthur attacked the house with zeal. An army of footmen and maids discarded their pristine uniforms for working clothes in preparation for the destruction to follow. They followed him about the house, obeying every barking order. I heard them stomping about, up and down the stairs as they opened up older sections of the house. A pile of debris outside the front door became higher and higher as old moth-eaten furniture and threadbare drapes were stacked up along with broken cornices and carpets.

I heard him ripping up floorboards and plaster, shouting for hammers and crowbars while I sipped tea with Sophie and Alice. Pip's head rested on my lap and I stroked his ears. My gaze followed the stampede through the house as Sophie tried to get me to pay attention to her.

"Joy! Really, dearest, you need to pay attention to our list. I want my grandbaby to have everything they need, and more. They are going to be spoiled absolutely rotten by the time I'm done with them," Sophie declared.

"You might have to limit her enthusiasm, and her visits." Alice wrote down another unnecessary accessory Sophie insisted I needed.

"Sorry." I blinked and turned back to the conversation. "I doubt they need a pony for a few years, though."

"We've moved from ponies onto wet nurses," Alice pointed out.

I shook my head. "No need for that." I'd have my baby at my own breast.

Alice and Sophie both looked at me with something akin to shock.

"What?" I asked, laughing at their comical faces. They both gaped like a fish out of water.

"Oh, you're joking with us!" Sophie laughed at last.

"No, I'm not joking." I looked at them oddly.

They were silent for a moment, staring at me before glancing at each other.

"She's from the country," Alice reminded Sophie quietly.

"Ah, yes. Put it on the list, just in case she changes her mind." Sophie whispered loudly. I shook my head. I wasn't going to change my mind.

"Really, both of you are making a baby much too complicated. A crib, blankets, gowns, diapers, and soakers." I pointed at the list.

"I've already got those down," Alice assured me.

"Put on more soakers." I tapped the list playfully. "Can't have too many. We might check with whoever does laundry to see what they need."

"Another body just to wash baby garments." Alice snorted and wrote on the list.

I laughed with her when Pip's head lifted off my lap, his gaze raised towards the ceiling. I followed his gaze before noticing the lack of noise. Things were silent except for a loud rhythmic pounding and some loud shouting. The servants' footsteps and stomping had ceased. A feeling of unease crept into the room as Pip walked to the doorway, his tail limp.

I stood up, following the noise. Alice and Sophie came to attention.

"What's going on?" Sophie wondered.

"Maybe they broke for lunch," Alice answered softly. Her voice contained all the doubt we were feeling at the sudden pallor that had taken over the house.

I walked towards the door. Sophie called out, "Joy, dearest! Just let Arthur handle things."

I ignored her.

I arrived at the staircase and saw several maids standing there, staring at the upper rooms with linens and dishes in their arms, arrested

PART 3 - THE CURSE

mid-stride by the noise. I walked past them, weaving in and out between their frozen forms as they whispered.

"Cracked…"

"Poor Missus…"

"Never seen him act like this…"

I made my way up the stairs to the bedrooms, past more servants who were still, staring and whispering.

"Do you think he's drunk?"

The shouting and pounding became louder when I entered the nursery. It was a big open room with large windows to let in plenty of sunshine and air. The flooring was torn up, along with the plaster. There was no furniture and dust swirled in the air. A few servants stood just inside, hands wringing but silent while they watched the scene before them.

Arthur was pounding into the fireplace mantle with a large hammer the length of his arm and a sizable head. Chunks of stone and mortar flew with every strike. He was covered in sweat and dust, his face was red, and the glare in his eyes bordered on madness. He was shouting at Byron who shouted back just as loudly every time Arthur threw him aside. I wondered about their history together. They were more than master and servant.

Byron saw me and his eyes widened. "Your Grace, you shouldn't…"

I paid no attention and approached Arthur. He was so focused, so set on taking down every piece of the mantle and chimney he didn't notice me when I stood behind him.

I heard Sophie gasp and call for me to retreat from the doorway. I waved her away and watched Arthur obsessively pound and chip, over and over. I could hear him muttering things that didn't make sense.

"Got to find it…do not understand…where are you hiding…"

I timed his swings carefully and when he lowered the hammer down, I rushed in. Alice gave a little cry of alarm when I wrapped my arms around his waist from behind and rested my cheek against his broad back. I held on tightly as he went to take another swing, feeling his muscles move against my chest and face. He swore and grabbed my hands, dropping the hammer to pull me off.

When his fingers touched my pink diamond ring he froze. I held on, listening to his rapid breathing and heartbeat. His fingers gripped mine tightly.

"Joy?" His voice was weary and wondering, like someone waking from a dream.

"Yes. It's me."

"What are you doing?"

"Embracing you."

He exhaled quickly. "Yes, I can see that."

Acutely aware of our audience I carefully proceeded. "I'm going to take Toady for some exercise and wanted to know if you would like to join me." *Or not so carefully.*

He gave me the reaction I was looking for, spinning around and glaring at me. "Are you daft, woman? You are not touching that horse in your condition."

I looked up into his red, weary face. I could see his heart still pounding under his shirt. But his gaze was starting to clear.

"You're right, of course. A curricle ride would be better," I pushed.

He blustered a moment, "You are going to drive me into an early grave." His color became better and his breathing slowed.

"Perhaps a walk then?" I gently lowered his arms from my shoulders and gave him a cheeky grin.

He glared at me and then glanced around the room at the wide-eyed servants along with Sophie and Alice. He looked startled at the sight of them all, and sighed in defeat. "Yes, Madame Wife, I believe a walk will do me good."

He led me from the room. I caught Byron's eye before we exited and he gave me a subtle nod. He would take care of things on the servants' end. Sophie and Alice just let us pass while we made our way down the stairs.

He stopped briefly at the door to retrieve his walking stick, tapping it hard against the ground with every step we took away from the house. My arm rested in the crook of his as we walked towards the cliffs and the ocean.

"I always find the sound of the waves so soothing." He didn't respond but glared at the horizon. We stood in silence. I searched for something to say. I watched the waves below, washing up and down the white sands.

"Is there a path to the beach?"

He scowled, furrowed in thought. "Yes, but I don't want you taking it alone, it's steep and can be slippery."

PART 3 - THE CURSE

Sunshine bore down on us while we made our way to the path. Stairs had been cut out of the cliffside and a wooden railing was put up for safety. Arthur went down first, resting my hand on his shoulder for balance.

The crashing waves met us along the shore. The tide was coming in and the beach was mostly empty of birds. I took a few steps on the sand and inhaled the salty air. Arthur rested a hand around my waist.

"Did I frighten you?"

"Did you frighten *me*? No. But you did the servants."

He scowled.

"You're searching for something," I guessed.

He froze.

"What is it?"

"Misery and death." He stalked away from me. I watched him approach the water, pick up a small stone or shell and hurl it back into the waves.

He repeated the action several more times while I waited, rubbing my arms for comfort. The words of the servants kept repeating over and over in my brain.

"*...Cracked...never seen him act like this...do you think he's drunk... poor missus...*"

It was the last statement that bothered me the most, and I hugged myself a little more. My husband stared at the waves so long the tide came up and licked his toes.

Arthur turned back to me. I could feel the verbal battle coming.

"You're looking at me as if I'm some kind of monster."

"Are you?" I asked softly.

"No."

"I'm sure the fireplace mantle in the nursery would disagree."

"Then it's a good thing it's an inanimate object." He dropped his walking stick, took my hands into his, and knelt before me. He then rested his head against my belly and wrapped his arms around me to hold me close.

"Everything I need is right here. You, our baby. And I'll fight...I'll destroy anything that threatens to take it away." He pressed a kiss against my stomach and I rested my hands on his shoulders.

"I will too…" I vowed, reaching up one hand to run it through his hair. "But I need to know what I'm fighting. Please tell me."

He shook his head. "You can't ask me, Joy. Don't ask again." He looked up at me, his eyes tired and red, his face in turmoil. I brushed one dark lock back from his eyes and cupped his cheek. He was starting to scare me. Where was the light-hearted man I knew?

I also saw the determination in his face. He wouldn't share this burden, whatever it was.

"Did you sleep last night?" I brushed my thumb along his beard.

He shook his head, "I couldn't rest."

"Nightmares?"

He shook his head, grabbed his walking stick, and rose to his feet, brushing off my question like the sand upon his knees. "I suppose a nap would do me good. I'm sure Sophie's going to give me a scolding when we go back to the house, and I would rather put it off."

He scanned up and down the beach and led me towards a spot of shade towards the cliff. He settled down into the sand and I laid next to him, resting my head in my customary spot on his shoulder. His arms settled around me and he exhaled, kissing the top of my head. "Perfect. Warm enough?"

I nodded against him and rested while his breathing became even and a soft snore escaped his lips. I slipped out of his arms once he was asleep and wrapped my arms around my knees. Watching the waves with a million questions in my mind, feeling like a piece of debris in the ocean, battered and tossed without any way to change my direction.

PART 3 - THE CURSE

CHAPTER 25

I can't find it.

I've ripped up floorboards and torn down walls. Where is it? Why is it hiding? It never has before. It's always displayed itself. Always. Just to taunt me further with my ineptitude. Is it searching for her?

I have to find it first. Somehow, I have to send her away. If I could just sleep. If I could just close my eyes without seeing their cold, dead faces.

A distraction came the next week when Sir Reginald Lockton entered the doorway during breakfast.

"Reggie?" Arthur stood, the disbelief in his voice profound. "What are you doing out of town? Are you in trouble?"

Reggie looked mildly offended. "It says a great deal about your opinion of me when that's the first thing out of your mouth when I come to visit." Reggie took my hand. "He's such a brute, dear lady. One wonders why you put up with him." He kissed my fingers lightly. Arthur made a quiet growl and resumed his seat.

"Sophie told me you needed my attention at once." He moved to Sophie's side and placed a kiss on her upturned cheek.

"Is that so?" Arthur glared at his mother.

She simply sipped her tea and shrugged. "Reggie is here to finally take your advice and learn to run his estate properly. It is disgusting the way he neglects it. I convinced him it would be in his best interest to do better or he'll soon be looking for a rich bride who will nag him into an early grave."

Reggie sat at the table comfortably next to Alice.

"Some of us are ill-suited for the marriage mart." He patted his stout belly. "The ladies can't see past my paunch to realize what a catch I am." He grinned at Alice. "Therefore, I must man up and take care of myself."

"How admirable of you." Arthur said dryly. He eyeballed his friend, then his mother. I reached over and covered his hand.

"It will be lovely to have you here, Reggie." I gave Arthur's hand a hard squeeze to remind him to behave.

"Ha! I have at least one of you fooled that my presence should be desired, not endured." Reggie laughed as a breakfast plate was brought to him.

Arthur released my hand and eyed everyone at the table. "I'm being managed, aren't I?" He crossed his arms and rested his gaze on Sophie.

She took another dainty sip of tea. "My dear boy, you could use a little management. You were absolutely beastly this whole week." She gave him a pointed look. "Now now, Mother knows best. You can drag Reggie all over the estate, get him in shape financially and physically, and then I can take him back to town and find a wife for him. It'll take your mind off all the things you are needlessly obsessing over."

"Needlessly?" Arthur's voice started to rise.

"The only thing wrong with Ironwood is you." She gestured around the table. "Everyone else is calm and in perfect health. Just ask. Joy, dear? Are you feeling well?"

Arthur's jaw ticked. I placed a hand on his knee under the table and rubbed my fingers along his thigh to reassure him. "As long as I eat my toast before I get out of bed every morning, I'm fine." He captured my hand in his and laced our fingers together, but he still looked like an angry animal caught in a trap.

Sophie looked triumphant. "You see, Arthur. She's fine."

"*Mother* knows best, eh?" The two locked eyes in a cryptic battle of wills.

"Toast in bed every morning? Now that sounds like a capital idea," Reggie interrupted, lifting a piece to his mouth and taking a large bite smothered in butter and jelly.

"Reggie dear, don't be difficult." Sophie rolled her eyes.

"Just echoing a good idea when I hear it." He grinned. "I think it's a… wait. Is this some womanly thing I should know about? Something gents shouldn't do? Toast before clothes are strictly feminine?"

PART 3 - THE CURSE

We all stared at him. The silence grew uncomfortable. Sophie was looking put out, Arthur looked at Reggie as if he were daft. Alice finally blushed and pulled him close, whispering something to him. He was confused until the knowledge swept over him and his face lit up.

"Another little Marco on the way! Best news I've heard all year." He stood and kissed my cheek and slapped Arthur on the back. "No wonder you're out of sorts, old man. I'll get busy putting your humor back to rights, you'll see."

Thankfully, his presence did make a difference to the mood of the household. He followed along behind Arthur as he continued to strip the house from top to bottom. Whenever Arthur would grow surly or get an obsessed look in his eye, Reggie was there with a joke or a suggestion to bring him back to reality. He'd rouse Arthur from a fit with a good-natured slap on the back, sometimes enough to knock him into a stumble.

I threw myself into taking stock of each room he'd cleared, the damage he'd caused and what needed to be fixed or replaced. He was still searching for something, as was apparent by the loose floorboards, missing cornices, and piles of sandy mortar. He even broke furniture apart looking for secret compartments or something in the upholstery.

Another week passed before I was given leave to bring in my brigade of workmen and craftsmen for the bulk of the house while Arthur scoured the attic. The house was full of noise and smells of construction. Pip escorted each new arrival in and out until he flopped into an exhausted puddle at the end of the day.

Ironwood felt alive and happy as if the old place was welcoming all the changes, the cleaning, and the modernization. The village was happy with the new revenue, and I was happy with a new project to focus my skills on.

The only one who wasn't happy was Arthur.

"It's just not here," I heard him mutter one night to Sophie after dinner. I listened in while appearing absorbed in my work. They stood against the fireplace on the other side of the room from me, and it was hard to hear over the cheerful crackling of the blaze.

"We need to be vigilant. But there are so many things that are different this time. Maybe it's the baby and won't show up until she's delivered?" she whispered.

Arthur was silent.

Sophie rested a hand on his arm. "You're becoming obsessed, and neglecting your wife."

Both of their eyes were on me as I worked on a new dress for Eva. I forced my eyes not to stray from my stitching.

I heard rustling and footsteps and saw Arthur's legs standing before me. I looked up into his weary face. He'd grown thin and dark circles appeared under his eyes. He'd been pushing himself hard to find whatever menace the house held.

"Yes?"

"I seem to remember we started the book *Ivanhoe* before we left London. Would you care to continue?" He passed the book back and forth in his hands.

I smiled and moved over a few inches to make room for him. "I would like nothing better."

He sighed and planted a kiss on my cheek. It was a silent apology of sorts. I patted his knee in response, and let his voice take us both away to the time of the Crusades.

PART 3 - THE CURSE

CHAPTER 26

I slept in her arms last night. Actually slept while she stroked my hair and face. I heard her speaking calming things when I'd wake up from a nightmare like I did for her in London. I felt so helpless at the time, and now I understand how huge a gesture it was for her.
Sophie's right. A change of plans is needed.

"These are bigger." Arthur nuzzled my chest. His beard tickled my skin and I laughed while pushing him away.

"So is this." He pressed a tender kiss to my slightly rounded belly before resting his head there. I played with his dark wavy hair.

Here was my Arthur. The man I married. Passionate, playful, a bit rash. Not the tired, obsessed creature who had been tearing the house apart looking for some horrible doomsday object no one would speak about.

How had my life come to this?

"I can see your brain working," he said.

I stroked his beard. "That's a change. Usually I can see yours."

He moved up next to my head and leaned over me, tracing my freckles. "What are you thinking about?"

I don't really know you like I thought I did.

"I'm glad you're feeling better," I spoke truthfully. Yes. Let's pretend it was an illness. A passing moment of madness to never happen again.

He kissed my forehead before getting out of bed and dressing. I reached for the blankets watching him with his morning ablutions from the comfort of my pillow with my toast and tea.

"Aren't you getting dressed?" he asked over his shoulder as he placed his razor to his neck.

"I'm waiting for you to finish." It was our normal routine. He dressed and left, I waited and followed. He was always faster than me, and I found it easier just to stay out of his way.

"Get ready, we'll go to breakfast together." He turned back to the mirror.

I glanced at the chamber pot and back at him. "No, I'll just wait."

He followed my line of vision to the chamber pot and shrugged. "I don't mind, go ahead."

I'm sure my brows disappeared into my forehead. "I mind. I'll wait."

He put his razor down and wiped off his face, "I'm not leaving this room without you."

"What?"

He shrugged and turned back to the mirror. "I need to keep an eye on you, that's all. Make sure you stay safe."

My mouth gaped. Was he seriously suggesting I couldn't even use the chamber pot without him being in the room?

"That's not going to happen. I need some privacy."

He gave me a serious look. "I'm not leaving this room without you."

I blinked in shock as the weight of my bladder increased. "Are you being serious?"

"Absolutely."

"Arthur."

"I'm not budging on this, Joy." He returned to his shaving.

He wasn't leaving the room without me? What new madness was this! And I wasn't using the chamber pot while he waited, no matter what he thought about keeping me 'safe'.

I stormed off the bed and retrieved my robe, tying the sash with a flourish. He wasn't leaving the room without me? I was definitely leaving without him.

I focused on the door to my own bedchamber. It was standing open as usual. I'd never slept in there and used it mostly as a storage room for all my fabrics and mannequins. The staff kept it clean but didn't bother laying a fire or bringing hot water there in the mornings. I usually shared with Arthur.

There was a perfectly good and empty chamber pot waiting there.

I marched across the room. Arthur watched me out of the corner of his eye. "Where are you going?"

PART 3 - THE CURSE

I didn't even look at him as I grabbed the key out of the lock and slammed the door between our rooms shut. I heard him shout my name and pound on the door as I raced for the empty chamber pot. He continued to raise a riot on the other side. Concerned voices gathered in the hallway. My cheeks flamed as the entire household congregated outside our bedroom doors.

I unlocked the door and threw it open to face my angry husband.

"What is wrong with you? Didn't I just..."

"Stop!" I shouted back pointing a finger in his face. "I refuse to get in an argument with an irrational person."

"Irrational?"

"Yes, irrational!" I leaned in. "Or would you like to explain to the entire household why I can't use the chamber pot by myself? Because I won't."

He clenched his fists as I stormed past him to find my clothes. There was a timid knock at our door. Arthur stomped to the door and flung it open. Sophie stood there in her cap and wrapper, her eyes wide as she peered through the door. The servants, Byron, Alice, and even Reggie all stood behind her.

"Just a little disagreement between me and my wife," he said tersely and shut the door in her face.

"That was rude," I said as I tugged my dress over my head. Grunting, I reached around to try to fasten it myself and found his fingers there helping. I pushed them aside.

"Stop it. I want to be angry with you."

His hands fell away as I struggled with the buttons. He let out an exasperated sigh and dove in again to help.

"Stop being so stubborn. Let me help, then you can be angry with me. I suppose I deserve it."

"Yes, you do," I agreed, but dropped my hands so he could finish the fastening. I walked away from him and finished dressing as he watched.

I stomped towards the door when I was done and threw it open. Thankfully, the hall was empty of occupants.

Arthur took hold of my arm and stopped me before I left. I wouldn't look at his face. I stared at the wall and waited for him to speak.

"Talk to me, please. Tell me how to make this better."

What are you hiding? Why the odd behavior? What does Sophie know that I don't? Why don't you trust me? Instead, I bit my lip, and took a deep breath. "You're the one who doesn't want to talk about it, and I'm not to ask. I'm just following your command, husband."

His hold on me dropped and I continued on my way to breakfast alone.

I was the first to arrive and allowed the servants to seat me and bring me a plate. I sipped my tea as Arthur plopped into the chair next to me and growled for some coffee. Pip's nose landed in my lap under the table and I stroked his head, feeling myself relaxing a little.

I kept my gaze on my tea and plate. I was fairly certain I couldn't talk to my husband without an argument ensuing, so I tried to keep my peace.

"How long am I to be punished?" Arthur snarled.

"It depends on you and your attitude," I said calmly. I wrapped my hands around my cup and let the warmth seep through me.

He sighed. "Can I apologize?"

"Do you mean it?"

"Of course I mean it."

I looked at him now. "Will it happen again?"

His face fell. "I can't say I won't ever be unreasonable again. I was being overbearing."

"Extremely," I agreed, turning back to my plate and the task of keeping the nausea at bay. "Let's move on."

The sound of laughter filled the room as Reggie opened the door and escorted Alice in. Both of them had pink cheeks from the outdoors. He led her to a chair and helped her sit.

"Another fine morning walk with a beautiful lady." Reggie declared. Alice had taken his health in hand and had insisted on him joining her for morning walks. His color was better, his breathing better, and his paunch was disappearing.

I watched as she deftly removed the cream from his reach and pushed a bowl of berries into its place instead. He scowled a moment but relented at her beautiful smile. "I've walked all over this rambling estate with you, Lady Alice. Surely I deserve a little cream in my coffee?"

"Cream or sugar, but not both," she told him, piling his plate with eggs and toast and rationing his bacon.

Reggie grinned at Arthur. "I've never been so delightfully managed." He tucked into his plate.

PART 3 - THE CURSE

"Enjoy it while it lasts," Arthur groused. I shot him a glare as Sophie entered the room.

"Good morning!" she said brightly as she seated herself at the table, briskly shaking her napkin into her lap. "Is everyone doing well?"

"Spectacular!" Reggie answered as Alice worded an agreement.

"And the newlyweds? Quite a little row you had this morning." she commented as her tea was poured.

"Yes," I said sharply.

"Quite," Arthur agreed, just as sharp.

She gazed at us, her silence willing us to elaborate. I'd stab Arthur in the eye with my jelly spoon if he breathed a word of the details.

"Just a small disagreement. It's over now." Arthur's attention went to his plate.

The silence hung about the table.

"I got a letter from Abigail," Alice spoke up. "She's coming as soon as the term has ended and wanted to stay until after the New Year."

I smiled at the thought of her youthful excitement filling the halls. "It will be wonderful to have her. Is Charles coming as well?"

"I haven't heard from him yet, but I'm sure he will." She sighed. "It will be hard to wait for the holidays."

"Mmmm," Reggie agreed with his mouth full. He swallowed. "I have a smashing idea. You should throw a ball while they are here."

I blinked. Sophie gasped with delight. Arthur looked downright murderous.

"Oh, come off it, Ironwood. Your wife has done a splendid job of bringing this old pile of stones up to snuff. She deserves to show off her hard work. And your mother throws the best parties in the known world." Reggie waved his toast in the air. "And I get to eat myself silly for a night." He winked at Alice. "It's a brilliant idea."

We were silent and still as Arthur's face contorted. After a long moment, he sighed. "I'll not put my wife under any more stress."

All eyes were directed to me as I chewed on my lip. I'd never organized more than a family picnic. But this was my duty, wasn't it? As his wife and partner? As the Duchess of Ironwood?

I needed to step up and push myself to be more. My health had been improving, and I had more energy lately, even as my belly was starting to round. "I think it's a lovely idea. Sophie and Alice can teach me all I need to do."

"Of course we will. She'll hardly lift a finger," Sophie promised, reaching out to squeeze my hand across the table. "A holiday house party. It's just the thing we need, especially with Abigail and Charles coming."

I looked at Arthur. "I can do it."

He scowled. "Will it put me back into your good graces?"

"It wouldn't hurt."

"Oh, very well. But I'll be watching you closely."

He'd already made that point quite clear.

PART 3 - THE CURSE

CHAPTER 27

Sophie promised to watch her, after my colossal misstep. She was right... again.

I can't be everywhere at once. I wish I could. I wish I could lock us together in a gilded cage.

Alice and Sophie threw themselves into planning the house party. We had a planning meeting to plan the planning. There were lists everywhere.

I hated the lists. I hated them because I couldn't even make one. I'd hold them in my hands and watch the letters squirm and writhe about the pages. Sophie's letters were big and bold like she was. She'd draw a line through each completed task with a flourish, which made the letters scramble about even more as if they'd been skewered. Alice's letters were thin and dainty and straight. She preferred checks rather than lines. I felt like an onlooker rather than the mistress of the house.

"You're rather quiet," Alice noted as they finished up the guest list. I couldn't even help write the invitations.

"I'm feeling my ... limitations." I tried to be kind.

Sophie's face fell. "Oh, dear. We've kind of just run roughshod over you in trying to help, haven't we?"

"I feel rather useless," I admitted.

"Joy! Please don't feel that way," Alice pleaded. "You are the most capable woman I know."

I stood to leave. "I should probably focus on the things I do best and let you two organize things."

"Please stay, Joy." Sophie tugged me back to her side before I could escape. She never left me alone if Arthur wasn't with me.

"And do what?" I asked crossly.

She smiled. "Make us and this house beautiful, of course." She set down her list and rose to her feet. "I think it's time Ironwood gives up some of her secrets, don't you? Come along, Alice."

Ironwood's secrets! Now there was a topic I was instantly interested in.

Sophie started leading us through the house, up all the flights of stairs to the attic. She recruited some maids to join us with more light.

It was dark and musty when we entered through the door. The candlelight revealed furniture draped in white dust covers, stacked trunks, and a great many shadows. Our footsteps echoed on the wooden floor as we made our way across the room.

"I haven't been up here before." I took hold of a dust cover. I pulled it off and coughed a little. An old scuffed sideboard sat there, laden with old papers.

"Arthur wanted to make sure the floor wouldn't fall out from under us before we dove into the mess of Ironwood's history." Sophie tugged off another dust cover revealing an old cradle. It was scratched and needed new bedding, but was beautifully carved.

"We'll definitely need that." My spirits lifted as we discovered more treasures that needed a little care. Anything we couldn't use would be distributed to the tenants. I called for some footmen to help with the carrying. Space slowly opened up as I found decorations and portraits hidden between the spaces of furniture.

Alice wandered to a stack of trunks, dusted off the top and opened it. "Old clothes," she announced.

I was next to her in an instant, ready to dive into fabric and lace.

"Let's wait on those," Sophie suggested. "I'm not as young as you ladies and I'm starving." She began to make her way out of the attic.

"We should wait for Abigail." Alice shut the trunk. "She loves to dress up in old things." She started pulling me as I protested. "And you shouldn't stay up in a dusty attic for too long," she chided.

I relented and let her lead me away.

I thrived doing what I knew best. I had furniture reorganized and re-covered, portraits and paintings hung on freshly washed and painted

PART 3 – THE CURSE

walls, tapestries and drapes cleaned and hung. Ironwood was regaining its color and history. I loved the sight of it.

Sophie and Alice returned to their lists and called out things for me to approve of as I directed a footman to straighten a painting of a young family. The wife was sitting with her arm around the waist of a young boy. His hair was dark and curly while her updo was large and white as the style had been in those days. She had a small smile on her lips that matched the boy. The husband stood behind them both with a gentle but protective hand on her shoulder. His white wig didn't reveal his coloring, but he had a fine physique and a bit of sadness around the lips and eyes.

Arthur and Reggie appeared just as the frame was straight and I stood back to admire it.

"Your wife is a miracle worker. This old stack of stones looks better every day." Reggie gave my hand a cheeky kiss before Arthur slapped him away.

Arthur looked up at the portrait with amazement. "Where did you find this old thing?" He walked up to it, gazing at the figures with a reflective look.

"In the attic. There is a treasure trove of things up there." I slid my arm around his waist. "Don't you like it? I can have it removed."

"Hmmm? No, no, it's fine." His arm wrapped around me as we studied it. "I just hadn't seen them in years."

"Who is it?" I asked.

"My...Grandparents. David and Olivia. This was painted before Sophie was born."

"Oh! I didn't know you had an older brother, Sophie," I said.

She looked up from her lists and gave Arthur a wicked little smile. "Yes. My brother Arthur. Such a pest."

"You were named for him?" I looked up at my husband.

"Sophie's not good with originality," he smirked.

"Not good with originality! I should take you over my knee." Sophie protested. "I could have given you some ghastly name like Cyril, or Albert!"

"Ghastly," he agreed.

"But since you would be the heir to this giant mess, I went with a family name instead." She huffed.

I grinned and gazed up at the little Arthur Marco the First hanging on the wall. "You look a little like him. You have the same curly dark hair and eyes." I looked into his face for confirmation. The same dark eyes as the portrait gazed back at me.

"Thank you, Madame Wife. I have it on good authority from Sophie he was a splendid man." He became somber. "He just died too young."

Sophie muttered something under her breath as Arthur gave her a kiss on her cheek. "Don't let my wife wander Ironwood alone," he spoke softly before pressing his lips to her skin.

"Never," she promised back.

More secrets. Unearthing Ironwood's treasures had done nothing to answer any of my questions.

I stuffed down my thoughts and turned back to the portrait. I looked at the faces of Olivia and David. His eyes were sad. Something I'd also seen in my husband. Had Sophie's father been keeping secrets too?

PART 3 - THE CURSE

CHAPTER 28

Ironwood is changing. It's becoming a home. Joy is a miracle worker.
Every day I relax a little more. Every night I sleep next to a warm and loving wife and hope for it to continue.
I'm still terrified of it, still waiting for it to strike. I still search for it, night and day.
As it continues to elude me, I'm starting to wonder if the curse has passed. If the person who stole it has taken on the horrible legacy for their family.
Better theirs than mine.

Time moved from summer to fall as I had Ironwood cleaned up and polished like new.

Winter was just hinting at an arrival when I turned to the task of re-outfitting the inhabitants.

I already had new designs for Sophie, Arthur, and even Reggie, but Alice was giving me trouble. How did one dress a lady who worked as a companion?

I turned the pages back to the dress I was designing for Eva. Something we could adjust easily as she grew...

"We've lost her, Arthur. She hasn't heard a word you've said." Sophie's voice broke through my thoughts.

I looked up to see my husband's bemused smile. "You've cheered the servants. All the maids are tittering away at the thought of their new costumes." Ironwood's livery had desperately needed updating and I had decided they needed two sets. Wool for winter and muslin for summer.

"Just doing my best to deplete your fortune," I said.

He leaned down and kissed my nose. "You'll never be able to," he whispered.

I raised my brow in a challenge, and he raised his to accept. We'd see how he felt once I decorated the entire village for the holidays.

"I was coming to inform you that Abigail and Charles are here. Alice took off immediately, but you were lost in a fog of fabrics and lace, weren't you?"

"Guilty. I have ideas for them too. Alice is giving me the most difficulty. I hope I'll find inspiration soon." I shut my sketchbook and took his arm to go greet our guests.

"I also received letters from your family," he spoke as we walked. I could see by his frown the news was not in my favor.

"They aren't coming?" I guessed.

"It seems all your sisters are in confinement, like you. I would point to a conspiracy, but I know how much you like to... procreate... so it shouldn't surprise me much they are all in the same condition." He ducked my playful swat. "Thomas is looking to propose to a young lady and doesn't wish to leave her. Your father is down with a cough and your mother refuses to leave his side. They all promise to descend on us in spring, so be forewarned. I even got a small missive from young David in his best handwriting asking me for a private tour of the beach to look for pirate caves."

"In other words, all is normal with the Horton family."

"I'd say so, yes," he agreed as we entered the hallway.

Alice was embracing both her siblings, her eyes bright and her face flushed with pleasure. Arthur pulled me near his side and kissed me quickly. I leaned into him, comfortable and warm.

I would miss my family, but it was time to make memories with my new family. Abigail ran to us and gave us a tiny curtsey before wrapping her arms around us and thanking us with her usual youthful exuberance.

It was shaping up to be a lovely holiday season.

***

Abigail and Eva had become fast friends. Sophie had promised to take us up to the attic in the afternoon. The girls were antsy, waiting for her. Alice and I were glad to let them both play and enjoy each other before class distinction would separate them.

PART 3 - THE CURSE

"But where is she?" Abigail whined, and bounced from foot to foot. Eva was barely better behaved, chewing on her lip.

"She's resting. Women of Sophie's age need more rest than ill-mannered girls like you," Alice teased. "Didn't that school teach you anything?"

Abigail rolled her eyes. "Don't talk about school. I'm on holiday. Please can we go up without her?"

I didn't see any reason why we should wait. "Let's go see what Ironwood's history of fashion holds."

The girls squealed with glee and raced up to the attic, where they descended on the chests of old clothing with giddy madness.

Abigail threw open a chest. She and Eva dove in headfirst, rummaging through old gowns and gloves, petticoats and veils. There was an abundance of headwear dated back to the 1500s. Their giggles and gasps were infectious. I laughed as they pulled on gloves that went to their shoulders.

"Goodness, look at this!" Alice pulled a heavy gown to her chest. It was old and looked to be from the time when panniers were worn. The garment was in good condition though, no worn spots or holes. White and gold with silver embellishments, it made her skin glow like the angel she was when she held it up in the dim light.

I knew then she had to wear it. Ideas and images flashed in my mind of how she would look and what I needed to do to accomplish it. I itched for my sketchbook.

Instead, I pulled out a petticoat and gasped at the weight of it. "However did they move?" I fluffed out the skirt.

"That's not even half of it. There are more instruments of torture to add." Alice pulled out the hoops, corsets and other assorted devices.

"Try it on," I urged, needing to see her in the gown.

Alice looked around the attic. "Here?"

"Abigail and Eva will stand guard, won't you girls?" I pulled them into service.

"Of course. Try it on, Alice! I want to see it," Abigail pleaded as she stood sentinel at the attic door.

Alice and I giggled as we tried to figure out which device went where and how to attach them. Corset, then panniers, then petticoats, and finally the gown. It took both of us to lift the heavy thing over her head. I fastened it up and took a step back to examine our efforts.

Alice looked as if she'd stepped back in time.

Abigail laughed. "You need a giant wig and a patch for your face." She circled around her sister. "Here, these too!" She slid a pair of long white silk gloves onto Alice's hands.

"She looks like a queen," Eva said reverently.

I reached out to fuss with the skirts, pleats, and layers. Alice kindly held still as I flitted about her. "I'll take that out...too much flounce. Wonder what it would look like without the hoop..." I mumbled.

"Oh look!" Abigail's voice pulled me out of my musings and we walked over to see her discovery.

It was a box of jewelry that contained huge gaudy pieces of necklaces and ear bobs, rings, bracelets, and everything in between.

Alice picked up a large brooch. "Paste."

"I wouldn't think they would keep a king's ransom in the attic." My focus was still on the gown. She didn't look comfortable wearing it. How to make it more amiable for the ball?

Alice rummaged around the box with the girls as I fussed with the gown. We both laughed as they wrapped themselves in ropes of pearls and sparkling hair combs, talking silly to one another as they pushed giant rings on over the gloves.

"Oh, this one isn't too horrible." Alice held up a blue sapphire necklace on a plain silver chain. It was a square cut the size of a baby's fist and ringed by round diamonds.

"This is a nice piece for being false." She turned it over in her hand. The blue of the sapphire made a stunning contrast to the silver and gold. "You need to wear it with the gown for the ball."

"I can't wear this to the ball! It's lovely, but horribly outdated." She made a laborious turn with exaggerated grunts and groans. "I can hardly move in it."

"You will when I'm done with it. You won't need any of those contraptions," I promised, unfastening the stays. I had a new project, and it would be a masterpiece.

› PART 3 - THE CURSE ‹

CHAPTER 29

Joy is in her element. Not even the tenant's homes or the buildings in the village have escaped her touch. Everything is decorated and attuned to her artistic eye. I was given a wardrobe for the evening and warned not to deviate from it. Ironwood is aglow again with life. It feels happy, whole, like a home. Like when Mother was here.

Joy has still not heard it. I have not seen it.
Could it truly be gone?

Our party was a much smaller affair than the one I attended in London, which suited me just fine. I wasn't a stickler for all the details like Sophie was.

"We should have had a bigger crush than this. We sent out the announcements too late." I silently disagreed as the ballroom filled with more and more people. Any more bodies would make dancing impossible.

Arthur was already working the crowd, charming as ever with Charles on his heels. He sent me a warm glance and a nod when I caught his eye. He was worried about me tiring too soon.

I knew I would not last as long as the ball. My feet were already sore from standing. My modified gown did nothing to hide my motherly figure. I wore the baby as proudly as the jewels Arthur had foisted around my neck. Guests offered their warmest wishes and congratulations.

I kept looking over my shoulder for a glimpse of Alice. She had shooed me out of the room when I went to help her dress. I wanted to see the final product on its owner. I had a feeling once the ladies saw it they would be searching through their own attics for gowns to restore and modify.

Arthur had told Abigail she could gather sweets for her and Eva, then watch the rest of the night from the upstairs balcony. Her eyes were bright as she came rushing down the stairs. "She's coming down. She looks like royalty. Reggie is going to faint when he sees her."

I laughed and lifted my eyes to watch Alice float down to the ballroom. She did look like royalty. Radiant and beautiful with her hair up in tidy curls, dripping with pearls and diamonds. The sapphire necklace nestled comfortably at the base of her throat. There were a few gasps and a murmur of words as she stopped before me and Sophie.

"Perfect!" I wanted to hug her and fuss with the fabric but kept my hands to myself. "Doesn't she look magnificent?" I asked Sophie.

Sophie's face was pale. "Oh, oh my!" She gasped and swayed a little.

Both Alice and I reached out to steady her. There were a few murmurs from the crowd as eyes turned towards the commotion.

"Sophie? What's wrong? Shall I fetch Arthur?" We directed her into a chair.

"Where..." She pointed at the sapphire. "Where did you get that?"

Alice glanced down and touched the stone. "In the attic with the other costume jewelry. I thought it was still in the attic, but today I found it in the pocket of the gown. Must have slipped it in there and forgotten about it."

Sophie groaned and shuddered again. I took her arm to catch her if she was going to faint.

"Arthur!" I called loudly as the crowd began to gather around us.

He pushed his way through the crowd, frowning. "What's this? You not feeling well, old girl?" He took her hand gently.

Sophie pointed at Alice. Arthur turned his gaze to her and all the blood rushed out of his face. His eyes widened as he straightened and reached out to Alice. We all gasped as he grabbed the blue stone and tore it from her neck with a loud snap as the clasp broke.

"WHERE DID YOU GET THIS!" He shouted in her face with the stone clutched in his fist. The room let out a gasp before falling silent. All eyes bore into us and I felt my cheeks burn.

Alice touched her neck where a red line was forming on her skin. "It... it was in the attic, with the paste..."

"I searched the attic and it wasn't there. Now tell me the truth!" he demanded.

Part 3 - The Curse

"Arthur!" I shouted, placing my hands on his shoulder. "She is telling the truth, I was there. It was mixed in with the other glass pieces the girls have been playing with."

Arthur turned on me. "What were you doing in the attic alone? I told you to wait for me or Sophie…"

"I'm not your dog or a child. And I refuse to be treated like one," I snapped back.

You could hear a pin drop in the crowded room. Oh, this was good fodder for the gossips!

Reggie came to the rescue once more. "I say!" He peered from behind Alice. "Awful lot of shouting for what's supposed to be a holiday party. If you're done berating the girl, it's time for us to open up the dancing."

Sophie had regained some composure. "Yes, yes you're right." She stood and cleared her throat. "So sorry to disturb everyone. There's a small misunderstanding. We've been searching for this heirloom for years!" She laughed and fanned her face. "It just shocked me to see it."

Heads bobbed and chatter was low and rushed like angry bees. The chatter stopped when Byron started popping corks loudly across the room, and the voices became more amenable as they crossed to get champagne.

Arthur was shaking, staring at the jewel in his hand. I put my hand on his arm and he jerked violently out of my reach.

"I think you should leave," I told him quietly. "I won't have you ruining the ball for Alice. I don't know what this is all about, but I do know in all the time I've been with you, I've never been ashamed to be at your side, until now."

Arthur stared at the jewel in his hand. He then looked up at me. I met his gaze just as boldly, feeling my heart squeeze painfully as the man I thought I knew slipped farther away. He glanced at Sophie, who nodded her agreement as the music began to play. Without a word, he stormed away.

The music picked up, and I was happy to see Reggie dancing with Alice, saying something humorous to bring the color back into her cheeks.

Sophie's young bucks soon pulled me into more wagers as I helped her direct them to the few wallflowers who needed a turn about the floor. The young ladies were soon involved in their wagers as well, making a lively group. I laughed at some of their antics before Reggie swept me into a dance.

"It's not right the hostess should have to sit out." He took my hand carefully in his for a minuet.

"I'm afraid my belly is rather intimidating."

"As intimidating as your husband. Don't know what's gotten into him tonight." He shook his head.

"Don't apologize for him. His behavior was ghastly." I maneuvered the small turn carefully around him.

"I think it's the trinket he's been turning the entire house over for. Things should be better now," Reggie assured.

I glanced over at Alice who was chatting with the neighborhood ladies. Her smile was back and her cheeks nicely flushed with the heat of the room. "I hope so."

I finished the dance with Reggie and Sophie immediately apprehended me.

"That's enough for you tonight. Your feet will be horribly swollen in the morning if you don't stop." She led me to the staircase. "Off to bed with you. Alice and I will see to the guests."

I nodded and made my way up, smiling at Abigail and Eva who still peered through the balcony slats at the party below.

"Don't stay up too late," I chided them softly and was given promises that were sure to be broken.

I made my way to my room. Our room. I stopped outside and took a deep breath before pushing the door open.

Arthur wasn't there. His coat and cravat I'd ordered him to wear were tossed carelessly on the bed as if he'd left in a hurry.

I was too tired to deal with him tonight. The thought of a conversation with him made me want to fall into a weary heap on the floor.

I made my way once again to the adjoining room, still warm since we'd been using it all day for last-minute details on our gowns. Reviving the fire with a few pokes, I looked at the large bed I had never used and rang the bell for someone to help me undress and bring a warming pan.

Arthur could sleep alone tonight.

PART 3 - THE CURSE

CHAPTER 30

I was careless. I was foolish. And death has come again. Again and again! I'll never stop paying for the sins of my fathers. Oh! Let this child be a girl!

"Are you two the first here?" I asked Charles and Abigail as they pounced on plates of bacon and eggs and toast. I put on a smile for them and reached for the tea at the table.

"Everyone is being lazy," Abigail complained. "I called out to Alice twice from the hallway and she didn't even move."

"She had a long night, with plenty of emotion." I buttered my toast.

"Good morning all," Arthur greeted us as he entered the room.

Everyone looked at him in silence. We were waiting, wondering which Arthur Marco would greet us today.

He furrowed his brow. "What? Am I banished from the breakfast table as well?"

"You were abominable last night." I scowled.

"So much so my lady didn't even come to our bed." He sat next to me. "And I do apologize. I'll set things right with Alice first thing." He then took my hand and brought it to his lips, his eyes meeting mine. "I'm truly sorry, Joy. Things will be better now, I promise."

Why now? I wanted to question him further when Reggie wandered in next, looking halfway put together, his waistcoat unbuttoned, his cravat half tied, his hair disheveled and smelling of spirits.

"Oh dear," I said as Arthur released me.

"Coffee," Reggie croaked.

"I see someone has found my private stash of French brandy," Arthur commented.

Reggie slumped into his chair. "I needed some courage. But it didn't help. I still couldn't work up the right words to ask her to marry me." He ran his hands through his hair before taking the hot cup.

"Reggie's getting married?" Sophie bustled in looking fresh and radiant for a woman of some years who'd just stayed up all night. She grinned at Reggie eagerly. "Who is the lucky lady?"

He slammed the empty cup down and groaned, "Alice."

Abigail squealed gleefully as Arthur laughed and Sophie gushed immediately about plans to be made.

Charles looked put out. "Don't you have to ask me first?"

Reggie nodded. "Quite right, quite right, old chap. As the acting head of your family, I respectfully ask for Alice's hand in marriage." Charles frowned in thought.

"You should be asking me," I interrupted. "I'm not sure I can let her go without a fight."

Reggie laughed. "So much fuss! The lady is in high demand." He clasped a hand over his chest. "I humbly appeal to your romantic nature, dear lady, to let me have my heart's desire and take care of the lovely Lady Alice Graves for the rest of my life."

I chuckled. "When you put it that way, how could I refuse?"

"I hope *she* won't refuse," Reggie said.

I rose from the table. "I'll go rouse the lady in question. I'm sure she would like to be part of this conversation."

I might have skipped a little to her room. She'd been admiring Reggie to me quietly, but afraid her family's circumstances would put off any suitors. She hadn't held much hope for anyone courting her.

I opened her bedroom door, peering around carefully. "Alice?"

I received no response. I walked in and opened the curtains slowly. "Wake up! We are having the most wonderful breakfast this morning, and a certain man you've been eyeing wants to ask you a life-changing question." I enjoyed the sun on my face for a moment before turning to the bed.

She hadn't moved.

"Alice?" I asked again.

She was so still.

I sat next to her and reached out to touch her peaceful, resting face. It was cold.

"Alice?..."

Everything happened so quickly after that.

I shouted for Arthur over and over as I shook Alice's body and slapped at her cheeks. I lifted her still form into my arms and crushed her to me, shaking her.

I remember the room filling with people, the gasps and shouts and moans. Hands pried me away from Alice. She fell back down onto the bed and remained motionless, eyes closed, face in a peaceful half-smile.

I remember Arthur barking orders, and Sophie pulling me from the room as Charles fell to his knees at Alice's bedside. I remember Abigail screaming in the hallway, holding onto her tightly as she began to sob.

And I remember the unholy wail from Sir Reginald Lockton as he lifted Alice's body into his arms and wept into her hair.

CHAPTER 31

She won't sit still. She says she can't organize a ball by herself, but she can organize a funeral singlehandedly. I've let her. Otherwise, she breaks down into sobbing, and I cannot bear her tears. Coward that I am, I let her work herself to sleep every night.

I've started my own memorial for Alice to join the others. I waver between sorrow for her and relief it's not Joy.

I'm worried about Joy's health. And for the baby.

I tried to destroy it again, smashing it over and over. The hammer just bounces off, like it did a hundred times before. I've hid the wretched rock away and have commissioned a case for it, something in thick glass so I can see it, but no hands can touch it. Please let it remain silent!

I was exhausted.

Still, I pasted on a smile and waved at the coach as it took Abigail away. She leaned out the window with a tear-streaked face and smiled back with the same false grin. Although our eyes were bright with tears, we'd managed to perfect our ladylike smiles.

I hugged myself and looked at Charles who stood next to me. He'd also donned black, including his cravat.

"Are you ready to go tomorrow?" I asked. He nodded, still keeping his eyes on Abigail's coach.

Arthur was taking him to Bath to inform their father of Alice's death, and then press for guardianship of Abigail and Charles. Arthur didn't expect him to put up much of a fuss.

PART 3 - THE CURSE

"I hope the news doesn't kill him," Charles spoke softly. "Or maybe I do." He pinched the bridge of his nose, his eyes shut tight. "It's all too much. I feel my head is about to explode."

He stood like a statue as I embraced him, my arms wrapping easily around his young wiry frame as I thought about the injustice of his position. I told him I had loved Alice too. That I would miss her. And I would never let anything happen to him or Abigail. His breath hitched and he mumbled an excuse about packing and rushed away.

My head felt like it was going to explode. I made my way back inside the house, tightening my shawl around me. A nap sounded perfect and I knew there was a nice warm fire in the library.

I entered the room, prepared to take up a spot on the couch when a stiff breeze brought a chill from the open windowed doors that led to a covered patio.

Sophie was sitting outside at the little table with no coat or even a shawl. Her ears and nose were tipped pink with cold. Sitting on the table was a bottle and a glass full of amber liquid. She rimmed the top of the glass with her fingers and hummed something before taking a sip of liquor.

She looked younger somehow, her eyes watching the morning sun as she enjoyed the breezes from the sea. But the closer I came to her the more her wrinkles became more pronounced, her lips became thinner. Her eyes were bright with unshed tears as a trembling hand brought the glass to her lips again. She had to be cold, sitting out here without covering.

"Sophie, dearest, come inside and warm up."

She jumped a little at the sound of my voice. "Oh! Joy, dear. Have a seat, and join me." Her words slurred. She snapped her fingers at me until I was seated next to her.

"I don't like you in black." She waved at my dress. "And she was a sort of servant, so you shouldn't be donning bombazine for more than a week."

"She was my friend." I watched the waves reflecting the sun into the horizon. I removed my shawl and wrapped it around Sophie's shoulders.

Sophie sighed and tucked it around her. "I never thought to see one of Arthur's brides in black. Usually, I'm the one in mourning for one of them. It just feels wrong to see you dressed like that." She shivered.

I frowned. "His brides? You mean Diana."

She nodded. "Diana, Catherine, and the mighty Luisa. Oh, she was my favorite! Spaniard. Took us all by storm. So passionate. She had a temper but was quick to laugh and play with me. She was loads of fun. She had Arthur by the nose. He was devoted to her every whim. He was so devastated when she died." She trailed off again, looking at the waves and taking another sip of brandy.

"I think you're drunk, Sophie." It was the only explanation I could think of for bringing up mysterious brides who didn't exist. Maybe she was thinking of the other Arthur, her brother?

"Hmmmm?" She looked down at her glass and then at the nearby bottle. "Daresay I'm fully foxed," she agreed. "Sure you don't want a sip? Oh! The baby! I forgot. None of the others ever lived long enough to produce babies." She shook her head. "Except Diana. But we know he never touched her. He only married her as a favor to me. Thought she'd be safe enough in London…"

I felt a chill travel up my spine. "Safe from what?" If she said ghosts again, I would scream. Sophie hesitated.

"What are you ladies talking about?" Arthur's hands slid across my shoulders and put gentle pressure there. I stiffened under his touch.

"Alright there, my Joy?" he asked. I looked up at him. His lips smiled at me but his eyes did not. They were wary as he searched my features.

"You came up so quiet. Just surprised me." I patted his hand gently. He took a step towards his mother.

She looked up at him with tears in her eyes. "You can't let this happen again, Arthur," she snapped at him.

"I know, old girl." He took the glass from her hand and pressed a kiss to her forehead. "Let's get you to bed. I know you haven't been sleeping well."

"I like her, Arthur. She's the best one you've had. Keep her safe!" she shouted at him as he lifted her to her feet.

"I will, my love, I promise." He looked at me and I chewed on my lip as he moved his mother into the house, calling for some servants to assist him.

I stayed still, my mind in a flurry of questions. Catherine and Luisa? Two other wives I had never heard of? How could he possibly have had two more wives? He was hardly old enough to have buried one.

Arthur returned shortly to the patio. He draped my shawl back over my shoulders and took the seat Sophie had vacated. He looked out at the sea in silence. I could see his mind racing again as his body sat still and calm, a storm waiting to be released.

PART 3 - THE CURSE

I turned back to the waves as my mind wandered over what Sophie had said. To keep me safe? Can't let this happen again? A slow feeling of dread started at the tip of my toes and spread up my entire body. I shivered.

"Cold?" His eyes were weary now, burdened with a load of grief and frustration.

"Just a chill. I was planning on taking a nap in front of the fireplace." I rose to my feet. "I think all this excitement and activity has finally caught up with me." I turned to leave.

"Joy." He stopped me.

"Sophie is old. She gets confused."

I nodded. "She had a little too much to drink."

He smiled at me. "Exactly. Don't think too much about what she says. I can't understand half of what she remembers. I was born late in her life, and there are things I don't even know about."

It made me feel a little better. "I understand. I'll try not to upset her."

He reached out for me and I closed the space between us. He tugged me down for a kiss I barely returned, then planted one on my bulging belly as well. "I'll clean up here. Get some rest." He turned back to watch the sea.

I closed the patio doors and made my way to the couch. The cushions were nicely heated from the fire and I sank into it, finding a cushion for my head. As the baby grew, I found sleeping in bed becoming more uncomfortable day by day. The couch was a warm and comfortable place to catch up on my rest.

I pulled my shawl across my body like a blanket and quickly fell into a peaceful slumber.

"Is she alive?" A timid voice woke me. I didn't open my eyes though; they felt so heavy I didn't know if I could. I just wanted to go back to sleep.

"Aye, she's breathin'. Don't know what we'd do with another body around here. Although, it's usually the missus that he kills, not their friends."

Now I was awake. I tried to appear asleep. I heard the maids bustle about quietly with their work but I wasn't going to stop their loose tongues.

"You really think they were just friends? Maybe he'd been sneaking into Lady Alice's bed. And that's why he killed her before she could tell the missus...you saw how angry he was at the ball."

My blood froze. Arthur. They were talking about Arthur.

I wanted to rise up and demand answers. Instead, I kept my breathing easy as my mind raced. They thought Arthur had killed Alice. Why?

"…Nah, he won't kill her. Not yet with the babe. Now, after it's born, I'll expect we'll be planning another funeral."

"Poor missus. She's a nice one. Bought us all new clothes, never complains, always thankful…"

"She's a Marco bride. They all die young."

I opened my eyes after they left. My breath was shaky and the fire gave no warmth. I gazed at the flames as my mind reeled.

Marco brides all die young? Like Diana? Who else had died?

It couldn't be true. I remembered the picture of Arthur's grandparents. She'd not died young. The healthy young boy at her side proved it and she'd gone on to birth Sophie.

I needed to find the source of these rumors. Arthur was leaving tomorrow. I could question people in the village, the tenants, maybe even a few servants if they would speak to me.

I jumped when a body sank onto the couch next to me.

"Sorry, didn't mean to frighten you…my Joy, you are so pale!" Arthur leaned towards me and rested his hand against my forehead. "Are you feeling ill?"

"No, no, I just woke up from a nightmare." I endured his touch.

He leaned forward and kissed me softly where his hand had rested. "I'm sorry to hear that. Luncheon is ready, and I don't want you skipping meals." He stroked my belly gently.

I flinched, but nodded. "Of course."

He rose to his feet, and offered me his hand. The hand of my husband, my lover, and my friend.

Was it also the hand of a murderer?

PART 3 - THE CURSE

CHAPTER 32

I showed Sophie where it was being kept. I locked the doors behind me and told her I was taking the keys with me. She told me she would set a footman to guard it, day and night and that she'd try to keep Joy distracted while I was gone. I hate to leave her, but I must. Charles and Abigail were important to Alice, and I owe it to her.

"Don't get up," Arthur said as I went to rise from our bed.

I looked around, wondering how I'd gotten here. I hadn't slept in our room since the ball.

"You moved me." I yawned.

"You were passed out on the couch in the library with an unfinished dress on your lap. I just brought you to bed."

"Your bed." I sank back onto the pillows.

"Our bed," he corrected, looming over me. "I want you back in our bed. I can understand you being upset with me the night of the ball, but it's been over a week. Are you still punishing me?"

I exhaled. "No, it was just such chaos with Alice's death. Abigail needed me, and I didn't want her to be afraid to come find me in the night if I was with you." It was the truth. I really had no reason not to join him again. Unless, he just wanted a convenient place to murder me in my sleep.

I pushed the unpleasant thought aside as I rose again, he gently pushed me back.

"Get some more rest. I'll take care of Charles," he promised.

"I should say goodbye." I tried to sit up again. Having another body in my belly made the maneuver difficult.

"Joy..." His voice rumbled a warning.

I gave up, flopping back on the pillows. "What?"

"Charles would rather you not hover about him right now. It makes him uncomfortable," he said as he dressed.

"Very well. I'll cease my hovering." I watched him as he tied his cravat into a simple knot. "How long will you be gone?" How long did I have to investigate?

"I hope not more than a week." He shot me a look. "And I expect you to rest the entire time."

I gave him a weary smile. "I feel like sleeping for a week, so the timeline is perfect." I planned to begin my queries as soon as his carriage was over the horizon.

He stilled for a moment. Was I not convincing enough? His eyes narrowed. "I mean it, Joy. No gallivanting around tombs with Eva, no riding Toady, and no curricle rides. I should forbid you to even pick up a needle."

"You're being a bully."

He harrumphed as he pulled his coat on. Then he leaned over me, caging me in as his dark eyes peered into my face. "Will you miss me?"

The words rang in my head. Would I? I reached up and touched his face, stroking his beard. His eyes were warm, but worried. Silence yawned between us as I worked things over in my mind.

"Things really have not been the same between us, have they?" I whispered.

He rested his forehead against mine. "It's completely my fault, I know." He kissed me softly. "Just...be here when I get back. Let me try and fix things."

"I'll be here," I promised, stroking his face once more before he left the room.

A warm furry body leaped on the bed when the door closed. I laughed a bit as Pip nuzzled into my neck and his body plopped down next to mine. "He didn't say anything about gallivanting around with you, did he Pip." I received a wet doggy kiss in response.

I dozed for another hour with Pip curled up next to me. Once all was quiet, I tossed off the bedding and readied myself for the day.

Reggie was alone at the breakfast table. He was staring at his plate heaped up with bacon and eggs and ham. A stack of toast accompanied it.

"I took too much," he said as I slowly sat down. He pushed the food away. "I keep waiting for her to ration me with her beautiful smile. I loved to banter with her in the morning." His head dropped into his hands.

Part 3 - The Curse

I leaned forward to comfort him but he drew back sharply. "Right, I'll be headed back to Town this morning. Arthur's gone. Sophie's under the weather. You don't need me moping about the place as well."

"You may stay as long as you like."

He stood next to my chair. "Thank you, dear lady. For all your hospitality and kindness." His voice wobbled. He leaned over and kissed my cheek, lingering while he swallowed his feelings. "I'll be back when the new little Marco makes his debut," he promised in a much firmer voice.

"Be well, Reggie."

He left the room without glancing back.

The servants swept in with hot food and Eva joined me, looking downtrodden as well.

"Everyone is so sad," she commented as Pip laid his head in her lap for an ear scratch.

"We all miss Lady Alice."

Eva sniffed, reaching for Reggie's discarded plate of bacon.

"We should visit with people today." I was ready to get some investigations started.

"Who?" Eva asked through a mouthful of eggs.

"Don't talk with your mouth full," I chided, handing her a napkin. "Who is the most elderly person at Ironwood?"

"Sophie," Eva said without hesitation.

"Don't let her hear you say that. Who else?"

"Mrs. Franks."

The housekeeper wouldn't do. I was positive she was keeping all the secrets of Ironwood from me as well.

"What about someone who doesn't live in the big house," I pressed.

Eva brightened. "You mean like Granny Polly? I love to visit her. She always has cake and milk to share and her house always smells like candy."

Perfect.

Granny Polly's home was tucked away beneath some large trees. Smoke puffed lazily from the chimney. Her home was tidy and neat, with a large pile of firewood outside the door waiting to be chopped.

I took both of Eva's hands before knocking and peered into her face. "Eva, I want to make Polly comfortable. Let's not tell her I'm Mrs. Marco. I don't want her to make too much of a fuss." I wanted to quiz her openly about Ironwood without her knowing who I was.

Eva frowned a little. "Then what do I call you?"

"Miss Joy is fine."

She glanced doubtfully at my round belly and raised her brows. I laughed.

"Mrs. Joy then," I corrected.

She nodded and dropped my hands to knock loudly on the door.

"Just a moment!" I could hear shuffling behind the door before it swung open. A plump little lady covered in wrinkles and bundled up in a cap and shawl greeted us.

"Who's this?" She squinted at my face.

"Granny Polly! It's me!" Eva said.

A smile made her face wrinkle even more. "It's Miss Eva. And a friend?"

"This is Mrs. Joy. We've brought you some preserves." Eva raised the basket.

"Oh how nice."

Polly sniffed. "We need something sweet for a visit. Let's bake a cake." She shuffled into her house.

"Yay!" Eva whooped. I told Pip to stay outside and closed the door behind us.

She and Eva performed a perfected baking choreography. Polly called out the ingredients and Eva scrambled about the kitchen to find it with a big grin on her face.

"What's going on up at the big house?" Polly asked. "You working up there?"

"I'm a seamstress." I tried to stick with as much of the truth as possible.

"I'll bet you've been right busy making all that new livery," Polly said, her old shaky hands cracking eggs with expert precision. "I heard about the new mistress making changes. 'Bout time too. I hated wearing those awful black creations."

"You worked at the big house?" I prodded as Eva carried a bag of flour to the table.

"Started as a girl in the kitchen and worked my way up to Housekeeper for the Dowager. Oh, the parties she would throw! Once, she brought an entire menagerie to Ironwood. Monkeys, lions, birds, and even an elephant!"

I laughed. "What a mess!"

"Exactly so! And the food bill was horrible. Do you know how much an elephant eats?" Even Eva was starting to giggle.

Part 3 - The Curse

"It was a grand time to be at Ironwood, with all the sadness in the house we were glad of it." She shook her head and started measuring out flour.

"One hears whispers about things," I prodded gently. "About ghosts and such."

"Ghosts?" Polly wrinkled her nose further and shook her head. "Never saw nothing close to ghosts. That house is just sad. Centuries of sadness builds up over time until it lives in the rocks and mortar."

Eva frowned. "Why is the house sad?" She slid her body up on the table and began mixing the sugar and eggs together as Polly sifted the white flour.

"The house can't keep a mistress. They all die here at Ironwood." She shook her head. "We were all shocked when it was Lady Graves who died last week and not the Marco Bride."

Eva glanced at me with shimmery eyes, then focused on her bowl. "I don't want Mrs. Marco to die."

"Don't fret." Polly stroked her hair gently. "She's got a babe in her belly. Never heard of one dying when they were in confinement."

"How many have you seen die?"

"Three." Polly scowled. "This is a horrible conversation for making a cake. I'm afraid we'll turn the milk sour with such talk."

But I pressed forward. "Oh please, all one hears is rumors. I like to squash them when I can. Was one the Dowager's mother?"

"No, she actually lived to a nice old age, now that I think of it. Pleasant lady. It was the Dowager's brother. He lost his mum at a young age and his father remarried Lady Sophie's mother." She took the bowl from Eva and slowly added her flour mixture.

So the lady in the portrait was not Sophie's mother. But Arthur had said it was his grandmother, I rubbed my head where a definite ache was building trying to keep things straight.

"Now the first Master Arthur, he lost two wives. Right nice ladies they were. Smart and spirited! Catherine and Luisa. Both died within months of coming to Ironwood. Broke Master Arthur's heart when Luisa was found. When she died, he vowed to never marry again. He left for the continent and met his end there, leaving it all to the Dowager."

"So she did have an older brother named Arthur," I verified.

"Yes. He looked just like the present Lord of the manor. Except he didn't have that disgusting beard. It's not seeming for a man in his position to look so unkempt." She scowled into her batter. "Open up those preserves now, Eva."

The conversation turned to the preservation systems at the "big house" as Granny Polly called it. From the ice house to the wine cellar, she recalled all the old nooks and crannies she'd once overseen.

"Are there any secret passages?" Eva asked. She'd asked Arthur and Sophie the same questions. They'd both laughed her question off as nonsensical.

"Of course there are. What's a big old house like that without secret passages? When new additions were made there was always a hidden hallway added on. Helped out the servants greatly to not have to tromp all over creation."

I latched onto this discovery in a hurry. I hoped my interest seemed nothing but innocent curiosity. "Oh, please tell us. Eva and I would love to explore them."

Granny Polly shrugged. "Ask the housekeeper. I'm sure she keeps some of them open for the rest of the staff to use."

There was no more talk of the big house. Granny Polly talked about the neighbors and other tenants, keeping a mental track of who might need some additional help. The cake baked, Pip snuck in and sniffed around for rodents. The little house was warm and cozy. I loved the way her face lit up when Polly told her stories of Ironwood's history. We ate the cake, and said our goodbyes as we left her comfortable home.

Eva's face lit up with excitement. "Secret passages! I can't wait to find them! I only wish Abigail was here, she'd love to explore too."

"I'm sure the house has endless secrets. We'll seek them out together and then you can show them to Abigail when she visits," I promised. I was as excited as she was to find them and hopefully shed some light on my husband's odd behavior.

PART 3 - THE CURSE

CHAPTER 33

I've been pushing everyone relentlessly. John Coachman pulled me aside and politely told me that the horses needed rest. The dark circles under his eyes told me that he needed some as well. I'm anxious and reckless. I need to get back to my wife.

"What on earth are you doing?" Sophie demanded as she entered the library.

"Looking for secrets!" Eva announced. "Granny Polly said the house was full of them. We're starting in here."

"Secret rooms and passageways," I admitted, reaching down to rub Pip's head as he sat on my feet.

"Oh that Polly! I should have sworn her to secrecy when I pensioned her off." Sophie planted her hands on her hips and scowled at us. "I suppose I should show them to you before you tear the house apart. I know I can't keep you from looking, and I don't want you falling off a ladder!" She shook her finger at me. "Just stay out of the locked rooms. They aren't safe."

"Is that where you're hiding the ghosts?" I quipped.

"Cheeky. Give me your promise or I'll have Arthur seal up every secret passage."

"Of course we will," I agreed. I would break down every lock later in secret if I had to.

She gave both Eva and I another look to assess our honesty, then walked to the fireplace that was cheerfully crackling away. She stopped at the bookshelves built into the walls and pressed down on the bottom shelf with her foot. It lowered about an inch, before springing back up as the shelf swung open like a door. Eva gasped with delight.

The House That Death Built

"All these books are fake." Sophie touched the spines. "The words are all written in Mandarin so no one would pay much attention to them. Otherwise the shelf would be too heavy to move. Look around Ironwood for things that don't make sense or are forgettable. It's where her secrets are."

"We should make a map! I'll go get some paper!" Eva darted off towards the study with Pip at her heels.

I walked towards the open door and peered in. It was cold inside, but not musty or dirty and looked to be in regular use. The width was plenty wide for one person to walk through, but two side by side would be a struggle.

"Do be careful." Sophie took my arm. "Joy, please understand. If a door is locked, it's locked for a reason. It's not to hide something, it's to keep us safe."

"From the ghosts? Or from the past?"

She closed her eyes and pinched her nose. "Arthur is right, you really are too clever." I could see the sadness now Polly had spoken of. This house was wearing on her.

Eva returned before I could question her more, triumphantly holding her mapmaking equipment with Pip at her side. "I'm ready!"

"Almost. It's a little chilly in there." Sophie wrapped her shawl around the girl. "There, now. Off you go, and take care of our Joy."

"I promise." Eva pulled me into the passageway.

We spent the day exploring. Eva took careful notes and made a simple map of what led where. She was even thoughtful enough to put pictures of things for me instead of words. Pip sniffed out every corner and cranny that smelled suspicious to him. I watched for footprints and dust. The well-worn paths were clear and clean and the servants were more than happy to share the paths they knew when we ran into them. Most of the passageways were connected in some way and I could see how they became installed with each new addition made to Ironwood.

"Mark this door, Eva." I touched another locked door. We were in the oldest part of Ironwood now. The floorboards creaked and groaned and plaster crumbled around us when we brushed the walls. This area wasn't used frequently and the hems on our clothes were soon covered in a fine layer of dust.

"Why do you think there are so many locked doors?" she asked as Pip sniffed around the frame.

PART 3 - THE CURSE

"It's an old house. Sometimes the floorboards get rotten and you might fall through and hurt yourself. They lock the doors to keep people out until it can be fixed."

"Are you going to fix them all?"

"Yes, I will. Ironwood is the best project I've had in a long time, much more fun than the London townhouse." I shuddered to think of all the pink still to be removed.

"Can I visit you there?" She made a note on the map.

"Of course you…" I broke off when I saw the dusty footprints heading down the passageway. Someone had stepped in a chunk of plaster and it had marked their every step. They ended at a door where half a footprint disappeared behind it. Someone had used this place recently.

I reached for the knob to give it a turn and found it locked tight. Pip sniffed at the door and gave a mighty sneeze that made me jump.

"Bless you, Pip!" Eva laughed as I looked up around the door for any sign of a key left on the frame. Nothing.

"Mark this door with a star, would you please?" I rested my hand against it.

"What is special about it?" Eva made a careful mark on the map.

"This door has secrets."

Her eyes were wide as she made the little mark. I drew a star in the dust on the door to match our map.

We pushed on through the tunnel, finding it exited in the attic. Perfect.

She and I made our way back downstairs to find Sophie waiting with tea and warm cake. She looked relieved as we entered the room and sat down.

"You're both positively filthy. We should have the passages cleaned out and checked for dangers if you insist on exploring further." She took out a handkerchief and swiped at the smudges on Eva's face. I wiped my own nose and grinned at the dirt on mine.

"It was so much fun. There are secret passages everywhere! Even into Mr. Marco's room. Do you think he knows about it?" Eva asked.

"I'm sure he does." Sophie finished wiping off Eva and sat back with her tea. "I had hoped you two would be so exhausted you would give up the idea of further exploration."

"Not a chance." I sipped my own cup of tea as Eva dove happily into her cake. She went home sleepy and stuffed as Sophie looked over the map we'd made.

"That was brilliant of you to make symbols. What's the little star for?"

"It was just a little marker Eva and I made in the dust to mark our path in case we doubled back," I lied. They were tripping off my tongue easier and easier.

Sophie handed me back the map. "No ghosts?"

"Not a peep of the supernatural," I assured.

"Well, I suggest you get cleaned up and take a nap before dinner. You look like you've been rolling in plaster and dust."

"I'll take your advice." I lied again. Instead, I made my way to the attic and the passageway. I had a room to explore.

A Roma family who had lived on my family's farm one summer had taught Thomas to pick locks. He was so proud of his accomplishments he couldn't keep it to himself. Luckily, I was the first one he boasted to. I pointed out the flaws in his exuberance and what would happen when our parents found out. He begged me to keep silent and I agreed if he taught me as well. It was the best use of a hairpin I'd ever found.

I eased the door open. It creaked a little on its hinges as I slipped through the doorway and shut it quickly behind me.

I could see my breath as I entered the room. I hugged myself and tried to rub some warmth into my arms. It smelled like oil, paint, and other strong chemicals. I held my nose for a moment to get used to the odors.

There was a fine layer of dust over everything. No one had cleaned in here for a long while. I could see footprints in the grime on the floor.

Faint light tried to creep in through curtains. I could see shapes enough to avoid hitting them, but not enough to make out what they were.

The threadbare curtains were cold as I threw them open to welcome the light. The sun brought me comfort and warmth as the dust swirled and settled. I turned to see what secrets the room held.

Portraits covered the walls. Portraits of beautiful women held by beautiful frames done by different artists. Women with golden hair, auburn tresses, chestnut manes, and black-haired beauties. Sharp and shining eyes; greens, browns, blues, and even one gold. Full lips, rosy cheeks... and not a freckle to be found. An entire gallery of women, each wearing fashions from a different time.

I turned slowly to take them all in, feeling smaller and bewildered with every portrait that gazed out at me. I recognized the face of Diana Hampton. I stopped, turning to study it. She was radiant in her favorite shade of pink with soft lips and bright eyes. She was smiling broadly. Happy.

There was an unfinished one on an easel, covered by a cloth. An old chair covered in splotches of paint sat before it, the only real piece of sitting furniture in the room. Everything else was cupboards and shelves full of paints and brushes and chemicals.

I made my way to the easel and slowly pulled the sheet off. Alice's face radiated back at me. Her eyes sparkled with the inner energy I had come to love, her face warm and radiant instead of the cold friend I had buried. Her portrait was not finished, just her face. The rest of her had been outlined and was waiting to be put in place. The only other detail done was a large sapphire hanging from her neck, the one she had found in the attic and had worn with my blessing for the ball.

I took a step back from the painting and glanced up at the others. They were all waiting patiently for Alice to join them in immortality. But who were these other women?

I shivered again with foreboding. Were these the Marco brides? All of them? Some of them? I glanced up at the first portrait and saw from her neck the same sapphire that had adorned Alice's the night of the ball. It was in all the pictures. Some wore it as a brooch or a hatpin. One had it on a ring. It was clearly something all of them had one time possessed or wore. What was it doing in each of the portraits?

The setting sun cut my time short. I slipped out from behind the tapestry that hid the false door in our bedroom and embraced the warmth coming from the fireplace. A bath had been set up in front of it. Sophie was always so thoughtful, or she was pointing out the fact I was absolutely disgusting and dirty. Probably a bit of both.

I sank into the tub and leaned back as far as I could into the hot water, closing my eyes.

The portraits swirled around me. All those faces of all those women. Beautiful and young.

And they all wore the sapphire. Was it the missing piece of the puzzle?

I resolved to try interrogating Arthur one more time about the mysteries of Ironwood. If he didn't answer to my satisfaction, I'd seek it out myself.

CHAPTER 34

I don't care what the doctor says, we are leaving! At once!

Arthur entered Ironwood with his usual flair. His hat, cape, and walking stick dropped onto the floor before Martins could take them. He strode into the sitting room where I was working on some small embellishments for Eva's new dress and tossed them out of my hands. He embraced me tightly and proceeded to kiss me until I became lightheaded.

"Arthur, please!" I begged as he started to plant kisses along my jaw to my neck.

"Please what? Give me any task," he promised between kisses. "I live to serve you, Madame Wife."

"Please let me catch my breath." I finished. He knelt down and rested his head on my bulging belly with a deep sigh. I ran my fingers through his hair as he embraced me and the baby.

"She's active. I was just kicked in the face." Arthur grinned and pulled away from me to greet Pip who flopped on his back for a belly rub.

"Or *he* is just protesting being manhandled by his parents," I countered.

Arthur rose and pulled me gently into his arms. "*She* will just have to get used to it because I intend to manhandle her mother as often as I can," he murmured in my ear before kissing the skin right behind it to make me shiver.

"Really, Arthur, make love to your wife in private," Sophie chided as she entered the room.

"Leave the room and it will be private." He accepted her embrace.

"How are the Graves?" she asked immediately.

PART 3 - THE CURSE

"Abigail is settled and well at school, I stopped by to check on her when I returned. Charles is squared away at his institute and Lord Graves is too ill to take care of his affairs. He has a younger brother who is taking over until Charles is of age. I threatened their new guardian with hellfire and damnation if I hear one snippet of unhappiness from the siblings. He was sufficiently cowed."

"Excellent work. And now that you are back, I need to return to Town," Sophie announced. "The thought of tripping over you two lovebirds kissing in every room frankly makes my stomach turn. And I miss my young bucks. Who knows what deviltry they are getting into without me?"

"You're just upset that you aren't there to get into mischief with them," Arthur pointed out.

"Of course I am. I have never liked country life for long. I'll be leaving tomorrow."

"I can help you pack," I offered.

She shooed me off as she left the room. "Nonsense. You and Arthur need some time together. I'll see you at supper."

Arthur took me by the hands and kissed each one of them as he tugged me carefully towards the couch. He pulled me onto his lap, resting his head on my shoulder.

"I missed you. More than anybody should miss somebody."

"I missed you as well," I said, wrapping my arms around his. I settled into his warmth and inhaled his scent. It brought me a feeling of comfort, even as my stomach churned with the thought of confronting him.

He let out a deep sigh. "Are you still out of sorts with me, my Joy?"

An invitation I couldn't pass up. "Not out of sorts. I'm just so very confused by your behavior."

He was silent. I could hear his mind gathering thoughts to put into words as he stroked my skin. "This house has secrets," he finally spoke. "It has a deadly and dangerous past…"

It was the same 'mysterious' and 'dangerous' speech I'd heard before from multiple people. I wasn't going to hear it once more.

"I know about the Marco brides," I blurted out.

His arms stiffened around me. "What?"

"The mistresses of Ironwood… how they die young. About your uncle Arthur's wives and his mother died young." His arms tightened and he inhaled sharply.

I forged ahead, I needed to try one last time for a rational explanation from my husband. "There's talk of murder, Arthur. About Alice's death not being..."

He pushed me onto the couch and stood. "We're leaving," he growled.

"Arthur please! Just tell me! What are you so worried about? You are so worked up and irrational! My brain can't keep up with your swinging moods. You are charming and loving one moment and then brooding and angry the next! I can't live like this! I need to..." I reached out to stop him as he marched to the door.

He turned on me. "Go and pack now! We're leaving with Sophie in the morning!"

"Why? Why must we go? Tell me, please! I'll listen, I promise," I begged.

He broke away from me, resuming his angry path to the door.

"Just tell me what happened to Alice!" I screamed at his retreat.

He stopped walking and clenched his fists. He turned to face me. "I won't be deterred this time, Joy. I suggest you ready yourself to leave. I don't care what the doctor says. I'll drag you from this house kicking and screaming if I have to." His voice was calm and cold, his glare fierce and stern.

"Please," I whispered once more.

He gave me one last glower and stormed away.

Defeated, I sank back down onto the couch. Pip whimpered and rested his head in my lap. I stroked his nose. I could hear Arthur's voice booming through the hallways, shouting for the servants to attend him.

I let out a shaky breath and swallowed the tears that were close to the surface. "We don't have much time, Pip. We've got to find that necklace." It was the only thing I could think of to confront him with. The one thing that connected all the Marco brides and my dear Alice.

It wouldn't be in the passageways. The only secret there had been the portrait room, and I'd checked there for it. Twice.

I stood on trembling legs and rubbed my arms. *Think, Joy, think!* I made my way to the bedrooms. The servants were scurrying about, fulfilling the orders the Master of the house had demanded.

I hated it.

I hated it when he plunged my peaceful household into something of chaos and apprehension just because he was the Master here. I hated the feeling of anxiety whenever he was here. Ironwood was beautiful and peaceful. Arthur Marco was not.

PART 3 - THE CURSE

Most of all, I hated the feelings I was having towards him. That maybe, just maybe, our marriage was a mistake.

I climbed the stairs slowly with my thoughts, Pip plodding alongside me. I glanced up a moment to make way for the servants as I looked out into the gallery.

The double doors had been closed all week. There had even been a footman guarding it. Pip and Eva had wanted to play catch indoors one cold day and I thought it had the best room for him to run. The footman had apologized but had turned us away, saying a broken window had littered the long hall with glass and no one was to enter until it had been cleaned and repaired. I'd not thought much of it, taking my two charges to the ballroom instead. I remembered someone always standing at the doorway for the rest of the week. Cleaning wouldn't have taken so long.

Look around Ironwood for things that don't make sense or are forgettable. That's where her secrets are. Sophie's words sprang to mind as I walked towards the gallery. It didn't make sense for someone to guard the gallery for an entire week. I knew it had to be Arthur and Sophie's doing. They didn't want me to go in there.

I was going to find out why.

The big double doors were unguarded, and opened just a crack. I pushed my face in and called out a timid, "Hello?" I was met with silence.

I chewed on my lip as Pip and I entered the gallery, watching over my shoulder to make sure no one was going to stop me. I shut the door with a soft click and faced the gallery.

First I noticed all the windows were in perfect order. I stung to know the entire house was in on the conspiracy against me. I headed to the closest window and threw open the long drapes to let in more light.

Faces of the Marco ancestors lined the wall. Busts stood on podiums made of marble and metal. Antique heirlooms rested beneath cases of glass. I walked silently down the wide red carpet as Pip sniffed around at things in the shadows. The room was cool and hugged myself for warmth, wishing for a shawl.

I recognized some of the faces from the portrait room. All the women were dressed in formal attire for their posing, their hair done in the styles of the day. They all stood in proper positions, holding still for their immortalization, none smiling. It wasn't anything like the portrait room where the faces had been full of life and emotion. Those paintings hadn't been for posterity, but as a memorial.

None of them hanging in the gallery were wearing the necklace.

I made my way through the Museum of Marco. There were weapons and artifacts from the Crusades, old blueprints for buildings and fans studded with jewels. A few articles from the Orient and even America were nestled on dark velvet beneath their glass cases.

And that's where I found the necklace. It was tucked away in the corner where no light reached. It was beneath a large portrait of an ancient man in full armor, looking down the gallery with a sneer.

I focused my attention on the stone behind the glass case. It was the one thing that connected all of the women in the portraits to my Alice. The thing that had outraged Arthur at the ball where he'd practically attacked her for wearing it.

The big blue stone shimmered at me. I shook my head to clear my thoughts. How could it shine so brightly in the shadows?

I touched the case and leaned over it, trying to get a better look at it laying on black velvet with a broken clasp. What was the mystery behind this object? Sophie spoke of ghosts and Arthur ranted about curses. Was this it? The big secret they'd been hiding? A piece of jewelry?

I had finally found it, along with more questions than answers. I wanted to open the case, to take it out and confront everyone with it and demand they tell me all of Ironwood's secrets.

"Joy!" Arthur's voice startled me. I spun and saw him in the doorway. A look of horror washed over him, and the color drained from his face. He held onto the frame for support as he fell into the room on his knees.

"Oh please...Dear Lord in Heaven...I have never asked for anything before..."

I had never heard him pray before either. His face, always so proud and fierce, was full of fear. The cold began to grip me as well.

"Did you touch it?" he whispered. His eyes were swimming, searching my face, then down to my belly. "...the baby..." He rose and grabbed me tightly by the arms. "Tell me now Joy! Did you touch that bloody stone!"

"No!" I pushed him away. Anger I could take. I had plenty of dormant anger and confusion to unleash on him. Sleepless nights at his side and days of searching for information about dead women ignited me further.

"I did not touch your precious stone!" I glared at him and shoved my fear down. "Would you kill me if I had?"

He moved faster than I could, jerking my body towards his. I let out a shriek and threw my arms up to protect us. Pip let out an excited bark.

I was wrapped up in his crushing embrace before I could struggle. He was kissing my hair, my face, and crying, speaking my name over and over. My Arthur. Crying. Instantly, my anger deflated and I was engulfed in confusion.

I lowered my arms around his waist and rested them lightly against him. "I don't understand. What is wrong?"

His eyes roamed over my body as if he was making sure nothing was out of place. "I can't watch you die. I could not bear it if it happened to you too."

"What happened? Arthur, you are not making any sense." I shivered a little as he kissed my face fervently.

He held me close and glared at the jewel in the case. He pressed me harder into him. "Did it call to you?"

Call to me? "Arthur..."

"Did it wake you up at night begging to be found? You should have told me. You can tell me anything, everything! I would not have thought you mad. It called to all of the others, except Alice. She was just unlucky enough to find it."

"I have not heard anything," I answered.

"In your dreams? Nothing wakes you and begs you to search the house to release it? Nothing whispers promises of endless riches or your wildest desires if you would find it?" He looked down at me. I shook my head.

"No! Nothing."

"Then what brought you to it?" he demanded.

"You did!" My anger was back. "You! With your secrets and your sulking. Your lies and stories that even I can't keep straight." I stepped away from him. "I know about the other brides. There were more before Diana. And now Alice."

We were both staring at each other with heavy words unspoken between us.

"Did you kill them?" I whispered.

"What?" He looked shocked.

"Alice, Diana, Luisa, and Catherine. Your mother wasn't drunk and rambling. She was telling the truth! All of them died when they came to Ironwood. Someone is killing them!" I felt my throat tighten. "Was it poison?"

"Poison? No, it was the stone. Joy, you have to listen to me. I know it sounds insane, but my family is cursed. All Marco brides are cursed to die once they touch the stone..." Arthur reached out for my hand and I stumbled out of his reach again, finding it hard to breathe.

A stone? An inanimate object killing his wives? Did he think I was stupid?

"Are you going to kill me too?" I instinctively hugged the unborn inside me.

"I have not killed anyone!" His voice was loud enough to shake the rafters.

Fear and dread clutched at my heart. I needed to escape. My eyes darted around the room for something to defend myself with, and they rested on the glass jewel case. It was heavy and might be enough to stop him long enough for me to run from the room and get help.

I lunged towards it.

"Joy, no!" His arm shot out and grabbed mine, jerking me away from the case. I stumbled backward and spun to catch my balance. I crashed into the wall, striking my head hard against the portrait frame of the sneering man. The world dimmed around the edges as I felt something warm drip into my eyes. I pushed myself up from the floor slowly, found the world was spinning too much and collapsed again.

Arthur's face swam before mine and I heard Pip whining. "What have I done?" he whispered. He reached out for me and I cringed from his touch.

"Don't," I moaned.

"Please, Joy. Don't move. You're hurt." He knelt next to me.

"You hurt me," I reached up to wipe the blood from my vision.

"I'm bleeding," My words felt thick. I pushed my torso up from the ground and tried to get my bearings. My head pounded and blood dripped from my head.

"I'm sorry, my love, so sorry." I froze as he touched me.

"Don't hurt me, Arthur. Please. At least think of the baby..." I managed to beg. I curled into a ball around my child as Arthur pulled me towards him. His hands were gentle as he scooped me up into his embrace and lifted from the floor.

Part 3 - The Curse

He carried me from the gallery. He kicked the door of my bedroom open and laid me on my bed. I sank into the pillows as he pressed a handkerchief to my wound. He held my chin firmly in his grasp.

"You'll be alright." He cleaned up my face. "I'll take you away from this cursed place. We'll go back to London. We can go visit your family. Anywhere but here."

"No..." I groaned. My thoughts were becoming clearer as the pain in my head increased. I hated London. Ironwood was beautiful and quiet and everything I loved. It was Arthur who wasn't himself.

"We have to." He caressed my cheek. "I need to keep you safe."

"I'm safe here. The only one who has hurt me here is you," I said.

He froze as my words penetrated. His hand slowly lowered from my head wound to caress my face. "It was going to kill you."

"What was going to kill me?"

"That bloody stone!" He paced the room, tossing the soiled handkerchief aside angrily.

I was bewildered. "What are you talking about?"

He let out a frustrated growl. "I'm cursed, Joy! Just like my father and his father. All the way back to James and Marguerite de Marco!" He sat on the bed next to me and buried his face in his hands.

"You aren't making any sense," I moaned, creeping away from him.

He leaped to his feet. "I know!"

He opened his mouth to speak a few times and closed it. He stormed across the room and grabbed a chair from my desk, bringing it to the bedside. I kept my grip limp as he stroked my skin; his movements were fast and irritated as he organized his thoughts.

"I was seven years old when I first saw the stone. My mother had it. She was lying on the floor in my father's study. She was... so still. I thought she was asleep at first until I touched her cold cheek. She had it clutched in her hands, tightly to her chest. She didn't want to give it up, even in death."

"You aren't making sense, Sophie's..."

"Sophie isn't my mother, she's my sister. My younger sister," he stated. I tried to pull my hand away but he held it tight.

"Look at me, Joy. Look at me!" I met his gaze. It was wild and fierce, filled with desperation. "You wanted my trust. It goes both ways, remember. I'm telling you now, I'm telling you everything. Everything you wanted to know."

"This doesn't make sense," I protested.

"I know, but you must listen. Please, just listen?"

He gazed at me with desperation. I wanted to calm him, so I nodded. He let out a breath and released me. He stood up to pace again, running his fingers through his long hair.

"I said the same thing when I married Catherine. My father begged me not to marry her. He told me this fantastical story about how our family coffers had never run dry and the men in our family could have immortality, all for the price of a life. He warned me the stone would kill Catherine, just like it had his wives, just like it had my mother."

He pointed at me. "I'm sure my face looked just like yours does. You think I'm mad."

I did, but I was scared to admit it. He was on a thin tether about to snap. I didn't want to see what would happen if it did.

"I promised to listen," I whispered.

He slid back into the chair next to me and took my hands. "Yes, you did." He kissed them softly. "I don't deserve you. I truly don't. If I wasn't such a selfish bastard, I'd let you go. But you make me happy, and after so many… many years, don't I deserve to be happy?" He looked at me earnestly. I gave a hesitant nod.

"Father told me it would kill her, kill any woman who became a Marco bride. I had taken the curse on when I found my mother with the stone. I took it out of her hands when I found her, trying to rouse her. Father's face turned white when he saw I had it. Once I touched it, the curse passed to me. He tried to keep it from me, from her. He'd done so well, raising me in Spain and never letting her touch English soil once they had wed. But she missed her family and wanted to visit, wanted to introduce me to them. She wanted to see Ironwood. Father thought enough time had passed, that the curse had ended." Arthur shuddered. "He was so wrong. My mother is Olivia Marco, the one dear little Eva brings flowers to every time she visits the crypt. She's not my grandmother, she's my mother, Joy."

I couldn't speak, I couldn't move. I just sat and listened as his wild tale continued.

"After her death, he raised me here. He took on another wife when I went to Cambridge, Sophie's mother. Now that the curse had passed to me, he was safe to marry. I loved having a little sister. Soph was a ray of sunshine…she's what kept me sane."

PART 3 - THE CURSE

"Sophie knows about this?" I couldn't stop my voice from shaking when I spoke.

He took to his feet and started pacing again. "Of course she knows. She's watched herself age while I stayed young. She sat with me through Catherine's funeral, then Luisa's. She took on running the household and all my affairs while I ran off to try and die."

My eyes widened. "Arthur, don't say that."

"I didn't believe in the curse when I married Catherine," he repeated. He glared and clenched his fists. "She and I were good friends. We had fun together, we talked and danced and played. We agreed on life and politics. She asked me one day if I wanted to be Prime Minister. I laughed at her. No, I didn't but she did. She was a genius, I just hadn't seen it. She told me if I would be the face, she would be the brains. The woman was incredible when it came to schemes and machinations. I agreed and we were married. We spent all our time in London, and everything was fine until she came to Ironwood for a summer house party. By the end of the week, this extraordinary woman had gone insane."

"I found her in the crypt, dead. She was barefoot and in her nightgown, her hair disheveled, her face gaunt. She was leaning against my mother's tomb, clutching the stone in her hand. My father had buried it with my mother to hide it. Her hands were bloody, her nails broken. I don't know what she did to get it out."

He spun and looked at me. "And you swear you don't hear it?"

I shook my head. "Hear what?"

"Voices...a voice. Something that keeps you up at night. Something calling you and promising all your dreams and wishes. Something threatening you. Something crowding out the space in your mind until you'll do anything just to silence it!" He was standing over me, shouting again.

"Arthur, stop! I haven't heard a thing! Nothing."

"But that's what it does! It promised Catherine all she wanted; titles, riches, to be the most powerful woman in the world. All she had to do was find it.

"I thought she'd become unhinged. Her schemes had become too much for her and materialized in this strange obsession that killed her. Father warned me it was the curse. He begged me to listen. I was mourning. I still didn't believe him and ran back to Spain to get away from it all."

I could see memories gathering in his mind. "It was there I met Luisa."

I didn't know how much of this was true or how much of it was madness, but I knew what I saw on his face.

"You loved her."

"I loved her," he agreed. "Everyone loved her. She was fun, she was loud, she was exuberant, she was wild, she was life itself wrapped up into a beautiful package. She was passionate. She taught me so much about life and love and…" his breath caught. "Things weren't safe in Spain, so I brought her home. Father had finally started aging. I thought he was going to die of apoplexy when I walked in the door with her. He demanded I leave. I thought it was because I had brought home a Spanish bride. I was sure Luisa would win him over with time. She made it two weeks before she died. She starved herself, searching day after day for it, swearing she had to find the stone to keep her family safe back in Spain. I tried to take her away to a doctor but she fought me, hissing and scratching and locking herself away, running from me anytime I went near her. Father had hidden it in the library this time. Sophie found her, clutching the false book he had used as a hiding place. She was sitting in front of a dead fire with a smile on her face like she'd won something precious."

"I was willing to listen to my father now. He showed me the journals he'd written about the curse. Of the accidental deaths of his maids, just like Alice. He wrote about his own three wives and their deaths, including my mother's." He took long steps to the door. "I'll get them, show them to you, once you read them…" he stopped before his hand touched the knob.

"But you can't read them, can you." His fist bunched up and punched the door in anger, making a loud crack that echoed through the room.

I jumped as he hit it again, and again. His knuckles were bleeding as he brought them through his hair, grabbing at his locks in frustration. He turned and looked at me.

"Please don't look at me like that. I could never hurt you. I'm just…I didn't think this would be so hard."

"I think you need to rest, to calm down." My voice wobbled.

He shook his head. "No, you need to know. All of it. I can't die, Joy. I've tried. I wanted the curse to end with me. I tried blowing my brains out, drowning, even beheading. The damn blade bounced off my spine! Can you believe it! Even the executioner was shocked." His laugh was unnatural.

PART 3 - THE CURSE

I was trying to curl into a ball, plugging my ears. "Please, please stop."

He took my hands again. "Why do you think I wear my beard?" He pressed my hands into his cheeks, pushing them into the lines on his face. "I can't die but I scar nicely. When I was attacked by Boney's spies they didn't just attack me, they slit my throat ear to ear." He ran my fingers along the long scar beneath his beard. "Feel it? It's right there." I tried to pull my hands away but he pulled them down to his chest. "Here, where Carter shot me. You were right. It wasn't just a simple scratch, it's a bullet buried deep into my chest. It's still in there. I hid it from you as best I could, but you knew it was something more. You're so damn clever! Why do you have to be so brilliant? Why can't you just…" He collapsed and buried his head in my lap, his fists pounding on the mattress next to me.

I put my hands on his head and calmly stroked him. His fists stilled and he clutched at my hips as I carefully caressed him. One of his hands slid up and rested on my rounding belly as I continued to soothe him silently while my own emotions quietly boiled in turmoil.

His voice was softer now. "I left for the continent and let Sophie run everything. She faked a pregnancy; then excused a child who was always with the nurse, or at school, or abroad. I came back when Nathaniel died, posing as her son and heir." His voice was calm and strong again. "I was determined to live alone. To be the last. Then Sophie asked me to marry Diana to save her family's finances. Sophie was positive that we could beat the curse. We talked and schemed and worked out every detail to keep Diana safe. I gave her everything I could to keep her happy in London. Then Diana met Carter. She came here to hide. I raced here to stop her, and when I arrived all appeared to be well. The safe was locked and it was there in its case. I still don't know how she got it out of my safe, how she stole the key from me while I slept. I found her dead in her bed the next morning, wearing the stone around her neck."

"I think you know the rest." His head slumped into my lap.

My tears fell into his hair as my heart started to break. I didn't believe a word he'd spoken. It was too incredible.

"Please, my dearest. Everything I've said is true," he said.

I knew he believed it. I knew that he felt it in his bones what he said was the truth. This fantastical, amazing story was the explanation for Alice, for Diana, and whoever else he'd seen touch it and die. He believed

Sophie was not his mother, that he was almost a century old, and that he was cursed. There was nothing more I could say.

I inhaled a shaky breath. "I'm tired, and my head hurts. It's all so much. I…I just want to rest." I pushed him away from me and rolled over on the bed, giving him my back. This conversation was over.

He ran his hands on my back, stroking me softly. I held as still as possible, hating how soft and warm his hands were on me. Hands I had thought were safe.

I heard him swallow. "I'll leave you to rest. Think about what I said. I'm sorry, my love, I should have never let you stay here, even if you were sick. I'll send for Sophie. She'll come, and tell you everything I've said is true." I felt him reach out and stroke my hair. I didn't flinch at his touch, but let the tears fall from my eyes instead.

I shook my head. "Leave Sophie alone. I'm too tired…" My heart was breaking in two.

"Sleep then, we'll talk in the morning." He bent to kiss my cheek. I did flinch then. He stilled a moment, then backed away and left the room.

I lay awake long after Arthur had left. I faced the window and watched the sunset. Tears rolled silently down my face and soaked my pillow.

I had married a mad man.

Even worse, I was in love with one.

My heart was firmly entwined with his and would always be. I loved Arthur Graham Marco and I felt it keenly down to my soul.

And he was insane.

The baby kicked, and I bit my lip. I caressed my belly and it stilled.

Its father belonged in Bedlam.

I sat up and wiped my face, exhaling a shaky breath. I would give in to Arthur's demands that I leave Ironwood. Only it would not be with him.

It didn't matter that I loved him. It didn't matter that my heart was slowly breaking. I could not stay with a man who was not safe. All those nights of him rescuing me from my nightmares worked into a knot of nausea. I hadn't been safe at all.

My belly wiggled again, reminding me I wasn't alone in my choice. I needed to leave. I couldn't raise our child with a mad man, who lived and made choices as though he was cursed, and who thought our child would someday inherit a curse. It was too much for me to wrap *my* head around, let alone a child.

Part 3 - The Curse

It was dark now and the house was settling down, servants retiring for the night. I lit a candle and carried it with me around the room.

There was a small portmanteau in my wardrobe and I opened it, packing underthings, a nightgown, and a clean dress. Unworn bonnets and money filled the rest of the bag. Luckily, I had gobs of it. Arthur kept throwing it at me, claiming it was pin money and no self-respecting husband would do less. I had hardly spent any of it. Half of it went in the portmanteau and the other was divided between my reticule and my clothes.

My hands shook as I gazed into the mirror to clean off the dried blood and search for any bruises. The wound was hidden in my hairline, and wouldn't be noticed.

More tears ran down my face. I wondered if they would ever stop. There were no sobs, no gasps for breath or deep wails, just a steady stream of tears.

Flinching as I picked up my barely used hairpins I did a horrible job of pulling my hair up, with pieces of blonde curls sticking out in odd places. It wouldn't matter once I put on a dreaded bonnet.

Sitting at my desk, I took out a dusty piece of paper and a pencil. I was about to write my first letter.

The traitorous tears splashed on the page as I drew, angry with the fact I couldn't write words and was reduced to drawing pictures like a child. Arthur took shape the way I last saw him, wild and irrational, dark and frightening. He faced a sorrowful pregnant woman, cradling her unborn baby. A big fat tear fell from my eyes onto her belly, smudging it. I finished with my signature, remembering fondly how Alice taught me to write it. Fishhook, circle, then a slouching scarecrow without a head. Joy. I folded it up and left it next to my pink diamond ring on the desktop.

Now I just had to wait.

I could hear Arthur in the next room, muttering and pacing the floor. He came to my door several times, stopped, groaned, and stormed away.

I waited.

Late in the night he went to bed, the light from under his door went out and all was silent. I heard his familiar soft snoring and made my escape.

Picking up my things, I carried my boots as I tiptoed out my bedroom door. Careful to be silent, I found my way through Ironwood in the moonlight. I said farewell to the beautiful home I had grown to love so much. I touched the banister on the staircase fondly and ran my hand along the walls as I made my way to the kitchen. It was quiet and warm there, with a loaf of bread set out for breakfast. I took it and a small wrapped cheese for my travels.

Pip slept in the corner of the kitchen. He looked at me with puzzlement but accepted the tearful petting and kisses I gave him. "Be good, you. Take care of everyone. Now, stay." I admonished, giving Pip an extra hug and kiss. He sighed and rested his head on his cushion when I stood up and walked out the door.

PART 3 - THE CURSE

CHAPTER 35

I've lost her.
I've lost everything.
I'm lost.

A small cottage with two bedrooms and a large garden suited my needs in the small village of Abbots Leigh. I informed the landlord, Mr. Poole, I was Mrs. Lucy Taylor, recently widowed, looking for peace and quiet and a nice place to raise my child. That part was true enough and he accepted it without much question. He said the house would be ready to move in as soon as I was.

I stayed at the inn all week. Sunday I made my way to the church to announce my presence to the community. I sat in the back pews and listened to the vicar's short but inspiring sermon. He caught my attention as I left the church to make introductions.

"Mrs. Lucy Taylor. I'm renting the small cottage on the river from Mr. Poole," I lied.

Mr. Yandle gave me a sincere smile. "It's wonderful to have you here with us, Mrs. Taylor. Staying at the Riverside Cottage? Beautiful gardens. Will Mr. Taylor be joining us as well?"

"Mr. Taylor is no longer with us." He sobered and apologized for my loss. I thanked him and he asked after my health with a pointed look at my belly.

"I am feeling well, thank you. But I could use the names of some people who could help me set up my home."

He nodded sagely. "I know just the person. I'll have her contact you."

The next day I moved into Riverside Cottage. It was a little dusty and the linens all needed a good airing, but it was ready for new occupants. I had just unpacked my clothes when there was a knock at the door.

My stomach clenched with fear. Was it Arthur? Had he found me?

I carefully opened the door a few inches and peered outside.

"Oh good, you are here. Let's get to work." A tall, middle-aged lady with silver hair peeking out of her bonnet pushed the door open all the way and boldly walked in. She sniffed the air as she tugged off her gloves and bonnet.

"Dusty. I knew Poole was too cheap to give it a proper scrub before you came. We'll have to do it ourselves." She shrugged off her pelisse. "You can never trust a man to think of all the things a home needs, especially a skinflint like Poole. I'll make him take a cleaning fee off your first month's rent." She hung up her belongings by the door while tugging on a mobcap.

I was still trying to find the right words for the hurricane who had just entered the house. "I'm sorry, but who are you?"

"I'm Mrs. Kissinger. The vicar told me you needed some help setting up your house and I knew no one else would do it properly, so here I am." She held her arms out wide.

"Oh." I recalled Mr. Yandle's promise. "I apologize. He said he was going to contact someone, but he didn't tell me you were coming."

"Of course not. That would take too much time. It's better if we just get started." She waved her hands at me and marched to the kitchen.

I followed her. "I don't mean to intrude upon your time...."

"Pshaw. What I do with my time is my own business." She searched through the cupboards and closets for cleaning supplies and stacked them on the table. "At least things are properly stocked. I saw the linens hanging outside. Let's go flip the mattresses, shall we? You didn't try to do it by yourself, did you?" She gave me a one-eyed glare that focused on my belly.

I covered my bulge with my hand, "Uh, no, I just…"

"Good. While I think it's perfectly fine for a woman to get plenty of exercise while she's expecting, lifting things is something you should not be doing." With a broom, a rag, and a dustbin, she brushed past me and started marching up the stairs to the bedrooms.

I followed her, trying to protest. "Mrs. Kissinger, I'm not quite sure what you are doing here."

PART 3 - THE CURSE

She clicked her tongue as she set down the broom and dustbin and started wiping down things in my bedroom with the rag. "Cleaning, obviously. You'll get worn out too fast trying to get it done by yourself, trust me. I gave birth to five healthy boys and I remember what it was like. You need a clean environment to bring your baby into. You'll need food too; the cupboards don't even have a tin of tea in them! I'll have little Daniel Young down the road set things up for you with the butcher and the grocer and send him with a list. He's much more reliable than Johnny Spout, even though he's two years younger."

"Oh...that sounds...good?" I was feeling as if I'd been hit by a carriage and had been left dazed in the road.

"Oh, and firewood. I saw a bit of a pile, but we'll need much more to finish out the winter. It's been a mild one this year, so far, but February is always the coldest," she informed me while buffing a spot on the window.

"It usually is. But I still don't know what you are..."

"Just a little drafty here. We'll have to get it patched up. Can't have a baby in a room with a draft." She moved on to the next window.

"Mrs. Kissinger," I said firmly, and was rewarded when she stopped and looked at me. "I really think we should..."

There came a sharp knock at the door.

"Go see who that is, and I'll start laying your fire up here." She shooed me out of the room.

Exasperated, I stomped down the stairs. This time I didn't hesitate to open the door.

I must have had a fearsome look on my face. The vicar took a step back from me when I glared at him.

"Mrs. Taylor," he said with a somewhat worried expression as he glanced over my shoulder.

"Mr. Yandle." I returned his greeting.

"I might owe you an apology." He flinched as a voice carried from upstairs.

"Is that the vicar? Tell him to take off his coat and start chopping wood. You have barely enough to get through the night!" Mrs. Kissinger commanded.

"I'll see to it at once!" he called, returning his gaze to me.

"Yes, I think you might owe me an apology." I agreed, folding my arms as he stepped into the house.

"I underestimated Mrs. Kissinger's...enthusiasm...when I told her about your situation," he confessed. "You see, her husband was the vicar before me and she's always been one to take things in hand with…" He trailed off.

"Exuberance?" I suggested.

"Exuberance, yes." He doffed his coat and hat.

"I see." Then I shrugged. "I am used to doing the managing, not being managed. She's a bit intense."

"Her heart is in the right place, I promise you." He rolled up his sleeves. "Sometimes we need to learn to accept charity, not just give it. Especially a young widow in your… ah… condition."

I smiled at the ridiculousness of it all. "Very well. I shall graciously accept her help. And yours too." I added, pointing to the axe resting near the fireplace.

He gave me a cheeky salute before walking out the door with the axe.

By the end of the day, the cottage was warm, clean, and filled with the smells of baking. Mrs. Kissinger had been right, my ankles were swollen and I tired quickly. She popped me into a chair with a blanket by the fire, put my feet up with a cup of tea and commanded the small army of volunteers the vicar sent over after he'd finished with the wood. I met little Daniel Young, a wiry boy with big eyes and hollow cheeks. I vowed to see them plump and full before the baby was born. He ran errands for everyone the rest of the day and was pleased with the coins I gave him.

"I think that's the last of it." Mrs. Kissinger plopped down onto the sofa next to me and rubbed her hands at the fire. She looked pleased with herself and with the state of my cottage.

I managed a small smile. "I thank you, Mrs. Kissinger."

She snorted. "It pains you to say that. I know an independent woman when I see one."

"Because you are one," I parried.

She chuckled. "You would have enjoyed seeing my discomfort when my Henry died. They all rallied around me and I could hardly pick up a spoon to feed myself without someone trying to do it for me. It was enough to make me want to join Henry in the casket." Her face went soft and somber. "Forgive me, my dear, that was a heartless thing to say. I know you are still in mourning."

PART 3 - THE CURSE

I shrugged. "No one ever knows what to really say to one in mourning, so we all say the wrong things."

"How long has he been gone?"

More stories, more lies to keep straight. "A month."

"And you have no family to stay with?"

"He was my family." I wiped away a little prick of a tear. I missed him.

She was silent a moment, then rose to her feet. She patted my shoulder and gave it a squeeze before retrieving her cloak and bonnet hanging by the door.

"I'll come by tomorrow to check on you," she promised as she dressed for the outdoors. "Keep your feet up and get some rest."

"I will. Thank you for all you've done today."

"Lock the door behind me," she directed and slipped out into the fading sunlight.

I did as she asked and faced the empty cottage that smelled of lemon, lavender and beeswax. It was silent except for the crackling of the fire. Sinking into my chair, I pulled the blankets tightly around me as the baby started rolling in my belly.

"Awake now?" I rubbed it softly. It answered with a kick and I was glad for the little company.

I sat in silence the rest of the night, wiping the tears from my eyes while rubbing my belly when it moved. Every unfamiliar sound made me jump while the house settled. It was only a matter of time before I knew what each creak and bump was, but they were much more frightening when one was alone.

And I'd never truly been alone before.

It was a daunting idea. One that made me shudder and pull my shawl tighter.

I'd always had a sibling at home or Martha for company. In London there was Sophie or ... Alice. My Arthur.

Tears started coursing down my face until it was impossible to keep up with them. My chest heaved faster as I gulped for air. I wished for someone to cry with, for someone to hold me, to be able to hold onto someone. Even if it had just been Pip.

At the thought of my beloved furry companion, I burst into loud sobs and fell onto my knees from the chair. My chest hurt as I moaned and curled into a ball. I shook and railed at the world and the unfairness of it all. I screamed into the carpet my pain and uncertainty.

I stayed there on the floor until I was completely dried out of tears. My mind was completely blank and my body was weary down to my bones. My chest still trembled a little when I breathed, but it was slowly smoothing out.

My heart was numb. I was having thoughts but they weren't producing feelings.

This was a preferred state of being. Anything was better than the state I'd been in. That Joy was a hysterical mess. and I vowed to never let her return.

Calmly, I sat up and slowly pulled myself to my feet and ran my hands over my belly. The baby was quiet, and only gave me a little nudge at my prodding. I didn't blame him. If I'd witnessed my mother break into hysterics, I'd keep myself scarce as well.

My new found numbness allowed me to eat a little supper, bank the fire, climb upstairs with a warming pan and bury myself into bed.

PART 3 - THE CURSE

CHAPTER 36

I've searched everywhere. I've followed every lead. I've left no stone unturned.

I thought her death would destroy me.

Trying to live with the unknown is more than pain. It's fear and guilt and pain all mixed into a ball of despair that's lodged into my chest. It pricks me with every heartbeat.

Be safe, my brilliant girl.

Mrs. Kissinger became a regular visitor at my door every morning. With her gentle but firm prodding, I went through the motions of living. I kept the house tidy, I kept food in my growing belly. I brushed my hair and clothes, I even picked up a needle and thread and worked on making a new set of clothes for Daniel Young and found a little pleasure in it.

But everyday forward was still a struggle. Every single day I missed my family, I missed my home, little Eva, my Pip, and especially my husband. I wavered back and forth over what I had done, if it had been the right choice, if there had been a better way. I picked apart every decision I made, calling myself an idiot in one moment and in the next remembering the fear I had of a 'madman's curse' and what it had done to my Arthur.

"You loved him, didn't you," Mrs. Kissinger said to me one day.

I still do.

I managed a small smile and set a cup of tea in front of her. "He was my best friend."

We both looked out the window in quiet contemplation. The world was starting to warm and little green sprouts were poking up from the ground.

The House That Death Built

More birds made their presence known to potential mates. Lambing season was in full swing and little babies romped around the fields besides their mothers. The renewal cheered me now as it did every year.

"When I lost my Henry..." Mrs. Kissinger's voice trembled and she cleared her throat. "I honestly thought my life was over as well. When you lose a spouse you love you lose half of yourself. Half your memories are gone. Things are turned from 'we' to 'I' in a heartbeat. I don't think the rest of the world really understands it. It's like suddenly losing a limb, but everyone expects you to carry on as if your leg is still attached while you bleed to death."

She smiled at me with tears swelling in her eyes. "Grief is so frustrating. Just when you think you are over it, something triggers a memory and you're an instant watering pot."

"What memory did you have?" I asked.

"Something silly, really. I saw the crocus coming up. They come first you know. Little yellow and purple heads can push up through the snow if it's time. Henry used to gather me a tiny nosegay to wear at church when they appeared. I miss them. I mean, I know they are outside dotting the landscape and I could make my own. But they weren't chosen by him. Those were special." She shifted her gaze back out the window.

Daniel Young broke the quiet by announcing his arrival for the day.

We welcomed him in and I gave him a sticky tart while Mrs. Kissinger found the list for the grocer.

"Miars comnn p rudd behoond me." He mumbled as crumbs fell from his mouth.

"Stop talking with your mouth full," Mrs. Kissinger chided him, brushing the crumbs off his coat. "Now say it again like a proper young man and not a heathen."

He swallowed. "Vicar's coming up the road behind me."

Mrs. Kissinger frowned. "Oh, that man." She shook her head and handed Daniel the list. "Off with you now."

"What's wrong?" I stood up to get another cup of tea for the vicar.

"The vicar's taken a fancy to you."

I froze as my heart stopped. "What?"

"I know. I've tried to discourage him," she said, hands on her hips and staring out the window to look for our spiritual leader.

I groaned, and collapsed into a chair. "No. No, no, no, no. This can't be happening." I wasn't even a real widow!

PART 3 - THE CURSE

"I'm sorry, my dear. I know you're not ready. Henry's been gone for five years and I'm still not ready."

"But I'm..." I gestured wildly at my huge belly.

She scoffed. "Makes some men even more amorous."

I groaned louder and rubbed my eyes into my skull. "How do you know he feels that way?" Maybe she was wrong.

"The way he takes your hand into both of his on Sundays when you leave the church. He only does that with you. His face lights up when he speaks of you. Just the very way he looks at you, my dear. The man is besotted."

"What shall I do?"

Mrs. Kissinger huffed and shrugged. "Be polite but distant. Hopefully he'll catch on."

The knock at the door stopped our conversation as she welcomed Mr. Yandle with a big smile.

"Daniel Young told us you were coming. Mrs. Taylor has just made a fresh pot of tea." She directed him to sit while I poured.

"To what do we owe the pleasure of your company?" she asked as we settled in.

"Checking in on my flock. I've come to thank you both for the work you've given the Youngs. It helps ease their burdens."

Mrs. Young came over twice a week to help with the laundry and cleaning. I always sent home 'extra' groceries so they wouldn't go bad with her. Daniel looked warm and happy in the new set of clothes I'd made him. With the extra food we gave him every day, his face and form were filling out the way a growing boy should.

"It's nothing." Mrs. Kissinger waved off. "The Youngs are a wonderful family. Just down on their luck since Mr. Young's accident."

Mr. Yandle nodded. "He's getting stronger and better every day." He turned to me. "And how are you feeling, Mrs. Taylor?"

It was a regular question he asked me, a polite way to inquire about my condition. "Healthy as can be," I assured him.

"I'm greatly relieved you have Mrs. Kissinger as a friend now. Promise me you'll contact me if you need anything." He turned back to Mrs. Kissinger.

"We will," she promised. He then spoke of the weather, the lambing season, the onset of spring. Nothing in his demeanor or conversation hinted at anything towards intimacy. I was relieved and relaxed once more in his presence.

Until he came back the next day.

And the next.

By the fourth day I wondered aloud if I should fake a headache when Daniel reported the vicar was coming up the road.

"No, that will only concern him even more." Mrs. Kissinger shook her head and set down her tea cup. "You're going to have to take him in hand and let him know where he stands." She was quiet for a moment, staring out the window at the man in question as he came up the road. "He is a good man, Mrs. Taylor, and you are so young. Mr. Yandle is healthy, strong, kind and smart. He would make a good father…"

"No, no, and no." I wasn't about to become a bigamist with a man of the cloth!

She shrugged. "Then you really have no other choice than to let him down gently."

I exhaled. "I think the vicar and I will take a walk today down to the river."

"It is a lovely day," she agreed, going to fetch my pelisse and bonnet for me.

His eyes lit up when I suggested the walk. I rested my hand on his elbow and was struck by the oddness I felt at touching another man's arm. It felt completely wrong. Not just in my head, but physically it felt strange and I struggled to keep my hand in place. He smelled nice, but wrong. He was handsome and kind, but still wrong.

I missed Arthur.

We admired the little patches of color poking up from the ground. Tulips and daffodils peeked out to find the sun, joining the bright crocus.

"Mrs. Taylor, I welcome this chance to speak to you in private," he said as we approached the banks of the river. It was flowing quickly, filled with odds and ends of debris that winter had released.

I watched it rushing by as my heart pounded and my gut wrenched. What to do? What to say?

"I have come to greatly admire you these past few months," he continued.

Oh, I had to stop him.

"Mr. Yandle, I need to confess," I interrupted him, tearing my eyes from the water. His brow furrowed.

PART 3 - THE CURSE

"Confess? I'm not a priest, Mrs. Taylor," he spoke carefully.

"No, but I'm sure there are many who confess to you their various sins all the time, don't they?"

He nodded slowly. "Yes, they do. I can listen and pray for their forgiveness, but that's the extent of my authority."

"And your confidence to keep their matters private, is it to be trusted?"

"I am. I promise." I could see his mind racing in the familiar way Arthur's did. Did all men have that look?

"I'm still married to my husband, and he is not dead," I said quickly.

The vicar dropped my arm like it scalded him. He gawked at me. "Mrs. Taylor! How can this be?"

"My name isn't even Lucy Taylor." I continued. Oh, the flood gates had opened and couldn't be stopped. "I will not tell you my real name."

He gaped at me a moment. "You're hiding," he guessed.

I nodded.

"You've come here all alone, running, and in your condition?" he asked.

I managed a small smile. "Luckily, my condition has been the easiest part of this situation."

"I think we should sit. I should sit."

There was a fallen log that served as a bench at the water's edge. He helped me down and took a spot beside me.

"Are you warm enough?" He really was a kind man.

"Yes, as long as we stay in the sunshine." I tipped my face up to the glorious rays and wished I could rip off my bonnet to enjoy them to the fullest.

He watched the water and gathered his thoughts, rubbing his hands up and down his breeches as he spoke. "Your husband, did he beat you?"

"No. No, he did not." I remembered the cut on my head, and the forceful way he'd pulled me from the glass case. "But he can be unpredictable."

"Unpredictable," he repeated quietly.

We watched the water churn with dead leaves and rotten logs.

"He shouts?" he asked.

I barked a short laugh, thinking of my Arthur and our many spirited conversations. "All the time, and I shout back."

"But he never hurt you? Physically I mean."

I shook my head. "No. Not physically." Just my heart. My poor twisted heart.

"As your spiritual leader I should be encouraging you to reconcile with him."

"He's mad."

"Mad?"

I nodded. "He...believes he is cursed. So much so our relationship has suffered." Oh, how it suffered. "I know there are plenty of recourses for men whose wives are afflicted, but it's quite the opposite when the wife is the sane one." I realized that I was rubbing my round belly as I spoke. The motion soothed me.

"I see." The vicar's eyes rested on my round form.

"He became unsafe to live with. And I had to leave." I rested my hand on my bulge. "For all our sakes."

He pursed his lips. "Forgive me for this, but I have noticed you are not hurting for funds. Did you steal from him before you left? Is he going to come chasing you down for it?"

I gasped. "No, I did not steal anything from him. I simply took all my saved-up pin money."

His eyes widened a moment and he gave me a disbelieving look. "Pin money enough to run an entire household?"

"He is very generous," I defended.

"Generous," he stated flatly.

"Yes."

His eyes narrowed. "You still love him." It wasn't a question.

"I'll always love him."

He studied me for a moment more before choosing his words carefully. "You are married to a wealthy, generous man. Who you love. Who doesn't beat you. You're carrying his child and heir, and you ran away because he's 'unpredictable.'"

I sounded like an idiot even to my own ears.

"Yes," I said firmly. Maybe he didn't understand what unpredictable was capable of, but I did. Unpredictable was Dibble trying to kill Eva because her father wouldn't lie to the Hamptons and strangling me for not telling him her whereabouts. Unpredictable was Carter, who pretended to be my husband's friend, before he pulled a gun on me for some notion of revenge.

I had the scars from 'unpredictable'. My child would not. Would never. Ever.

PART 3 - THE CURSE

I didn't notice the tear that had escaped my eyes, but Mr. Yandle had. He slapped his thighs and stood up, pacing away from me quickly. He stood a few steps away, his back rigid. I saw him clench his fists a moment before turning on me. "This isn't a ruse is it? Some bounder of a tale to frighten me off?"

"I would make up a more believable tale than this." I promised, wiping my eyes. My voice was strong and didn't waver as he took in the measure of me.

"Mrs. Taylor." He glared harder at me as he used my alias. "If I find you are indeed lying to me, I'll drag you back to his side myself."

I nodded. That was fair.

He plopped back down next to me and buried his face in his hands. I could hear him muttering to himself.

I allowed him to vent for a moment before apologizing. "I'm sorry, Vicar. They say confession is good for the soul, but I can clearly see it's not."

"No one ever asks if it's good for *my* soul," he groused.

"I'll refrain from any further admissions of guilt in your presence," I promised, and sank back a little on my elbows to enjoy the sunshine.

"And I suppose you feel better? Your heart is lighter now, having freed yourself of this burden."

Actually, I did. To finally not have to lie to someone was a great relief to me.

"And now I'm stuck with the burden of a runaway wife in my congregation. One who is about to give birth and won't give me the knowledge of who she really is."

Oh dear, I hadn't thought of that.

"I have put you in an awkward position, haven't I?" I admitted.

"Yes, and I'm not sure if you are telling me the truth even now."

I shrugged. "I am. And I know it. If only I and the Lord know the truth, then I'm satisfied."

"And now she brings the Almighty in on it," he mumbled, and stood. He held out his hand to me to take. "Come, Mrs. Taylor. Your cheeks are getting far too rosy from the cold air and I don't want a scolding from Mrs. Kissinger."

Mrs. Kissinger looked more anxious than angry when we returned.

"How was your walk?" She helped me from my pelisse.

"Enlightening," Mr. Yandle said with an overly bright smile. "And now I'll take my leave from you ladies. Please call on me if you need anything."

"It went better than I thought. I was sure I would see a brokenhearted man returning to the doorstep," Mrs. Kissinger remarked.

"He took it well." I hoped.

He seemed to. He treated me simply as a member of his congregation. He still came by and chopped firewood for us, but was teaching Daniel the technique for splitting logs. His visits were formal and polite as they should be.

Everything was fine until Mrs. Kissinger got her newspapers.

Her daughter-in-law visiting from London brought them. A whole stack of papers she'd brought from last month's press.

"I do so love to read them. As ghastly as it is, the gossip rags are better than any novel one could put out." She tucked into her first paper. "Henry always chastised me for my morbid curiosity of the peers, but then he followed their escapades just as closely. Shall I save them for you when I'm done?"

"Oh, no, thank you." I plied my needle into a handkerchief I was making for her. A little butterfly garden began to take shape on it, and I was pleased with the progress. I was happy to note the little project was bringing me a little pleasure to work on. Take that, my broken heart!

Mrs. Kissinger pouted. "Don't tell me you are going to frown upon my morbid pastime as well."

"Not at all, I just...I cannot read."

Like all the others she started in on my character being too well bred to not read, I promised her I had been taught but it didn't take. The dear lady swore then that she would teach me.

"Please, try to understand." I set down my work and caught her gaze. "I am physically unable to read." I pointed at the open paper on her lap. "Where you see letters and words, I see squiggly lines that mesh and writhe about the page. It is an inherited condition."

She blinked a few times. "Upon my word, I've never heard of such a thing."

"It's not a situation one broadcasts," I returned to my butterfly while she contemplated my revelation.

"Would you like me to read them to you?" Her voice was timid. I could tell she was afraid I'd take offense.

PART 3 - THE CURSE

I smiled broadly. "Mrs. Kissinger, I would love to hear you read to me. Anything and everything."

She smiled back and jumped into the paper. We both laughed over detailed exploits about who was seen with whose wife or husband. Whose son or daughter was seen without a glove or how the moral fortitude of so and so was being called into question because of their love of cards.

Mrs. Kissinger laughed hard about the story of one young Lord who ended up in the Serpentine because of a new-fangled contraption called a 'dandy horse'. I enjoyed watching her animation as she read more than the stories themselves. She would always gasp loudly and rush into each scandal, her eyes wide as she tried to guess who the writers were really talking about.

I heard a knock on the door and she set down the paper to answer it.

"Ah, Vicar! Welcome." She took his hat.

"Have some tea." I offered, pushing myself slowly out of my chair. I found it more difficult to maneuver every day.

"Stay seated, Mrs. Taylor," he chided. "I can pour my own tea."

I obeyed and gave him a grateful smile.

"And how are you ladies getting on?" He took a seat next to the fire and sipped his tea as Mrs. Kissinger brought him a plate of tiny tarts and sandwiches.

"We're taking gruesome delight in the misadventures of others." Mrs. Kissinger confessed as she sat back down.

He raised his eyebrow. "Oh, how so?"

"Scandal columns in the papers," I divulged. "My companion has a great love for the peerage misconduct."

He snorted. "Sometimes that's all they are good for; an example on how not to behave." He gave a little shiver as the fire started to warm him. The day was cold and rainy.

"Stay and warm up," I told him. "Are we the last of your visits today?"

He nodded. "Just checking on your fuel supply. Daniel has done a nice job keeping you well stocked. I was coming to see if there were any larger logs he couldn't do."

"We're good for the rest of the week," Mrs. Kissinger promised, browsing the paper once more. "Are you good for a story, Vicar, or shall I stay silent?"

"Maybe I'll be inspired with the subject of my next sermon."

I turned back to my project as Mrs. Kissinger's voice filled the room once more.

"Oh, now this is dreadful. The Duke of Ironwood is undergoing a formal investigation on the disappearance of his wife."

I felt all my blood drain when she read off Arthur's title.

Was the room spinning?

"Apparently his first wife also died under mysterious circumstances, as well as Lady Alice Graves when she was in his custody as his wife's companion." My project fell from my shaking hands.

"'As we all know, Privilege of the Peer does not extend to murder. Although he claims his innocence and is always dashing off when he hears a report of her whereabouts, this author is going to take a well-known phrase and turn it to point out, 'the gentleman doth protest too much.' We are all anxiously waiting for some sign of the Duchess, or what remains of her.'"

Mrs. Kissinger asked and set the paper down in her lap. "Now that is truly dreadful! Mrs. Taylor, are you well?"

The room was definitely spinning. I clutched the chair I was sitting on to remain upright. My belly churned as the revelations kept hitting me over and over. Arthur was accused of murder? My murder? Diana and Alice as well?

"My dear, you are so pale. I didn't mean to upset you!" Mrs. Kissinger was on her feet and rushing to my side. So was the vicar. And he was livid.

"Go fetch her some water and a vinaigrette," he barked at Mrs. Kissinger. He knelt in front of me, his eyes blazing up at me.

"Are you her? The missing wife. The…"

I bristled at the title. "Don't call me that!" I tried to push him away but he caught my hand easily.

"And the other two women. Did he kill them? Is that why you are here?"

"No! He didn't. He wouldn't," I protested. My breathing sped up as the room threatened to topple onto me.

Vicar Yandle grabbed my head and thrust it down towards my feet, at least as far as it would go. The baby kicked in protest.

"This is intolerable. This isn't a little misunderstanding, this is a murder charge! He is a bloody peer," he hissed.

"Vicars aren't supposed to say those words!" I moaned.

"They aren't supposed to shake the brains out of their parishioners either, but I am so very tempted." He released his grip once I started breathing normally again. He rose to his feet and peered down at me. "This is not something we can discuss in front of Mrs. Kissinger."

I couldn't agree more.

"I'll return tonight after she leaves," he said quickly as we heard her footsteps on the stairway.

I nodded, grateful to have an ally on what I should do next.

Mrs. Kissinger provided me with a cold glass of water and a few whiffs of her vinaigrette. I told her over and over she hadn't upset me. I promised it was just an odd occurrence.

"Probably brought on by the baby in your belly," Mrs. Kissinger concluded. "I remember all the strange things my body did in the last month of confinement."

"Then I'm sure I'm in for more unexplained episodes. And I will gladly submit to your expertise." That made her flush with pleasure and the matter was dropped.

The vicar took his leave and Mrs. Kissinger put her papers away. I tried to encourage her to continue. Any further information I could find about the investigation on Arthur would hopefully allow me to help him. She dismissed my wishes and instead read from the Bible aloud for the rest of the day. I endured the Good Book for a while then asked if she had any novels to read instead. Happily, she started into more storytelling until the light was no longer good and she left for the night.

When darkness had truly settled over the countryside there came a faint scratching at the door. I opened it and let Mr. Yandle enter.

He wasn't glowering at me now. He kindly helped me sit and then took a chair next to mine.

"I've had time to think about this predicament," he started. "At first, when you told me he wasn't safe, I was admittedly confused. But the story Mrs. Kissinger read today puts things in a new light. Were you afraid for your life?"

I shook my head. "Not from him, not really. He always treated me with love and kindness until I confronted him about his odd behavior. He believes his family has a cursed object. I went to touch it and he forcefully pulled me away and I stumbled and fell, hitting my head. It was more like a parent pulling a child away from a hot stove than any ill intent."

"Then why did you leave?"

"For the baby." I rested my hands on my belly. "I could live with a mad man, but I will not subject a child to the same thing. How could I? A father who believes in a curse that is passed down from father to son? A man who is whole and rational one moment, then raving and unhinged the next? No. I won't expose a child to such conditions."

He nodded. "And the death of two women?"

I shook my head. "He blames the curse for their deaths. His first wife died from an unknown illness and Alice…" I stopped a tear and took a deep breath. "Alice appeared to have died from an aneurysm. I had the doctor do a thorough exam of her before we buried her for everyone's peace of mind."

He was silent, staring into the fire.

"I think the most important thing you need to decide now is if you want your husband tried for your murder," he said.

"I don't."

"But you don't want to be found."

"I can't."

He pinched his nose. "I know Mrs. Lucy Taylor has no family. Is the same true for…"

I cut him off. "Mrs. Marco. And yes, she does. A perfectly lovely family she misses very much."

"I suggest you write them a letter, appraising them of your good health and of your husband's innocence."

"I will need your help. I cannot write." I hoped it would be enough of an explanation, but the skeptical look he gave me said otherwise. I explained for the second time that day of my frustrating condition. His face softened and he agreed to write it for me.

"We cannot have it postmarked here," I stated.

"In Bristol there's always a ship bound for somewhere that can take a letter and deposit it elsewhere. And you have enough coin to cover the cost of the subterfuge," he pointed out.

"That will work, thank you." I motioned to the small desk near the window. He helped me to my feet and I lit a candle so he could see.

Together we composed a letter to my mother about my health, my concern for Arthur and the investigation, and my promise to write again after the baby was born. Mr. Yandle's writing was straight and consistent, no blotches or smears. I complimented him on it as I signed my shaky signature Alice had taught me. Fish hook, circle, slumping scarecrow without a head. It would convince anyone who knew me my letter was not a forgery.

"I have never received a compliment on my handwriting before," he chuckled as he folded the letter.

"Trust me, I have stared at plenty of letters, trying to figure them out. Yours are very nice," I assured him.

He just shook his head. "You are an odd one. Get some rest, Mrs. *Taylor*." His emphasis on my alias had my hackles raised again.

"Do you not believe me? That my husband is mad?"

He was quiet as he contemplated the letter in his hand. "Mrs. Taylor, I have been on the Lord's errand since I was a young man. I have seen many miracles and signs of His goodness and mercy." His voice lowered, "And I have also seen the signs and afflictions of His adversary, who also works in unbelievable ways. I don't know your husband, so I cannot say he is mad. But I do know the Lord's enemy, and I wouldn't be surprised if this was his work."

I was speechless. Was he saying it could be true? That the far-fetched fantasy I had told him could actually happen? I could only blink at the vicar as he walked to the door.

He looked at me before he left.

"Get some rest, Mrs. Taylor."

CHAPTER 37

She reached out to save me.
I was ready to shock the world and let them try to hang me, to let everyone know of the curse when my body snapped back into place and I walked away from the gallows whole, but Joy stepped in to save me. She really is too good for a damned soul like mine.
I also received a letter from a vicar.

In a word I was miserable.

To elaborate, I was sure I couldn't get any rounder. My belly looked as if it were about to burst. The baby was not at all happy with the tight confinement and kicked me in the ribs repeatedly to let me know his displeasure. Laying down cut off my breath and there was simply no comfortable position to rest in. I was tired and at the same time I had bursts of energy and the sudden urgent need to tidy everything.

When Mrs. Kissinger walked into the cottage from her morning rounds and found me on my hands and knees scrubbing the floors, she called for Daniel to fetch his mother.

"We'll need another woman on hand for the birthing," she said as I rested back on my haunches and stretched my back.

"I'm not in any more discomfort now than I was yesterday," I told her. "And hanging my belly down is the only way I can get a proper breath, so I might as well scrub while I'm down here." I went back to it.

"It will be soon," she promised and bustled about the kitchen to make a fresh pot of tea.

"How do you ... Ow! Ow! Ow!" My belly started to cramp and tighten.

PART 3 - THE CURSE

Mrs. Kissinger gave me a knowing look and took the scrub brush from my hand. "You see?"

I'd had these pains before. They were a little harder this time, but I expected them to disappear as they usually did. My belly softened once more and I stood up and took a deep breath.

"Go sit by the fire and relax, I'll bring you some tea and toast." Mrs. Kissinger shooed me out of the kitchen.

I grumbled but obeyed, finding my favorite chair that faced out the window. I snuggled into it and rubbed my belly, wondering how Arthur was. What would he say about my size? Would he be anxious or calm? Excited or scared?

I wiped an errant tear from my face. The stupid things fell with alarming regularity nowadays.

Mrs. Kissinger placed the tea next to me and slid her arm around me. She smelled of lavender and wood. She smelled like home. She was warm and soft and kind, but I wished my mother was here instead.

"Now, don't be scared. Everything will be fine." I didn't have the heart to tell her my true thoughts.

Another pain started up and I flinched through it. The sensation wasn't too bad, nothing worse than my monthly cramping had ever produced. I was certain I would get through this without too much drama.

Hours later I was in my bed, sweating and sobbing as the pain escalated. I wanted my mother, I wanted Arthur and I wanted this whole ordeal over!

"Almost there," Mrs. Kissinger encouraged as Mrs. Young held my other hand. Together they held me up as I bore down. Finally something shifted and in a rush of blood and fluid, a screaming, writhing little person appeared.

"A boy!" Mrs. Kissinger declared as I flopped back onto the mound of pillows that propped me up.

"Oh he is absolutely perfect!" Mrs. Young picked him up with the rags she had on hand. She rubbed him vigorously which only made him scream louder as Mrs. Kissinger dealt with the cleanup. Mrs. Young wrapped him up in a clean blanket and handed him to me.

Trembling, I took him into my arms. "Hey. Hey there, that's enough," I shushed him while inspecting his tiny perfect body. He quieted at the sound of my voice and blinked at me.

I was instantly in love with that little, wrinkled, ugly, squalling baby boy.

I kissed him and soothed him, and I began to weep as he nuzzled into me and relaxed with a tiny baby sigh. I wished his father was here to share in my joy.

Two pairs of arms surrounded us. Both Mrs. Kissinger and Mrs. Young hugged and petted me softly, not saying a word. They silently supported me in the way I think women had supported each other for centuries when their fellow sisters were going through grief and pain.

"Out of bed with you now, so we can clean it up and set you both to rest," Mrs. Kissinger commanded once my tears had subsided.

Mrs. Young took the baby as Mrs. Kissinger led me to the nearby chair. They rested him against my chest and piled us with blankets. She opened the door and called down to Daniel to bring up the warming bricks.

I changed into a clean nightgown and they placed back into warm clean sheets with a baby rooting at my breast. It was almost perfect.

Almost.

"What will you name him?" Mrs. Kissinger asked. She brought me a drink of cool water and told me to sip.

I swallowed and let out a shaky breath. "Graham. Graham Thomas Ma...Taylor," I said at the last moment.

"Perfect name for a perfect baby." She planted a kiss on the top of my head. "You did good."

I held Graham tighter, wishing his Papa was here, wondering again if I had done the right thing.

Mrs. Kissinger tugged the curtains closed and I shut my eyes as the room darkened, taking a deep breath. A full, glorious, deep breath that I would never take for granted ever again.

Graham and I spent the rest of the day and night in bed together, with Mrs. Kissinger and Mrs. Young taking him from me to change and cuddle when they brought me food.

After a day of respite, I was ready to get out of bed to tackle the household once more. Mrs. Kissinger let me and Graham move to the warm space by the fire into a rocking chair and presented me with a pile of mending I could do while he napped between feedings.

"I know you have energy now the little man is here, but I still want you to rest," she commanded.

PART 3 - THE CURSE

I reluctantly obeyed, and set to work on the projects she had brought while Graham snoozed on my lap. I was reluctant to let go of him for any length of time, afraid something irrational would happen to him if he were out of reach. Were all new mothers like this, or was I just overly paranoid?

A knock at the door brought the vicar again into my home. "I've come to meet the newest member of my congregation."

I smiled and readjusted Graham's little body for viewing as Mrs. Kissinger went for tea.

Mr. Yandle peered down at him, "Well now, that's a bonny wee laddie."

I laughed a little at the accent he immediately dropped, "I suppose another letter is needed."

"Yes, please." I tucked Graham up against my chest.

"Healthy, is he?"

"As far as we can tell. He eats like a greedy pig and has a lusty cry that wakes us all in the night," I reported.

Mr. Yandle chuckled and took a seat. "Good, we'll wait until he's a bit bigger for his christening. Has he a name yet?"

"Graham Thomas Ma…" I trailed off as sudden tears sprang to my eyes. "Taylor. It's Taylor."

"I can record it as Marco Taylor if you wish."

I nodded and wiped my face. Again. These spontaneous tears were becoming quite annoying.

Mrs. Kissinger brought in the tea tray and soon took over the conversation with the vicar as I rocked my son and listened. There was a peaceful feeling in my home, which I was grateful for. I let them plan Graham's christening and listened to the village news until Graham declared he was hungry.

"I'll see you tonight, then?" he asked as Mrs. Kissinger went to fetch his hat. I watched him leave before giving my son his next meal.

The vicar returned after darkness had fallen. He closed the door himself and went to the desk. "I'm happy to report word from London has reached me about your husband."

"Have you? Is it good news?" I was anxious to know if my letter had helped at all.

"Your parents have exonerated him, for the time being. They showed the investigators your letters and told them they were positive they were not forgeries. Rumors are still flying rampant, but the officials are satisfied for now."

"Hopefully another letter will put things to rest." I kissed Graham's little soft head as I returned to my rocking chair at the fire.

"I believe it will. So, Madame, do we announce the birth of the heir to…"

"Don't say it." I stopped him. "I wasn't born to that life, and it makes me squirm just hearing it."

He looked amused. "Very well. A letter to your husband? Or to your mother again?"

"My mother, please." I was sure the vicar was tired of my tears. I was. Trying to write a letter to Arthur would be nothing but a disastrous, bawling mess.

"That you delivered a healthy baby boy…"

"Healthy child. Don't include the date," I corrected. I couldn't give Arthur anything to follow.

The vicar looked displeased, but wrote the words. At least I hoped he did.

"The mother is doing well, and the child 'eats like a greedy pig and has a lusty cry that wakes us all in the night'?"

I smiled as he quoted me. "Yes, that will do."

He scribbled a few more words as I found some coins to pay for the letter. He took the money as I leaned over the desk and scratched my signature to it again. He folded it up and put it in his pocket and sat back in the chair, giving me a thoughtful look.

"Have you given any more thought to the idea your husband might be telling the truth?"

I shook my head. "No. I've been busy with this little one." I rested Graham's sleeping head against my shoulder. He gave a tiny baby sigh that shuddered his whole body.

The vicar rose to his feet and straightened his coat. "Give it some thought, Mrs. Marco."

PART 3 - THE CURSE

CHAPTER 38

I hate that vicar. I hate that he can see my wife whenever he wishes while I search the masses for her face. I hate that he has seen and held my child while I yearn to do the same.

I hate him for giving me hope.

Springtime was waking up the world. Blossoms on fruit trees were starting to fill out the branches, and I checked on the kitchen garden and investigated the hot house. Riverside Cottage gardens had been neglected for a few years and needed some tidying up. Spring was a busy time if one wanted to eat during the winter.

Mrs. Kissinger stayed with me for a few weeks until she was certain I could handle the household and the baby at the same time. Mrs. Young still came by twice a week and I saw Daniel daily. He gladly jumped at the chance to earn a little more money for helping me in the gardens.

But one morning, he was late.

I waited for his usual arrival time with tea and cakes, feeling a little niggle of worry when it came and went. I decided to wait for him no longer when Graham had started another of his naps. I had work to do.

I was elbow deep in dirt when I heard the creak of the garden gate. I blew the loose hair from my eyes as Daniel walked through.

He was a mess. His cap was missing, his shirt sleeve was torn, and there was a bruise forming on his cheek next to the tear stains.

"My dear boy! What happened?" I rose to my feet and peeled off my work gloves.

He sniffed. "Nothing. I'm fine." He rubbed his face on his ripped sleeve.

"You are not fine." I pulled out a handkerchief from my apron pocket and wiped his face.

I examined his bruise, and noted the distinct finger shape to it.

"Who did this to you?" I asked softly. I was afraid it was his father. Mrs. Kissinger had told me about his temper since his accident, but he'd only raised his voice. Never his fists.

"No one. I tripped." He sniffed again.

"Tripped? Then where's your cap?" I asked. I could see patches of his scalp were red and bald. My anger increased.

I took him by the arms. "Daniel. You must tell me who did this. You are safe here, I promise. I'll do all I can to help you." I rubbed his arms softly as I pleaded.

His eyes filled with tears again and he sobbed. "It was Johnny Spout." He threw his little arms around my neck and wept. I held him until his tears subsided.

I set him out some tea and a large portion of cakes at the table in the kitchen. "Take off your shirt so I can mend it," I told him, finding him a shawl to keep him warm while I worked.

He obeyed me and started on the food while I examined the damage. His ribs were also red, and he had a large scratch on his arm where his sleeve had torn. I managed to keep my temper as I sat down with a needle and thread to work on his sleeve.

"What happened between you and Johnny Spout?"

"He saw me paying the grocer for this week's food, and he got mad, saying it was his job and I was stealing from him." He wiped his eyes.

"You've been my errand boy for months without a peep from Johnny Spout," I pointed out.

"'Coz he's lazy. He don't care that I'm doing this job. He'd rather be fishin' or playing cards." Daniel took another sip of tea and shuddered. "It's his brother, Richard, that's causing trouble. He's back from the sea and he makes Johnny's life hard, so Johnny makes everyone's life hard."

"Richard Spout is a navy man?" I asked.

Daniel shook his head. "No, the navy tossed him out. He's on a merchant ship now. He's usually not here for long, but when he is there's always trouble."

I scowled at the shirt I was mending. "What does Mr. Spout think of his older son?"

PART 3 - THE CURSE

Daniel shrugged. "He and Mrs. Spout don't think he can do anything wrong. It's everyone else's fault when there's trouble. Everyone but Richard's."

My little friend was miserable. I wouldn't place any more burdens on his shoulders. "How long is Richard Spout here for?"

Daniel shrugged again. "Usually not more than a few weeks."

"I will run my own errands while he is here," I said.

Daniel's face fell. "Oh no! Mrs. Taylor, I need to work!" My heart broke a little at the fear on his face. His family depended on what little he brought in and I wouldn't deprive them of it.

"Of course you do, and I'll find plenty of work for you to do, don't doubt it. You just keep coming here every day, and we'll wait until Richard Spout leaves again before I send you on my errands again."

He calmed down and ate his cakes while I finished his shirt. We spent the rest of the day calmly working in the garden and washing windows. He thought it great fun to climb the walls to reach the glass as I fretted below on the ground. Daniel left my home that afternoon in better spirits.

I bundled up Graham the next day and went shopping for the first time since his birth. The air was warm and sweet with the smell of spring, and I laughed as Graham kicked his heels with excitement whenever he saw something new.

I completed my errand to the butcher quickly, excited for my next stop. I probably looked like a grinning idiot as I opened the door to the dressmaker's shop, sighing loudly with pleasure at the familiar sights and scents surrounding me. Graham was rapidly growing out of the gowns I had on loan from Mrs. Young and I wanted to get ahead of his needs.

The dressmaker and I picked out lightweight material for summer and wool for winter. I enjoyed my time there, smelling and touching the fibers and textures, gushing over prints and embellishments with the dressmaker. I'm sure I spent too much money, but I gave in to almost every suggestion she gave me, especially when she assured me a bit of white lace at the collar would not be too unseeming for a widow to wear. I couldn't wait to wear color again.

Graham started to protest our lengthy time at the shop, so I paid for my purchases and strapped him back in his sling to carry home with my parcels.

I hadn't made it too far when a little voice chirped at my side. "I'll help you with those, Mrs. Taylor."

I looked down to see Johnny Spout at my side, attempting to take my parcels in hand.

"Oh, no thank you, Johnny. I'm quite well balanced at the moment, if you take something away I might tip over," I said with a false smile.

He gave me a miserable look as a shadow fell over us both.

"She's terribly overburdened, Johnny, just take them for her." A deep voice commanded.

I knew at once this was Richard Spout.

He was built like a burly sailor, with muscles and scars to show for it. He leered at me, his eyes bright with power.

I looked down at Johnny Spout and saw the bruises on his neck and behind his ears. Carefully hidden places most wouldn't think to look.

"After all, now that her errand boy is no longer working for her, she's gonna need someone to help her," Richard said.

I instantly loathed him.

I smiled at Johnny with genuine warmth, and handed him my parcels as Graham was kicking up a fuss. "Just around the corner to Mrs. Kissinger's house. I'm meeting her for tea," I told him.

He nodded and began plodding in front of me. I shushed Graham as the menacing shadow followed us both to the Kissinger residence.

"Just here on the porch." I directed Johnny. He dropped my parcels without care and I was glad there was only fabric in them. "Thank you, Johnny." I dutifully fished a coin out of my reticule and gave it to him.

"Have a good day, Mrs. Taylor," he mumbled and shuffled off.

I knocked at the door and waited for it to open, aware of the eyes still boring into my back from Richard Spout. He didn't move from his spot on the street, and tipped his head to watch me. I gave Mrs. Kissinger a warm greeting when she opened the door.

She was a little surprised at my impromptu visit, but welcomed me smoothly inside when she caught sight of Richard Spout standing in the street with his miserable little brother at his side.

She brought in my bundles and shut the door. "Oh my dear, this isn't good." She walked to the window and peered out carefully between the curtains. "He's still here, watching the house."

"He's waiting to see if you toss me out for not being invited," I guessed, pulling off my bonnet.

PART 3 - THE CURSE

"I would take in a pack of stray mangy dogs if that man was following them," Mrs. Kissinger said.

"As bad as all that?" I unwrapped Graham from his sling and sat down to feed him.

"Worse. He's a villain through and through, but no one can ever prove his crimes. I wonder why he's taken such an interest in you?" She closed the curtain. "I'll make it my business to find out at once."

I knew the formidable lady would follow through. Although I was a bit worried, she quickly steered the conversation towards my purchases and raved over my choices.

"He will be the most fashionable baby I've ever seen," she declared, repacking my parcels. I was pleased with her response. I couldn't wait to dive into them myself.

Mrs. Kissinger refused to let me walk home alone. She didn't leave until she'd checked all the windows and locks. It only made my anxiety grow.

The next morning, I didn't leave the house until Daniel had arrived. I made him circle the property and report if there was anyone else about.

"Just you and me," he said. His face looked better after a good night's sleep and his wounds were less severe. We took Graham out to the gardens and started our work when we heard Mrs. Kissinger calling for us.

"Daniel, go and bring her here, please." I picked up Graham. He'd been kicking his feet in the sunshine and gave me a grin when I picked him up and I kissed his fat baby cheeks.

Mrs. Kissinger looked relieved to see us. "I just found out what's been going on with Richard Spout. It seems he was running a banking errand for his father and saw your name in the accounts. He's after your money."

I snorted. "My money? There's only enough for Graham and I to live on."

"To someone who can't keep two pennies in his pocket it's a fortune."

"I don't see how he is going to get it," I scoffed.

Mrs. Kissinger scowled. "Oh, he'll find a way of trying."

She was right.

The next Sunday when I was saying goodbye to Mr. Yandle and thanking him for his sermon, Richard Spout appeared at his elbow.

"I say, Vicar, please introduce me to this good lady. I haven't had a chance to meet her since my return." He grinned at me, as I tucked my son closer to my chest.

The vicar looked unhappy as he made the proper introductions. I didn't extend my hand, using Graham as an excuse but bobbed at Richard Spout.

"Ah yes, the new resident of Riverside Cottage. It's a pleasure to meet the mysterious lady," he said.

"Not mysterious, just private," I assured him, and gave both men a brief nod of dismissal. "Have a nice day Vicar, Mr. Spout."

I turned to take my leave. Graham reached up and grabbed one of my bonnet ribbons and started chatting to me with intelligent sounding baby nonsense.

I looked down into his dark eyes. "I know, the only man I need in my life is you." I felt the lie down to my toes. If his father was here, he'd place a warm, comforting hand on the small of my back as he led us to the carriage. He'd have Graham in his other arm, carrying on the baby conversation with a witty banter that would make me laugh.

We would be a family.

And I wouldn't have a single fear about Richard Spout.

Who was following me.

"I'd like to walk you home, Mrs. Taylor," he said from behind me.

I shook my head. "That's not necessary." I didn't stop my stride.

"A single lady, all by yourself. You must be lonesome." He came up to my side.

Really? That was his best approach?

"No not really, I have Graham. He keeps me plenty busy." The baby tapped his tiny hand against my cheek.

"He's a handsome little chap. Would you like me to carry him?" Richard Spout held out his arms.

I visibly recoiled. "No, no thank you. He's wary of strangers right now." I tightened my grip around my son as Richard Spout lowered his arms.

He smirked. "Perhaps I should pay you a visit, then I wouldn't be a stranger."

I stopped in my tracks and faced him. His brows raised with surprise. "Mr. Spout. It sounds like you are making an attempt to court me. I must discourage you at once. I am a widow who was very much in love with her husband. I will never take another husband. Ever. All I want is to raise my son in peace." I didn't lower my gaze.

PART 3 - THE CURSE

He met mine in a silent battle of wills. He didn't back down, and neither did I.

"Things can change," he said with a superior smile.

"Things won't change," I replied. "I've already turned down a better gentleman than you."

His face transformed into anger. He sneered and his cheeks flushed as he glowered at me with malice. Here he was, the real Richard Spout.

"Everything well here?" Mr. Yandle approached us. We hadn't even made it out of the churchyard yet. Other parishioners were watching the scene with avid interest.

"Everything is fine, Vicar. I was just explaining to Mr. Spout I had turned down your advances, and there was no chance I would even consider him."

Mr. Yandle turned to Richard Spout. "It's true, the lady knows her own mind. I would encourage you to press your suit elsewhere."

"Someone needs to be a father to that boy." Richard Spout glared at me.

"Someone is a father to this boy, he's dead. There will never be another to take his place." Graham started to fuss in my arms, and I was thankful for the interruption. "Excuse me, gentlemen, I need to take my son home and care for him.".

"As you should. He's a healthy boy. Be a shame if something happened to him," Richard Spout called after me.

Mr. Yandle's expression was as incredulous as mine.

"What did you say?" I demanded.

That smirk was back on his face. He gave a casual shrug. "Babies don't always live very long. I'd enjoy every moment I have with him." He gave us both a nod and sauntered away.

"Mrs. Taylor. I think you should…" The vicar started.

I cut him off. "I know exactly what I should do, Mr. Yandle. And I will do it."

"Let me know if you need my help," he offered.

I knew he wanted me to write to Arthur. I should have my husband come and take both Graham and I away.

But he didn't know about Dibble or Mr. Carter. He didn't know what an obsessed man could do.

I did. When Mr. Spout made his move, I would be ready.

CHAPTER 39

I sent him my journals, all of them. I thought about having the man who came for them followed, but I don't want Joy to run again. I don't want her to run anymore. Not from me.

The day was drab and gray, one of those days when the air around you pressed against your skin, your lungs, your heart and mind.

No one remained to visit after the vicar's sermon. I think everyone knew it was time to go home and brace for the weather.

I was making a mental list in my mind when someone grabbed my elbow. I stopped and turned to face Richard Spout. He hadn't spoken to me in the last two weeks, but he was always in my sights, on the edge of everything I did.

"It looks to be a rough storm coming. I will come by and make sure your house is buttoned up tight." He didn't release my arm.

"Unhand me at once!" I jerked away from him. The other members of the congregation stopped in their tracks and gawked at us.

"Just trying to help out the widows and orphans, like the good book says." He kept his gaze on me and called out, "Isn't that right, Vicar?"

"What are you trying to do, Mr. Spout?" Mr. Yandle sighed. Others approached us to listen in. Mr. and Mrs. Spout were at the forefront, looking on with interest.

"I'm trying to do the neighborly thing and help Mrs. Taylor. But she's rejecting my assistance. Don't you think she should accept a little help?" His voice was carried to everyone nearby.

PART 3 - THE CURSE

I held Graham tightly to me as my cheeks flushed with embarrassment. He wanted a scene? I'd give him a scene. No one would be confused about where I stood in relation to this man.

"Mr. Spout, I could not think of anything more vile than to let you into my home. You are a wastrel and a bully. Things are much better in our little parish without you, and I suggest you return to your ship as soon as you can so we can all enjoy life once again."

His eyes bulged in anger as the crowd gave a collective gasp.

Mrs. Spout gasped and took a step towards me. "How dare you!"

I turned on her. "How dare you, Mrs. Spout. How dare you let your older son beat his younger brother. If you were smart you would cut ties with this abominable man and take notice of Johnny so he doesn't grow up to be just as bad." The crowd murmured.

The vicar groaned behind me. "That's enough, Mrs. Taylor."

"Don't be a coward, Mr. Yandle," I retorted, enjoying the wide-eyed look he gave me. "If you want to be complacent while a child is beaten, you may. I will not keep silent. Nor will I waste any more of my breath on this family." I pointed directly at Richard Spout. "Do not come near me or my son ever again."

Mrs. Kissinger came forward and linked her arm with mine. "I think Mrs. Taylor has made her position clear. Now, everyone go home and prepare your houses for the storm."

The crowd broke up as Mrs. Kissinger led me to her rented hack. "I think I should give you a ride home today."

With a sigh I accepted. I hadn't realized I'd been shaking until we sat down on the bench and the coachman had shut the door.

"That was either incredibly brave or incredibly stupid," she told me, taking Graham from my arms.

I hugged myself. "I won't be bullied by him. By anyone."

"Yes, well, you've certainly brought things to a head." She rocked Graham gently. "I'm not sure what will happen now. Mr. and Mrs. Spout are well respected, even if their son is a wastrel. Some will take their side; others will take yours." She sighed. "I didn't know he was tormenting poor Johnny."

"He hid it well. They both did." I took my son back, nuzzling his baby cheeks and inhaling his sweet scent. Both actions calmed me.

"Button up your house tight tonight, and bring in any food that's ready to harvest. It feels like a damaging storm is coming," she directed me as the coach came to a stop. "Would you like me to send Daniel over to help?"

I shook my head, "No, I don't have that much to do."

"I would feel better if he spent the night," she added. The threat of Richard Spout hung over her words.

I shook my head. "Let him stay with his family. I'll lock things up tight," I promised.

I put Graham down for a nap and made a quick walk through the gardens, gathering up any ripe or near ripe food. I fastened all the shutters and double checked all the locks.

The oppressive air still pushed in through the cracks and crannies. I closed the unused chimney flue and lit a few candles for extra light, keeping the fire in the sitting room going just for the cheerful glow.

Graham was a welcome distraction when he woke up. I smiled at his cheerful baby babble, and he grinned back when I babbled nonsense at him. We played for the rest of the day, enjoyed a small simple supper and went to bed early.

The storm woke me from a sound sleep. Graham was crying his little heart out after the first booming report of thunder.

I rose from my bed and picked him up from his crib. "It's just the storm, little man." I shushed and bounced him as he hiccupped into my chest. The thunder clapped while rain pounded down hard on the rooftop.

"Let's see if it's quieter downstairs." I picked up his favorite blanket and another for myself. We could snuggle on the couch until the storm passed. I bundled him up onto the couch and bent to light the fire from smoldering coals.

Another loud crash made me jump. It wasn't thunder that had just shook the house.

Someone had pounded on the door. It was a single, hard thump that shook the windows.

Graham whimpered on the couch and I set down my kindling, waiting in silence, hoping it wouldn't happen again.

A few moments later the giant thump crashed against the door. The locks shuddered and I was certain they wouldn't hold much more abuse.

"Let me in, woman!" A voice shouted, followed by another thump. "It's not fit to let a man stay outside on a night like this!"

PART 3 - THE CURSE

I bundled him up tighter. I held him close to me and bounced him, silently praying they would go away.

The thunder clapped again and the rain fell harder.

The door rattled hard. "Let me in! I'll show you what a good husband I can be!" The voice roared.

I stifled a sob. Richard Spout.

He was here to carry out his unspoken threats. Under the cover of darkness and noise when I couldn't call for help. Fear gripped my heart as other memories flooded back, of Dibble's hands around my throat, of Carter's pistol in my ribs.

"Why me... why me?" I sobbed into Graham's neck. What did I do to attract such attention?

Graham started crying, my fear mixed with his own made him inconsolable. The sound of his fearful wails slammed something inside me. All other emotions were shoved aside to give way to the absolute knowledge I would do anything to protect my son.

"Don't be scared," I shushed and went into the kitchen. The front door wasn't going to last much longer.

I retrieved the pistol from its hiding place above the mantle. I hadn't wanted it to come to this. I had hoped to never use it, that it would sit like a harmless paperweight and gather dust out of sight, out of reach. I sniffed one last time and took Graham back to the couch and laid him down. His cries grew frantic as Richard Spout cursed and swore at me.

"Just wait, little man. I have to do something." His wailing filled the air, mixing with the thunder and the pounding of the door.

Even though my heart was battering my ribs, I felt calm. I knew what I had to do. I was Joy Horton Marco. And no man would ever make me afraid ever again.

The doorframe gave way under the assault and the door violently smacked against the wall with a loud crash.

The soaking wet Richard Spout stood in the doorway, illuminated briefly by the lightning. He looked smug and ugly.

"Mrs. Taylor," was all he said before I leveled the pistol and put a bullet in his head. He flopped over backwards onto the porch.

The shot rang in my ears as I dropped the pistol and returned to my son.

The House That Death Built

His little form writhed and I felt the angry tears on his face as I cradled him to me. I bounced him and sang to him, kissing him over and over until the ringing stopped and I could hear his little sobs at last. He sniffled and gasped, overtired and on the verge of an unhappy sleep.

"Go to sleep, sweetheart," I urged him. "Mama's got a mess to clean up."

Richard Spout was a heavy man. It took me three tries to roll him onto a quilt. I was thankful for the mud that let me drag his body easily over the terrain towards the river.

I prayed the whole time I struggled with his corpse. I wasn't sure the Almighty was going to forgive me, but He would be the only one that ever knew of this. The rain was a blessing at the moment, washing away most of my sins of the night. The lightning had stopped but the rain still pelted me as I tugged and pulled his tall form into the river. I rolled him off the quilt and watched his body sink into the water. I hoped the current would take him far away.

I left the river and dragged my quilt back again through the mud, smearing any footprints I might have made. I stood outside and let the rain wash over me. The night's peril caught up with me, and I bit my lip to keep from shaking into a hysterical mess.

"Don't be an idiot, Joy. You don't have time for that," I scolded and stormed back into the house.

Graham was still asleep. I was grateful for that small blessing as I started a roaring fire, building it up big and hot to try and heat my bones. I still shook as I looked down at the muddy quilt and my stained nightgown.

Dragged the tub back into the room in front of the fire, I stripped and wrung out the wet things into the tub and tossed the muddy water outside. I cleaned up my muddy prints with my nightgown and went back to the kitchen to fetch more water. I filled the tub and went to work scrubbing and rinsing by the light of the fire. I worked until the grey light of pre-dawn started working its way into the house and the rain had stopped.

When my nightgown and the quilt were free from mud stains, Graham woke up. I fed him quickly and stripped him out of all his clothes as well. He wiggled happily in his naked state and I was thankful for babies and their short memories. I dunked his clothes into the wash water and spread them out next to the drying quilt and nightgown.

We dressed back into clean clothes and I laid him back on the couch. He burbled happily as I shut the front door and started moving all the furniture I could get my hands on in front of it. I stacked them up around the door in a neat barricade. I then glanced about the room to look for any further damning evidence.

The gun sat like a useless doorstop in the middle of the room.

"That would be condemning." I returned the gun to the kitchen to clean, reload, and put it back in it's hiding place above the mantle.

I built the fire back up in the sitting room, and returned to Graham. Clean and full, he snuggled into me as I wrapped the blankets around us on the couch. I shuddered and shut my eyes, hoping to get some rest.

A dreamless sleep engulfed me for a few blissful hours. The sun was fully up when Daniel came knocking on the door.

"Mrs. Taylor! Mrs. Taylor! There's been a murder!" he shouted through the doorway. "What happened to your door?"

The river hadn't taken Richard Spout away far enough.

Graham fussed a little as I padded to the door. "You'll have to come around back, this door is blocked," I said when he peeked in through the two inches my barricade allowed.

"Blimey!" was all he said before racing around the house. I met him at the kitchen door and unlocked it. He ran right past me and into the other room to inspect my construction work.

"It was Richard Spout, wasn't it?" he asked softly.

"I don't know." I spoke my first lie of the day. "Someone was attacking the door during the storm. I'm not sure who, but I was too scared to let anyone in. They were so violent. I stacked up the furniture until they left."

Daniel's eyes were wide. "They found Richard Spout this morning in the river, all stuck up under the bridge. No one would have seen him but his arm was floating out just where you could see." He wrinkled his nose. "He's all white and blue, so they thought he drowned. But when they pulled him out, they saw that someone shot him right in the head."

I gasped. "That's horrible!" I would give the performance of a lifetime today.

"Everyone's in a fit about it and the constables are sniffing around at everyone. I'll go get my papa to come fix your door." He rushed back out the door.

"I suppose we should get dressed and put the kettle on. I'm quite sure we're about to have company," I told Graham. He squawked loudly at me. "After your breakfast, of course."

I had just finished my own breakfast when Mrs. Kissinger descended on me. She came to the back door, so I knew she must have talked with Daniel.

In her typical way, she swept past me and marched straight to the matter. "This is just awful." She declared at the state of my front entrance. She shook her head at the sight. "My dear girl. You must have been so frightened!" She took Graham from my arms before patting my cheeks and forehead. "Are you well? Do you feel faint at all?"

She was such a dear lady, but so silly sometimes.

"I'm quite over the shock," I said as Graham immediately attacked the ribbons on her bonnet.

"Such brute force. Oh, this is a muddle!" She untied her ribbon and handed it to Graham. He happily started gumming on it as she pushed her way around the stacked furniture.

"They broke right through. The frame is in shambles. Well, Mr. Poole will have to pay for it. There's no reason a woman shouldn't feel safe in her home. I'll make sure he gets a stronger door with bigger locks." she said.

"It was the frame that gave out," I pointed out. "A new door and locks won't do much good."

"Hmm, just so. The whole thing must be redone. You and Graham shall come stay with me until it's finished." She took my son and started the climb to the bedrooms.

"I'm sure that's not necessary. Daniel is sending Mr. Young over right now to fix things," I shouted up the stairs at her.

She turned around and came back down without breaking her stride. "That is a smart idea. He'll do it up just right and tight. We will still send the bill to Mr. Poole," she insisted.

I didn't argue, and followed her into the kitchen where she handed Graham back to me and started making tea.

"It's just dreadful business everywhere. Little Molly Pratchet found Richard Spout's body on her way to the baker's this morning. Saw his arm flapping out from under the bridge. She ran home and told her parents and then the whole village knew. I think everyone was there when they pulled him free."

"Were you there?"

"Of course I was there. You should have heard the uproar when we all saw he'd been shot. Right in the head!" She shook her head and sipped her

PART 3 - THE CURSE

tea. "Now Mr. Poole is pulled into constable business, and he's completely worthless, while Mr. Spout is at his heels looking for someone to blame. Doesn't even think of looking at his no-good son to be accountable for his own death."

"You think he shot himself?" I hadn't thought of Richard Spout as suicidal, but it could be a valid story to deter people from my part in his 'unexplained' death.

She snorted. "Richard Spout? No, he's much too in love with himself to do such a thing. But the kind of people he kept company with are always just barely on the right side of the law."

There came a rapping at the front door and Mrs. Kissinger leapt to her feet. "I'll bet that's them now." She tossed off her bonnet and stormed to the door.

"Mrs. Taylor! What in blazes happened to my door?" Mr. Poole's voice rang through the hallway.

"You'll have to come around, gentlemen," she shouted back. "Mrs. Taylor was attacked last night and has barred the front door." She pointed to me. "You go wait in the sitting room. And look a little more distressed. You are taking all this far too well."

If she only knew. I was happy to let her handle things and play the damsel in distress.

A bewildered Mr. Poole was the first in the room, followed by an angry looking Mr. Spout and Mr. Yandle.

"What happened here?" Mr. Poole demanded.

"Don't shout at the poor girl? She's had a terrible night." Mrs. Kissinger raised her voice to match his. They both glared at each other and I wondered, not for the first time, what kind of history these two had.

"I think we all should sit down and quietly listen to what Mrs. Taylor has to say." The vicar's calming influence had everyone taking a seat. Mr. Spout sat in a huff and glared at me.

I swallowed. "Someone attacked my door last night. I don't know who it was. It was during the storm, and the thunder was so loud I could barely hear the voice shouting. It was too violent to be anyone seeking shelter. I was frightened so I barricaded the door. The door frame broke, but my barrier held. I was in the kitchen doing the same at the back door when they left. I suppose it was too much trouble to break in."

"You're sure you don't know who it was?" Mr. Poole asked.

I shook my head. "No. The storm was so loud, and the pounding on the door drowned out the sound. I could hear shouting, but Graham was crying and… it was all very upsetting."

"What if it was my boy? Running from a murderer!" Mr. Spout rose to his feet.

I cringed as Graham started to cry and all the men looked uncomfortable at the sound. Mrs. Kissinger took the baby and started bouncing him. "There, see what you've done. I don't know why you're even here."

"It's my boy that's dead, isn't it? If she had opened the door, he might still be alive."

"We don't know if it's your son that was pounding on the door. It could have been the murderer for all we know. And then she could be dead too!" Mrs. Kissinger scolded him. I was so glad she was here.

The room went quiet except for Graham's sobs. No one looked at each other as the implications of a murderer running loose around the village took hold.

Their murderer was right in front of them, with no way to tell them that the real threat was dead and thrown into the river.

I pressed my hands into my eyes to ward off the incoming headache. "If you have no more questions for me, then I am asking you to leave. I didn't get much rest last night and if Mrs. Kissinger is willing, I would like to take a nap while she watches over Graham."

"Of course." Mr. Poole rose to his feet.

Mr. Spout glanced around the room suspiciously. "That's an odd place to hang your laundry, Mrs. Taylor. Any reason not to hang it outside?"

I gave him a weary smile. "I will if the weather's nice today. Early this morning Graham's soakers failed and we had an impromptu bath and laundry wash. I didn't want any stains to set in," I said. As I'd hoped, any bodily functions of a baby were enough to make all the men red in the face quick to leave.

"Mr. Young is coming to fix the door. I'll have him send you the bill," Mrs. Kissinger told Mr. Poole.

"Hmm? Oh, yes, I'll gladly pay for it," he said before exiting the cottage. Mr. Spout gave me one last glare and left.

Mr. Yandle lingered behind. He glanced at me and Mrs. Kissinger. "Might I have a private word with Mrs. Taylor?"

"Oh yes, of course." She carried Graham out of the room, cooing to him softly.

He watched the door close and glanced at me. "Where's the pistol, Joy?" Joy? "I beg your pardon."

"The pistol. I know you purchased one two weeks ago when Richard Spout started harassing you."

I glared at him, but marched to the hiding spot where it rested. "Are you having me followed, Mr. Yandle?"

"Just watching over you, Mrs. Taylor."

I took it by the barrel and handed it to him. He silently checked it, saw it was loaded, and returned it to me.

"You've thought of everything," he said as I put it back in its place.

"I don't know what you mean." I didn't look at him. I kept my eyes on the mantle as he came up behind me.

"I know you did it. I know why you did it. I just don't know how you did it all by yourself," he whispered.

"I'm sure that would have been impossible." I didn't dare turn around. The guilt was written all over my face, with a little bit of anger. He underestimated me, like everyone else. The illiterate yeoman's daughter couldn't possibly do anything of this magnitude on her own.

"Your husband said you were brilliant. I didn't believe him at first. He's right. You are brilliant. Terrifyingly so." He stepped away from me.

I still didn't turn around. The ground fell out from under me when he mentioned my Arthur. I gripped the mantle for support. He'd been in contact with Arthur?

"Good day, Mrs. Taylor."

CHAPTER 40

I received another letter from the vicar. It had a return address. It said, "I believe you. Come get your family out of my parish." I'm equal parts elated and terrified of what that could mean.

I lay Graham down on a blanket, making sure his little body was in the shade. He kicked and gurgled happily as I moved to weed the little herb garden next to the kitchen door. I listened to his happy babbling as I plucked out my first weed. I glanced back at him periodically, making sure the shade hadn't moved with the sun and he hadn't squirmed too far. He had rolled over a few times, but his favorite move was to spin in little circles on his back.

I had a pile of weeds and was about to move to a new location when a shadow fell over me. I glanced up to greet my visitor and felt my heart stop.

Arthur.

He stood over Graham, staring at him. He looked horrible. His frame was thin and his hair disheveled. His beard was no longer neat and trimmed, but long and unkempt. His clothes hung off him. His eyes were hollow and rimmed with black shadows.

"Arthur..." I managed to speak. I watched him carefully as he hovered over Graham. What was he doing here? How?

He swallowed and spoke, his voice was trembling and hoarse. "A boy or a girl?" His eyes never left Graham's little form.

"A...A boy," I said, slowly rising to my feet. What was he going to do?

"Healthy?"

PART 3 - THE CURSE

"Yes. He's very healthy and strong," I said, carefully peeling off my gloves. My hands shook as the gloves fell to the ground. I clasped them tightly in front of me.

Arthur smiled a little. "I'm glad. I was so worried about you both." He turned his gaze to me. "You look well, Joy."

"You don't."

He ran his fingers through his hair. "No, I probably don't. I haven't been...taking care of myself." He looked down at Graham again. "Does he have a name?"

"Graham Thomas Marco." I left off the false name I'd given the vicar.

"You named him after me?" he asked with wonder.

I didn't reply. My traitorous heart leapt in my chest, telling me to enfold Arthur in my arms, to make the look on his face disappear. I physically ached to hold him, to be held by the man I loved. I clasped my hands tighter to keep them still.

"How did you find us?" I asked.

Arthur moaned. "You are so damn clever. You led me on a goose chase all over England. Even your parents had no clue where you were or how you were posting your letters from a different town each month." He reached into his pocket and pulled out a letter. "The vicar wrote to me. He wanted me to come and get you."

Mr. Yandle had betrayed me. Or maybe he just didn't want to harbor a murderer in his midst. Either way, I'd physically hit him when I saw him again.

"I was wandering around the village when a Mrs. Kissinger pulled me aside and demanded to know my business. She was rather surprised your husband wasn't dead. She told me where you were."

Of course she did. I was sure to get an ear full later.

"She's a good lady. She doesn't like that I'm alone," I said quietly.

"I don't like that you are alone," he growled. "I went crazy when I couldn't find you. I feared the worst. I had everyone searching up and down the house, the grounds, the cliff...I was screaming and yelling...out of control. And then I found your letter. I felt as if you had struck me. I couldn't believe that's how you saw me until I looked up into the mirror and I saw the same monster you had drawn looking back at me. I had been trying so hard to protect you from the curse that I had become the 'disgusting beast' you once accused me of being."

He lowered his voice. "I don't blame you for leaving, Joy. I'm glad you did. You kept yourself and Graham safe." He looked up at me. "I'm here alone, and I'm not going to try and drag you back with me."

"Arthur..." My hands betrayed me. I reached out for him; there was so much to say.

"Don't touch me, Joy! I cannot do this if you touch me," he shouted, backing away from me. "I came to tell you I'm leaving England. I'm going to Spain. I won't be returning. I've made arrangements for you and Graham. He'll inherit everything and you'll have a nice estate up North by your family with as many sheep and spaniels as you wish. You won't need a thing." He swallowed. "I know you think I'm insane, that I belong in Bedlam. Perhaps I do. But I won't force you to live with a monster."

I was ready to try. I'd lived without him and it was nothing but pure pain. Could we possibly meet in the middle somehow? I was already in love with a madman, could I find a way to live with him too?

"I love you." He gazed at me when he said it, and I could feel his sincerity down to my toes. "I'm done being a selfish bastard. All I want is your happiness." He exhaled a shaky breath, staring at Graham until his eyes went glossy. He shook his head from his daze, gave me a long look and turned around, walking back towards the drive.

Tears streamed down my face. My heart took over, shoving my brain and all logic aside. I rushed to him, and slammed into his back, holding onto him tightly. He staggered when I wrapped my arms around him and pressed my cheek against him. His scent surrounded me and I felt the space where my heart used to be filling back up.

"All I want is you!" I burst out in sobs. I clutched him tightly to me. "Please, please don't go."

He trembled as I cried into his coat. One hand slowly came up to rest on my arm; his other hand joined it and gripped me tightly.

"I don't care if you are mad. I've tried to live without you. I thought it would be the best for me and Graham. But I hurt, Arthur. I hurt because there is a hole in my heart where you should be, and I can't bear to be without you anymore."

"Dare I hope..." he whispered. He slowly turned in my arms, his hands cupping my cheeks.

I looked up into his face, into those hollow eyes. The calm and rational Joy was gone, replaced by the broken-hearted woman I'd become. I was a shadow of my former self, and so was he. I cried, letting big tears stream down my face as ugly sobs racked my body. "I want to come home. I'll take care of you, if you trust me. No more hiding, no more secrets. I'll listen to all your stories about the curse on your family. I'll even try to believe it. I love you."

He groaned, pulling me into his form, a hand in my hair and the other firmly around my waist. "This is the first time you've ever told me you loved me," he said in awe. "I hoped you would grow to love me. You acted like you did, but you never said it."

"I do love you!" I cried, reaching up to touch his face. "With all my heart and soul. Please, Arthur. Let's stop torturing one another. Let's go home and be a family, with all our problems and mistakes and imperfections and our curses."

His arms held me so tight to him I lost my breath. I felt his lips on my hair, and I lifted my chin. When his lips met mine, all my heartache and fear disappeared. No matter where we went, no matter what the future held, this was home.

And I'd fight for it.

CHAPTER 41

I have them. They are whole, they are safe. My heart swelled with joy at the sight of my son. I didn't think I could feel any happier until Joy said she wanted to fight the curse with me.

We made love silently, fervently, and with tears of joy from both of us. We landed in our familiar heap, with my body draped over his, both of us breathing deeply with contentment.

Arthur's fingers ran through my curls as I settled into my place in the niche of his shoulder. I sighed and buried my face against him, inhaling him completely and feeling my heart settle before resting my hand on his chest. I stroked the scar from Carter's bullet. Was it really still lodged in his chest?

"How are we going to do this?" I knew my Arthur. I knew he'd try to control everything. I didn't want to start with an argument.

Arthur groaned and wrapped his arms around me. "Your husband is a worn out and broken man. I yield. I'll do whatever you ask if it means you and Graham are by my side."

Well, this was different.

I glanced up into his face, stroking his long beard and looking into the dark eyes that were starting to show a little life again. "Anything?"

He kissed me. "Anything."

"First of all, you have to gain some weight and shave a little. Your beard is out of control. I think I have burns on my skin," I commanded. It brought out a chuckle.

"Done, Madame Wife. What else?"

"I want to go visit my family."

"We can leave in the morning if you wish," he said. "Although I'm not sure how much they will embrace me. Your brother still packs a sharp punch."

"He hit you?" I rose up on my elbow to look at his face.

Arthur nodded. "Knocked me off my feet. I think your father wanted to, but he just left the room. Your mother showed me your letter and ordered me to leave. She said not to return unless you were with me. Your family is frightening."

I smirked and rested my head back onto my spot.

"I want you to buy this house and give it to the Youngs. And Mrs. Kissinger's home too," I said.

"Ah, now that you have the full weight and power of my purse once again you seek to deplete it," he teased.

"You said I could try," I reminded him.

"I suppose I owe the Young family and Mrs. Kissinger for your wellbeing?"

"They helped bring Graham into the world," I told him, tracing my hands along his too thin ribs.

"I will set them up for life," he vowed. I kissed him.

"I think a home, a job for Mr. Young, and an education for Daniel will be all that is required. Mrs. Kissinger will be harder. I don't think she'll accept anything."

"Oh, she will," Arthur promised sternly.

That was a battle I wanted to see.

A thought struck me and I rose up on my arms. "Where's Pip! Did you bring him?"

"That poor dog. He's gone into a deep state of depression without you. Really, Joy. I should scold you endlessly for leaving that poor creature behind."

I laid back down on his chest. "I couldn't bring him."

His arms tightened around me. "I know."

"Where is he?"

Arthur exhaled. "Back at Ironwood with Eva."

"We are going back there," I said.

"Joy…" he growled.

And now the fight would begin.

"Arthur." I matched my tone to his. "I love Ironwood. I want to live there." I pressed my finger against his lips to keep him from interrupting.

"I know you have demons there. I want to fight them with you. As your wife and partner. I won't have any whisperings of a curse spoken to Graham unless I can see it for myself. It's not taking control of anyone else," I said. I was willing to go this far. I'd believe in him, I'd be cautious and careful, I'd do what he asked as long as he would tell me why.

He closed his eyes as I removed my finger. "Promise me you'll tell me if you hear it."

"I promise." If it would ease his mind and save our marriage, I would promise him almost anything.

"I know you don't believe me, Joy. I know you think I'm mad."

"So?"

His brow quirked. "I never took you for one who suffered fools willingly."

"If I meet a fool I won't. I don't think you are a fool, Arthur. I …" I sighed as I tried to gather my thoughts. "I don't know what I think about your story, about your wives and Alice. About your age and Sophie. And that your vast wealth comes from sacrificing to a gemstone."

"It sounds incredulous to me and I've lived it," he said.

I nodded. "But the vicar told me about the forces of good and evil in this world. If I believe in God and his angels, then the opposite should be just as true, shouldn't it? And I should fight against those forces, shouldn't I? Especially when it is trying to hold onto someone I love so dearly."

He embraced me. "I get chills all along my whole body when you say you love me, my Joy." He kissed me. "A compromise then? You promise to let me know if that damn stone talks to you. You'll never touch it. We'll keep this curse from the next generation."

I kissed him back. "And you promise to trust in me. Bringing me any fears you have about this curse of yours so we can fight it together."

He tucked a curl behind my ear. "Done, Madame Wife."

PART 3 - THE CURSE

CHAPTER 42

What an idiot I was. This woman saved a child's life from Dibble. She faced down Carter and obsessed over my wound rather than hers. She stood up to me and refused to be my gilded prisoner. Why did I think she would back away from a horrible family curse? Why did I fear her rejection so much when she lived a life of rejection because of her reading?

I am still an idiot. A hopeful idiot.

Arthur settled my affairs for me in Abbots Leigh. He bought Mrs. Kissinger a carriage, horses, and a hired coachman so she wouldn't have to hire out to drive her on Sundays anymore. She hesitated a moment, giving him a calculating look before accepting. I was almost disappointed there hadn't been more of a showdown between the two.

The Youngs were gracious and happy to accept Riverside Cottage. Daniel whooped and ran around the house like a savage, making Graham laugh as Mrs. Young cried happy tears. Mr. Young was quiet. I saw his pride rise up a moment to reject it, but Arthur cut him off. My husband humbly thanked him for taking care of me and Graham, and begged him to accept his gesture. I think the sight of a peer making such an honest gift of thanks soothed him.

Arthur met with the vicar as well. I watched Mr. Yandle return a stack of journals to him, shake his hand and ask for the Lord's blessing on our family. "We need it," was Arthur's reply. I stayed quiet, still angry about the vicar's betrayal of my trust.

His eyes met mine, as he spoke to Arthur. "There was a murder in our quiet village while your wife was with us. Richard Spout's family are fervently looking to find who did it. Don't bring your wife back to Abbots Leigh."

Arthur's eyebrows reached his hairline as he agreed to the vicar's request. Back in the carriage, he turned to me. "You wouldn't know anything about a murder, would you Joy?"

I didn't want to relive the details. I had sworn my secret would stay between me and the angels that would condemn or forgive me. "No, I wouldn't know about a murder. I do know that Richard Spout was a villain. He was probably killed for attacking a widow and her infant son."

"Probably?" he pressed.

"Murder is an unpleasant subject and I don't wish to speak of it ever again."

He contemplated that before he kissed my palm. "What a beautiful, brave wife I have."

It was a quick trip across the country to my parents. Graham was a grumpy travel companion until Arthur took him up on the box when the weather was nice. I heard him gleefully giggle with the wind on his face and babble at all the new things he saw to his father. Arthur calmly and patiently explained the world to him, protesting when Graham would untie his cravat or knock his hat off.

They were inside the carriage when we pulled up to my parents' home. I knew my mother would ring a peal over my head if she saw an infant riding on top.

Before the coachman could even move, she ripped open the carriage door with a look of malice until she saw me sitting next to Arthur with Graham. Her face softened and tears swelled in her eyes.

"I brought them back, Mother Horton," Arthur said softly.

"Don't lose them again," she replied before snatching Graham out of the carriage and making all sorts of loud exclamations over his beauty and size. She smothered him with kisses while Arthur and I disembarked.

We spent two weeks there, catching up with my sisters and their families who flocked to visit when they heard I had returned. I worried a bit about Thomas and Arthur until they both came home roaring drunk at an unholy hour of the night. Arthur had a split lip and Thomas had a black eye, but they were bosom companions once again.

I would never understand men.

Arthur was quiet when we approached Ironwood. I could feel him tense up when the carriage started down the drive. I squeezed his hand and kissed his cheek. "Relax," I said.

PART 3 - THE CURSE

He took a deep breath when the carriage stopped. "I trust you, Joy."

Sophie burst into tears when I emerged and wrapped both arms around Graham and I in a tight embrace that made the baby squawk. Eva attacked from behind and blubbered at me, her face buried in my skirts. Arthur struggled to keep us all upright.

"Oh, look at that little lad. Arthur, he's perfect!" Sophie gushed and touched the baby's cheeks. She kissed my cheeks as well. "My dearest Joy. I am so sorry. I feel as if I failed you."

"We'll make it better," I promised.

She nodded and wiped her tears, taking Graham from me. "Come in! The staff are dying to see their new young master. Someone else is dying to see you too."

Pip barreled into me once the door opened. I fell down to my knees and burst into tears as he whined and wagged and cried and licked and pressed his form into mine.

"I missed you too!" I wept into his soft fur when he had calmed a bit. "How's my handsome boy?" I crooned as he licked my tears and I rubbed his silky ears.

"I thought I was your handsome boy," Arthur teased. He knelt down beside us with Graham so Pip could sniff and investigate our newest family member.

The rest of the day was a whirlwind of activity.

Arthur watched over me carefully as we unpacked, ate, walked the gardens, played with Pip, installed Graham's crib into my bedroom, and finally found our way to bed.

He didn't say anything, but gave me a meaningful look before I doused the candles.

"I'm fine. I promise." I kissed him soundly before we both fell asleep.

***

I knew you'd come back. They always come back.

I awoke from a sound sleep. The voice lingered in the air. It was deep and rich, with a hint of malice.

I rolled over to Arthur, who had one hand on my hip. His eyes fluttered awake when I moved. "Nightmares?" He pulled me closer to him.

"No, I just thought I heard something."

"The baby?" He glanced at the open door to the next room where Graham slept.

"Maybe. He might be making noises. I'll check. Go back to sleep." I tapped his arm for him to release me. With a grunt he rolled over as I slid from the bed.

Graham was fast asleep as well, his little baby breaths coming fast and loud through his nose. I watched him and admired his beautiful little body, how his lips searched to suck for an imaginary breast even in his sleep. Nothing was ever so perfect.

I turned to go back to bed when I heard it again.

They all give in, eventually.

It was coming from all around me, resonating around in my head. I looked under Graham's crib, in the corners, starting to panic when I couldn't find the source of it. I was about to shout for Arthur when it spoke again.

I'm not there, stupid girl. You know where I am.

I froze.

It wasn't possible.

"No," I whispered aloud.

It laughed.

I've been silent, waiting for the next heir to be born. Alice made a nice distraction while I waited.

"It's not...it can't be..."

He thought he could hide you in London. Mr. Carter was most helpful to remind him that no Marco can escape my reach. I thought he had learned his lesson with Diana. Carter was so easy to manipulate once he fell in love with her.

I swallowed and returned to our room, shutting the door to Graham's quietly.

Did you like Mr. Spout? He was so wicked. A few suggestions in his dreams and he was eager to do my bidding.

I was shaking as I stood next to the bed.

No matter where you go, you can't escape me. I'll have you soon enough.

"Not me. Not this time."

I knelt on the bed and softly shook Arthur. "Wake up," I said gravely.

PART 3 - THE CURSE

He rolled towards me and blinked. "Something wrong?"

I swallowed, realizing the world as I knew it would end when I spoke.

"I hear it."

EPILOGUE

I found a gray hair! I think Joy finally did find me mad when I plucked it and presented it to her like a prize pig. I don't understand what is happening with the curse, but I'll accept every tiny victory we have.

I watched Graham run across the lawn. He stopped when his little brother cried out and returned to help his three-year old sibling regain his footing. He held young Oliver's hand and they made their way towards their play platform that Thomas had built for them.

Pip followed behind them, slowly. He'd lost a few steps lately with age. He was also fighting off the exuberant chewing of our new puppy, Angelica, who bounded ahead of him and leaped up on the platform.

Arthur had offered to buy all her littermates, saying he was just keeping his promise of people 'tripping over spaniels' when they came to visit. I assured him two at a time was sufficient.

I sipped my tea and watched the boys convert their little play place into a ship. John Turner and Lily had recently visited with their children and Graham was all things sailor at the moment.

Sophie snored in the chair next to me. She often fell asleep in the sunshine, even after complaining that it was going to give her spots and then she'd be mistaken for a heathen like Graham. It made him giggle.

Everything was right.

Oh, it wasn't perfect. Arthur would always be his overbearing self where his family was involved. I had to rely on Sophie's help for running a large household while Eva went to school to become my new companion. The boys had their moments of youthful insanity and Sophie still invited her young bucks to invade our privacy when she felt restless. But on the whole everything was right. Everything except…

I can give you that. A baby girl, so healthy and beautiful.

I rolled my eyes and muttered into my tea. "Shut up."

Arthur peered up from his newspaper. "What's that, my Joy?"

"Nothing," I said, setting my tea down. "Just thinking of our family and your stupid rock had to cut up my peace."

Arthur slowly set his paper down, moving carefully. He always did when the cursed object spoke into my mind. He slowly leaned over and took my hand. "And what is it saying now?" he asked, squeezing my fingers.

I smiled at him. "It's being ridiculous, as usual. I was thinking a little girl would make a nice addition to our brood, and it's promising me to magically make it happen." I squeezed his hand back, "I know the only one who can give me a daughter is you."

He sat up straight, and kissed my palm. He settled it over his heart and said in his most solemn voice, "I shall do my best to serve your needs, Madame Wife." His eyes sparkled. I laughed and the infernal rock was instantly silent.

It wasn't always easy to ignore. It had taken me some time to brush off it's threats and promises but once I realized it had no real power over me it became easier to disregard.

Until we lost little Andrew the day after he was born. I gave in that day.

I left bruises on Arthur when he had to physically restrain me. I'd struggled and screamed like a madwoman while he and Sophie had pleaded with me to see reason. Meanwhile, the cursed object was whispering promises in my mind to bring my baby back to life. My screaming had echoed throughout the hallways of Ironwood. Even the servants wept. After that, there was always a footman guarding the gallery. If I went in there, even if Arthur was with me, the footman would move to block my view from the glass case where the infernal rock sat.

We couldn't leave Ironwood for long, either. After a few weeks it would try to influence someone else to destroy me. I think it enjoyed that more than tormenting me directly.

Thankfully, I loved Ironwood.

Arthur rose to his feet. He gave Sophie a kiss on her cheek that woke her. "Mind keeping an eye on the boys, old girl? We've business to attend to."

Sophie blinked sleepily. "Wha- where are you off to?"

Arthur put an arm around my waist and I slipped mine around his. "My wife demands to expand the dynasty," he announced.

She grumbled and waved us out of her sight.

Arthur tugged me along, making ribald comments to make me giggle while we made our way through the house. The servants pointedly ignored us, small smiles on their lips.

My husband threw open our bedroom door, ushered us inside and then locked it.

I put my arms around his neck, touching a bit of gray that was appearing at his temples. I remembered how overjoyed he was when he saw proof that he was aging again.

As he leaned in and kissed me, the thought struck me again.

Everything was right.

ACKNOWLEDGEMENTS

I am so thankful to all those who supported me and this work. Shout out to my Fab Five friends who always made writing fun growing up, Amyjo, Bojam, Robere, and Sarah. I had two awesome editors willing to take on this monstrosity, thank you Julia and Danielle for making my words look pretty. My Beta readers who didn't shy away from it and became my author buddies as well, Victoria, Miranda, Brooke, Rachel, Amanda and Courtney. Everyone at The Writing Gals Critique FB group, you guys are awesome! My family, especially my picked on hubbyman, Dell, for his willingness to support whatever I do.

ABOUT THE AUTHOR

Mel wrote, illustrated, and published her first book at the age of five. It was not a huge success and she only sold one copy to her mother. Undaunted, she plunged herself into reading every book she could get her hands on. She found a love for ghost stories and gothic tales, suspense-driven works of fiction, and of course a little romance never hurt. Now she combines all three of her favorite genres and writes up tales that feel familiar until you find out things are not what they seem. She lives in the Wasatch Mountains and enjoys time with her children, her husband, and her 100-pound lab/mastiff/dane, Boudica, who thinks she's a lap dog. She also has a serious addiction to yarn, fiber arts, and crochet hooks.

Connect with me on Facebook, *@Author Mel Stone*

Visit *authormelstone.com* to check out my blog and sign up for my newsletter to get access to a free short story, featuring Sophie and Nathaniel.

Printed in Great Britain
by Amazon